UNALTER

BOOK 01

ASCALI

JOE REYES

Copyright © 2022 Joe Reyes
All rights reserved
First Edition

NEWMAN SPRINGS PUBLISHING
320 Broad Street
Red Bank, NJ 07701

First originally published by Newman Springs Publishing 2022

ISBN 978-1-63881-925-7 (Paperback)
ISBN 979-8-88763-178-3 (Hardcover)
ISBN 978-1-63881-926-4 (Digital)

Printed in the United States of America

CONTENTS

01

The King's Pyre

The sun was sinking in the sky as the Square finished filling with folk who dwelt in the city and from beyond as well. Edward Frauer arrived at the king's pyre later than he'd expected, now gently squeezing his way through the crowd of standing foul-smelling commoner folk. He brought himself deeper into the cluster of living bodies, closer to the wooden stage upon where he now found sight of his family, seated high with the rest of the councilmen and their kin. Lord Frauer was expecting to see all three of his sons sitting beside his lady-wife and the rest of the men in brown robes with families, yet only one of his own offspring he viewed to be present up there. His youngest son sat impatiently beside his lover, Lady Sophia Frauer.

After passing through the honor guards at the oak stairs leading up to the stage, Lord Frauer paused to give himself a moment so he could catch his breath back while wiping the sweat from his brow. He made his short climb, step by step until he reached the top, and then reinspected the crowd of the lords and ladies to find sight of his wife and youngest son again.

Lady Sophia and young Dallion were seated within a row of chairs close to the edge of the low stage just above some of the many standing commoner folk. The families assigned seating had been far from the pyre being prepared at the center there. Edward's wife was putting thought to why Jason, Arthan, and Lord Edward were tardy, while little Dallion was gazing at both the red and blue stars coming above in the soon-to-be night sky. When Edward finally had made his appearance, he placed his hand upon Sophia's shoulder, interrupting her deep thought of the absent sons, Jason and Arthan.

"Lady." said he, while she sat looking past the other seated people ahead, trying to get a view of the unlit, deceased king's pyre. While still standing, Edward immediately made mention of his sons who weren't here. "Both of them late as expected." said the lord as he picked up Dallion and moved him over to an empty chair close by. Edward took his seat in between his wife and his boy, thinking carefully about what he should say to his lover now as to avoid her becoming angered.

The seated, surrounding councilmen and their families had been loud in conversation, as were the commoners standing below. Edward had to raise his voice a bit so Sophia could properly hear him. "There will be an explanation. They will tell us when they arrive. They always have good reason." said Edward to his wife.

She wasn't pleased. She looked to her lord-husband, watching him as he reached past her breasts to pinch Dallion's nose in a playful manner. Lord Frauer looked to his wife after he had caught notice of her angered, watchful eye. When the lord and lady looked upon each other, she said to him, "Why are you in seek of an excuse? They both know how much the king meant to you. They dishonor the family by not attending his burning. You've arrived late yourself, for what reason?"

Edward ignored his wife's talk with an awkward laugh, which she found insulting. He watched the two empty black oak chairs beside her, wishing the rest of his sons were with him, for they assisted him when his lady-wife would often become displeased.

"Father, where is Jason and Arthan? Did Jason say to you he would be back in Ascali by this time? Jason said to me he would be back in Ascali by this time." Dallion was giddy as always just before his brother's return to the city.

Edward told his son that both of his older brothers must have lost track of the hour of day. Dallion said nothing in return, only placed the wet sleeve of his little shirt in his mouth to chew on some more.

"Edward!" called Councilman George from the row of chairs behind the Frauer family. "Where are the boys?" asked he loudly.

Edward shifted himself in the dark chair to adjust his view on George back there. "My son is right here." George laughed as loud as he could have up at the night sky.

"Joker! I have eyes. I meant the sons *not* here in the Square."

Lord Frauer truly did not know the answer to this question that seemed to be in everyone's thoughts, including his own. *Where are my sons?* he asked himself in thought.

Lord Frauer ignored the man in brown, with those ugly gray whiskers of his, turning himself back around, joining his family in facing the old dead king clad in steel and white silk on the stack of wood.

Lady Sophia closed her eyes in a contained state of fury before she spoke. She opened them now, saying, "George mocks us, and he's right to. Where are they?"

"I don't know. Perhaps Jason had some trouble on the road. As for Arthan, I cannot say. We'll question them when they arrive. Lady, it's not a problem." Edward Frauer placed his hand on Sophia's to calm her. "George doesn't even have a family, so he's only just envious." Edward reached on over to remove his son's wet clothing from his little mouth while sitting comforting his wife with his left-side hand.

"Lord Frauer, everybody else's families are here except yours!" George shouted from behind. If not for the massive audience and loud dialogues surrounding them, Frauer would have been uncomfortable and humiliated, though nobody was listening to Councilman George.

"George, I said it isn't a problem!" loudly replied Edward, without turning back around.

"As you say, Lord Frauer." George smiled and then leaned back into his own seat to search for more of his fellow councilmen to attempt to make angry, to jest at. Just as Lord Edward felt he was beginning to calm himself, Lady Sophia pulled her hand away from her husband's, as Edward did not realize how hard he had been gripping hers. She massaged the pain away from her palm whilst looking upon her husband in disgust. He took a deep breath inward, as the ceremony was to begin in very short time.

Grand Councilman Lewis was ascending the steps of the stage with a cane in one hand, a text scroll in his other. As small as he was, he stood easily viewable over the common people of the city after taking his final steps up there and to the edge of the wooden stage. On this stage, the grand councilman was huffing and puffing from loss of breath after making his climb up the stairs and taking this little short walk. He continued on all the same. With the commoners low in front of him, and then the rested king and the councilmen and their families behind him, Lewis unrolled the scroll to read aloud so all occupants within the Square could hear.

"Sons and daughters of our realm, Midlön, the reign of our great King Harold Apollo has ended! He served the realm with pride. Rested King Harold had pulled us from the darkness of the Gray-age and blessed us into the white. His name sh-shall be remembered forever. God gave rested King Harold no siblings! As known to the folk, his one and only male heir has passed many years ago, now leaving him with no successor and ending the line of House Apollo. A faithful ruler he was, an honorable man who sadly never married. God loved him all the same though! He will stay in our hearts forever."

Aside from his occasional stutter, Grand Councilman Lewis had a pleasant and powerful voice. His appearance though, always had the poor old man looked like a sickly little pale goblin from the made-believe knights' tales; even in Lewis's youth he'd appeared this way some have claimed who'd known him in that long ago mark on the timeline. *Well done so far with the words, Lewis,* Edward thought to himself.

Grand Councilman Lewis continued on with his speech about the dead past ruler, the body lying beside him on the tall wooden pyre. Rested King Harold Apollo was dressed in his finest silks with his plated shoulder pieces fastened as he'd commonly wear them in his days of living young and old. The brute-sized elder man seemed to glow a bright white, shining silver and somehow blue too; colors of his house. The grand councilman then announced and introduced to all the closest friends of the bright rested king, *as if nobody had knowledge of who anybody was in this wretched city.* Included in this list of well-known folk would be Edward Frauer and many others so that they might speak aloud to the people of the city regarding their realm's loss.

Simple and short, he had planned for his wording. "He was my dearest friend, inside and outside of the council. I will never forget not just what a good king he was, but what a good friend and father to his children he'd been." Edward told this to the folk as he stood upon the stage. Edward didn't find joy in rising to speak; his dull speech made this fact clear to all. Lady Sophia thought that strange, for such a person as her husband who had kept a good friendship with the recently dead ruler, to have no interest in expressing the memory of his close relationship for all to hear.

Even the Gray sisters (daughters of the previous wicked king before Harold's rule) were eager to speak aloud to the people of the city. Their wishes for Harold's soul were kind, followed by a poem sang for all to hear. There was beautiful princess Audrey too, Harold's daughter, who read a speech aloud to the crowd. Edward found her words very touching.

"I know if my brother were among us this moment, duty and love would have him step forward to succeed my now-resting father. He would have been honored to take charge of that beautiful Golden Throne. Sadly, my brother is rested and gone too. There are no more men of my house left to…left. This is to be the end for the Apollo family."

She let loose tears as she read from her scroll. The princess had much more written upon her text parchment, much more planned to say to the folk. Unfortunately, she had walked down off the stage, silently crying before she could finish.

Edward's son Arthan Frauer was meant to give a short speech on how inspirational King Harold had been to him, yet when Grand Councilman Lewis had named young Arthan for his turn, he was far from the Square, coming now southward down Brey Street, rushing to get to the ceremony. *How could I let this happen?* Arthan asked himself as he dashed past the commoners and their rotting wagons. The young man could never seem to keep track of the time of day. Arthan knew his mother and father wouldn't be pleased with him, especially this time.

"Out of the way!" shouted Arthan at a drunken potter stumbling in his path. "Make way! Make way!" Arthan then lost his footing, leading to a hard fall. He hit face first onto the filthy cobblestone road. Brushing the dirt off his family robes and mouth, he stood up and came faced to Rodrick Drake. "Out of my way, Rodrick! Did you just trip me?" Arthan shouted at him, asking him this.

Rodrick Drake answered, *"'Out of your way?'* or what? What's a boy like you gonna do?" Rodrick stepped closer to Arthan, speaking again. "You stepped in shit, Arthan. Wipe it with them soft hands of yours, boy." Rodrick grabbed Arthan by the wrist.

Arthan knew he had no time for arguing. "Don't call me boy. I'm older than you, fool!" Arthan pulled his arm away from the young antagonist's grasp, and then Rodrick cursed at him, spitting in his direction. Off went Arthan to the king's ceremony, with a scratch on his face and a shoe covered in poop and Rodrick's saliva.

Just as Edward's son was making his way through the crowded passage to the Square, the grand councilman was finishing his speaking in total. "May Aeon light his path in the afterlife above. The soul of Harold in this smoke shall ascend into the night sky. When the sun has fully risen, the drifting soul within the holy fumes will be gone in completion. The sun will have absorbed his precious soul, and Harold will have truly joined god in the great heaven. Rest in love, Harold."

"Rest in love, Harold." the thousands of people had repeated, commoners and the lords and ladies alike.

The fire elementists then revealed themselves, ascending onto the stage wearing their blood-orange robing to prepare to light the pyre with magic.

Arthan shuffled his way through the folk as little Lewis with his long white beard surprisingly continued his talking loudly. "Now is the time for a new king to rise! Rested king Harold left no heir of his family to claim the throne, and so his successor will be chosen based through the law of our tradition. Our precious Steward! Gregory Royce, the right hand to rested king Harold Apollo shall sit the Golden Throne!"

The crowd applauded the handsome and new-soon-to-be king as he now made his way onto the stage. Arthan clapped with both hands best he could as he was still moving through the thick crowds as all cheered for their new ruler.

"People of Ascali!" Gregory screamed as he danced his way to the center. "I, Gregory Royce, shall treat you all with as much respect and honor as our beautiful King Harold did in his days of living and ruling. As the old steward of the realm, I had advised and aided King Harold many a time, helped him in keeping the peace, keeping his rule. I have gained much knowledge from the years I have spent at his side, believing as a mighty Royce that I can do just as well ruling the realm, if not better than precious he!" Gregory Royce's long black hair, accompanied by his equally long beard, had flailed and cracked like whips as the young man danced in between sentences as if at a ball. He spun his hair around in circles as if he'd happily gone mad from drinking or lost his mind to the lust of music.

While this young and royal man spoke, whipping his hair in circles, Edward sat shaking his head in discomfort. He knew Gregory well from all the past hours he had spent with him on the king's council. Edward saw him to be nothing but a young man who simply lusted for attention and valued nothing but the theatrical arts and spectating of the fighting arena. "This will not last." Edward whispered to his wife.

"What?" Sophia asked him.

"His reign, everybody's lives. Now that he's in control of the treasury vaults, we are well and truly doomed."

Her husband was whispering in her ear until she said, "Be quiet, Edward, please shhh."

Gregory stood with his fists curled up, placed at each hip, the way a hero would pose for a statue carving. "I name my younger brother Lord Arol as my steward and successor until I find my queen and impregnate her." He discontinued his heroic pose, dancing a bit more beside the dead King Harold's corpse and the wood he lay upon.

Arthan made his way in deeper, past the cheering people of the city, trying to get as close as he could to the stage. He could just barely see his family seated behind the new soon-to-be king, Gregory Royce. He watched the stage as the acceptance speech was being made. The second empty chair beside little Dallion, meant for his brother Jason, caught Arthan's eye. *At least I am not the only son absent,* he thought to himself as Gregory Royce was finishing his words.

Grand Councilman Lewis opened a golden chest carried by an honor guard. The elder drew forth the crown of the kings. He placed the shining diamond-filled steel device atop Gregory's head. After that slow and dramatic action, the crowd screamed loudly. They were shouting and applauding their new ruler. The young and kingly man's head seemed to dazzle white as the old Harold Apollo's crown rested atop that long jet-black, greased hair. Arthan was still busy making his way closer to the stage, violently brushing his nose on the chests and backs of folk as he squeezed through a fat family of eight.

The hooded elementists began chanting now. After some loud spells were said and they performed their queer hand movements toward the stacks, the wood cracked, and then the body of Harold Apollo burst into a blaze of flames with all the logs as well. Newly crowned King Gregory Royce stood again with his fists upon his hips, smiling while Harold lay in the fire. It was tradition for all to watch the a dead past king burn for hours until the flames died down to embers and the sun showed itself. Arthan stopped moving in forward; he had to settle for where he now was standing.

The young Frauer boy was breathing heavily on foot, silent amongst the crowd while those around him muttered prayers. All then fell silent to his ears; this happened just when Arthan's eyes met his father's up above in the distance there. Edward smiled at his son from upon the stage, but Arthan's lady-mother didn't look pleased when they'd seen each other. Arthan then looked away from her to give a wink at his little brother, Dallion, like always. Before Arthan could see if Dallion winked or waved in reply, Arthan then dropped his head like all the rest and prayed softly to himself. "*Aeon, forgive me for my tardiness and dishonor. My hopes are that I have not brought embarrassment to my house. May you light the path of our rested king, guide him to your realm of heaven up above, as I hope you will do for me one day far from now to come.*

Many hours passed by. The stars, both red and blue alike, were fading away. The sun was rising, and the folk were tiring. In the older days of the realm during the Gold-age era, if one did not remain standing until the sun had made its reveal, they would be shamed and punished. Now on this day of the timeline, some slept for the royal burnings, others stood through the night, and some stayed awake but seated.

Night turned to morning, ending this long silence. Flames were now gone, and the old king was nothing more than ash and blackened bones among the lifeless wood. The courtyard, known as the Square, was beginning to clear of folk. Some still remained sleeping as if they were of the houseless, while others took a knee or sat on their asses even long after the fire had died out; most made for wherever their homes were.

Not all had god's power to stand risen the entire night for the burning, but Arthan had, and now it was his time to leave. He made his exit with aching feet, moving slowly amongst the surrounding commoners, trying to avoid his family for a short time and succeeding in doing so. Arthan glimpsed his lord-father carrying his sleeping little brother off the stage. He had seen this just when the sun had fully risen above the city walls; but quickly, the gathering crowds then soon blocked his vision of his family. Arthan knew he would be reprimanded, but now wasn't the moment for this scolding; he wanted his knightly brother by his side for when the trouble with Mother and Father came.

Arthan Frauer quickly left the Square by Small Street; a thin western path on the edge of the Square's border, leading to a portion of the city's walls, west of Gold-Gate, which was built within the walls itself at the south part of the city. When he approached the big closed doors built into the wall, Arthan looked at the massive entrance and laughed inside his head, a habit of his when he'd catch sight of its enormity. It wasn't truly gold, this gate. It went by that name in the days of the Gold-age, after it was painted the color gold. Years later, King Harold had the golden paint scraped off when he had taken charge of the throne. The city's gate now appeared dull, dark, and fearsome like the day when it had been first constructed at the end of the Spawn-age. The monstrous metal door still went by the name of Gold-Gate, though many years had passed since that real golden glamour was there. Arthan climbed the steps of the south city wall, just beside the massive gate by the two main watchtowers to be seen. He waited for his brother's arrival there while enjoying the morning breeze, as well as the faint music coming from one of the new restaurants close by.

Hours went past until Jason and his knights could be seen in the distance riding their white armored horses toward the city of Ascali by way of the main road.

"Opener!" a city guard shouted.

Arthan was sleeping against a barrel of oil on the battlements when he heard the whistle blow. Seconds later the gate swung open slow as ever to welcome the knights inside. Arthan rushed down to greet them with excitement. "Jason!" he shouted when he finished descending the stone steps of the walls.

His brother clicked his teeth together; the mount obeyed. Sir Jason, upon horseback, turned from his path and made his way towards his brother Arthan; the knights with matching mount armor had followed.

This brother of Arthan's atop horse seemed a giant up there, until he dismounted and walked to him, armor clanking the entire time. The brothers viciously hugged each other as the steed licked the back of Arthan's head.

"Ah, Pax!" Arthan broke from his brother's grasp and kissed the horse on its white plate armor, just under an eye. Arthan was beginning to now sweat from his blood rushing because of this excitement. He sopped up the wetness on his face with the back of his blue sleeve, and then as a jest, he punched Jason on a shoulder piece. "And you! Two weeks, you idiot, two weeks? How could you bear the wilderness for that long?" asked Arthan.

Jason, along with his armored knights behind him, removed their helmets. He strapped the armor to his horse's saddle. Jason was grinning like an idiot the entire time he did this, while those behind their captain there held emotionless faces. "Kept you waiting, did I?" Jason asked his brother with a big smile. Then Jason said, "The road isn't the wilderness! Two weeks, you ask? You know I've had longer missions than this one. I'm late, and I owe father an apology. I bring dishonor to the family, fool, I'm stupid, stupid-" Jason was looking downward as he began to ramble on.

"Have you completed the mission?" Arthan asked as this knight brother of his stood insulting himself.

"Yes." Jason replied with a snappy glance back up. Arthan's brother began to smile again. "Alec, pass me the bag." One of Jason's knight's put away a skin of rum at the side of his mount, then tossed Sir Jason a heavy sack discolored with blood.

"Then you have done nothing but *honor* the family, Jason. This is brave work of yours, but please, I do not want to see such things that would be in that bag."

Jason laughed at Arthan as he patted the sack. "Yes, always getting ill at such things." Jason sniffed the bag, then strapped his prize to the horse. The smelly bag sat dangling beside the dented helmet that had protected Jason's face and head, many times in the past.

"Looks heavy. How many?" asked Arthan.

"Five, all of them the chiefs. The outlaws will trouble the realm no longer." Jason fed his horse, Pax, an apple.

Arthan applauded his brother and said, "Very good, very good. Well, all of this, such good news then…yes. What do you say, you come see Father and Mother with me? I wasn't at the ceremony at the correct time mark either, and I know they won't be too angered so long as you're there beside me."

Jason laughed at Arthan. "Lost track of the hour?" the knight asked his brother.

"Yes, I did. I hadn't thought it to be as late as it truly was. Why did *you* not come on correct time? You were expected to be back here in Ascali by midday yesterday."

"We had to handle some trouble along the way." one of Jason's knights answered for him in the back, the elder one with the raspy voice closest to Gold-Gate, mounted with the rest with a big bow fastened at the side of his horse.

Jason turned back to smile at him and the rest of the men, then faced Arthan again. "Yes, we visited Castle Hammer for rest and refreshment on the way back from the outlaw hideout. Lord Hardain told us of rapists hiding in his woods." said Jason.

"And what did you do?" Arthan asked.

Before Jason could answer Arthan, a voice behind Jason said, "We found them, and now they will not trouble Lord Hardain's people anymore, or anyone, for that matter." Jason turned back laughing.

"Shut it, Brandon. You make us sound wicked. We didn't kill them. We chased them off. But the Hardains and border guards will finish them off. Martin back there shot them full of arrows! They could be bleeding still even now! Haha!" Jason had said the last bit of his tale, laughing hysterically as he told it. Arthan stood there watching all knights share in the humor as Jason mounted back up.

"I'd love to see Father and our *loving* mother with you, but I've got to get these heads to the new king before they rot any more." Jason told Arthan this while patting the bag.

He mounted Pax and told his knights that it was time to look upon Gregory as a king for the first time.

"What weekday is it?" Jason asked his brother.

"The burning was today, so it's the first of the week." Arthan answered.

"Ah, of course. Thank you! I'll see you at midday for a meal at the house. Don't be late now, you pretty."

And with that, Sir Jason and his five knights galloped through the Square, then into and up Brey Street, away from Gold-Gate. The knights became lost in the crowd of commoners and wagons.

Arthan walked home alone to his father and his mother.

02

House Frauer

"Smell that? Brandon!" Jason asked his youngest riding knight. "Yes! Onion shrimp soup! Which I'll have inside me after we gift these heads. Oh a nice big bowl! *Or* do we get some now?"

"No…" almost the entire riding company said at once. They were eager to be finished with their quest, but they also thought on how nobody in the city made a bowl of onion shrimp soup the way Benjamin Drake made his at the shop on Brey Street. As Jason and his knights galloped up the sloping city road, the sweet onion smell that came from Benjamin's shop brought all their mouths to a water. After two weeks on the road with eating mostly only dried salted meats, the knights craved to feast on a hot meal; now wasn't the time for this though. The new king required their attention.

"It's a shame we missed the burning." Lance said as they rode.

Jason wasn't concerned with consequences of missing the ceremony, and so he told his men without worry, "I take full responsibility for our disrespect. Remember, my loving father sat the council with our new King Gregory before his crowning. They were close when Gregory was steward through these last many years. Our new ruler will be nothing but thrilled when we show him these trophies, presented by the son of his good old friend." Jason spoke loud so all five of his company could hear him whilst they galloped up the street.

"Thrilled is right. I heard this Gregory of ours gets a hard one for the blood." Brandon said, riding behind Jason.

Jason laughed aloud.

"Brandon is right." Borran told them all. Borran continued on saying, "My cousin was sayin' that the Royce family is mind sick. He says House Royce ate man flesh, all the way back in the early years of the Gold-age. He says, says it's a good thing it's only Gregory and Arol left, 'cause nothing good never came of their fathers, or fathers of their fathers."

Jason looked back and nodded as he took a sip from his hidden wineskin, then tucked it back within the satchel at the side of his trotting horse. He then turned back again now to look at big Borran to say, "The beginning of the Gold-age was hundreds of years ago. Who knows what truly happened. Me, I don't care if his ancestors ate man flesh, not even ballsacks, and don't *we* get hard for blood?"

Jason pulled a new doeskin sack out to drink from, this one filled of river water. He took a sip then spoke, "So listen here: he's our new king, and we shouldn't be talking ill of him, nor his dead family. We respect those who can fight well, yes? He is skilled in combat, King Gregory. We will treat him with respect, exactly the same way we had treated old King Harold, with his great sword he had the strength to swing so well. No more ill talk of King Gregory. We could be punished for talking poor of him in this way."

"Who's gonna punish us? We're the king's knights!" Brandon yelled while laughing.

"Ooyah!" Jason's knights all said aloud at once, followed by bursts of laughter.

Jason couldn't help but join in the humor as well. He rode with them laughing, drinking his water and then some more wine again.

The armored knights rode in their wide formation, trotting far up Brey Street as the smell of onions sadly left their nostrils. After passing under the bright stone archways, they brought their mounts up upon the city's High District, where only the wealthiest lords and their ladies could choose which homes their families would dwell within.

"The White Knight! The White Knight and his gallant companions have returned!" the young woman on the street shouted directly at Jason as she exposed her bare chest to the six riders.

The knights saluted to the woman, crossing Silver Street, and then entering through some thinner paths in between the homes of these rich folk who dwelt here. Girls and children threw flowers down upon the riding warriors as their envious lords watched from the windows too beside their daughters and wives. The knights eventually reached the Great Keep, where they would soon find their new king in the Throne Hall.

The two silver-plated honor guards saluted and made way for Jason and his men. The defenders each clapped the stone floor with their dark spears in hand. After that gesture came the opening of the giant iron doors. The guards moved their shields aside to welcome Jason's men into the large greeting room they'd have to pass before entry up to the main hall.

"Welcome in, sirs." said each of the guards at once.

The Throne Hall, built within the center of the keep and up at the highest point of the city, Jason's favorite structural creation here in Ascali. This fortress of a keep in which the chamber was constructed within had been crafted in such a way so all folk of the city could have their gaze of the marvelous wonder where their king dwelt, no matter where you placed yourself in the city. This tall Great Keep could always be seen to all folk within the walls of Ascali, upon the walls of Ascali, and visible still beyond from afar even if one would not be present inside the city.

After Jason secured his wine and water safely under a cloak, settled safely upon his precious steed, Pax, he unclipped the bag of heads from the horse's saddle. The knights then dismounted, leaving their beasts for the keepers in the yard to tend to. The men reapproached the pair of guarding knights, then stepped through the iron doors to walk down the short welcoming hallway, yet this hall was oh so very tall. Silver glowing torches hung from the chandelier above, seeming like a mile away upward when Jason looked overhead as they made their way through. At the end was where they then found a familiar set of even bigger half-blue-, half-white-painted doors, colored for House Apollo. The iron entrance behind them shut, then this blue, white pair opened up, leading to the most hated set of stairs in the world. Front them upon the floor was the white carpet. Almost a quarter mile long, the carpet extended outward and upward, resting upon each of the many steps of the staircase; the staircase with one hundred and fifty steps. When they had finished their climb, the knights thought themselves blessed to be formally inside the Throne Hall once again. All shared Jason's opinion on the beauty of the royal locale, besides Sir Martin, who had been only annoyed at the amount of steps one was required to take to reach the chamber with this route.

At the far end of the hall, the Golden Throne could be seen, shining bright. The tall seat sparked with the light of the sun pouring in from behind. Past the throne, to the far and opposite end of the room, was the famous wall made entirely of unstained glass. All the northern portions, the folk, and the patrol upon the outer city walls of Ascali could view bits of the room through this glass side of the Great Keep. Inside, when sun fell completely, the hundreds of torches on the walls made the metal chair glow an even brighter color than the sun ever could. Those later hours had always been Jason's preferred time to make his visits here, when torchlight lit the chamber, not the sun. The knights halted upon the white carpet to await permission to approach their sire.

Bright rays of daylight pierced through the glass now, making the throne and the king's crown sparkle and dazzle warmly. The white device sat upon King Gregory's freshly shaven head. He was standing beside his throne, massaging his own hands with fingers all dressed in rings. He spotted his new prizes in that old bag at Jason's side so fast.

"Sir Jason of House Frauer, White Knight of Ascali, Champion of the Arena, the Captain of Eagle Party and his five swords." Councilman Adam announced them all with his lisp, above from an indoor and crumbling balcony.

The party made their way toward the king.

This new ruler of theirs waited for them to reach the front of the throne at the steps for them to line up in formation and give their salutes before he finally spoke. "Kneel, please." asked King Gregory.

The knights all happily smiled, and then bent their knees to pledge loyalty to their king. "We are yours, my king." Jason said to break silence while they fell in low.

King Gregory looked to his left, pressing the palm of his hand to the throne. "Sir, I don't exactly know who *'we'* are. Of course I know *you*, the mighty Sir Jason Frauer, the White Knight, Champion of the Arena. Knights, his father is a good man and *dearest* friend of mine. Please introduce this fellowship to me, Sir Jason."

My father? A dearest friend? Jason wondered if that was actually true. "Yes, of course, an introduction of my men! Before we begin, I want to compliment you on your new appearance."

Gregory ran his fingers upon the smooth skin above his ear. "The black locks were hideous. They suited me as steward, not as king."

"I agree. You look stunning, my king!" Jason said loudly with a big smile, still kneeling, and then he began, "So! We are the Eagle Party, as you know. This is Sir Brandon Trentor, Sir Martin Praxus, Sir Lance Flux, Sir Borran Estrain, and Sir Alec Donlyne. We serve at your command. We are knights of the throne, in charge of keeping the great peace by completion of personal, *private* missions for our good king who…now is you. I hope-"

"I see. Oh, this is exciting!" King Gregory spat while he shouted, clapping his hands now. "I do apologize. Rested king Harold never told me much about his personal band of warriors or of any *private* missions… I may have been right-hand man to him, but this, well, that's the purpose of a *private* mission, yes? To keep the task private." King Gregory laughed.

The knights remained kneeling. One by one they presented themselves with their swords at the ready.

The new king giggled. "After all I've endured serving Harold, my life of politics, I now feel…almost as if, if I have never seen anything of these sorts before. I'm just viewing the rule on the realm all from a different…let's say, set of eyes? In the council, the king's secret knights are the last thing on anyone's mind, you see. During sessions, Harold hardly spoke of you six and yo-" King Gregory quietly burped in between sentences as the knights stood upward in a now more relaxed position when they had realized King Gregory was not acknowledging their kneeling gesture or the half-unsheathed swords they held out to him.

"So…when I want evil lords killed in secret, I come to the six of you to have it done? Please educate me, haaa, there's loads I still don't know yet about being king. I suppose it just feels a bit odd now that I *seat* the throne instead of aiding an owner of it… Watching over poor sweet old Harold was splendid."

Sweat dripped from Jason's moppy brown hair. *The new king won't shut up. I can't speak, I can't fight, so why do I stand here?* Sir Jason was only good if he could use that clever mouth of his or a sword; Jason was not a comforting listener, and he admitted this often. The knights slid their blades entirely back into the scabbards at the hips as they gave their attention still to the rambling King Gregory.

The king went on, "Again, I am sorry if I appear to have a disgusting attitude. This is all going to take some time for me. I stood on my feet for six hours watching the old man burn in the Square… I am fatigued! Oh, poor old Harold. Am I speaking too harshly now?" The new ruler grinned as he took a look to the right and high above, where his very own brother, the new steward, was seated atop a silver chair on one of the stone balconies, half asleep and so quiet that some of Jason's knights hadn't even noticed him up there. Arol Royce yawned, facing down to his kingly brother.

The silence was broken by one of the knights, "You are the king. There is nothing to forgive. Speak as harshly as you would like." Jason's smallest yet most clever knight, Sir Alec, told King Gregory that.

"Thank you for your kindness." the king said to the short, thin knight in return. The king made a winking gesture, specifically toward Sir Alec; he then addressed all six knights while the steward above and few surrounding councilmen listened on.

"Speak with me, talk to me, sirs. Tell me why is it that you have come? You are my first visitors. I'm assuming the answer lies within that sack?" The king planted his butt in his new golden seat and took a sip of iced water from a chalice, it's metal matching the glamour of the throne.

Jason unhooked the bag from his belt beside his white cloak. He raised the sack of heads high so that the king, councilmen witnesses above, lord-steward, and honor guards among them all could see. "Proof that the Eagle Party has put an end to the bandit outlaws. The ones that have been harassing the folk in the northwest of the realm. King Harold set us to do this before his passing. We know he would be proud. We hope you are, King Gregory." the leader of the knights told this all to the new and young king of theirs.

"What's in the bag?" asked the king of him.

Sir Jason replied with, "The heads of the chief outlaws! We slew them all, my king, and a great number of their lesser men as well. Without the chiefs, they have no lead, no organization. Their order will soon fall apart, and they will scatter." Jason spoke true words, and from the look painted upon the king's face, he seemed pleased.

Old Sir Martin took a step forward next to Jason to add in, "The bandits will argue, fight for who takes control of what remains of them. There will be many among them seeking power and succession. This will cause breaking in their companies. Most will hide in smaller grouping. When the hiding is done, they'll fight, they'll kill each other, not in the roads, not by the villages, but in the woods and caves. There's nothing left to fear, for god will do the rest."

"Sir Martin is right in this." Jason said.

The king clapped again, louder and longer this time. "Dump the bag." commanded he.

"I'm sorry, my king?" one of the six knights said.

"*Dump* the bag. I wish to see these chiefs with my own eyes."

It was a simple command, nothing old King Harold would have asked of them though. Sir Jason would soon come to realize that this disturbing demand was nothing out of Gregory Royce's character to ask.

"My king, the floor will be stained with filth." Jason said.

Gregory's maroon eyes rolled to the back of his head. When he returned them to look on Jason, he said to him, "It's granite, Sir Joker. Please spill the contents of the bag upon the floor. It will be easily washed."

Jason unlaced the brown bag and turned it upside down. Out fell what remained of the chiefs; onto the floor of the Throne Hall they landed. The new steward in his silver chair high up laughed while looking away in disgust. The king smiled to the few councilmen above, clapping his hands once again, his rings echoing through the hall as they collided with one another, again and again. The witnessing councilmen on the stone balconies soon then applauded the knights down below. "Well done! Well done! Sir Jason Frauer. Your father will be proud when you tell him of this."

"My father grows displeased when I discuss my missions with him. He always asks that I keep these sorts of matters to myself. Thank you all the same! I would not have the ability to have done it without my men at my side."

The king grinned, rising now from his throne to take a closer look at his gifts. The knights moved back so that the king could examine the heads. King Gregory Royce in his red high-top heeled boots, stomped down the steps that lay in front of the knights. When he reached the floor, he towered over the remains of the bandits as thick blood leaked from where their necks had been. The king pointed downward with a finger full of red and black rings. "This one here, this ginger one. He has a wolf claw inked on his face." The king placed his hand over his mouth. The stench of rot filled his nose as he stood confused at the markings on the head.

"You know this ink mark, sire. Ranger from the South, at one point in his life." Jason stated.

Borran then added, "A runaway of some sort."

"I see. Well, I do hope his soul burns in Retilliath… I hope… and I hope his family dies horrible deaths! Like he did. Ah! I thank you again for this. I want to purchase you all pleasure ships someday; not today, someday! What a great way to start my first midday as the new ruler of the realm, with enemies of my lands dead before my eyes. The realm of Midlön just feels a bit more, a bit at peace after this beautiful act of justice that the six of you courageous knights have committed. Sirs, you all have my leave to go."

Gregory stepped over the heads and hugged each one of the six knights, lastly kissing Jason lightly on the lips; a very odd thing for a king to do, in comparison to past traditions. All of the Eagle Knights remained at the silent ready after Gregory had released himself from Jason; all besides Borran. Borran laughed oh so slightly at the king's queer expression of thanks to Jason. King Gregory returned to the side of his golden seat. The knights descended the many steps, leaving their new sire. They all returned out through the blue and white doors, then out from the tall black ones to once again breathe the city air.

The silver guards gave their salutes to the Eagle Party, as the six knightly men walked their short distance to the mounts. It was there where they found the keepers, feeding vegetables to the beasts and brushing their coats in between the white armor platings. Jason dismissed those tending to Pax and the rest of the beasts after handing each one of the keepers a gold coin. He grabbed hold of the saddle to bring the horse by the path leading back through the many homes of wealthy folk. Before he prepared to take his leave, Jason gathered his men together for a brief word. "My knights, my friends, we have had a brutal two weeks together out in the wilderness and upon the roads. Well, our misery has truly made the realm a better place I suppose. I will greet you all tomorrow bright and early. It's time that I returned to my family now."

The knights all bid Jason farewell. After that, they'd all left him for ride to Benjamin's shop to feast on soup.

Seated atop Pax, Jason made his way through the High District's alleyways, eastward down to where he could reach Silver Street. This was where he would find his family's house, front garden, and stable. When he reached his home, the knight dismounted and went through the thin iron gate of the property built in the fence. He led Pax upon the stepping stones of the little garden, turned right, and opened the door of the small wooden structure. Jason removed the war plating and saddle from his horse. He placed them in the old pink chest just outside the small stable here, beside some blue flowers that his father, Lord Edward, planted long ago. He locked the box back up, and then tended to the animal by taking the time to brush him down within the single stalled stable. This big old friend of his stood there happily in the shedlike construct on all fours as Jason Brushed him. Sir Jason recited poetry while he used the hairbrush until he looked through the doorway up into the sky, seeing where the sun had placed itself. After twenty or so minutes of this, Jason gave Pax a kiss on that huge nose of his and then brought himself inside to greet the family.

"Jason!" both his father and mother shouted as he shut the entrance door behind him, quickly making his way past the dining area and into the kitchen now.

He gave his hugs and kisses before apologizing for not making the ceremony in time.

"It's fine. Really, it calls for no punishment. You had more important matters that required your attention." Jason's lady-mother said as she hastily cut into the burnt baked peaches. "Go get settled in and be quick. Supper is on the way."

"Yes, Mother. Where's Dally?"

"He grew tired." Jason's father began. "We sat and waited all the night while rested King Harold burned. He's sleeping, but I'll wake him for the meal in short time." Edward Frauer told his eldest son.

Jason made his way down the pink hall, then into his bedchamber to remove all his apparel and to store provisions he had journeyed with. He unpacked all the contents that lay inside his back satchel, mini bag, and many pockets. After that, he took a long while removing his white plate mail and underarmor too made from dwarvish Drull chains. He wiped the travel grease and filth from his body with a scented rag before changing into a blue tunic and trousers, a color of his house emblem.

As the now unarmored knight was lacing up his more comfortable and clean boots, somebody had entered his bedchamber. "Was it pleasant? Speaking with Mother and Father?" Jason asked his brother Arthan after hearing the soft footsteps from his furry slippers at the doorway; he was still tying up his footwear while he waited for Arthan to say something back to him.

Arthan replied with, "Just as I expected. Father didn't seem to mind. He was tardy himself prior to me. Mother was angry."

Jason scratched at a small stain on his boot, then he turned to face Arthan. "As expected, yes? Well, brother, better to be late as you and Father were, than to not have arrived at all, like my wicked self. Is the food already served?"

"You don't seem bothered? He wasn't just our king. He was friend to father. We should have been there, right? And yes, Mother told me to tell you the meal is ready. She burnt the peaches and the meat too." Arthan watched Jason on the bed, adjusting his boots once again.

Jason finished with his footwear, then he jumped up to go to the doorway by Arthan. "You look grim, brother. Come, let's get some wine in our bellies before we eat Mother's shit cooking." Jason lightly slapped Arthan on the cheek and walked out his own room with him, through the pink back hallway of the house to reenter the main chamber. Jason searched for a seat at the family table.

"Jason's returned!" little Dallion screamed with baggy eyes when he saw his elder brother arriving to join him for feasting.

Arthan looked through the cabinets at the kitchen to find an opened bottle of wine.

"Awake now? Yes, yes, I have returned! Protecting Mother, Father, and Arthan while I've been off? I trust you to scare off any witches and thieves when I'm not here to do so. How've lessons been?"

The child frowned as Jason found his place at the family table. "The lessons are boring. I want to do sword lessons instead of history classes. Didn't you have sword-fighting lessons when you were at my age?"

Edward helped his wife bring the food out, and then he and she both sat in to join the sons' conversation.

Sophia said, "Jason took his history lessons *and* sword-craft lessons when he was your age, but you can barely keep with the language and history! How can you expect to practice with swords too?" Lady Frauer waited for the little one to give answer while she herself began to pour drinks, passing the water jug and then the big plate of blackened meat.

"I can do both if I want to. If Jason did it, then so can I."

"Then tell me what did you learn today?" the lord-father of the family asked as he filled his dish with supper.

Dallion paused to think, then said, "We learned about the ages. First was the age of Origin." Dallion then smiled because he knew he was correct.

"*And* the four after that?" Lady Frauer asked her youngest son, who seemed oh so confident.

Dallion hesitated, followed by that precious youthful smile of his fading away. He took a sip of milk, then he slammed his stone cup on the table as Lady Sophia was cutting and passing meat to Jason. "I cannot remember." Milk spattered across Edward's plate of roasted meat and blackened peaches.

"He *does* pay attention in class." Arthan said jokingly when he arrived at the table with a jug of wine in hand. He poured for four stone cups.

Edward laughed and ignored the small bit of white mess on the surface of his meal. Arthan sat eating with his family while Lady Sophia cleaned the splashes of milk wearing her *"bitch face,"* as Jason would refer to her current expression as.

The family of brown-haired, brown-eyed, pale folks sat now enjoying one another's company in comfortable silence for a minute or so. The Frauers all shoveled food into their mouths without any more dialogue, until the quiet was broken when halfway through the meal, Dallion asked Jason about his mission, an awkward topic of discussion. Arthan and Lord Edward shared a hatred for the talk of violence and anything that had a relation to the topic of suffering. Jason was devouring his roasted meat. It looked as if he was inhaling the portion of the slain animal when Dally asked him of the quest.

The hungry young man took a brief moment to wash his food down with a cup of wine before telling his tale. "It wasn't difficult! We battled the bandits, defeated their leaders. We would have been back much sooner if we hadn't stopped at Castle Hammer to fight more bad men who had been annoying the folk who dwell there. Always we try to travel as fast as we can, but we needed to answer the call for justice. There's only six of us, little brother, but we do what we can for the good of Midlön."

"You know, your father and I are so proud to see you can complete such tasks at your age." Lady Sophia said to Jason.

"Thank you, Mother, but this was only a minor achievement! This journey, in comparison to our last, the previous mission that King Harold set forth for us-" Jason's eyes met with Edward's.

"Let's not speak of that one. Harold told few of us councilmen what he sent you out into the wild for; not appropriate at the table."

Arthan agreed with his father, even without knowledge of what this mission was that they had just been discussing.

"Daisy says there are hundreds of bandits in the Northwest. How did you kill them all?" Jason's little brother asked him.

"Dally, we didn't fight *all* of them. Once we killed the leaders-" Lord Frauer stopped Jason there.

"Enough talk of this mission for me. You defeated the bandits, and that's the end of it, my sons. Dallion, no more questions of it, please. You do not wish to hear such things." Edward smiled to Dallion and to Jason.

Arthan hardly touched his meal. The young man was sipping his wine, listening to his mother grow slightly angry, and Dallin more curious of his brother's work. "Ed he hasn't seen him. He's wonders these things. Let them talk." Sophia said.

"No, it's fine, Mother. I would rather not have the thought of all that in my mind anyway, after I've had to live through it once and so recently. Sorry, Dally, maybe I'll tell you about it another time." Jason smiled to his little brother.

The family sat in silence again for a short time as each of them feasted on the seasoned pork roast and peaches.

"So what do we think of this new king?" Arthan asked nobody in particular, with lips already stained violet for the remainder of the evening.

"He's a Royce, not one of the better-known houses in Midlön." said Edward to Arthan's random question.

"What's wrong with them?" Dallion asked his father.

"For starters, it isn't really much of a house in these days. It's only Gregory and Arol, both sons of Oreg Royce, a drunken cripple."

"Oreg was once one of the greatest knights whom ever lived, Father! I learned about him when I was even younger than Dallion. The man was talented before he was injured." Jason argued.

Edward told him, "He may have been talented in his youth but he became old, as every man does, and turned into a drinker after he twisted that foot. What's worse than a drinker raising children? A crippled drinker raising children. That's why Arol and Gregory are so soft in the head." Edward said this to everybody at the family table.

"They seem quite ordinary, in my opinion. I haven't seen much of them though, so my input is of no value." Arthan put in.

Edward shook his head with a mouthful of food. "I've sat with both of them on the council for years now. I know Gregory better than any average folk, common or high. Lord Gregory was rested King Harold's steward for a time in Harold's last decade of life, and the brother, Arol, always had been just another councilman like me...*had been*, until now. He'll do well as lord-steward, I suppose. I could think of better men though. I have not one bit of idea of what Harold saw in Gregory though. He's nothing but a whore for attention." Edward put a finger to his mouth and faced Dallion, "Shhhhh! No repeating my foul words."

Both father and all three sons laughed.

Edward Frauer took a sip of wine before he continued chewing his food and speaking on. "Gregory made a terrible steward. His love for killing and for war, it disgusted me and many others." Edward's family was eating in silence while listening to the lord of the household speak of these Royces. "Grand examples: He always urged Harold to allow the men of the arena to use live steel in place of blunt blades, always insisted that we went to war with the Dwarvish of the realm of Fordge, by right of conquest and expansion, as if we were villains. The wicked ideas he would have, they left me in thinking, *how could Harold have this man, this boy, as his personal advisor and successor?*"

"What about Arol?" Jason asked while pouring more wine for himself and for Arthan.

"Oh, don't get him to begin ranting on Lord Arol... He was just finishing." Sophia said, rolling her eyes back, gulping down her drink. "More wine for me as well, my child." Sophia held a stone cup outward for Jason to fill while she readied for Edward to rant onward of those he despised.

"Arol may appear a good man, if you're a woman looking for a handsome lover...but he's oh so lazy, so slow. Arol appears as if he has the mind of a man thrice his age. He's been on the council just as long as his brother, and I've hardly heard a word from him. He's always half asleep, always eating and drinking; pure waste of a soul. I don't like the man, never have. Both of them are just idiots. Perhaps you can't hate a man for being an idiot though, I don't know."

Arthan took his final bite of food after his father finished speaking, then Arthan asked after swallowing, "The king, he can fight though, yes?" He was no longer hungry for some apparent reason. He was prepared to leave the table with a half-filled dish but was enjoying the dialogue with his family.

Edward replied to his son with, "Yes, Gregory can fight because he's lucky that his knightly old father taught him how to use that red sword before twisting that old food of his, else Gregory he'd be useless, absolutely useless."

"You know Gregory is the only councilman to ever have fought in the arena?" Jason added in.

"Is he better than you?" Dallion asked Jason, chewing.

Lord Edward and Lady Sophia laughed at the boy's question.

"Nobody is better than Jason." Sophia said, grinning at her mighty, heroic-looking son there at the table.

"Well, Mother, I've never fought Gregory, and I don't plan to. I don't care whether it's just arena play or if he became my greatest and worthy opponent like in the fiction tales of the evil royal rulers, I wouldn't strike my king."

To that, Edward said, "You have been victorious in all but two of your arena matches. Those losses though, they seem now like ages ago, do they not? Even *then* you were strong, fast! And now even more so. As in these current days, I don't think there's anyone out in the lands who can beat you my boy, in a single melee." Edward did his best to give great compliments to his son.

Jason held his wine up for a drink salute, ignoring the painful reminder of his arena losses that his father had just made mentioned of. Jason said, "Maybe you're right. Perhaps I can't be beaten by a warrior of Midlön, but what of the other five realms?"

To that Arthan said, "Perhaps one day you'll find out. Fight more foreigners maybe." Arthan held his stone cup up too for the cheers gesture, wishing he knew how to fight like his brother.

03

DESMOND

Desmond remembered both his little arms from long ago, wrapped around his father's leg. The hairy muscled man stomped like a giant from the old books; his boy Desmond clutching onto him during each step he would take. Desmond's entire little body would swing with the motion as this man who raised him would take his walks within the village and yellow fields; his son would often be attached to a leg of his in this manner. This child always felt deeply comfortable wrapped around his father's big leg, whereas most other babes would be seen always at play climbing to shoulders of their parents to ride high. These thoughts and memories were from a time twenty-five years into the past; a time of warmth.

Desmond was cold now, yet strangely comfortable wrapped around the log in the river, in the same fashion he would wrap himself around his father's leg, more than two decades ago. Of course Desmond was much larger in this current day of the timeline, and this soaked old log, triple the size of his father's leg was the only thing keeping him from death. Death had taken his father from the world, almost ten years in past to this day, although this wet log seemed to bring him back to life.

Desmond imagined the log to be his father's leg with using detailed comparisons. The moss would be his thick hair, wood felt as his brute-like muscles had when he'd been alive. Other hours Desmond saw the old man drifting with him, clutching the soaked bark just as he did. "*Desmond-*" he would begin with. He never could hear or remember what the ghost of his father would have to say to him after reciting his name though.

Desmond drifted downstream, not caring if he collided with one of the hard rocks, not caring if the rapid white waters, or the eels found him. He finally opened his eyes after hours of deep thought of family, to raise his head up a bit higher out of the water to gaze upon what he could see of the lands as he moved within the current, low in the river. Desmond thought he would come to see more brown stones like from hours past. There was no yellow grass either... *Beautiful,* he thought. *Is this real? Have I died?* He quickly submerged himself under the soft current of the river. When he brought himself up and removed the black strands of wet hair from his eyes; he accepted that he had truly not been in a dream, not dead, nor in his homelands anymore. The grass he watched as he drifted, seemed alive with color. The stones were no longer brown, they were white and black. At home, death and the herbal natures worked as one, but Desmond saw he was no longer in his home now.

The foreign man chose to live, to survive for longer than this day. He used his strength to grip some of the white passing rocks. He climbed out from the waters of the southern river, abandoning his precious drifting log and the ghost of his father. Breathing heavily, the muscled man emerged onto the green grass, then right after that though he collapsed down. All that he could see for miles, grass. Luscious green grass, not like the dead, dried grasses from his homeland, far up the river to the East. This was soft, gentle grass; it was alive. Midrealm Plains stretched out before him. He watched it as he lay on his front side, drenched with river water. The fields and hills seemed endless as the Easterlñ gazed up, finding strength returning to his leg muscles again. Desmond watched the millions of blades of green grass extend out in the distance. The hairy, half-nude wet man took a deep breath inward, then began his journey north with nothing but the rags he wore at his waist.

The dark-haired man walked the unknown green plains for an hour's worth of time, the sun drying him all the while. He hadn't made any halt in his progression forward yet, not until he ceased walking after feeling the rumble at his toes. He took no more steps forward as of now so he could carefully listen to the sound of the horses' hooves in the distance; this was the first time he's looked back, first time he's stopped even once since his journey out of the river and onto the grass had begun. Black-bearded Desmond turned himself around, watching as two men in gray chain mail, one holding a banner, and the other wielding a crossbow, were riding upon horses, fast toward him. He watched the bolt of cloth on the oversize banner flap in the mild wind as he patiently awaited their greet. A black cross on a red backing was stitched on both sides of the flag; unfamiliar artwork to the foreigner.

"Halt! You have entered the realm of Midlön. In the name of the new king, Gregory Royce, we ask what business you have here?"

"Travel. Coming from that way." Desmond replied, then pointed a finger toward the mountain range to the East where he came from.

"I told you he's a foreigner." The man in chain armor with the crossbow told his armored friend holding the banner. He spoke again, "We watched you climb from Southern Satnis River. We've been following you. Why did you not enter the realm through the Mubey gate? Are you spying? Why swim the river?"

"I wanted to swim. Is it a crime to enter Midlön with swim?" asked Desmond to this horseman with the bow.

The men sat atop their mounts, whispering to one another for a short time. Desmond watched them quietly talk for a brief moment, unmoving. The one with the banner finally spoke, "Not against our law, but it is our duty to ask. You have hardly any clothes, and you looked weary after you climbed from Satnis River. We apologize for our rudeness, but it all appeared irregular."

"That mop on your head and that beard of yours could do for a trim as well. Not to mention you smell of absolute dung, even from up here I'm tortured by your odor." the other rider, with the crossbow, told this to Desmond.

The foreigner was appearing to be growing bored, but the riders mistook these harmless expressions as a sign of impatience.

"May I continue on with walk?" asked Desmond of them. "Not until you tell us where it is you're headed." they demanded to know.

"I'm going to the nearest place I can find a drink of water and food." Desmond said up to the men.

The one with the crossbow spat and giggled while the other began saying, "Useless searching for such things if you have no coin, but you'll find Willowhold to the northwest. About a day's walk it is, if you're quick and have a belly full that can last you that long of a journey."

"Thank you, my lords." Desmond said, in an attempt to sound respectful.

The man with the crossbow put his weapon away, then he took a bite of hard bread he pulled from a satchel. "I do love that you're trying, though we aren't *lords*, you halfwit, we're border guards. Don't cause any trouble, and find some clothes." He chewed, looking now to his companion beside him. "Hour's ride tailing this one with no more rum on us, and this is all we get? Not fun." The men rode back southeast toward the river. Desmond then continued on northward.

These strange moments are a part of Desmond's first day in a different realm for the first in his lifetime. Eastfell had been his home since birth. *Home*...until his people recently discovered the dark magic that ran within his blood. The Easterlñs had no choice but to cast him out by their law, to send him down the southern river into the mountains. Desmond was strong, a great swimmer from years of recreation at Eastfell's great lake with his father and sister. His fishlike skillset he had obtained enabled Desmond to use patience to float down the river, remaining alive after his banishment. Gently as he could, he had swam through the rapids for what seemed to be an entire night, until he finally passed through the full mountain range to eventually grab a hold of that giant drifting log which seemed to spawn the ghost of his father.

That night of his banishment, when the currents finally had brought him out of the white speeding waters of the mountain and into the gentle flow of the main river of this realm to the west, the sun had risen and then he began resting as he had drifted clutching the mossy log. He had floated all morning in thought and hallucination, before finally opening his eyes and climbing up onto the fresh green land of the realm named Midlön. Desmond was banished from home, told he could never enter the realm of Eastfell again. Now here he found himself, miserably walking in the plains of Midlön.

Hours in this new world seemed like they lasted as long as days. It had been quite some time since he'd had his encounter with the riders in chain mail. Desmond shuffled through the grass the way an elder would walk through quick-mud. The beauty of the colorful lands was dazzling to the man, but the thought of never being able to return home again clung to the back of his mind. This sadness, hunger, and thirst made the man move slowly. He returned to this thought of his banishment every half of an hour's amount of time; as much as he tried to deflect the pain, he could not. He would think, *Even if I found a woman here, or man to fall in love with, I could never call this realm home, never walk as one of these people.*

Desmond drank from the clear streams, tried to pick what mushrooms he could find beside the creeks, the ones that were not rotted or poisonous. At sunset he slept under a tree, and when sunrise came, he walked; and then he slept, then did the same the next day. Already he missed the warmth of the village he'd been raised in, dwelling there living until his last day in Eastfell. The thought of his old, exciting visits to the grand wooden city of Aildube brought him now to tears when he came to realize he could never see its beauty, not ever again. He missed the dryness, the special way the sun touched the lands. He longed for his family, the family who would never want him in their lives again; perhaps his father would have thought differently of this curse within his blood if he had been alive to witness it. None of that could matter to Desmond now. He knew he had need to find civilization, to find some life in place of remembering a dead father, a mother, and sister who'd abandoned him. Desmond had need to find a way of retrieving larger amounts of food and the will to make a legacy in this new, strange realm. O*therwise why live?* thought he while walking.

The sun fell, and so Desmond found rest just beside a muddy pond surrounded by tall grass where the dirt was soft. The man struggled to sleep, always tossing, switching which shoulder faced the sky. He turned over, trying to make himself comfortable, then he began to shiver. He couldn't bear the coldness much longer; he needed warmth again. Desmond arose and found small bits of twig and leaves to begin a fire.

He sat staring at the flames after he crafted the blaze. His black eyes lit up and shining from the fires reflection. The heat on his face gave him reminder of home; back when he would look up to watch the sun. Desmond looked up now and saw nothing but blackness; not one single star in the sky, red or blue. He was lying down, facing the fire. He watched the empty sky for as long a time as he could, then he finally lost himself to sleep after he thought of his father's love and the rhythmic swing of holding his leg during a walk in the past.

He woke to the sight of dying embers, joined with the sounds of vicious growling, sky still black. Desmond turned and looked beside himself across the pond, where he saw a pair of shiny, colorless eyes stalking him in the tall grass; eyes black as death, just like his very own. He stood up and began to whisper to the animal. He spoke in his own tongue, the words of taming. The beast continued to growl, and so Desmond moved forward slowly, still whispering. He knew that performing his craft incorrectly could mean death for himself, so he was sure be correct. One error, and the beast would go mad. Out of the grass leapt a dog of great size, releasing from its mouth loud, mighty howls. Desmond, without fear, spoke his words more sharply, more harshly. The ancient Eastern taming words had failed him when he was a child many times, he had now mastered them.

Desmond spoke louder and louder, and the hound then howled louder and louder, until finally his speech was finished. The creature turned its own head from side to side quickly, as if shaking off a foul smell, looking like a sort of sneeze. The beast resumed focus on Desmond, without a growl this time. It then slowly padded toward him, and then stopped to put its head down into the soft dirt. Desmond patted the beast on the back, then with a firm grip, lifted it by the snout to examine the animal's eyes.

"Araisha." Desmond told the hound in his language. *Araisha,* the name of an old lover of Desmond's from his early years during his second decade of living. "Araisha, find food." Desmond said in his own language.

The dog backed away and howled just before dashing off into the grass. Desmond found more twigs for the embers and two thick branches too by a fallen tree not far off. He wanted to be ready for what his new companion would bring back for him, and so he began to revive the small fire. Desmond's eyes went from black, back to brown as he calmed himself, letting the dark magic fade away some.

Scalding hot grease dripped from his fingers as he ate the rabbit off the ashy wooden skewer. For today, he had consumed nothing but little fruit, mushrooms, and water from what ponds and streams he could find within the green plains. Now though, his newly acquired dog here had just brought back the fattest little critter he had ever seen in his lifetime when she returned after the hunt sendoff. He felt thankful to fill his stomach with meat once more. *Midlön rabbits are far bigger than those of Eastfell.* He sat, eating with Araisha sleeping beside him, using her for the warmth of her body and fur. When the sun rose, the spell of taming that Desmond had performed was now sealed in; the dog was his for now. He killed what was left of his fire, then woke his companion and started northwest once again.

The people of the East practiced ancient taming techniques for hundreds of years. With large amount of patience, about almost any sort of beast could be mind settled and controlled, if the right words were spoken in the right manner and, most importantly, with a bit of magic in the blood. Of course It could only be done if spoken in the eastern tongue, and only if spoken just the correct way. Desmond had used the words on wild boar, and the oversized scorpions to lure them into traps, tricking them into a deceiving approach so he could thrust a spear into their heads.

Desmond once discovered that he had the ability and skill to tame one of the large spotted sand-cats, to keep as a pet and companion for hunting when he was just fifteen years of age. His mother and father soon put an end to the beast's life when they discovered it within the village. Now he felt currently all that he needed was his hound here Araisha, the perfect companion for the start of his new life. Araisha would hunt for him, keep him from becoming lonely, and even soon defend him from threats even in this upcoming night. Desmond found himself eating more often with his new friend catching his meals. The two, man and animal, traveled through the cloudy plains, both with filled stomachs.

When Desmond had climbed from Southern Satnis River to enter the realm, it had been bright and beautiful, yet each day now grew darker from constant clusters of incoming clouds. These clouds caused the view of the stars to be blocked during the hours after the sun would fall.

On this cloudy and starless night of his journey, while he was feasting on meat that he had roasted over a poorly made spit, his thoughts returned back to his old home toward the east *again*, but his mind this time didn't settle on his family, they settled on his gods. On that night long after the sun had fallen from the sky, Desmond began an Easterlñ ritual which all followers of their religion must complete to be cleansed of their past errors, recent and or of long ago. When the men of his village exiled him from their realm, Desmond had wounded two of them with their own weapons before he was brutally cast into the river. It took four strong warriors to restrain him, to throw him away as he fought and struggled to stay with his remaining family who hadn't even had a want for him anymore themselves. Desmond desired forgiveness from his gods and so he lit three small fires. He made the three burning stacks just under an old oak tree, using scraps of rabbit fur and some leaves to help the branches catch flame.

He prayed for forgiveness with the dog beside him until all the red glow and smoke had vanished from each three small blazes. After his prayer, he blew the ashes away with the breath of his lungs, starting with the last one he had made. In the eyes of the Easterlñ religion, Desmond now has been forgiven for all the errors he had committed since his last fire ritual, but that wouldn't stop his people from seeing him as a corrupted dark being, *Because the darkness will forever be in my blood*. Still it made the man feel much warmer in his heart, knowing that at the least his three gods will always find a place for him and offer love in the next lives to come.

He lay down backside to the dirt with a full stomach, watching some of the newly visible red stars appear, and then quickly melt away into the black clouds above. Just as he was about to close his eyes and let sleep take him away, he heard his companion growling. Desmond sprang up onto his feet, looking in the direction Araisha was faced. Three dark figures were approaching quickly. They were men, and they were awkwardly carrying objects, *Tools perhaps?* but more than likely they were holding weapons.

"Who's there?" one of them said from afar.

Desmond didn't answer the voice. The light from the incoming moon was making the walking bodies appear brighter, easier to view now that they'd become closer. Desmond, his dog, and especially those glowing embers had been easy enough to see in these lands here from close and or from afar.

"I said who's there?" yelled the biggest of the three. He was giant-sized, like Desmond's father. This big man walked with a limp though, whereas Desmond's father had chiseled fast-moving legs.

The dog howled, and Desmond prepared himself. "He's got himself a wolf, he does. He's a homeless." said the one wearing an oversize black cloak that looked as if it should have belonged to the one that was giantlike.

"Leave me alone." Desmond told the men.

The man with the cloak revealed his sword, orange and rusty but easy to view in the night even without a shine. He was attempting to frighten Desmond, but the foreigner stood his ground, keeping his eyes fixed on the crusty blade in the darkness of the night. "Don't be so hasty as to draw steel, brother." the large man told the one with sword in his belt just after grunting from an ache in his foot.

The last one and smallest of the three kept his hand gripped on the hilt of a weapon, a sheathed dagger; it rattled and shook. Fear of the mysterious-looking Desmond was growing inside this small one of the men.

The dog snapped at the giant man, the one who limped. This giant man with his bad foot walked backwards two paces, as the one beside him with the big cloak pulled the sword from his belt. "My brother here has his blade drawn, and he isn't afraid to use it. Keep the dog calm and cough up what you got, and we'll let you live." he told Desmond this.

"No." was Desmond's answer.

The big man sighed, "You're from the East, I can tell by the accent. It makes sense. He doesn't know us, lads… I don't exactly know how it be in your realm, but here we're *raiders*. I'm sorry, we're the bad ones, the Hardain wood rapists they call is in the Northwest of Midlön, and there's plenty more millions of us right down the road. We have weapons, and there is more of us than you. Be smart now if you don't wanna get boned and killed."

"They call us *bandits* here. That's what we are, we can do bad things." said the small one, as if Desmond didn't know what the word *bandit* meant.

The little man shuffled back and gripped his knife tighter when he'd caught Desmond's attention and gaze. Desmond might have been an Easterlñ, but he understood Midlön speech very well. "You three, leave right now or I'll fight you." he told them.

They looked at one another and then all smiled; even the tiny fearful-looking one. "Take his head off his shoulders." the big one said to the one in the cloak. The bandit with the sword stepped forward, and so Araisha leapt to meet him.

The hound bit onto the bandit's cloak, dragging him down before he could even swing his sword once. The hound's next bite was to the bandit's arm, giving Desmond enough time to rip the sword from the antagonist's hands when his fingers went loose from the pain of the dog's bite. Desmond thrust the pointy end into the disarmed man's gut as the dog held his arm within her jaws.

Araisha let him loose as Desmond removed the sword from the inside of his stomach. The bandit lay crying, bleeding in the grass as the other two watched in shock while Desmond moved forward with the iron in his hand. *These two shouldn't have let him come at me alone.* Araisha pounced on the small one before he even had time to unsheathe that silver dagger. Desmond took care of the large one in seconds, only because the rapist fell backwards, pissing when he saw both of his allies fall. Araisha feasted on man flesh that night, and Desmond won himself a rusted long sword with some new garb. At sunrise, the Easterlñ man and the hound continued on northwest together.

04

The Council

Arthan woke from a dreamless sleep to the smell of eggs and burnt lamb. He began his day with a morning prayer just before heading through the pink hallways and then into the kitchen for breakfast. *"Aeon, god of light, hear me now and today. Lighten my soul and brighten my house today. Guide me in this world. Lead me to greatness today. Cast out and keep away the terrible of today. Ascend me to your heaven when my time ends, not this day. In Aeon I trust all days."* Arthan recited that same prayer most mornings since he learned it when he had been a child. He studied with great focus for years during his time in post youth lessons, where he had learned deeper knowledge of the ways of god under the training of the priests. He had dwelt among them in the Cathedral of Aeon for half of a year after graduation from the Institution. The cathedral was constructed on Silver Street, as was Arthan's house. The Frauer family was known to be religious, just as any of the greater and noble houses of Midlön had been expected to be.

Still in thought of god, Arthan stepped through the kitchen arch where the pink hallway ended. In the dining area he found his mother and father cleaning the table. He noticed both of his brothers, Dallion and Jason, were not present.

"Slept in again?" his mother asked, eyes set on the wood she'd been scrubbing at.

"I'm sorry." Arthan said back to her.

His father left the dining table to put the plates away in the dishwash tub. Edward prepared a handful of soap for himself while he watched his son idle at the hall entrance.

"It's all right. Here, it's cold, but I saved you lots." Arthan's father told him, pointing to a plate beside the oven with the many strips of meat upon it.

She had overcooked *and* overseasoned the lamb again with too much pepper; he coughed from the strong scent.

Sophia stopped scrubbing, now throwing the scraper into a bucket of filthy water. "You should learn how to wake on time." After saying that to Arthan, she looked right to her husband. "Edward, beginning today, if he isn't up while we eat, then he doesn't get a thing."

Arthan took a seat at the half-cleaned table and made himself appear expressionless, as he learned to do throughout his years. "It's just breakfast. It's not a large problem, Mother."

"It *is* a problem! How do you think it makes me feel that I work hard to cook my children meals, when instead of consuming them while they're hot, they sleep long after god has put the sun back in the sky? Go to sleep in the nights earlier, then you shall wakeup earlier in the mornings, so we can feast as a family. This is a privilege! Ability to dine every morning with you… Oh, Aeon, save my soul."

Arthan revived his dead face, looking to his mother to speak to her as he chewed the burnt breakfast. "I'm sorry. I know it's no good reason, but I can't help my sleeping on some days. How does one even choose when to waken? I could use for a strong spell or potion to help me. What of Jason and Dally? Oh, forget I mentioned them. To you they always have good excuses as to why they miss these meals."

Sophia's face turned a dark red. Arthan's father remained calm as he smashed some peanuts beside the sink where he could catch a breeze coming in from the window. For such a clouded day, it was hot in the kitchen and also in the dining area of the house, as well as the entire city, more than likely. Arthan was wearing his thick tunic, beginning to sweat now from the top of his forehead where that shaggy hairline of his started. Lord Edward smashing peanuts, looking upon his dripping son, decided to add in to the talk to answer his question, *What of Jason and Dally?*

"Jason left early to see his men. Dallion just walked out the door for his lessons only a minute before you've woken just now." Edward told Arthan this.

Of course Arthan had nothing to say in response. Young Arthan looked down at his plate, at the hideous dark-green flakes of burnt pepper on his blackened food.

He remained silent while Edward tried to calm his wife. "My lady, are you well there? Please relax yourself. This isn't how I want to start my morning, not ever. Sleepy Arthan meant no disrespect, of course. Perhaps he didn't get a good night of sleep. Remember when we were his age? We'd sleep half the day away at times."

Sophia ignored her husband, striding off down the hallway, angry.

"Father-" Arthan began.

Edward took a bite of some cold buttered bread. He chewed and interrupted his son while he stuffed some peanuts in his pocket. "Don't worry about her and her deep, dark depressions. Listen, I have a gift…well, a surprise for you today. I want you to go clean yourself and put on your finest clothes." Edward paused to swallow the bread in his mouth. He resumed speaking, "I'm taking you with me to the keep and into the council chamber."

Arthan was lost in confusion. He planned to spend this very morning at the library in the Wizards District, like he always had on the second day of the week. He wiped the sweat from his forehead with the already used napkin on the table. "Father, the council chamber is no place for me. What reason could you possibly have for-"

"I told you, it's a surprise." Edward said.

Arthan had hatred for planned surprises, the idea of them disgusted him, but he knew he wouldn't get an answer out of his old father, so he didn't bother to ask again. Instead, Arthan said, "I will get myself prepared."

Edward smiled at that. "Please do. I don't plan on making King Gregory wait for us. Half of the council would be there already."

Arthan dashed for his bedchamber to clean and dress himself. He didn't know if he should think to be nervous or full of eager excitement. He slipped on a pair of dress shoes just before he tore off his sweat stained tunic. He then took out his finest blue silks from the chest, the ones with his house emblem embroidered on the chest: a blue tree, black background. Arthan would have appeared a proper lord, if only his oily brown hair hadn't looked all that wet. He washed with hair soap, but it didn't help one bit; not that it mattered, his father made no comment about the grease, or on his unshaven, uneven-looking hairy chin and lip.

Edward and Arthan left through the door without giving Lady Sophia a farewell. After they passed through the little front gate, then stepped foot onto the stone street of the city, Arthan inhaled deeply as he always did when he left his house to begin his day. *Foul city air, lovely.* They quickly met with a passing horse walker wearing one of the yellow cloaks to mark their profession. They mounted two of his city ponies in exchange for gold coins to give to him, father and son now heading up and onward after bidding him thanks.

The ride would be quick. The Frauers dwelt on Silver Street in the High District. Their house was built on the east end of the street, close to their destination. Short travel up the winding street now leading northward, would have them soon coming to the steps to the Great Keep, where the Throne Hall and council chamber would be resting. This royal structure of course could be seen entirely from where Arthan and his family's house was built. From almost everywhere in the city, one could get a grand view of the Great Keep's exterior and all its fortifications. If one was within the city's northern portions, it was possible to get a glimpse of the interior of the Throne Hall through the huge glass wall built at the back end of the chamber; a glass wall appearing as one enormous unstained window. From the Frauer household though, the front of the keep was the only viewable bit of the massive construct.

The Frauer family wasn't always settled in Ascali the way they had been in these current days of the White-age. After Harold Apollo took hold of the realm's throne and put an end to the Gray family's reign, he welcomed Edward Frauer into the council and knighted his eldest son, Jason, the youngest knight in the history of Midlön. Edward Frauer passed his own castle of Fort Bluewood to his younger and only brother, Lord Carlyle Frauer. Lord Edward then brought his wife and sons to the capital city, Ascali, where he would now live out his days advising the royal family in the council chamber by the day, and then raising his sons at the Frauer residency on Silver Street with his wife Sophia in the evenings and nights.

Arthan and his father spoke to each other as their tiny mounts trotted onward bringing them to meet the king and the rest of the council.

"Who walked Dallion to his lessons?" asked Arthan of his lord-father.

"Who would you assume? Sir John, as the usual. You know he means to begin to train Dallion in the combat arts next month. He's now eight years old. It's about time he's learned how to fight, wouldn't you say?" Arthan then chuckled at that, thinking of his pathetic self. "Do you remember me at eight?"

"Aye, more interested in studying magic and reading, lots of reading. You liked those horrible grammar books more than swords, sure. And now, you write well, sure…so those books weren't a waste, but all that magic studying! Haaa, it isn't in your blood. I've tried telling you in your child days, what seemed like a hundred times, but you wouldn't hear it."

Arthan's memory took him back to his time in youth when he would sit in the study reading the priest's spells from the book of light, waving a toy wand about, trying discover the power of holy magic-craft. He never found these powers though, and he was smart enough now to know that he never would.

The streets had a significantly less amount of folk about than the previous days; Arthan noticed this as they rode. He wondered where the people were, *Where had they gone? Inside their homes? If I could use magic, I would use it to see through these household walls.* So soon his mind brought him back to the thought of those magical powers that he never discovered as a child yet tried so very hard to long ago. They rode in silence for a bit until Arthan said, "I thought maybe if I read them over and over, tried hard enough…then the spells and enchantments, the charms…would work for me."

His father then sighed, sitting atop the saddle. "It does take practice and effort, but if a child's mother and father have no magical blood in their veins, then that child, *you!* has no chance of becoming what we all dreamt of: not a wizard nor mage nor even an elementist or a boredom-filled priest; not any kind of magical being whatsoever. Not one soul in our bloodline has ever wed a woman who practiced magic. Every boy without these gifts felt this way at some time or another; this yearning to use magic. Sometimes this desire never leaves them. I know it hasn't left you."

"I know this. It has never left me, I'll admit. I would do many things to gain the gift of magic." Arthan said sadly.

They rode in silence again, past empty jeweler stands and art wagons. The previous conversation was making Arthan slightly melancholic; the deserted streets were not helping his mood grow brighter either.

"It's not too late, you know." Edward said after studying his son's bodily behavior atop the skinny beast.

"For what?" Arthan asked, although he already knew what his father was going to tell him. He'd been trying to make it happen since Arthan could hold his little gardening shovel.

"It's not too late for John to teach you how to fight, or Jason, if that'd make you feel more in comfort."

Arthan was becoming angry already.

His father had brought up this conversation topic on him many times in the past, and they all had ended the same way.

"How many times must I tell you, Father, I don't want to learn swordplay. I'll never have need for it. I don't plan to rush in to a battle or to be playing in the tourneys. Nothing could convince me to attack another soul."

Edward shook his head in the negative manner, laughing a bit before saying, "What about defense? What if the time came when you needed to defend yourself or someone you love? Like a family of your own? What would you do then? Would you throw your books at them? Wave a magical wand in their face? I've raised my son to be an ass, but I do love you still."

Arthan occasionally expressed flashes of sadness, or extreme mind stress, always temporary and never lasting long though. The priests claim this to be a birth imperfection, and so they gave word to the Lord and Lady Frauer that this common illness had spawned inside her son while he grew in her womb. For years Arthan's mother, Lady Sophia, had brought Arthan to the cathedral for *"inspection"* by the healing priests. He'd always remembered, these men of god they claimed to be, poking at him with the tiny needles in attempts to provoke him, to study this illness in hopes to potentially find how to cure him of it.

Arthan was breathing heavily as he rode now. He took a hand off his reigns to place on his chest; he was doing his best to relax himself. These fine clothes he wore had been weighing him down, he now realized. He was sweating, thinking how dreadful plate mail would feel equipped right this very moment. *How could Jason bear it? I'm glad I will never need to wear such things.* Was he lying to himself though? Was he truly glad of this fact that he would never have need of any armor in life? Arthan knew that for a common lord his own age of twenty years living, at the very least he should know what the weight of chain mail upon his shoulders and neck is like, even how the proper balance of a sword feels in those clam-like hands of his. *Why should I practice a craft that I do not choose to pursue as a profession though? I have better use of my time.*

Lord Edward wasn't finished speaking about it. As the they trotted and trotted, the lord fed his mount some peanuts while interrupting his son's thought with, "Arthan I may be a councilman, but I myself at least know how to wield and properly use a sword. I know how to swing the axe above the fireplace, and not just at wood. I might not be the best… I might not be like Jason, but if the time came where I found that I *had* to fight…I know that I have the courage to stand up for myself, and for you. Not even the courage, I'm speaking about the arms training. A craft that gives me power to stand for your mother, and for Dallion. And! I'd stand for Jason, god forbid he was unable to defend himself one day."

Arthan didn't know what to say to all of this theater-like nonsense as he rode, baking in the sun when the clouds would occasionally allow the powerful summer rays through. He didn't have the urge to begin arguing about the drama of this all, nor feel like admitting to his father that he was a bit correct in the subject.

"Father, you might not be as talented as Jason, you say? Well, there isn't anybody who's better than Jason." said Arthan to the lordly man. Edward assumed his son was now trying to change the subject of talk; he could see in his eyes as they both rode through the clean streets, how flustered his own child was becoming in the moment. He let him win and gave rest to the discussion topic. *Today would be too good a day to ruin! I do hope this makes you happy my son.* Edward Frauer was speaking to himself in his own mind while the stranger pony he rode chewed on more peanuts.

Atop their little rented mounts, the father and son followed the rising street to the left where the winding turn was ending. Edward wasn't speaking of Arthan and his lack of arms training anymore, yet he remained on this rare conversation topic of combat though. He began talking of an infamous knight of Ascali, and then the new king too.

"Sir Lucifer Gray is one of the most talented living souls who practices sword-craft, so the records say. King Gregory is said to be *the* best of now. Just kiss-ass talk because the crown is his. King Gregory can swing a sword like an artist, though only in the duels though with the blunt tin swords. Gregory, he's never cut a man. Jason lost the tournament that one year against Sir Lucifer, so I wouldn't go so far as to say your brother is the best of the best, not until he rematches and defeats the old Sir Gray. Jason against the king though, oh, what a show that would be. Talented Gregory is, but as I have said, still never cut a man. Jason has butchered bandits, orcish, raiders, and rapists."

He said a lot just then and there, thought Arthan Frauer. He hadn't known what to say back to his father. He asked Edward, "What about that old Jack Blaydên? Can *he* beat Jason?" Arthan asked him.

Edward answered, "Jack Blaydên is rotting at a whorehouse somewhere in Eastfell, more than likely. The man competed in the arena only once, beat everyone bloody, sure, but it was only one year. It's a shame he wouldn't fight again. Oh, how I've always wondered if Jason would be able to handle him truly, and so has the whole city. But aye, that's probably why the old man didn't want to compete again. He defeated all of his opponents that first day, and after that see, he doesn't want to lose."

This *Jack Blaydên* the Frauers spoke of was the only living soul left from the first royal family of Midlön, the founders of the great city Ascali and creators of the realm's law and Book of Order. Sir Jack was known for his good deeds as a knight and for the story of the downfall of his royal house. Such deeds hadn't been what earned him his ultimate fame and fear though. This iconic, elder knight was renowned for his stunning first and last day in the Ascali arena! All the folk not just of the city, but of the realm knew these tales of Sir Jack and how he had defeated all foes in the tournament sands while the city folk cheered him on. Arthan had heard talk of Sir Jack Blaydên's skills, as anybody had, the same way all had known of the legendary Sir Lucifer Gray. Gregory Royce though, this talk and mention of the new king being skilled with a sword is new and unheard information to Arthan's ears.

"I didn't know King Gregory fought well." Arthan said, looking up at the gray stone keep, watching it grow larger as they rode closer.

Edward coughed. "Some say he's *the* best. Gregory's never cut or killed before, yet he's defeated some of the greatest knights in the arena with the tourney weapons. Remember, we're only speaking of men though. We can't forget the other beings within the other five realms. If we are speaking of *just* our *Midlön*, then I must say our new king, the young man knows how to use his weapons. It's rare to have a king who can fight. I think Gregory sucks in dialogue, but he's skilled with swords! Just speaking truths."

"Father! Hush, we're in the public of the streets. You cannot say he sucks."

Edward giggled to that, and then Arthan did too. "The deserted streets…" Edward said back to his son.

The paths on the empty streets were becoming steep. The stones seemed to rise higher and higher, slowly though. They still rode on and spoke to each other. "How long was he on the council for? Gregory I mean, before Harold died. Isn't it rare? to have a councilman who can fight? I mean fight well…well as Gregory."

Edward looked to his surroundings, this time to make sure what little people there were among them could not hear him speak poorly of the new king again. "Well, maybe that explains why King Gregory was such a terrible steward and councilman. A man can't be well at everything. If our new king wasn't such an ass of a halfwit, he'd be perfect for the throne. He has the look for the love of the folk, and the arms training that every king should wish for, god forbid war came! He could stand upon the frontlines with that mighty leading look of power within him. But his person, his soul…he sucks."

Arthan laughed and soon snapped from his awful mood. Both father and son giggled their way up to the Great Keep's eastern entrance, talking badly about their new king for the rest of the way.

Is it cruel to enjoy talking ill of someone? Someone in the royal family? Arthan didn't care much. He enjoyed sharing humor with his father, felt blessed to turn from sad to happy so quickly, hoping god above couldn't read his thoughts or hear his dialogue in these moments.

They rode up and up, finally then finding the silver-plated honor guards stationed at the eastern entrance's iron doors within this meeting yard.

"Sirs, let me introduce my son, Arthan." Edward said to the pair of knights.

They shifted their spears to opposite hands and settled them down after stomping the blunt ends into the yard ground twice. "Welcome in, lords." both of the guards said at the same time just before the black doors to the keep swung open.

They left their mounts with the nearby keepers, and then they entered the structure. After both father and son passed through the incredibly long, narrow hallway, seeming more like a tunnel to Arthan, they came to a small doorless entry. Another two guards wearing silver stood by this arch leading to the main chamber.

This security greeted them, in the same manner the last pair had. Arthan and his lord-father entered this dome room built low beside the tall Throne Hall, known to all as the *council chamber.* They seated themselves among the rest of the councilmen. It was customary that all souls of the council sat in a randomized fashion, to express equality throughout their order. Arthan looked above, watching the chamber expand overhead as he admired the architecture. He was fascinated by the hundreds of torches that lit the circular shaped room. A magical cold, silver-colored light bathed the walls and all occupants. The bright torches of the elementists making could last burning for days before a change be needed. Lord Edward remembered old king Harold Apollo expressing his love for his cold-colored torches; sadly, the new royal family would soon make a change to the fashion of them. Edward was looking at his son as the young man admired these lively, uncommon magical flamed decorations giving light.

As the room was still filling with councilmen, Arthan, in his House Frauer tunic, looked away from the fascinating silver-like fire above, carefully viewing all of these men in their brown robes now. He guessed there to be a hundred souls if not just a little more than that, he was correct. The council chamber held one hundred councilmen, who would all be seated around the three sparkling chairs in the center of the room: one for the king, one for his steward, and lastly for the grand councilman. Arthan looked down at his garb; the sight of it made him uncomfortable. He was dressed as a high-dweller, certainly not dressed as a councilman.

Arthan Frauer thought, *Am I the only soul not dressed in these dung-colored robes?* All four entrances were manned with pairs of honor guards; the knights in the heaviest of silver armor, wielding the largest spears and shields that a man can carry. These souls have sworn their lives to shielding the king until his or their death. Only the guards and Arthan wore different attire than the rest of the one hundred men in the chamber.

Edward and Arthan heard Councilman Martin say, "Good morning, Lord Frauer." just after the father and son took their seats beside this pink skinned man.

"Morning to you too, Martin. I introduce my son Arthan."

"Hello." was all that Arthan said to the councilman. Edward's son couldn't keep his eyes from the warts on the old man's right-side face.

"It's a pleasure to meet you, my boy. Here for training, are you? I'll tell you it's all a lot easier than it seems."

"No, I'm here…" *Why am I here?*

Arthan began to speak again just before his father cut his words off with, "Yes, he's to be a councilman. I want him to sit in on a meeting first so he understands how we go about it all. I've already discussed it with Lewis." Edward gave his son a pat on the shoulder.

Arthan was struck with confusion. He looked from Councilman Martin's largest wart to his father's brown eyes. Lord Edward laughed and smacked Arthan on the shoulder, hard. He didn't know if his father was just making jokes or if he truly meant what he had just said.

The three of them sat there surrounded by the rest of the councilmen, all moving to get their seats. Martin smiled at Lord Edward. "What a good father you are, Edward! I would bring my boys, but they're both embarrassments. Well, Arthan, I hope you do well. I would be glad to see you as one of us. Just be patient, wait until the right time to speak. You'll do just fine! Well, it's your first time. Don't speak at all, I suppose." The man itched that big pink wart, smiling, then turned to look on forward as the king entered, along with his brother, Arol, the new lord-steward, and Grand Councilman Lewis as well.

These new glamorous, royal brothers stood now in front of their chairs at the center of the room, just beside the grand councilman with his chair too. All then quickly fell silent. They were surrounded by the one hundred councilmen (and Arthan); all these men placed higher than their three selves. All had perfect view on the royal two, and Lewis down below in the center, similar to the arena's seating and viewing style. When the Royce brothers and the grand councilman sat their asses down in the metal chairs, everyone who was seated above arose from their places while saying, "*My king.*"

When King Gregory raised his hand for all to be seated, Arthan asked his father of what he had just spoken to Councilman Martin. "Father, do you mean it?"

All councilmen and Arthan sat down the same moment.

"Yes, I mean it. That was the grand surprise." Edward whispered, crossing his legs to make himself comfortable. "Just keep your voice down and listen. Don't speak, just listen… I'll tell you more after the session."

Arthan nodded, then he took in a deep breath.

King Gregory raised and then lowered his hand, bringing it now to rest upon the arm of his chair. He rubbed the gold with his oily thumb and then quickly adjusted his crown atop his shaven head before he began to speak. "Councilmen, I am glad to sit here, in this golden chair, as your king. Just last week, my bottom was placed where my brother sits now, in this silver chair beside me, as your steward, but now I sit as a king, yes." King Gregory gripped some of the golden medallions on his oversized belt with his left hand, looking to the torches placed among the dome ceiling. "I do hope I can treat all as good as our Harold had, but it will take time, yes, time. The truth is, I am a bit nervous. You all see this is only my first meeting I've called. I apologize for the hour. I do know it is early."

"There is nothing to forgive, my king!" one of the men in brown robes yelled from a top last bit of rows in the chamber.

The king, using those reddish mud-colored eyes the woman loved so much, found the councilman.

"We serve at your command and pleasure." another said from the opposite end of the dome.

The king then looked toward the direction of this second councilman who spoke, then laughed to all. "Yes, still. I would rest easier if I knew all were pleased with my decisions. Unfortunately, I can't bring the great pleasures to all. There will be arguments and disagreements in this very chamber, just as there always has been, but this… haa, that is what you all are here for! Now let us begin." With his pale shining head and his bright steel crown filled with diamonds, Gregory was glowing as he sat in his kingly council chair.

Then there was the goblin-looking Grand Councilman Lewis, who was now rising from his bronze seat, unraveling a scroll. "There be only one matter for today's session. The king wishes to ask the council for their great and valuable opinion on an important choice. Which soul should be named Shield to the King!"

Lewis sat back down in his chair as dozens of councilmen sprang from their seats, shouting what seemed to be hundreds of different names of renowned knights throughout the realm; hundreds of names shouted in a matter of seconds.

Arthan looked to these living surroundings, watched the screaming men in their robes yelling out to the king. *Gregory can't possibly hear all of them,* Arthan thought to himself. He didn't understand how the king was expected to focus on all these answers, all in one moment. Arthan had never come to think that this very chamber his quiet father spent so much time in would appear so ear-piercing, would seem so very stressful even just after minutes upon arrival.

"Silence! Please! Men, please!" shouted the king's brother, Lord-Steward Arol.

When the room became quiet again, Grand Councilman Lewis said to all, "Please stand if you wish to give your input on the subject. Stay seated if otherwise."

Almost all rose to stand.

"You there." King Gregory said as he pointed to one of the councilmen in the front row.

"My king, I believe you should have Sir Preston Estrain as your sworn Shield. The man is faithful. He has trained all four of my sons in the arts of combat. He is well known to me and to my family. I can assure you there is no better man." The councilman was afraid to look to his king as he spoke to him. Instead, he spoke to his own shoes.

Lord-Steward Arol then replied for his brother, the king. "Sir Preston is old. He's aged to his what? Midsixties, I believe? Is that correct, Grand Councilman Lewis? A strong young man is needed protecting my brother, just how Sir Brendan was only a lad in his days of defending young rested Harold in the earlier years of our White-age."

King Gregory agreed with his brother on this matter. "Arol is correct, as always. I wish to find a guard who appears closer to my years of age and spirits. Sir Preston, and even our Sir Brendan Callum continuing on for my care after Harold's *would* be suitable for me with their arms talents, but I hardly know either men's soul traits. I don't have the same…I don't know, I wouldn't have the same sort of bond as our previous king had with *his* shield if I chose Sir Brendan or Preston! Harold Apollo saw Brendan fight for him. He had seen his skillset not just in arena play, but in true combat! I hope he does well dwelling as of now, our Sir Brendan." King Gregory tapped the floor with his heeled boot repetitively. "But yes, yes, he will not be dwelling with me… Brendan's role as Shield has ended after Harold's life has." Gregory adjusted his crown as it began to tip and fall. "If I am to spend my time with a new man by my side to shield me, I would like him and I to have similarities to inspire a desired friendship. I want a man I can converse with. That's not too queer, is it? A strong man that will not only protect me, but also be a sweet friend to me."

Blind Councilman Brian rose up to be given permission to speak.

"Councilman Brian." Grand Councilman Lewis shouted as he pointed a shaky wrinkled finger to the man in brown.

Brian cleared his raspy throat then yelled, "My king, I believe the decision should be based on skill and ability to serve as a protector. Not age, nor how well you can share dialogue and recreational time with-"

"Awe please! Silence!" Arol kindly shouted. "It will be *based* on however my brother, your king! wants it to be based on! That's why he's *the king*. Now don't be silly, don't be. Do you have a recommendation or not?"

The white-eyed councilman grew a fat lump in his throat. He froze in standing silence, then finally coughed, breaking the quiet off with, "I, umm…yes, no, my lord-steward! I have no suggestion on who should be Shield. I was just beginning to remind all of the importance of skill…how well your guard can give protection to King Gregory. That factor is all that should be taken into consideration."

"Sit down." commanded Arol, with a lazy annoyance in his voice, too tired to argue with the blind man any longer.

"Skill and ability for protection." the king said aloud as he brushed at the black blanket-looking beard hanging from his chin resting upon his chest. "If that's all that is of importance, then I should have the brave Sir Jason as my Shield."

Arthan looked away from the three below, watching his father now as he rolled his eyes to the back of his head. *He knew I'd look right at him,* Arthan thought. Shouts came from all directions of the chamber. It seemed more than half of the room was in favor of Sir Jason Frauer being named Shield to the King.

The grand councilman chose Councilman George to speak next when he'd seen him rising for a word. "My king, Sir Jason is possibly the city's finest knight, and most skilled. His party has successfully completed dozens, dozens of private missions for King Harold. I believe that it would be a waste of such a good sword to have the young man dedicate the rest of his time to protecting you, when instead he could be serving the realm in the battles to come across our lands, continuing as a journeyman and quester. Jason serves for the good of the realm, good of all realms."

Edward had no love for that sly councilman George, but Edward was in full agreement with what the man had just told the new king. Lord Edward and Arthan both knew Jason well enough in their minds. Both father and son assumed their famous knightly Sir Jason Frauer would hate to have to stand guard all his days and nights for a king when in place could be out with the freedom to adventure alongside his knights.

Without permission to speak, Edward stood up to say, "I can assure you, my king, Jason would be honored to serve as your Shield, but he wishes no part as the role of a guard. His place is with his knights, to quest until his time comes to settle peacefully with a family of his own."

"I understand." the king said upward, just before Edward rested back down into his seat. King Gregory closed his eyes and sighed while itching his shining scalp.

"My king, might I recommend a tournament?" Councilman George asked his king.

"There *will* be a tournament. Very soon, I wish to have the arena open for post battle ground matches, dedicated to the coming of my sweet self to the throne."

Grand Councilman Lewis shook his head negatively. The elderly man sitting in his bronze chair yelled to all, "After this talk of Shield to the King, we can move onto the discussion of the tournament, although the king has stated that he and his brother can handle the arena matters in their private times. They will discuss our set fair price on the amount of gold that the grand winning prize will payout. Our last tournament, for the heigh-elf charity eleven months past, the winner Sir Lucifer Gray won four thousand golden coins. How much shall it be this year? Our royal brothers here will make that decision in private."

After listening to the grand councilman's words, and even during the old man's talk, George smiled his usual sly smile. His throat, ears, and his pointy side hairs shook as he spoke down loudly again. "Forget a gold payout prize! The title of the Shield to the King shall be the reward!"

All of the councilmen in the circular room exchanged looks at one another. "Whomever is last man standing in the melee for the free-for-all shall be proclaimed the Shield to the King. No gold, no glory! Only an honorable place beside our good king; to protect his royal self until death. This is a way for god to choose a victor worthy of the role. A victor who will spark a bond with our king as he has desire for, as well as victor who will be skilled in combat as a king deserves."

The steward and grand councilman had a hatred for George's idea.

Lewis said, "The arena brings competitors from all six realms of the earth! Not just Midlön. Aside from the orcish, any soul from all realms are welcome at an attempt for tourney play! It would be disgraceful! You would give even grunts that chance at a win for this role? What if some halfwit wins the match by luck or queer scenario? What if it's a soul not suitable?"

"I understand the grand councilman's logic." King Gregory's brother said to all. Lord-Steward Arol then turned his head to look on Gregory now after listening to the elder speak.

King Gregory yelled, "Brother, the winner *will* be suitable because our god will select this champion, give him or her power to win! Think on it, brother! Men of the council! How could the winner *not* be suitable if they've just defeated their opponents for me? How could a winner not be suitable if they've just won?" George nodded as mostly all councilmen decided they had a liking for this new way for a royal-protector selection method.

They applauded George's way of thinking. Councilman George added in, "We have had brave warriors from all corners of the realms competing in every tournament in the history of this city; even the reeking dwarvish have fought in the beautiful arena of ours! A warrior cannot win the tournament simply by chance, not by mistake, not by luck. If he or her wins, they earn this win. No matter what the outcome is, you will be left with a talented fighter. Therefore, instead of a mortal soul choosing your shield in a council discussion, our god Aeon will after this Shield quite *literally* fights for you in the sands… and wins doing so. Aeon will grant strength to the champion's sword. Aeon will give you, King Gregory, the most worthy competitor to win for you! He or her shall be placed as a most fit Shield! I myself pray this victor to be a woman! To have a woman as a protector for you will make the lovely ladies and she-peasants of the realm very happy to see that you have taken an interest in promoting the strength of their lesser kind."

The king clapped his hands together with those rings clanging all the while. He was rising to give hugs to the grand councilman and Arol while they remained awkwardly seated.

He pointed his finger far up to George, "You may sit, George. I thank you very much, for it is settled. The winner of the next battle royale shall be named my Shield!" King Gregory clapped hard, fast, and loudly.

Arthan watched the grand councilman and the lord-steward Arol clench their jaws, shaking their heads to each other in disapproval. They hated the thought of a stranger having the chance at being The king's future bodyguard. The half-breed heigh elvish and the full-blooded lew elvish came from their lands, close and far, to compete in almost every tournament for past decades. Foreigners from the nearby lands of Eastfell and even dwarvish beings from the cold island realm of Fordge afar would now have an opportunity at becoming the personal and primary guard to the king, as these souls tended to travel to Midlön to compete on game day every year. The

Shield to the King always had been a knight from the men's race of Midlön, never a foreigner nor other being.

Not including the orcish beings, any soul had the rights to attempt to join the arena games through the upcoming less extreme trials, known as *battlegrounds*. If a warrior finds himself or herself able to succeed in winning a battleground fight that all competitors were required to partake in prior to each tournament, then they were guaranteed a place in a one-on-one in the city's arena on game day; the one-on-one commonly known as a *duel*.

"Tomorrow I will set out for the close by villages of the realm. I wish to see their dungeons and fighting cages. I'm going to personally select the grunts for the upcoming game while the battlegrounds take place here and across the realm. I will not be gone long!"

Edward from afar, in his seat beside his son, shook his head to that. "What a fool." he whispered.

Arthan was worried; his father loved to talk ill of folk; shouldn't have been doing so of the king, especially here of all locale. The king could have had Edward's tongue ripped out for talking badly of him, like he was doing right this moment.

A councilman stood up from his chair, saying, "My king, are grunts so important that you must leave the city to select which will play in the upcoming arena battle? You can send men to make good selections for you, just as they have done for every other tournament for rested King Harold Apollo, and the previous Gray, and Blaydên kings from years past. You've only just taken possession of the throne, and now you already wish to leave the city so fas-"

"I'm not *abandoning* the throne. I'm simply leaving our great city of Ascali and taking a short ride. I will travel with my best honor guards, and we will bring with us only a light caravan. The Blaydên kings were all known adventurers, so shut your mouth, Councilman, for those kings of old inspire me. I'm not ruling the realm from a chair here at the capital all days of my life. Speed will be with me, and if anyone gives us trouble on the road, then they shall taste the edge of my sword. Councilman, have you seen me use a sword?"

All were silent.

"I'm skillful with it, haa! My brother will sit the Golden Throne until I make a return. I promise, I will bring back a party of men that will make this tournament a bloody mess. It's said Willowhold and the colder, southern villages have the worst dungeons in Midlön, nothing but scum. It's time I find out if there's any truth to that."

That there was the end of the discussion on the king's future personal guard. Arthan spent the rest of the meeting with his ears open to the councilmen's talk on minor matters. If the treasury vaults and doors of the keep had need of new paint layering…how much gold would be considered a fair amount to spend on a dwarvish-crafted stone memorial for the old rested King Harold.

"The man was more than a king. He drew us all out from the darkness of the Gray-age and showed us how a true king should stand and treat his folk." a councilman had said.

Lord-Steward Arol Royce told him that rested King Harold was simply just another dead ruler, like all of the others whom had previously seated the Golden Throne well and that he would be remembered just as equally as the other great kings had been when they'd came to pass.

"My brother is right, Councilman! When my beautiful self dies, I will be remembered just as rested King Harold Apollo will be, and just as rested King Lucan Gray before him was, and as all of the Blaydên kings before *them*. There will be no special statue, nor memorial of any kind for rested Harold. Master of Undercity will see that Harold's ashes are placed within the crypts beside all the rest of the other kings who have lived and died."

"My king, Harold Apollo wished for his remains to be returned to his family's castle of Whitehall…to Princess Audrey and his cousins."

To that the king frowned, then spoke. "I will honor his will. Have the urn sent southward, immediately to Whitehall."

King Gregory was readying to bring the session to an end. He shouted up to all, "Before I call this meeting to close, are there any other matters that require my attention?"

Edward stood. "My king, I wish to speak with you in private along with my son after the meeting, if it pleases you!"

This is about me, Arthan thought.

"It would please my brother if perhaps you told him *why* you would like to speak with him in private, Lord Frauer!"

Edward gave Lord-Steward Arol a foul look.

Just before Arthan's father was about to speak, the king said, "Forgive my brother, my lord! Arol feeling simple today? What's the purpose of him speaking with me in private if he's gonna announce to everyone *why* he wishes to speak in private?"

Arol Royce looked at his brother, the king. Arol laughed, then brought his eyes back to Lord Edward far above in the seatings. "My father wasn't the best teacher when it came to the manners! We Royces aren't known for our kind words."

Edward smiled down to Arol. "There is nothing to forgive, steward."

Arol closed his eyes, and then he let loose a great yawn.

The king said, "My lord Edward, I would gladly speak with you and Sir Jason. Did he tell you that he had just brought me a mighty gift yesterday? A bag of bloody heads; the outlaws got what they deserved!"

Arthan looked to his surroundings, noticing all were listening to this now awkward sort of dialogue. Other than the sounds of Lord Edward and Gregory's voices, the council chamber was silent as a crypt.

"Yes, Jason spoke to me of his mission, though I was talking of my other son, Arthan. He is with me now."

All eyes were then on him and only him.

"Stand, son." said Edward.

Arthan nervously rose, his cheeks red.

"Ah, I almost had forgotten you had two boys." confessed King Gregory.

"Three! My youngest is eight." said Lord Edward Frauer.

The king looked as closely as he could from far down in the council chamber to study Arthan as the young man stood there next to his father; in that fine silk blue family clothing he wore. All the rest of the councilmen wore brown wool robes, making it so extremely obvious that the young man did not share a role here. "You and your son are granted permission speak to me here and now! Everyone else, dismissed."

The chamber cleared out in seconds. Arthan watched the men leave through the four exits as he then descended the steps with his father to meet with the king, the brother, and the grand councilman.

"My lord, would you mind if my brother and Grand Councilman Lewis joined us in our...*talk?*"

Edward cleared his throat as he reached the bottom of the stairs. "Not one bit, my king."

Arthan, now beside his father, observed King Gregory Royce. He watched the very important, royal man standing there with his ringed fingers twiddling together. *Is that a sign of impatience?* Hair covering his cheeks and chin, ink black just like his brother's back there behind him. Both of them handsome young men, and strong looking. Then he focused on the king's eyes: deep maroon eyes. Sometimes they appeared orange looking, other times a bloody-mud color. He hadn't ever gotten a good look at a Royce man, until now. He watched them both and also briefly eyed that goblin-looking Grand Councilman Lewis. He resumed inspecting the handsome brothers now. *I wonder who the women chase after more, these two Royces or that lucky brother of mine.*

Edward was watching the king too. He was thinking now, *Last month, I would have seen him to be nothing but the steward, assistant to King Harold. Now he stands before me as the most powerful man in Midlön...as the king himself.*

"Do you mean to ask my brother out for a walk in the High District Garden? Or perhaps have him over the Frauer household for supper? Child, why do you look at him like this?" Arol asked Arthan from back in his silver chair. The lord-steward still hadn't moved since the session had ended.

Arthan was caught, his cheeks turning red again, and so he looked away, embarrassed. "The boy is getting a good look at his king. It's not everyday someone gets to view the body of a soul as fine appearing as mine. Young Lord Frauer, your father and I have sat together on this council for years. He's friend to me, and now so are you. Now what can I do for the both of you?"

Edward looked to Arthan and smiled. "I wish to have my son become an apprentice councilman."

It looked as if Lewis had been slapped in the face. Arol, though, seemed to be sleeping as he sat back there in the center of the dome room with his eyes closed.

"If Arthan wishes to become a councilman, then he may find his way back to the school and enlist himself just as you have done in past, and just as Lord-Steward Arol has done, and *I* have as well, long ago. He must enlist and be accepted *before* he begins his training." the grand councilman informed Edward of this.

The king let loose his giggle that he had been infamously known for doing. "Don't be so grim, Lewis. They come to me now, because that is exactly what they *don't* want to have to do! Am I right, my friends?"

"Yes, my king, we, we had hopes that you could grant Arthan here access to the meetings, a place among us to learn the council ways, without him having to tend to the three years of schooling. He is smart and knows his numbers, a master of grammar. He has spent countless hours in the study, learning proper realm mapping, dwarvish and elvish law too. It would be a relief if my son wasn't required to take the tests to apply the traditional way. Arthan has greater logic within his mind than the school's best students! And of course waiting for acceptance to gain entry, well it could take weeks, even months! I'm sure you remember this as I damn well do."

The grand councilman shook his head in disapproval while sleepy Arol had said nothing, only looked at the walls with half opened eyes as if he had no interest in the matter with these Frauers.

The king then asked Arthan, "Do you know why Harold Apollo named me his steward?"

"No." he replied to the crowned man.

"You know your history, well, you know of the Sealord's Rebellion? During the siege at Pirates Landing, I rescued Sir Harold from the outlaws. The rebels and pirates had him bound in a cell within one of their speed ships docked on the northern coast of the massive town. My brother and I disarmed his captives right in front of him as Harold the Knight sat blindfolded, helpless. I myself then cut the ropes that held Sir Harold's hands together. I removed the rag covering his eyes, and then he saw me and he pulled me close. He whispered, *'I owe you my life.'* so quietly after my brother and I told him what I'd done and how we'd saved him. Years later, King Gray's death took place, Harold was crowned, yes. King Harold found me within the council and assigned me the position as steward. Harold had no brothers or sons to succeed him, and so now I sit the throne."

Arthan didn't know what to say. He looked at his father, and then back at the king just before blurting out, "An interesting story, my king, but I don't exactly understand why tell it."

The king laughed aloud. Arol still didn't seem to hear much of anything, and Edward had a very bland expression on his face, making it so difficult for Arthan to read his father's thoughts. Lewis just stood hunched over angrily shaking his head as the king went on.

"Boy, I'm trying to tell you, you don't necessarily need to pass the tests or have knowledge of the books to be a councilman! Not even a steward. I saved Harold's life. My sword is what got me my place beside the king, and now I *am* the king"

"Yes." was all that Arthan said.

"My king, forgive me, but Arthan is no *boy*. He is much older than he appears, wiser than he would seem to you at this moment. We would both appreciate if you spoke to him as a man." Edward told the king this.

"My king," Lord-Steward Arol began, just after he woke from his sitting sleep.

King Gregory Royce asked, "What is it, Arol?" The grand councilman scratched the white hair under his chin while the four there looked over to Arol Royce.

"Well, I would advise you to see to it that Arthan enlists at the Institution. Are we just meant to take his father's word in? That this boy is fit to be a proper councilman?"

"Yes, we are. Like I have stated, I have known Edward for some time now. I'm sure he raised his son accordingly, and even so, you wouldn't lie to me when you tell me that Arthan is fit for this role, would you?"

"No, my king."

"Then it is settled," the king grabbed Arol by the shoulders and playfully shoved him up from out of his silver council chair. "Arthan is to begin training at the start of our next session. He is to attend dressing in apprentice's robes. He is *not* to speak unless spoken to, do you both understand?"

The information and instruction, it all came so fast, but Arthan understood well.

"Yes, understood, my king." his father and he said at once.

Grand Councilman Lewis prepared to exit with the lord-steward.

King Gregory was finishing up the talk by saying to Arthan, "Your input means nothing while you are an apprentice. During time in a meet, if we wish to hear what you have in mind, we will ask. No standing, no speaking unless you are asked."

"Thank you, my king, he understands." Edward said.

"Thank you, my lords. Now if you will excuse my brother and I, we have our midday meal calling to us…and lots of midday drink too. Lewis, you can go discuss paint with whomever it is you do that with."

They all left the chamber at once; the Frauer father and son through the east arch, the grand councilman and royal brothers through the west passage leading deeper and higher into the Great Keep. Arthan and Edward were silent until they reached their rented ponies to begin mounting up.

"Father, I am to be a councilor?" asked Arthan to Edward with a sort of shock as his father handed him a large satchel containing his new apprentice robes.

"*Councilman.*" he corrected his son as Arthan took hold of the new apparel. "Though, right now you are to be a good brother and go home to rest. You need to wake within reasonable time tomorrow: *midday* to retrieve Dally from his lessons. We'll talk when I return home. The day after tomorrow will be your first true session! I'll see you shortly my son!"

Edward galloped off to go somewhere, leaving Arthan atop his little mount in front of this welcoming yard of the Great Keep by the councilman's dome at the fortress's east end.

Where's he headed off to so fast? thought he to himself as he inspected the pink training robes in the bag. It made no matter. Arthan had perhaps finally found his profession in life, and he was too happy to think on anything else.

05

Fight at Willowhold

Desmond camped roughly half a mile outside the fences of Willowhold for an entire day and a night, his hound companion at his side. Sunrise was upon them now, yet the clouds shielded its beautiful golden rays. Now on this gray day, he sat cooking half of a rabbit while taking his rest in the grasses; giving him the great opportunity to study the commoners camped surrounding him and the ones down the hill, entering and exiting the village of Willowhold.

The people of the realm Midlön in the past and current days, rich or poor, rarely had ever entered Desmond's birthplace to the east; causing him to have a limited knowledge of their fashions. He saw the villagers from afar as they entered and as they left, some of them, the same in-and-out within hours, quickly. Others like himself, seemed to have come from afar to camp in the short grass here, prior to entry; some even camped after they exited the settlement.

Foreigners were not, and should not be considered trespassers here in the towns, villages, and cities of this realm; though, Desmond still had no urge to enter the locale with giving knowledge to these people of where he had come from. The dirty Midlön garb he had taken from the men attempting to rob him two nights past could now be put to use for blending among these ugly villagers. He still remained fierce looking, armed and clothed now instead of wandering in rags though. Desmond still carried the bloodied rusted long sword and the silver dagger he had looted from those now dead robbers. Desmond was greasy and covered in wet filth, as he had been when emerging into Midlön by entry of the river, days and days ago;

yet differently, now he appeared a filthy Midlön *commoner*, instead of a filthy outcast foreigner.

His eyes changed from brown to black while he sat watching the old fathers and young sons enter the village, some of them carrying hunting satchels and slingshots at their hips. The sagging, disgusting wives almost appeared the same age as the elder women of the village did. They carried empty jugs out past the fences to find the nearby ponds. Viewing from upon the grassy hills, Desmond saw this routine happen hundreds of times now with the fathers and sons and these women who looked triple their true age. He had been willing to sit upon the grasses with his miniature fire and his dog Araisha for as long as need be, doing his best to pose in among the other campers near. He was surrounded by traders selling dead frogs, jokers selling their tricks, and whores selling themselves. Desmond pretended to be a common hill dweller, all for eyework. Desmond watched down by the road into the village, all to study the people in hopes to learn from their behavior; yet just now, when Desmond's dead rabbit found by his hunting companion began to truly rot with a stink, it helped him make up his decision as to when he should take action, to enter the damp village known as Willowhold. *I should have roasted the entire critter, instead of only half,* Desmond said to himself inside his head as he looked upon the smelly little thing; sliced in half lying there as Araisha sniffed it. His last bit of food had gone to a waste, and so now he moved.

As hungry Desmond arose from the grass, he fastened that old looted black cloak around his shoulders, then stomped on the embers below. He left behind the rest of the dead critter, and Araisha's arm bone she had claimed as a chewing stick from the remains of the bandits they had slain together in the recent past. "Cannot be in the village with an arm." he told her in the Easterlñ tongue.

Araisha was displeased but did drop the bone beside the dead fire and the smelly rabbit. She wasn't happy, though she padded alongside him downhill to the settlement all the same. The man and dog awkwardly made their way beyond the stick fences, yet not any of the persons moving about paid them any bit of attention, that soon ended though. After they'd entered the village, there was a bald smith who seemed to be in a dramatic rush who appeared close by.

"Out of my way, all of you fools!" the bald big man said as he passed by, waddling toward what looked like an old smoky forge.

Desmond watched him; he wore a ridiculous oversized scarf, hardly anything else. *This is what the Midlön people call a town?*

Desmond had known the great city of Ascali he had heard of throughout his youth was of greater size in comparison to this cluster of wooden hovels, occupied by half-starved people. He was beginning to question if there was truth in those tales of the massive and legendary city, after sight of *this* place. As he walked deeper into the village, his eyes began to burn from the stale incense and the dirty smoke drifting throughout the air. His boots made noises from below with each soppy step he'd taken. The roads between hovels seemed to be made entirely of mixed mud and poop. Desmond appeared to blend perfect here, among the ash blackened villagers. Everyone of the persons seemed either incredibly young or disgustingly old and covered in all sorts of filth and ash, just as Desmond appeared wearing his mismatched stained clothing. *Dirty children and old people. If the Easterlñs raided, like we had in the old times...a town like this, wouldn't last an hour.* Desmond watched the pale skinned old and young. They were wandering, working, drinking among friends and family, all surrounded by smoke and falling ash.

"Wanna come to hear a song?" a starving looking man with a torn up shirt and pants said as he stumbled in front of Desmond and Araisha.

Desmond halted and put a hand on the man's shoulder to help him balance himself in the wet dirt road. "You're drunken? Or cripple?" Desmond asked.

"Both!" the man of Willowhold replied to Desmond.

The skinny man took Desmond's hand off his bony shoulder, now pointing a thin arm away down the road. "That tent over there! Come, my cousin has a voice of gold. Says he'll be getting more ale soon."

The villager was drooling as he looked in the distance toward the direction of the hovels he was pointing at, wobbling with a shaky leg. Desmond placed a firm grip on the villager's shoulder again, this time to gain his attention, not steady him. "I'm looking for foods, not song. Where can I eat food? I have more clothes than mine that I wear, and a good dagger to sell. Dagger, clothes to trade for food perhaps." After Desmond spoke, the man's eyes closed, so Desmond shook him by the shoulder.

The skinny man took a deep breath in, and then exhaled with annoyance. "We have ale here! Not food. What you're lookin' for is ale! Come, forget the song."

Desmond released the man so the poor embarrassment could stumble a few feet away just to trip into the mud. Desmond walked to the downed man to ask him, "Who leads here? Commander is?"

Araisha crept up to the man in the mud, sniffing an ear as he lifted himself from the filth. Desmond wiped the smoke from his own eyes as he watched the young drunken man spit out wet dirt from his mouth before speaking.

"Come, I'll take you to the Willowhold Hall. We'll get drinks." he said while on all fours, one leg twitching.

Desmond waited for the man to raise himself up. After he stood, Desmond watched the drunken villager walk ahead calmly, wiping mud and poop off of his hands and onto what little ripped up clothing he was wearing. Desmond yelled, "I do not wish to be having a drink. Who is command here?"

The man continued walking forward, hastily now. He yelled to speak to Desmond, without turning back to look upon him. "They're in the hall! But the hall is also the alehouse. Come! Come!" and to that, Araisha continued ahead to follow the man. Desmond withheld his typical groaning noise, following Araisha with the extra dead men's garb tied to his back. Both his long sword and dagger clanged together loosely as he took his steps.

Desmond and Araisha followed closely behind the drunk, leading the both of them to the Willowhold Hall, as these villagers referred to the keep by. Desmond observed the filthy thin young man walking ahead, ugly scars along the back of his little arms. On the way to this "hall," the sloppy young fellow kicked a nearby walking chicken and so was then yelled at by six old women in yellow slaughter-robes stained with animal blood. Desmond had to pick up his pace in hopes to keep up with the tiny man, outwalking these elderly and angry villagers. Luck was with Desmond, for he and his hound were both at a great enough distance from the fool as so the old women had no notion that the pair of them were following his lead.

Desmond and Araisha followed his trail some more, turned a corner around a broken-down old wagon filled with spoiled frog meat, to now find the drunken man had escaped all of the old women. This villager was now heading further uphill on the mud-poop slope, and so that was the way Desmond and Araisha went too, passing the wrinkled women returning to work wearing their bloody outfits. A bit uphill and away in the short distance, they saw this old keep: one and only true structure of the town, or village.

What they call a place like this, I have no desire to know. The Willowhold Hall was surrounded by many hovels, those hovels, *surrounded by sets of embarrassing wooden stakes in the hill that they call fences.* Desmond laughed aloud as he criticized the poorly constructed settlement in his mind.

The man they followed up approached the wet wooden building to begin pounding at the soft door. He spoke to the oak as he banged with his weak arms. When Desmond and Araisha arrived at his back, they were now close enough to hear him say to the wood, "Me again, with two folk who wish an audience with the mayors."

The hound barked a vicious communication of rage when the man turned around to Desmond after the three of them had waited in silence for a short time.

"Just a minute, good pup."

The man flinched and pressed himself against the door when Araisha had now showed her teeth with a loud, vicious set of sounds herself.

Desmond was growing impatient as the now-frightened and drunk man pounded and pounded at the door with that gross leg of his.

The man finally turned to Desmond to look him in the eye. "Please don't have your pup eat me..." said the fool, wobbling there wearing his torn-up clothes, the garb really covering nothing but half of his shoulder, one arm, his manly areas, and his ass. If another second had gone past, Desmond would have left this shivering idiot if not for the door behind the drunken fool opening just then and there.

The drunk had been leaning against the wood and so now fell backwards to the floor of the entrance as a boy in cheap leather armor gave answer to this soaked and swelling door.

"No more! Go away." he said in a high-pitched child's voice.

Desmond shouted, "Wait!" to the boy in pink before the youngling could have time to shut the wooden door. He must have been ten years of age, possibly younger; in that ridiculous oversized helm made of wet pigskin. This boy pointed at the drunk as he was rising from the filth of the doorstep, drooling.

The boy told Desmond, "He has enough coin. He's just too drunk is the problem…and you neither, 'cause no dogs!" The boy attempted to smack the door shut, yet Desmond was quick enough to catch it before the little one could slide the lock in place.

The boy almost lost his footing when Desmond opened the weak door with strong force, flashing his black eyes at the child briefly. Desmond watched the poor thing regain his balance, retreating as the crippled fool behind choked on his own spit. The youngling was entering his own little sort of defensive state of mind as he now stood with his back to a wall there at this entrance part of the wood keep. The child in leather struggled to unsheathe his short sword as Desmond slowly entered the establishment.

"What sort of madness is that over there?" shouted an old voice by the large fireplace, past the dining area to the furthest end of the hall.

The drunk fool spat on the wood, ignored the soon-to-be-armed boy, entering Willowhold Hall through the front door behind Desmond.

The drunk began saying, "Mayor, I have come-" The man slightly, but sloppily bumped into Desmond's shoulder, and so Desmond's elbow then met the nose of the thin man with great speed and force.

The child watched this and so then began instantly sweating, still trying to draw his sword. The *"mayor"* arose from his old leather chair by the fire to witness the bloody mess which Desmond had made of the drunken young man. The boy in leather finally slid his sword out from his torn-up little scabbard. The drunk crawled on the wooden floor, away back toward the door, leaving what looked like all of the blood in his head out upon where he had fallen; his leg twitched the entire time. With a palm against his red nostrils, he brought himself up from the floor and then he fled out from the hall, down the mud road and gone into the smoky, gray mists of the morning.

This large in stature, leader of the village, holding a sappy walking stick, waddled away from the fireplace over to Desmond, a cup of ale in his other hand all the while. Desmond watched this man's four chins move as he spoke. "Who are you? How did you come to be seduced by that ale-drinking fool?" the gray-haired mayor asked Desmond, just after ingesting down a horn of some ale.

"I asked him who was commanding. He brought me to here." said Desmond to the mayor with his eyes on and off of the boy's dull, thin sword.

The mayor now stood beside the miniature guard in pink leather. "I am safe boy, thank you. Go wake your father for a talking session. This man here, he means us no harm. He just wants a word with me, your father, and other uncle."

The youngling moved backwards toward a flight of wet and rotted wood stairs. He still held his useless blade in hand, as if it would save him should a conflict occur. This child looked as if he had just come out from the ocean, lake, or a river like Desmond had days ago, all drippy and shining. The mayor laughed at the boy running off upstairs, then he took a seat just across from the front door, beside a wooden end table with empty mugs sprawled across the top of its slimy surface. The boy left behind almost as much sweat on the floor when he ran off, as the fool had left blood from when Desmond elbowed his nose into dust.

Both the fool and the boy in leather armor had been away, gone now. Desmond finally thought he was alone with the mayor, and so he asked him, "You say to the child I am no harm. I am not to you. How do you know this is truth though?"

The lack of guards or armed security gave surprise to the foreigner Desmond. The mayor took the last sip of what was left of his ale, then he slathered back some of his dead-looking hair out of his eyes with a handful of spit. He placed the empty horn on the slimy end table, then locked eyes with Desmond as the foreigner stood there in front of the doorway. "I know you are of no harm." said the mayor.

Desmond took another step inside the messy keep as the mayor rubbed his own fat eyelids. "How you know this?" he asked as he observed his environment. He saw now, aside from this sleepy mayor with his big ass in that chair at the entrance here, and an elder villager behind the bar by the fireplace where the crooked ale taps were placed, Desmond was alone here in the Willowhold Hall. He thought he was at the very least, so he summoned Araisha inside. "Drovhee." he said aloud. The dog crept inside through the door just as the boy in leather retuned from the set of stairs, with his half-naked father with him. *I suppose I'm not alone with the mayor any longer.*

The old, dying-looking man who served the ale in the back of the hall didn't seem to even notice the large hound, or Desmond at the door either. He just stood there, at the ready to serve mugs, horns, and cups filled with the refreshment the village was known for; his eyes placed lifelessly looking to the messy tables and benches among the hall. Desmond could see it was the father and son at the wet willow staircase who had great concerns for him, and now for his dog too, which the boy had not seen *inside* the hall prior to warning his father about this possibly dangerous foreigner.

"He brought his attack dog inside!" the child yelled to his father as they both stood shivering at the stairs.

The pantless man took a few steps down to the floor while he smiled to Desmond. Desmond had lived to see about three decades in life, whereas this man and the fat one seated at the door, appeared to have lived to see five or so on; he wondered if they considered themselves fighters, warriors.

While looking into Desmond's now-ordinary-appearing eyes, the walking man said, "It's okay, my child, remain. Foreigner, what business do you have with us? In here…with a dog. We'd rather not eat dog here."

Before Desmond could reply to the man as he now came closer, the mayor said, "It's ok, he won't harm you, and he won't harm your son there. This Easterlñ wants food. He won't harm any of us. He won't be risking losin' a chance at some eating. Isn't that right?"

Desmond nodded to that, remaining cautious though. The father of the boy was still slowly coming forward, although unarmed he was. His son back there had remained upon the staircase with that sword in hand. The boy looked nervous but eager to use his weapon as he watched his father with no pants approach Desmond.

The big mayor lifted himself off of the chair, gripped his nasty walking stick tight, and yelled to the back of the hall, "Get some ales for the foreigner and myself and our mayor here and his son!"

Desmond took a step backwards as the man who had the son now had gotten a bit too close; Desmond was becoming confused and uncomfortable.

The man halted, yelling to the back of the hall now too. "None for my child! Extra for our guest!"

Desmond scratched his black beard. "I thought *you,* the mayor…" Desmond spoke to the heavyset man using the stick to steady himself.

"I'm mayor number two." he said as he waddled away past benches to where the ancient villager was readying the refreshments.

Desmond asked the partially naked man, "Then you're mayor number one?"

In the distance closer to the taps, a jug or some cup made from glass or ceramic had fallen from a table to crash in the center of the floor. This happened because of a little old villager's foolish attempt to remove himself from a tangled cloak on the hall bench. He had done all of this while throwing up a meal. This old villager then knocked over a plate, piled high with chicken wing remains; although he wasn't just a villager.

“I’m mayor number one!” shouted he, while the bones fell to the floor. “He’s mayor one that one back there. I’m three.” the half nude one said. This new shaggy, gray-bearded mayor by the bench had been head-sick from drinking the previous night, *that* or he’d just still been drunk even now.

The half-naked mayor introduced his son to Desmond. “Him there at the stairs is my son, our defender. *I* am the third mayor. My eldest brother getting our ale is the second. He’s the first!”

The one who had just awoken from the benches referred to as the first mayor was making his way past tables to Desmond and the third mayor. The little gray man with his mophead burped while he picked at his nostrils. The *first mayor*, as he was called, took a glance at the sweaty boy nephew of his wearing leather at the stairs, and then he laughed his way over to the side of the father. “Tell your son to relax himself, or to go upstairs. Or you can tell him to have himself some ale.”

The boy rushed to the back of the hall to assist the fat second mayor in bringing drink to the front entrance area.

When mayor number one saw the ale heading his way, he began rambling so fast Desmond couldn’t make sense of half of what he had been saying to him. “Ale on its way! What is the dog’s name? You’re foreign? Are you here to help us? Willowhold hasn’t seen proper shipments since the beginning of King Apollo’s illness, six years ago. This was six years ago I speak of! Where are you from? What is your place among your folk?”

Desmond shook his head in the negative fashion. The heavy mayor with two filled mugs in one hand and a wobbly stick in another approached them all. “Here you are.” he said to Desmond, handing him a foaming mug, and he then spoke again. “My brother here thinks you to be a messenger from the eastern realm, here to aid us.”

Desmond accepted the drink as he watched the boy hand a mug to his father and the first mayor. “I am no messenger.”

“An ambassador? A diplomat?” the first mayor asked the questions at the same time while drinking. His voice had been surprisingly high in its pitch for such an elderly man.

Ale poured down both sides of his cheeks to absorb into his graybeard while he spoke, squeaked and chugged.

The boy now asked, “Is it true there’ll be a tournament in Ascali soon? Are battlegrounds happening now? This very moment?”

To all of this, Desmond said, “I am not those things. I do not know any tournament. Never been to Ascali.” Desmond took a healthy gulp of his drink, then squatted down. He was at a height of the boy in leather and the first mayor now. He was giving Araisha the remainder of the ale out from the ceramic mug, waiting for some sort of response from any of the three. The heaviest mayor, the second, took a seat once again, drinking some more; also speaking while he drank, like his brother had.

“I said he wants food. You’re not just a foreigner, you’re a homeless. Homeless here, *and* in Eastfell, yes?”

Desmond grabbed the mug while the animal was still licking at the ale so he could take in the last bits for himself. He arose to tower over the plump mayor and his old, tiny brother beside him. *It isn’t the deadly child guard that concerns me, or either of these ones, it’s this man with no pants, and those strong shoulders of his.* The half-naked mayor, the youngest of the three, was the only one out of these persons that Desmond couldn’t rip apart with his bare hands. As he was thinking of ways he might have to kill each of them, he soon realized the three elderly men and the boy were all watching him, waiting for him to speak. He was supposed to be in the mid of having a conversation, in place of that, he was putting thought into how easy it would be to snap the boy’s neck with a bit of a twist if he came rushing at him with that shit sword. If that second mayor had the strength to lift himself off the chair and fight with *his* stick, Desmond wouldn’t know if he had the mindset to decide whether to shove the wooden device up the man’s butt, choke him with it, or kill him by sliding two fingers in past his eyeballs to reach the fat brain of his. *Hard to decide.*

Instead of putting thought into how to slay the most dangerous of them all, *Mayor number three,* Desmond snapped from his visions of slaughter, to act as regularly as he possibly could. *Araisha will handle that one anyhow,* Desmond said inside.

"What?" said Desmond aloud.

The little mayor and the third mayor both had laughed at him. The boy went on to take a seat at the steps of the stairs where he had come from moments before, shit sword still at hand. The youngling coughed, watching them all there at the entrance. The second mayor in his seat took another gulp of ale. He told Desmond, "I said, 'You're not just a foreigner, you're a homeless too, yes? You're here to ask for food?' You're dressed in bandits clothes, but you're no raider. Those Hardain rapists wouldn't take an Easterlñ as one of their own, yet you wear their garb. You robbed one of 'em for those clothes, yes?"

Desmond chose his words as carefully as his negotiating skills allowed him. "I was outcast from Eastfell for reasons I hate to talk of. I have a silver dagger for selling. I'll give the silver dagger, for any food, bad food, if you have. Burnt bread? Stale foods. Half bad food?"

"Damnit." the little first mayor mumbled the curse, then took down a gulp of ale. He spoke more, "That's trading, not selling. We don't want to trade. I really thought some fortune had finally found us, oh, Aeon."

The first mayor finished his mug of ale. "Wasted good ale on you we did. I thought you to be our savior. We hardly have food here for our own. We can't be handing out the chickens and frogs to just anybody. Half of the realm drinks our ale though. We make plenty of that right here in our keep! Willowhold makes Midlön's finest. Come have some more if you aren't our savior. Let's drink anyhow."

The first mayor dropped his mug, then he turned round to walk back there to the oldest man on the earth behind the rotting bar. "Another for me, and our smelly foreign beauty." the little village leader said, walking over to the taps.

Desmond attempted to walk and join the first mayor. Even though no food had been promised, the ale was refreshing and the only source of nourishment accessible at the moment for his hound and for himself. The fat mayor lifted his stick up to block Desmond's path though. "Our eldest brother is still quite drunk from last night. Why don't you leave the hall now that he knows you are not what he hoped you to be?"

He drank ale after saying this to Desmond, with his stick still held in place blocking the way. The boy at the wooden stairs stood up from the soft steps, beginning to sweat some more. The sort of naked third mayor gulped down the rest of his mug of ale, then told Desmond, "You can leave Willowhold now. You have nothing worth trading, and you'll find no work among us. Go back to the East."

"I was outcast from Eastfell, wanted to find food here. There isn't food for so far outside of this place."

Saddened, Desmond didn't wait for the man with his dick out to say anything back to him. Desmond walked back to the door with Araisha, wishing he would have gotten more than half a mug of ale in his stomach after leaving this old hall and village.

"Where's he off to?" Desmond was leaving as heard the first mayor say this, far off from inside the hall at the ale taps.

Desmond had then heard the reply, "Shut your mouth, inviting everyone to drink!" It was the almost fully nude third mayor yelling angrily to his drunken brother.

That was the last Desmond thought he would ever see or hear of them again, yet as he and his companion were moving through the mud to find the exit of the village, the third mayor walked to the doorway of the keep to shout out loud, "Easterlñ!"

Desmond stopped moving, turning to give his attention to this village leader, as did all the people now in this mud road. The mayor was not addressing any of these persons when he had yelled *"Easterlñ"* yet their heads snapped to look same as if he had been; some villagers even left their tents and hovels for a view at the scene. The third mayor looked to Desmond from afar. "You'll leave behind that dog of yours for us! Payment for drinking our ale and wasting our time with begging! I'll have one of the women make us a great stew!"

Desmond heard the third mayor say all of this, and so did his companion at his feet. Araisha bared her teeth before Desmond made any move, growling in rage and shaking with some fear too. Desmond turned to face the keep upon the hill with his one and only enemy in this world in sight, right at that doorway there. The man naked from the waist down leaned against the soft wooden structure.

He took a bite from a rotten pear, watching Desmond struggle with his thoughts from afar.

"Nobody let the foreigner leave with the beast! Whomever slays it shall feast with my brothers and myself!" yelled the man chewing on the black fruit in his mouth.

The heavyset second mayor and the third mayor's son in leather approached the doorway. "What are you doing? Causing dramatics?" the second mayor asked his brother with his stick keeping him afoot.

Desmond and Araisha stood unmoving in the mud as the people gathered around. Desmond watched his left, then to the right as the villagers whispered, speaking quietly amongst themselves. Most unarmed, but some with greasy black pots and pans, one or two with a dull knife or a gardening tool; hard to see now, with so many coming and coming. More and more approached quickly. Desmond and Araisha watched carefully.

From the keep on the wet hill, the second mayor yelled, "Please! Just leave so we can get on with it! My belly is rumbling now!" Desmond's hound was struck in the neck with a projectile. The stone came from the top of a hovel. Araisha reacted in extreme in anger with a dozen barks and howls up into the clouded sky, as for the beast did not know where she had been attacked from. Desmond saw a child up there squatting, holding an old hunting slingshot made to kill birds. This boy pulled the band back, then shot Desmond in the shoulder! It hurt for a second or three with a little sting, then when the pain faded, Desmond unsheathed and hurled his tiny bandit's knife up at the child. It came close to hitting the boy's foot, but the little one hopped away, falling down off the hovel into a pile of poop before Desmond's bent silver knife could collide with him.

Desmond was looking upward at the tops of the surrounding hovels and tents now. If he had any more children about, up there with these slingshots, he wished to know at this very moment. *Why did I just throw my knife?* thought he, watching above. Unfortunately, his deep inspection of the hovel tops left him blind to the dozens of villagers surrounding him on the ground. Araisha tried to warn Desmond that a young girl grasping a rock was approaching, but he was busy searching for more boys climbing hovels. The rock flew, striking Desmond in the back of his head. The bitch was weak, and Desmond was thankful for that. He placed a hand on the gash in the back of his head, and then glanced over his shoulder to look back at his attacker; this was when he was hit in the nose with a slingshot pellet. Araisha barked toward the girl and the holder of the slingshot too.

Desmond scratched at the bloodied thick hair on the back of his head, while he wiped redness from his nostrils. He was now looking at the weak stone throwing girl, and behind her, that drunken skinny idiot who led him and Araisha to the Willowhold Hall. The slim man with dried blood upon his nose and mouth loaded another pellet into the slingshot with a hard pull. He stood there wobbling on that weird-looking leg of his.

He yelled, "I was helping you get ale!"

Desmond walked toward the now crying bitch and this starving drunk fool behind her. "And then you hit me with your elbow!" the man cried out while pulling back the tight band. The drunk aimed well, considering how much ale he had put in his belly that very morning. His well aim did not help him though, for Desmond caught the pellet in the smoky air, just before it could strike his eye.

Desmond was still moving toward them now as crowds continued to gather from all directions. There were a fair number of villagers behind the girl, the drunk man with the slingshot included among them. Difficult to judge if any of these people were ready for a true fight or if not. The villagers of Willowhold seemed filled with dread, yet also they appeared to be horny for blood and dog meat too; some had swords now.

The girl who had thrown the rock sank to her knees as Desmond came closer. The mud seemed to almost consume her in a way while she sat there crying. While walking to the drunken slingshot man, Desmond flung her from his path. She flew, like a doll discarded in the strong wind of a storm, if dolls could scream. He was coming closer and closer to the man in torn clothes while the fool was removing a fresh pellet out from his pocket. Just as Desmond was getting himself ready to rip the device from his grasp, he heard, "Over here!" from an old woman covered in chicken blood. Desmond looked away from the drunk to this bloody lady at his right side, only to be smashed over the back with an empty jug by some young villager to the left! The ceramic shattered against his spine, forcing poor Desmond to fall into the mud.

As quick as he allowed himself, he turned over so he would not face into the wet road. The villagers began to swarm in around him, the starving one with the slingshot now the closest. The man aimed directly at Desmond's eye with the weapon, getting ready to launch another little pellet, which Desmond could easily catch again now that his face wasn't stuck in the road. Desmond tried to do that but was unable to after the big blacksmith man brought all the weight of a freshly forged pickaxe down upon Desmond's hand in the mud.

The Easterlñ was pinned to the road, while all three of the mayors watched from the keep at the hill.

The first mayor shouted, "I told you to come get some more ale! Why'd you leave?"

His brother, the third mayor, shoved him, telling him to be silent. The three brother leaders of Willowhold drank ale with the armed boy in leather under them. All the while they watched the villagers attack Desmond and the dog in the distance down there.

Towering over Desmond with his twitchy leg, the drunken man with red all over his face was just about to release his grip on the slingshot band; that was when Araisha quit barking at the Midlön people to leap herself up to grab ahold of the idiot's arm. When her teeth sunk into his skin, the drunken man turned himself upward and away. He quickly released his hold on the weapon band, sending a speeding pellet into the throat of a nearby old villager, wielding a shovel for a weapon. Desmond saw none of this, as he was trying to get that pickaxe out through the palm of his hand. The point of the pick was sunk deep through his palm, out the back of his hand and into the mud yet loosened bit by bit as he flailed around kicking his legs, trying not to shout in pain with this big shirtless smith above him.

The smith was saying, "Kill the dog!" while he had Desmond pinned, bleeding in the mud. Desmond stopped trying to pull the iron out from his hand, deciding he would now reach for his rusty sword, forgetting he had it until just here and now during this painful moment. He didn't have it though. It was gone. Few of the villagers around him had swords, but everything was happening too fast for him to see if any of those blades had been his missing one. *How? When?* It was sadly lost; he was finished searching for it already.

When he stopped feeling for the sword that wasn't there anymore, he looked to Araisha. Two old women were hitting her upon her back top with broomsticks; she didn't seem to even notice the strikes though. Araisha was growling, ripping a simple man's leg off as all the children on the road fled after the sight of the simpleton's blood and bone. When Desmond came to realize this big bald blacksmith wasn't releasing this pickaxe from the earth, not ever, he decided to bring the *smith* down to the pickaxe. Desmond softly grasped the man's dangling scarf to pull down upon it. Thankfully, the crusty cloth tightened without any rip or tear. The big villager held onto his axe with greater force now, this fighting craftsman thinking Desmond was finding some new, cleaver way to release himself from the iron trapping him, *except* Desmond wanted that pickaxe to stay exactly where it had been.

Villagers were shouting and attacking Araisha while this blacksmith used all of his strength to *not* pull away from Desmond. The smith knew, stepping back, meant releasing the pickaxe from Desmond's hand! And so this opponent of Desmond's leaned down toward the axe with great strength as this foreigner pulled him by his own scarf. Desmond then let loose the rag from his own grasp, now putting a firm grip on the back of the bald man's scarred head when it became close enough. The blacksmith held the pickaxe oh so tight, while Desmond used the man's own flow of weight to an advantage, along with all the strength in his own body as well. Desmond brought the big and talented villager's head down upon the pointed end of the pickaxe that wasn't sunken through the hand. The blacksmith's own iron found its way right into the blacksmith's own eye. He twitched and sat moaning like a dying goat. The unlucky man was locked into place there, face leaning into the device he had just crafted that very morning. Desmond was under all of this carnage, still unable to move with that pick in place as he saw his dog was now being kicked by angry villagers.

Desmond with eyes black as death itself looked far off and above to the Willowhold Hall where he saw the three mayor brothers, just now without the boy in leather with them. He thirsted for a walk up to that hill to slaughter them with dark magic, yet he found the will to ignore this urge. He had to be rid of this fight, this road, these mayors, these people, and this place. With his freehand, he gave shove to the shaking blacksmith. The craftsman villager locked into place, had become limp when the axe point popped out from what was once his eye. He fell over into the mud, halfway off of Desmond, one hand still loosely placed on the grip of his own pickaxe, as a point still remained sunk in Desmond's hand. Desmond kicked the heavy body away, and then he ripped the pickaxe out the village road, and finally his palm. His hand and arm looked like a work of dark art, black and red from filth and from his tainted blood. He was gazing now, upon his bleeding hand, watching himself holding the deadly pickaxe.

Desmond shook off the horrific pain of the hole in his palm, then gripping the pickaxe tight, he was now turning, approaching the mob of people chasing Araisha down the muddy poop road. They ran as the dog was dashing through the village, Desmond slowly following behind them all as he wiped mud from his eyes. He had to move faster if he was to catch up to the villagers trying to kill Araisha! Just as Desmond was getting ready to turn his stumble into a sprint, with his new weapon in hand, he heard wet footsteps behind him. Desmond halted and wiped some smoke from his eyes while he turned back around to face his new attacker, yet nobody was to be seen. Desmond wiped more smoke and mud from those darkened eyes, and then he looked down a bit lower to the road where he found the boy in leather with his shitty, little dull sword. The boy struck Desmond in the mouth as hard as he could with the weapon. Desmond's jaw broke, he fell sleeping, bleeding into the mud road of Willowhold.

06

Before a Night at the Inn

There was a parade in session, celebrating the crowning of the new King Gregory Royce. "Hail Gregory! Hail King Gregory Royce!" shouted the folk of Ascali walking upon Silver Street.

My damn route in the High District leading to the school! Arthan angrily said this to himself inside of his mind. The street was completely filled, packed with folk and the paid parade goers. The celebratory screaming gave stress to Arthan, the music even more! Jokers juggled balls, musicians played their instruments awfully, and blue-hooded elementists shuffled through the people as if superior beings, sending bolts of lightning into the sky. Today Arthan was tasked with meeting his younger brother at the school to escort his little self back to the Frauer house after lessons. This parade was making the young Arthan's mission extremely difficult.

Silver Street in the High District typically was the most cleanly, finest-looking portion of Ascali, yet today it was covered in chicken and beef bones, fake flowers, ale, and piss, with sweaty folk jumping above it all screaming in pleasure. In fact, both Arthan's household and the school (officially known as the Institution) were constructed on Silver Street, yet Arthan could not reach the structure easily, because of the disgusting parade on this disgustingly cloudy evening. Sun would begin to set soon, meaning Arthan was already late at that very moment in retrieving Dallion. Arrival to his destination by continuing his way westward on Silver Street from this end wasn't an option for Arthan he could now see, and so he ran as fast as he could southward. He almost tripped where he found the faded silver painted stone steps, yet he caught his balance and brought himself down to Brey Street steadily.

After some time in this direction on the busy steep street, just before reaching the Square where rested King Harold Apollo had been burned, Arthan would need to make a right turn to pass into the Wizards District to then reach West Street. West Street led back up to Silver Street's west end, just where the school was located! Sadly, before Arthan could even make it to Brey Street's alley leading to the Wizards District on the right, he was shoved with a pair of thick hands. Arthan crashed into the cobblestone street as his attacker approached calmly.

"Arthan's a councilor now, gentlemen." Drake said to his creepy little gang of commoner friends behind his ugly self.

Arthan knelt up, quickly found himself on his feet. He brushed off some dust that had attached to his apprentice robes. He took a short look at the annoying, bulky boy who had just caused his fall and then Arthan winked at him with his left eye. Arthan then ran off down to the purple brick alley to enter the Wizards District, yet before he sprinted away, Arthan got a good look at Rodrick Drake's reaction to the queer gesture he had just sent to the bully. Arthan had never seen him look so angered before, in all the years he'd known the gross, chubby stew merchant's son; never seen his face as it just appeared. *So furious, from just a wink?* What made Arthan perform that gesture? He asked god as he ran past a group of elementists, trying to freeze each other in recreation with poorly cast ice spells. *Stupid little wink, but Rodrick Drake had not the slightest notion of what to say to that.* Arthan had never felt so clever, so witty. He thought this over as he ran past a dozen little boys performing card tricks front some of the shops, him hurrying to West Street yet still observing the folk around as he moved, deep in thought.

As Arthan was still having these satisfying thoughts of bringing frustration to Rodrick Drake, he began to choke. *Wizards and their dusts.* Arthan coughed, removing the thought of the bully from his mind and was now screaming on the inside as he was forced to run through blue and purple clouds of incense. He had to pass hot steam too, and even some wizards weed smoke, all to make his way to West Street, and then eventually Silver Street; he was angry all over again, now because of these fumes in the air. The wizards and all their followers were incredibly theatrical, colorful, and often giddy. No desire for combat or violence, their dazzling magic was practiced as an art form used for entertainments. Some of the loudest and happiest-looking folk of the realms these souls were!

The music here is almost as loud as the damn parade. He walked with a frown on his face holding his breath in, shuffling through the folk, insulting them in his mind as he made his way deeper into the district. Arthan was more accustomed to the holy magics, which was practiced in a much gentler fashion. The priests were often quiet, soft-spoken, only using their magical crafts when absolutely necessary. Just beside the Institution lay the Cathedral of Aeon, where it was taught that the magical aspects of the world were to be viewed as a blessing, privilege, and gift from Aeon the one and true creator. A gift that should be sparingly performed; similar mindset of the mages of the military. The wizard aspirers, quite the opposite of all that.

"I shall cast a spell on you! Evil Councilman, prepare to be turned into an orange-colored sheep!" the young lady wearing a festive bear costume yelled this to Arthan.

She pointed a purple staff toward him as he tried his best to dodge and squeeze through folk on the street.

"Eat dung, woman." he said to her, softly, not even knowing if she heard the curse.

He ran past her, moving faster now, bumping into folk wearing their bright wizardly garb as he went by. Glitter fell from the above apartment windows, pretty, yet the smell of perfume distracted him as he then began to gag. Torches of blue, violet, and green were now being lit among the sides of the shops and apartments. It was becoming late in the evening's time, and Arthan hadn't even reached the West Street yet; he soon changed all of that. Arthan found himself then climbing this rusted red ladder in which he remembered from old childhood seek and hunt games with Jason, then the young man hopped onto the balcony paths of the old library. Walking up *above* the Wizards District instead of through it, he took a clever shortcut past more magical folk, them throwing up from too much drink, and some others playing dice games under a set of green torches. This route would then bring him to West Street, but from above, instead of from street level!

Walking alongside the library up upon the paths, Arthan caught sight and was distracted by three wizardly people performing whore-ish acts, pressed against a crumbling stone wall. Arthan watched and watched yet did not discontinue moving forward. His perverted distraction from the three horny folk caused him to violently trip down the old library steps west end, those very steps led down and out of the Wizards District to bring him tumbling upon *West Street.* Arthan recited the name in his mind when he gazed upon it, low from the dirt road, happy to finally be here.

"West Street…" *Second damn time I've fallen on a street today. Aeon, make the midday brighter.* Sadly, the stars, red and blue, were beginning to faintly shine in the blackening and cloudy sky; the midday was over, night was beginning. *Oh, Dallion, forgive me.*

He walked upon crowded West Street now. This stretch of city road was always busy with horse, wagon, and shipment transport. Loud, but in a peaceful sort of way, though; more beast and carriage noise in place of folks' voices and them dancing while moving about. Desmond preferred these sounds of horseshoes, wheels creaking, and nails being hammered in for the new shops to the horrendous music, markets, and just about all other folk throughout the remainder of the city's districts. West Street was where the folk of Ascali moved, and moved with haste; Brey Street, the Square and the eastern portions of Ascali was where the selling, dwelling, and crafting took its place.

Arthan turned his run into a sort of fast walk, and then decreased his fast walk, to a sweaty standard paced shuffle as so he wouldn't appear breathing too dramatically when he reached his destination. He wiped the sweat from his brow, using the pink sleeve of his newly acquired councilman's apprentice robes. He was almost struck by a fast moving carriage as he inspected the distracting, bright glitter upon his chest, now trying his best to remove the shiny bits, and some cobble he'd now just caught sight of as well. *Glitter…haa, and I wanted to be a wizard in my youth.*

He resumed walking again after dodging some more carriages, wiping more glitter and cobble from his chest as he soon came to West Street's top end, leaving the early night's traffic behind him.

Arthan climbed a ridiculously large set of painted stone stairs, coming now to the top of Silver Street, where the school would be seen. As Arthan approached the Institution, he could hear the folk and parade goers at the eastern end of the street to the direction of his house. The parade was coming closer to the Institution to finish their celebration at the west end of the city. Arthan sighed, then he quickly entered the school through the giant doors to search for his brother.

Arthan was greeted in the colorful school entrance hall, just moments upon his arrival. The man he met, he was young, with red hair and had a giant clean-shaven jaw. He wore an old robe, similar to the color of Arthan's but in a different fashion of pink. *Rosen-golden*, the dwarvish folk would call the tint. This redhead instructor wore a big silver necklace too. "Apprentice-Councilman?"

"Arthan…" he said in reply, trying to discard the sounds of the parade from his brain as he could hear every one of them out on the street from here inside the school, growing louder and louder with each second that passed. *I can ignore the fools,* Arthan thought to himself.

The redhead man had no shoes, Arthan remembered that strange custom from when he was a student in this Institution. The instructors and their lack of footwear, not even slippers, not even socks. "Arthan who?"

"Arthan Frauer."

"Ah, Apprentice-Councilman Frauer, oh. Dallion is your brother, yes. Please remain here Apprentice-Councilman Frauer, only a minute." The redhead man in pink silently stepped away, disappearing down a dimly lit hallway, leaving Arthan to the growing sounds of music and cheers from the parade.

Somewhere down a different hallway, a student could be heard making horrible sounds on the harp, as he or she was learning the ways of the instrument, terribly though. The child's horrible tune did not make the parade music any less frustrating.

Arthan patiently waited as he observed the art, above and below. The entire hall was painted, and painted on again and over again! All done by the children, the students of Ascali. Dome ceiling, walls, floors. Even Arthan put a bit of work into this beauty at some point in his youth, but that was long ago. He couldn't remember what he had drawn now, or which wall or bit of the hall it could have been upon. *I will ask Dallion where he has left his little work of art here, if I can remember to ask.* Where was Dallion? Arthan was beginning to wonder this, but that was just when his little brother appeared down the dark hallway, holding the hand of an old woman instructor; she had a silver necklace too and was barefooted. They were also accompanied by the giant jawed redhead one from earlier.

"Hello, Arthan!" Dallion threw the woman's hand away behind his little self, then ran to Arthan. He jumped in his older brother's arms to bury his face into his shoulder. Dallion asked him, "How was your day? I'm tired. Let's go home now."

Arthan patted his sleepy little brother on his tiny back as the old woman without shoes approached, her colleague dressed in the same fashion by her side. The woman said, "It is regularly Sir-Paladin John whom escorts young Dallion home in the afternoons. A change of escort is fine of course, yet night gathers now, and you've only just arrived."

Arthan closed his eyes and continued to pat his brother on the back as he held him. The elder instructor woman and the man with that giant jaw of his, they both exchanged glances.

The man was beginning to speak until Arthan said, "I slept late. When I woke, the parade had delayed me."

Arthan squeezed his small brother tight, comforting him as best he could.

The sagging old woman said, "Sleeping during such hours of the day, a bad habit for a lord of your age. I'm sure you don't need to be told this, Lord Frauer, but retrieving your brother from lessons is of greater importance than attending parade after sleeping in the daylight."

Arthan almost choked on the fluids in his throat. "I didn't attend the parade. The parade was in my way! It made it difficult to arrive at the correct hour."

The woman stepped closer to Arthan as he held his brother Dallion in his arms. She stroked the brown locks of the child's hair as his face had still been stuffed into Arthan's armpit. "There was a slight problem today. We shall discuss it with Sir John, or your lord-father, or mother. Please inform them that Dallion was found fooling about inside the air tunnels in the ceilings, within walls too…"

Arthan's arms had now been shaking from holding Dallion, yet he hid his weakness from these instructors well, listening on, pretending his best to care of the topic. *Dallion likes to explore. This isn't a surprise to me,* he thought. "I'm sorry, I don't know why he would do that. How did he get up inside of the air tunnels?"

The woman then answered, "Dallion claimed he was acting as a rogue on a quest to slay goblins. We need to speak with Lord Edward of this matter, immediately as to see the boy never does something of this sort again. It is very important he knows that there are no such things as goblins, only in the fables and tales."

"I apologize, this is very unlike Dallion to-"

"Go with god, Arthan Frauer."

"Thank you." Arthan replied, after they both said *"Go with god, Arthan Frauer"* at the same exact time.

He and his brother left the two instructors there in the colorful, inspiring entrance hall of the school. Arthan was already tired, and tired more now from holding his brother in his arms. He was sweating as he carried him outside and down the front steps. He was irritated as well because of all that horrid artwork he was forced to view and the instructors with their bare feet and awkward necklaces; they always had irritated him, even in youth. He was eager to be away from the Institution, being back inside after so many years had sent him into another ill mood.

Arthan had carried his brother in his arms, all the way down the front steps of the school, then he gently placed him standing on Silver Street while he stood himself, catching his breath. Arthan made a decision to place his ass down, to sit there upon the curbside of the street with Dallion for a bit, just to wait and catch his strength back. Dallion would have slept, and Arthan would have gazed at the moon and put thought to his first day tomorrow as an apprentice-councilman, maybe even what was to come for supper when he had arrived home if his mother and father weren't all too furious with him. Arthan would have lived in his mind and thought about many things as he always had done, but he couldn't do this now, just as Dallion could not rest, because of the loud, obnoxious parade in all the history of the realms! The parade taking place right in front of the Frauer boys, right there at the street entrance of the Institution.

Dallion looked up above to his brother as he sat there in his lap. "We can go to West Street, Arthan."

"What?" Arthan said back to his small brother.

Dallion then said, "We can go to West Street, then go past the wizards, then we can go home."

Arthan understood his brother. "I don't want to do all of that walking through the city, little one. When the parade ends, we will walk home. It's just down the street there. It's just the crowd is too thick at the moment."

"Yes." Dallion hugged Arthan and tried to sleep as the music played while more and more folk drank and walked cheering. Arthan was gazing at the attractive women as he wiped more glitter from his filthy robes.

Arthan watched a woman with long legs dancing with her lord-husband. During this viewing time, he had itched and harshly blinked his eyes, rubbed at the lids a bit, then the parade vanished. He opened his eyes, seeing about a dozen or so folk walking about, in place of five hundred. Some cleaning and others just casually moving through as they would any other night here in the High District of the city. Dallion was still placed upon Arthan's legs and chest, sleeping with his finger in his mouth. Arthan blinked a bit more to make sure he wasn't dreaming. He woke Dallion so they could begin their walk to the household. Arthan was not strong enough, or awake enough to carry the child down Silver Street at the moment, maybe not even at any moment, seeing his big brother's incapability; the child had not even asked it of Arthan.

They walked on the sleek stone street as they passed puddles of every form of liquid imaginable; and piles…piles and piles of bones. One would expect there to be some group, person, or persons tasked with cleaning the remains of this royal event, yet the dirty street just seemed as if it would stay a dirty street as of now and forever.

"Dally, it's smelly now like Brey Street, isn't it?" Arthan asked Dallion as they walked, holding his hand.

"Yes." Dallion said back to him.

Arthan and Dallion passed an elder man rolling a barrel of pickles.

Arthan asked as they walked by, "Excuse us, what's the hour?"

The old man took a bite from a massive shining green pickle. "Don't know, Lord Apprentice-Councilman." said he as he chewed with a leaking mouth of pickle juice and drool.

Arthan smiled and nodded, walking closer to his house with Dallion.

Arthan viewed some of the stars above past the clouds to try to make sense of the hour. He looked back down to his tiny brother to say, "It's late. Mother nor Father will be pleased with me. You must tell them you've had a pleasureful evening and that I hadn't been late upon retrieving you from lessons, yes? Let's just say to Mother that we've been parading. You've had a fun time with me, have you not?"

Dallion rubbed his eyes from exhaustion with his dirty free hand as he held onto his older brother's wrist with the other. "Yes, I've had fun! We should play a board match before bed or sing songs."

Arthan forced a giggle to that. "I'd love to do such things. I will not tell them of your rogue quest in the walls of the school, if you tell them how much fun you've had. Now let's have some more fun! I would love to play at a board game match with you, Dally."

They had almost reached the front miniature gate by their family's small stable when out the Frauer household door came Jason in motley, now walking down the wood steps. "You look like a red joker!" yelled Dallion to Jason coming through the short gate.

All three brothers now stood on Silver Street, chatting. "A kissable, wealthy joker; there's a great difference." said Jason.

Arthan observed Jason's ridiculous tunic and his tight dress pants. He touched and inspected the materials, saying, "Black and red? Demonic colors, you're an attention-seeking fool. You're dressed as if you've just come from Retilliath. Where's the blues of House Frauer?"

Jason smiled, handing Dallion a sweet piece of chocolate, rubbing a black-gloved hand around in his little brothers shaggy hair while talking at Arthan. "The eagle knights and I have made the wise decision to dress in this leather garb for tonight. I've grown bored wearing my whites. I want just my armor to be white, you see... The White Knight is a *'white'* knight, yes, but not in white always for forever. The folk even expect my noncombative apparel to always be white..."

Dallion began punching Jason in the leg, making sounds of swords clashing together, arrows soaring and striking also. "You don't have need to dress in whites to match your armor set. It is our house colors you should represent."

Jason sighed at Arthan's words, while Dallion battled his leg.

"I hate *blue*, brother. Anytime any folk in Midlön sees a bit of blue, their mind soars right to the wizards and their love for the queer color. Tonight in these reds, we shall be noticed, and you know how I do love the attention."

Jason flexed his muscles and laughed very obnoxiously loud.

"Quiet down..." Arthan said.

"Why? Don't want Mother and Father to hear us having fun?"

Arthan looked above into the windows of his house. Candlelight flickered brightly, and he could see torches had been lit from the glowing of the light through the glass. "They're awake and will be angry with me. Dallion should not be about the city at this hour. It has taken me the entire noon and night to bring him back to the house."

Jason then began to make it all seem easier, like he always had done when ill events had occurred. Any soul, including Arthan, regularly could and would present Jason with a problem, and Jason would explain how easy it was to solve or ignore.

"Forget about all of that. It's Sir-Paladin John's fault. He's the one usually picks Dally up." Jason said, putting a hand on Arthan's shoulder while receiving little punches to the leg. "Of course they're awake in there. You haven't spent all night retrieving Dally. It's still early. In fact, it's so early I haven't even arrived at the celebration yet myself, as you can see."

"What celebration? You're attending the feast in the Throne Hall?"

Jason now responded to Dallion's play by smacking him around on the face a bit while the child went to war with his leg. "I *was* invited to the feast, but not attending, no. Instead, the rest of the Eagle Party and I will be drinking at the Alligator Inn, on Brey."

Arthan watched Jason and Dallion play, pretending to battle as the conversation was taking its place. "Why drink there? It's all commoners and jokers and so many whores. Even beggars go there…"

"Then I shall give the beggars coin to go away or coin to drink with us. The commoners, jokers, and whores are *why* we're going there in place of the Throne Hall."

Arthan laughed at his brother, as in his opinion he was acting very foolish now. "It is a great honor, Jason, to dine with the king. How could you not attend something of that sort?"

Jason rose up from gently smacking Dallion to stand and look upon Arthan. He removed a potion from his back belt-satchel, then he drank from it. Jason said, "Listen to me, brother, the commoners' music is finer than anything you'd here in that Throne Hall, and the women more attractive in their garb at the inn's. These ladies of the High District, you can't get a good look at what's going on under those dresses. Here, have some of this." Jason handed his brother the vial of clear liquid.

Arthan accepted and drank. "What is it?" he asked Jason as he handed him back the potion container.

"It will help you feel better in the morning. You will join me tonight. I want to find you a filthy commoner woman. I want to show you what I speak of. This act here is me saving you from Mother and Father."

Arthan took a step back as Jason walked to the house stable to join with his mount, Pax. "I don't want to go out drinking. I cannot go out drinking. Me and Dallion have plans for the night. We are to play board matches, then we are to sing songs before we sleep."

Jason led the horse out onto the once clean Silver Street. "Watch your footing, boy. That's vomit there, isn't it?" Jason told Pax while he brushed his mane after leading him past the little gate.

"Have you just heard what I've said?" asked Arthan.

Dallion approached the horse and rubbed his belly. "Pax!" Dallion shouted upward.

"Me and Dallion plan to play a board game and to sing before bedtime, isn't that so, Dallion?"

"Yes, sorry Jason, me and Arthan are playing and singing before we sleep."

Jason squatted down to appear equal to his youngest brother's height. Jason gave Dallion a kiss on the cheek and then said to him gently, "If you let Arthan come with me, I'll let you have a present tonight, but this must be a secret."

Dallion jumped, three times in a row shouting, "Present! Present! Present!"

Jason had to calm him with a, "Shhh, Mother and Father can't know. That's why you need to be quiet."

"Quiet, like a rogue-assassin…" Dallion said with a stern face.

Jason laughed to that. "Yes, in fact, this present is of rogue-assassin relation."

Dallion's jaw dropped in surprise, question, and wonder, then Jason looked to Arthan, smiling, then back to Dallion.

"Under my pillow is my big shiny white dagger. You remember this dagger, yes? It looks like my sword but only smaller."

Dallion clapped his hands together, quietly though. "Yes, I remember from when you showed me the finger game."

"Yes, yes, Dally, yes, the finger game. Well, if you're sneaky enough, like a rogue, you can *have* it. It will be all yours until my next quest. You have to hide it from Mother and Father though, and you have to allow me take Arthan out to eat a meal tonight. Do we have a deal?" Jason put a gloved hand out for Dallion to shake.

The boy firmly gripped it with both of his little hands, shaking it hard and happily. "We have a deal." The little one said.

Dallion hopped over the gate to approach the front door.

Arthan shouted, "Wait, don't go inside yet, Dally!"

Jason tightened the saddle onto Pax. He was getting ready to mount up while Arthan stood there, still as a statue.

"Well, Jason, that was a clever way of saving me from the games and songs for the night, but I still won't be joining you."

Jason climbed on top of his horse while he listened to his brother in pink reject the offer. "The White Knight is going up and onto his nice white horse, and now you. Come, are you truly going to be a miserable little princess? I would guess you cannot think of a good reason not to join if I was to ask now…"

Arthan scratched his fuzzy chin. "I'm not dressed in the proper attire. I don't want to look queer on the back of your horse while you ride like I'm a wench of yours. I need to recover my strength anyhow. I must have a good night of rest for my first real day in the council tomorrow."

Jason put his hand out for Arthan to grab ahold of. "I need to be awake early in the morning as well, for sparring with my knights, and to see the king off for his travels, which is even *before* my sparring. Come, let's watch over each other, you and I, to be sure that we are leaving the inn to come back here for bed at a reasonable hour tonight." Jason wasn't giving Arthan anytime to think, nor to reply.

Arthan found himself taking his brother's hand and climbing the horse while Dallion made his way inside the Frauer household.

07
Arthan's Day One

Arthan felt as if he was the coldest he had ever been in his entire lifetime. The evil cold burned his skin. *Frostbite? No?* He then decided he had caught fire! He took a big breath in. That was when he had imagined he was not only burning, but burning in the fires of Retilliath. How could he descend into hell? He was always such a good boy, a good young man! Dreams of the past came into and out of sight while the fires of hell entered his mouth and then his lungs, devouring his chest. As he flailed around in the burning cold, the feeling of the fire became moist. *How long have I been wet for?* He was boiling in a cauldron, and the fear wasn't leaving him. *Am I burning? Am I drowning? Burning? No… Freezing, the sea! No, a bathtub?*

Arthan exploded out of the metal bathtub. He fell onto the damp wooden washroom floor, coughing up all the water inside of his chest. He choked on the dirty tub water as he lay shivering in the nude. The room was entirely black; he would have thought himself to be blind if not for a sudden lightning flash from the ill weather. Light rushed in and out through the cracks of the imperfect wooden walls. The frightened young man, unable to see, brought himself to his feet so he could walk about his washroom. It was so dark; he had to use his hands as his eyes. *His* household washroom he knew, always had its stained windows which, even through the night, gave view to the city's lamps out upon Silver Street; this meant Arthan was *not* in his household washroom. Even worse for the young man, it wasn't night hour either. If a window would have been here, there'd be the daylight pouring through it as of now; this he was thinking on.

The nude young man opened up the creaky door after he finally had found the knob with a shaky wet hand in the black. On the other side of this door he found a bright and well-lit, *occupied* bedroom of the Alligator Inn. Arthan was more curious of what was out the window of this chamber than he was of who the four folk sleeping under the greasy covers in the little bed were. With his cold hands covering his cold manly parts, he waddled out of the darkness into the inn's bedroom over to the window, still wet. He tried his best to look into the sky, through the glass. The sun would tell Arthan how early or late into the morning it had truly been now, yet the clouds of a rainstorm prevented this.

When the lightning flashed, he turned around and gave quick inspection to the four souls sharing the blanket at the bed. Three women and one man. *None of them look familiar to me. Can't see too well under those blankets though...* He watched them sleep for a minute, just standing there, naked and cold. He wanted to ask them their names, how he came to share this room with the four of them; but then he began to question if even he had a share of this bedroom or if they'd even known him to be in the washroom just not so long ago. He was dying in that tub without their knowledge? Had they welcomed him into this room? What happened? *Jason would know, but where is Jason? Where is my damn brother?* he asked himself as he stood there with his little sack in his hands. Arthan looked over to a broken chair in the corner of the room. Under the furniture was his pink councilman's robes, filthy. How he was able to catch notice of the garb under there oh so quickly, he could not come to realize. Perhaps god was aiding his eyes and mind in searching for the clothing to assist in this struggle. There were a hundred things entering in and out through poor young Arthan's mind this late morning. *Or is it the noon?* He still hadn't any knowledge of the hour.

Arthan spent the next five or so minutes back into the black washroom with the door wide open, trying this best to half-blindly scrub out vomit from his robes. His vision was limited in this darkness, and so in the process of cleaning the fabrics, he had cut himself on a broken rum bottle in the sink. Blood, vomit, but mostly soap covered Arthan's hands and forearms as he almost teared up in the bathroom at that very moment. He had no time to cry though; it was important that he got himself to the High District and into the Great Keep's side dome known as the council chamber. He scrubbed and rubbed and, when finished, decided not to give time for any of the clothing to dry out. *It could dry on the run to the council chamber.*

Arthan exited the darkness to search for his footwear in the inn's room as quietly as he could. Thankfully, his sandals were under the bed, the first place he had checked to search for them. Fortunately, they were just topped with a bit of ash from wizard's weed, no vomit. *Thank you, Aeon. You understand how I so hate the smell of vomit,* thought he.

After Arthan was now clothed and a bit more cleaned, he stepped out and away from the strangers. Quietly now, he shut the door to the room as not to wake any of them. He hastily but gently made his way downstairs, to the sort of familiar Alligator Inn's main hall. It seemed as if he remembered this drinking bar and dining area from a dream, yet it wasn't from a dream! It was from last night's rampage.

"Lord of rum! the *God of Iron* himself, Arthan!" shouted the young serving woman who had no teeth in her mouth, standing behind the bar. She said this as Arthan was stepping down to the first floor of the establishment.

Half of the occupants eating breakfasts raised their mugs of tea and horns of ale to Arthan, the other half had their heads placed into their plates, from after-morning drink sickness. Arthan nervously smiled, hair and face still wet from the copper bathtub he had fallen asleep and woken in. Without letting loose one word, he ran away from the folk, almost tripping into the unskilled, fat harp player by the door. He bolted right out of the Alligator Inn and into the rain, northward up and up Brey Street while the occupants of the establishment wondered why the crazed, rum-guzzling Arthan they had met last night seemed so very different on this stormy morning.

Clumsy Arthan hoped his clothing would dry off some as he ran to the keep; that was impossible though, with all the rain falling and all that sweat leaking from his skin because of this miserable sprint. *At least now they won't suspect I've just woken up in a bathtub with this rain falling about the city.* He sprinted up, up, up the cobblestone of Brey Street, then up some painted steps to make on into the High District. He sprinted upon Silver Street right past his own house. Last time he had run this fast, yesterday, he had been tripped and fallen. The last Arthan needed in his life right at this moment would be Drake giving him another trip like he had done plenty in the past. Arthan wasn't fit to battle or brawl, yet he felt an encounter with the bully today could lead to his very weak self potentially trying to rip the boy's head off with a twist using his bare hands. Arthan never saw Rodrick Drake though that day, just the casual folk of Ascali as of now, maybe a bit less on the streets than usual, because of the ill weather.

When he reached the east entrance to the Great Keep, the council chamber's tunnel, he gave himself two minutes at the near stable, resting low by the keepers, to wait until his heavy breathing had ceased. After he was finally able to inhale and exhale without looking irregular and fast tiring, he brought himself up to stand, preparing for an upcoming dialogue. He was readying to charm his way into the keep by asking the honor guards at the door for access, explaining to them his whole horrific morning story and somehow explaining it with leaving the *"rum-guzzling"* portion of last night's adventure out. Arthan used the mixture of rainwater and his sweat to wipe his hair back and out from in front of his eyes, removing himself from the stable pillar. He then began to cross the small yard path to meet the silver guards at the big iron doors to this tunnel.

"Boy?" a voice said from by the stables he had just walked away from.

When Arthan stopped walking forward and turned around to look at the man addressing him, he saw it was Sir-Paladin John wearing his big coat and that golden breastplate of course.

"Good morning." Arthan said to the old holy knight.

The knight replied with, "You out of all people in the realms here at this hour?"

"What? I'm a part of the council now." Arthan said back to him.

They stood there in the rain, speaking as John now moved closer to Arthan. He had arrived at the stables at a similar hour that

Arthan had, settling his old mount in himself, refusing to let any keeper touch the old horse.

"Haa, I meant why are you here early. The Arthan I know loves his sleep too much for an early arrival. Have you ever been early to, say…anything in your lifetime?"

Arthan was seeing now; he wasn't late, or was he? Should he have been more angry now? Or less? He was still trying to understand it all, understand what had happened last night, before he woke into this morning's awful tense scenario, trying to still understand the current hour. Arthan said, "Well, I wanted to have an early start. It's my first day. I wanted to be here early. I'm either late, or early, so better to be early. I am here early?"

John grabbed Arthan by his shoulder and brought him closer to the stables to shelter from the rainstorm. They stood back under the wooden structure while the keepers brushed the mounts behind them, being sure not to lay a hand on Sir-Paladin John's horse. "You're usually either late or late. Doesn't matter, let's hope this becomes a common habit of yours now. Being early and all."

Sir John took a step back from Arthan, removing a pipe from his coat pocket as he moved. The knight smoked leaf as he watched the rainfall with Arthan beside him under the stable roof. This Sir-Paladin John, he was a tall older man, and so his smoke drifted high up and away from Arthan, yet the odor had disgusted the young man all the same as if it had drifted down low.

"Thank you, John. I shall make being early a habit. You're always so wise. I wish you had trained me after all. I would have been rising up early in the days for the past ten years now." Arthan said this with flares of sarcasm, although Arthan truly did wish Sir John had shown him sword-craft deep in his soul; why he was picking an argument with the knight now, he didn't know.

"I wish I had trained you too. You have your brother's blood. If you had let me teach you the sword the way I have taught him, you'd be legendary as well. Rising out of bed early, yes." Sir John spoke as he puffed away on the pipe.

"Legendary." Arthan repeated him, giggling.

"Your brother *is* legendary, and Dallion will be also, after I'm finished with him. If I don't die by the time the training's complete. Look at my beard, Arthan, going gray. My students, they're getting so old. I'm afraid I am too. When Dallion becomes the age you and Jason are now, I will be an elder soul."

Arthan took a step away to avoid the grotesque smells of the holy knight's smoking pipe. "You should begin training me now. You'll be a skeleton by the time I've learned the basics."

They both laughed together when Arthan said that.

"Why are you here, Sir John?" Arthan asked him as he tapped on the tall old man's breastplate.

Some knights casually wore their armor as regular attire; others wore common clothing at times, like Jason had mostly. Sir-Paladin John, whatever attire, always his coat and breastplate worn over; whether it be in the moment of battle or peace. Never any more plate for protection, never any less.

"Are you attending the council session?" Arthan asked John as two councilmen could be seen approaching the yard, taking shelter from the wrath of the rain.

Sir John said, "I'm not permitted, no. I'm here to give news to my son after he's relieved of his duty for the morning."

"His duty?" Arthan asked John.

"Guard duty."

"Ah, yes, little John the Second is an honor guard. I've forgotten, I apologize." Arthan said this looking out into the rainy yard, a yard filling with men wearing councilman's robes. Sir John took a last puff of his leaf pipe, then placed the wooden smoking device back inside of his inner coat pocket.

"He enjoys the honor guard position. There's no higher rank of a guard in Midlön. Well, yes, aside from Shield to the King. He still doesn't appreciate being called the name '*little John.*'" The knight was looking into the sky to watch the clouds, trying not to become wet from the rain while he had his talk with Arthan.

More drippy councilmen approached for today's session as the big old knightly man and Arthan made conversation.

"Right, so you're here giving news to big Sir guard John. Is it good or ill news?" Arthan asked him.

Sir-Paladin John took a sad breath in and outward. He stroked the graying yellow beard under his chin. "Oh, ill news, unfortunately. My wife and I will be no more soon. We had a fight yesterday, you see, and I just, well, I just can't look at her the same any longer. It was a true fight. She struck me. I struck her back. I shouldn't have done this. God will punish me." He removed his pipe from his pocket again and began smoking from it after he had lit the leaf once more.

"I'm sorry, John." Arthan told him.

"No, I'm sorry. She's the reason I wasn't there for Dallion yesterday. The lad wanted to practice with the sword and shield after escort back to the household, and I've disappointed him… I was not there." John sucked deep on his pipe, then coughed a bit, but then he smoked more.

Few surrounding councilmen were appalled, horrified at the smell of the burning leaf, so they stood in the rain; most hadn't minded the odor though.

Arthan patted him on the breastplate to comfort him as best as he could. "Sir-Paladin John, give more worry to your son rather than Dally. This news, it's news that will shatter your boy's, his heart. Where will your wife go?"

Old John choked on more smoke as Grand Councilman Lewis made his way out of the doors, past the honor guards, and into the rainy yard.

Lewis shouted, "All councilmen are permitted early access into the chamber due to the ill climate. Please enter, lords."

"That's you, boy." Sir John said as he rested himself against a wooden pillar of the stable, ready to enjoy his long smoke session while the councilmen prepared for a session of their very own indoors.

"Aeon is with you, and your son." Arthan told John the paladin-knight before leaving him there alone at the stables while lightning cracked in the clouds above. *Poor old man, been married for thirty-five years and suddenly… What? What could have happened? "Forget about all that…" Jason would say.* Arthan was now thinking of Jason, of where he could have been this moment. The last Arthan was remembering of Jason was climbing atop Pax with him to head down to the Alligator Inn. *Forget about all that!* Arthan thought now, *that,* meaning Jason. He had a council session to mentally prepare himself for. Arthan entered the opened doors to walk his way to the council chamber with more groupings of councilmen clustered around him.

Arthan hadn't been planning to put any bit of effort into searching the chamber's seatings for his father upon entry. Lord Edward was expecting to arrive in a pair and to spend this day and days with his son Arthan at these sessions together side by side. Arthan decided Lord Edward would simply have to make do for this day without his son, as Arthan himself had to now without his father. *All these other councilmen had their first days without their fathers beside them, why shouldn't I be able to do that very same.* Arthan thought about such things as he walked through the long hallway leading into the dome-shaped chamber with brown robbed lords in front, behind and on both sides of him. *Oh, I just hope father still plans to arrive here for today's session, even after him not being able to find my horrible self this morning at home.* Would Edward Frauer assume his son missing, spending this session time roaming Ascali, searching for him? Or should he think better of his boy and come to look for him here at the chamber where they're both meant to be? Arthan would soon come to find the answer to this, as he was coming nearer and nearer to the interior of the dome. He could already the see the redness at the end of the tunnel hall. The chamber would appear different to all who'd known its previous light scheme, beginning this day.

Regularly, the glittering silvered blue torches were set throughout the council chamber above where Arthan now stood walking (colors of House Apollo). Today Arthan and every other councilman had been surprised to see the grand room glow a deep and dark red. All souls saw this when first arriving inside on this day.

"Welcome! Welcome! None of you be shy please! Let's be fast today!" Lord Steward Arol Royce shouted those words from far below, standing behind the three shining chairs, thick arms crossed. He wore a sleeveless silk shirt, red; black pants as well. He was yet again sounding as if in pain of boredom.

Grand Councilman Lewis was descending some steps to join the steward while the many dripping-wet men funneled in behind, up above the two and spreading lower and throughout the seating areas.

"Please enjoy the freedom to make compliments on my torches! I had the fire elementists here early. Put them to good work I did, all to surprise my brother for when he returns!" Arol was speaking to nobody in particular.

Not one of the councilmen had anything to say to the steward as he shouted there for all to hear while the men took their seats surrounding the dazzling chairs at the base of the dome room. The chamber bathed in red light slowly filled with robed men, quietly though and so slowly. Perhaps the weather, combined with the dim, demonic lighting had casted an ill effect on the folk of the city this day.

Lewis finally descended the last set of steps, reached the bronze chair, and anxiously waited for Arol to seat himself in the silver one. Just as Arol Royce sat down into the silver chair with a leg up on a handle, the grand councilman took his seat, catching his breath. The king's golden chair lay empty and cold in between the two. With all that happening down below, Arthan found a seat as fast as he could, placing himself high up and far back, slouching when he sat, as to be unseen by… *Who? Who am I hiding from? My father? The steward or grand councilman? Why would they want me to speak for this session? Why would they even notice me?*

He sat there still as a statue in the red darkness, hiding from nobody specific as the rest of the much older men took their time settling into their randomized placements. After a bit of time seated, Arthan noticed himself growing hungry, followed by a thirst now; perhaps his body had this crave the entire morning. Perhaps because of his vicious awakening, Arthan had no time to notice his body's need for these refreshments. His memory of falling to sleep at the inn or any action leading to it, had sadly faded. Arthan assumed he had been through a long night of great drinking and feasting, yet he felt empty inside. As councilmen surrounded and took their places, he looked down to the stains of vomit on his sleeve, wondering if it was his. *There could be a bit of what I ate and drank...* He tried to wipe some but was then was painfully reminded of the cut he suffered on his hand in the sink this very morning. He found fresh blood leaking from his wrist, and then felt some more pain.

He had hidden his suffering very well from the men surrounding as councilmen had arrived to take seats upon both sides of him now. Arthan covered his wrist with a long sleeve of his training robe, turning to look upon one of the men beside him, and then to the other. He smiled at them, giving a friendly nod to each man as they sat in.

"Nasty weather this morning, isn't it?" the older, clean-shaven man to Arthan's left side had said to him.

Arthan was looking to the councilman's wrinkled spotted scalp in the red light, getting ready to reply in agreement, when the lord-steward just then began to speak. Arthan and the man beside him and all the rest of the wet councilmen gave their full attention below.

Lord Arol sat and leaned as far back as he could with that leg still lazily placed over one handle of the chair. He made himself extremely comfortable for today's session. "I know all of you share the same thought!" Arol loudly and slowly moaned while picking dirt out from one of his fingernails. "Only few days after he rises to the throne, and the king is already off on a foolish, meaningless adventure!" Arol looked just beside his seat, where the empty chair could be seen coldly placed, glowing red, when regularly would be shining gold. "Please, if any of you should think to assassinate me, do it after King Gregory returns, for I fear Lewis could not bear even a day of ruling, if both my brother *and* I were not present!" Arol ceased his fingernail cleaning, then he looked above to smile at all councilmen he could see front him. Elderly Lewis sat unmoving, watching the councilmen too with a grim and saggy face. Arol laughed. "It was a joke. I'm a joker..."

Arthan heard some of the councilmen laugh; most sat quiet.

The council hadn't been accustomed to the royal family being so humorous and queer as the Royce brothers were known to be. *Witty,* as Arthan's lord-father would say. Old Harold Apollo was a gentle, laughing, loving ruler, yet he found the Throne Hall and council chamber no place for showing comedics, Lord Edward Frauer told this to his kin. These Royces, quite the opposite of that.

"So no more jokes. I see none here have a taste for them! On with the usual then? Grand Councilman, today's topics?"

The grand councilman unrolled a scroll, now placing one hand on the chair to steady himself to rise up for speaking.

"You don't need to stand, just read from the scroll." Arol said quietly.

Lewis fell back to sit, unrolled the scroll, and tucked his white beard into his robes just at the neck as so he could read without the hair in his view. Arthan watched from above as the shaking, wrinkly old councilman held onto the paper resting upon his lap and read it over, and then over once more before speaking out the contents written upon it.

"Men of Ascali, of Midlön, on this stormy day, we are tasked with discussion of an increased monthly cathedral donation. Kief requires word on sewage matters. Lord Flux requires word on masonry. Tournament matters to speak of. And lastly, House Orange and their insulting lack of payments!"

"Discussing these topics in the order upon which you have just read them to us?" Arol Royce the steward asked, then he yawned in exhaustion. "Oh so boring. We all should be thankful my brother is absent. These matters would bore him into an ill mood, should bore anybody really. You can all agree, yes? When I was a councilman like all of you, just last week! I was never able to speak such things! No one was… Well, now, please, all! Speak your minds, and speak the truths. It's time we make great change in this chamber."

Arthan was in surprise as to how loudly the voices from below could carry up and into the back of the chamber where he sat, even when one would speak softly down there. *Magic? Was it magic? Or was it just an echo? Already losing focus and thinking of magic! Wake up, Arthan! Not everything is magical.* His head was pounding, pounding, pounding. Whatever potion his brother had given him the night before their journey to the inn to *"help you feel better in the morning"* hadn't been taking affect for poor, thirsty Arthan. He put his fingertips above his ears and pressed hard into his temples, eyes closed. Trying to think away the head sickness. This constant red lighting in the room was making the young one nauseous, sending pain behind his eyes as well.

Below, on the floor of this massive room, Steward Arol Royce was sitting slumped, making complaints of the first issue at hand. Donation to the Cathedral of Aeon; the first topic of discussion for today's session. Grand Councilman Lewis had stated the elderly Ark Priest had been requesting more gold be gifted to the cathedral each month. Before any councilman in the chamber could give any sort of input on this matter, Arol made his statement, "Ask them their price, agree to it, gift them a single chest filled with a year's worth. In place of foolish monthly bags, we shall be donating on a yearly basis. Have the priests, hmm, let's have them sign a sort of contract stating that, hmm, I don't know, let's state, if asked by them for anything else of the royal family, we are owed every single bit of the coin back to our vaults."

The bold decision by the king's brother had intrigued Arthan and helped distract him of his head aching. When the king was absent, the steward acted and spoke for the king, and Lord-Steward Arol had spoken, boldly.

He continued on, "Fair, yes? We're to supply them with a year's worth of gold. A chest filled of gold! For god, they can leave us be for a year for it! Next topic!" the steward shouted loud, louder than he had needed to.

Lewis took a glance at the scroll on his lap and then looked to the steward, shouting, "Master of Undercity wants word!"

"Yes, bring Kief in." Arol resumed cleaning his nails, as he had been earlier in the session.

"First word!" the grand councilman shouted out.

An iron door in the stone wall opened from the bottom south side of the chamber, and out of it came the old hunchback man of Ascali, life dedicated to maintaining the below portions of the city.

"Kief, how do you?" Arol asked when the man limped up to stand and present himself at the base of the chairs.

"Well, could use a little sunlight." The many men of the council above laughed at the jest, for Kief, Master of Undercity, was fairly liked among most here. He had done his job well from below the streets for decades; and the appreciation for it had been shown always.

"What can we do for you, Kief? What can I or my brother do?"

The tall, old hunched-over man gave himself a second to speak while he rubbed at the stubbles on his sagging chin. Even from all the way above, Arthan could see his pale face had no hair about it aside from his thick, brick-like eyebrows. For an old tunnelman with such long unkempt hair down to his ass, it was surprising to see his face had been so cleanly shaven. *Clean garb for a man who lives in the sewage too.* Arthan, alike many folk in the city, had knowledge of this Master of Undercity's existence yet hardly any had looked upon him.

"My steward, I ask that I please be supplied with men to help shovel the shit out through the bars at the grand privy exits."

Arthan saw how Arol had squinted his eyes, tightening up his mouth in disgust, almost as if he had caught a smell of poop at that very moment. "The grand privy exits?" Arol asked the Master of Undercity, as if he hadn't known what or where Kief had meant by this.

"Where the shit is meant to leave Ascali at the east rock side under the walls there, to have a proper flow off down into the river. It's blocked off by shit. Nothing passes through the bars." Kief told the steward while all looked on from above.

Arol placed his face into his palm and shook his head negatively.

Grand Councilman Lewis said, "There are no men for this."

Kief quickly replied with, "Grand Councilman, if we do not clear the blockage, the streets will be covered in overflow filth, in shit. This will happen within a day or two's time."

Neither Arthan nor the rest of the councilmen could see from their places if Arol Royce was amused or annoyed sitting there in that silver, now-red-appearing chair of his. He just remained with his palm in his face, silent.

Grand Councilman Lewis spoke more. "You are the Master of Undercity, tasked with maintaining all tunnels, dungeons, and sewage. Order a group of your men to do these things."

"As you said, Grand Councilman, there are no men for this. When I ask my seniors to have their men tend to it, they tell me, *'I would never ask such things of them, even for tunnelmen.'* After I had kindly asked my chief advisor to command his best man to do this, he had a similar response as well."

The grand councilman made puffing sounds in anger, as if he had been smoking. The steward still sat, remaining silent. Grand Councilman Lewis said, "This is an annoyance. You mean to say you cannot control your own laborers down there?"

The Master of Undercity sighed. He rubbed his tiny bits of stubble again, and then itched his leg while saying to the grand councilman, "Grand Councilman Lewis, they all tell me they weren't hired to shovel shit, yet that's truthfully what they *were* hired for… Of course they're meant to tunnel, build, check for under structural rot, slay the large rats, keep the torches lit, feed the scum in the dungeons, yet when it comes to the *shit* tasks, they refuse, refuse me! I am the master there, yet they do not acknowledge this. I need a royal order."

Arol finally had spoken up, yet Arthan had been distracted as some in the chamber, including a few of the guards too, had been giggling from the many times old Kief had just referred to the privy waste as *"shit,"* a common curse for the foul substances, yet not commonly used in the council chamber. Arthan watched men hide their humorous reactions while the lord-steward went on. While some men above were quietly laughing, Arol said with his hand now away from his face, "You'll have twenty soldiers from the city's barracks. Twenty soldiers, few hours of shoveling, waste managing. Twenty should do it, yes? I'll be sure they give you the strongest. The folk of Ascali are shitty. There must be plenty of shit down there, only for the strongest to shovel away."

The pale-faced man released a grin, trying his best to disable his hunch to stand straight for expressing his gratitude. "Yes, I believe twenty men should suffice."

"My lord-steward!" shouted a councilman from across the opposite end of the chamber, away from where Arthan had been seated. A silence filled the room as the councilman far off waited for a reply by his steward.

"Yes, you can speak! What is it?"

The councilman nervously smiled. He held his hands together just at his belly, against his robes. "Soldier's d-do not wish to be shoveling sh-shit." The chamber filled with some more laughter, louder now.

Lord Arol smiled in return, yelling up to speak to this stuttering man. "Nobody wishes to be shoveling shit. Somebody needs to though. We aren't at war, yet we pay these brave men, feed them, and shelter them! Yes, our beloved men of the military. We can scramble together twenty of them to shovel some shit out past these iron bars and into the water."

The councilman was frightened of Arol Royce, yet he wasn't finished arguing his point. "Steward, these soldiers put their lives in harm's way f-for Aeon, and the realm, for the folk-"

"Not when we're not at war, they don't! If there's no battles to be fought, they'll shovel shit if the royal family and the council wills it! Which we do!"

This time mostly all in the chamber gave a laugh to the constant use of the word *shit* during the session's dialogues; even Arthan let a bit of a giggle out, still rubbing his head pains away with shaky fingers though.

Grand Councilman Lewis was the only soul in the chamber who seemed to not agree with this behavior from the new steward or from the council. "Is this what the council has come to? Demonic torches? Shit jests, laughter? We aren't an army of demon jokers! Let's be on with it. Royal order, twenty soldiers! Send a councilman to the barracks with a paper." The grand councilman yelled this, not happily. "Give them shovels in place of swords. Let's be on with the topic." the annoyed old man continued on saying.

A councilman below Arthan rose to leave the chamber and fulfill the delivery of this order. The steward then waved away the Master of Undercity, who would have still been standing there if not for the hand gesture for sendoff.

Arol was not finished speaking of this matter to the above man. As Kief walked away, he continued on with the nervous councilman up to the top, as the man had not taken his seat yet. "Councilman, someone must be tasked with this foul job. Don't make judgment upon me for ordering paid men to clean a mess, mess from us all. Please sit! Now! Grand Councilman, yes with haste, let's be on with the next…what is next?"

The councilman above finally sat himself down as Lord-Steward Arol and Grand Councilman Lewis spoke to each other loudly.

"Lord Flux would like speaking time!" the grand councilman told Arol, and for all to hear.

"What is it you said he would like of us? This is a matter of masonry? What of it? What does he want?"

The old man untucked his beard from the neck portion of his robes, looking to his lord-steward now. "He wants a moment of time with us!"

"Yes, although you know what it is these folk desire to ask of us, prior to them entering the chamber here, yes?"

"Yes! I and your brother the king approve these requests to speak here. We all know this. It's me they see first, me." Grand Councilman Lewis rubbed his forehead. Perhaps he was experiencing head pains as Arthan had been today. Lewis said, "He's requesting forty or so masons of the city, put to travel for work to restore the dam at Alhert."

Steward Arol hadn't seemed to be familiar with the location. "Alhert?" he asked Lewis.

"Castle Alhert, where the Flux family dwells! Do you not know this?"

"Ah, I see. Forty? A bit excessive, yes? He gets a dozen, perhaps two dozen." The steward pointed to ten random councilmen seated up above. "One of you above will round up some masons and present them to him!" *He favors his problem solving to be carried out simply and swiftly. Jason would make a good friend to Lord Arol, and Lord Arol a good friend to him.*

"Tell Lord Flux to return to his castle and to expect these masons in short time, no need for a word here."

"Word two! Dismissed!" shouted Lewis toward the closed iron door as a few of the councilmen above jumped from their seats and hastily walked to leave the chamber, rushing to carry out Arol's command.

"Next?" asked Lord-Steward Arol.

"The tournament!" yelled Lewis.

Arol removed his leg from the side of the chair and sat himself up straight, more presentable, more formidable as a steward of the realm should appear. "Ahh, my brother's most beloved topic of discussion, poor man. We'll inform him of what we speak of! Grand Councilman, what tournament matters are there to discuss?"

Lewis held his beard out to the side, as to not block view of the wording on the paper in his lap. He looked at the scroll, and then placed his white beard back into his lap. "Most importantly, the set and confirmed date!" shouted Lewis.

"The end of this current week!" said Arol loudly, then he leaned back into his chair and crossed his arms, smiling.

The chamber erupted in whispers and private discussions throughout the councilmen. Each one of the men in robes had been speaking softly to the man either at his left, or right while Arol sat down there biting his lip now. Old Lewis sat in the bronze chair, trying to catch his breath and slow his heart speed so it wouldn't burst in that ancient chest of his. Then there was young Arthan, watching the red flames of the torches above.

"This very week? Nonsense." the councilman on the left side said to Arthan.

From the right side, in the chair, Arthan heard from a different voice, "Hasty, hasty is good! Why wait weeks anyway?"

The councilman sitting at his right spoke to Arthan, and he spoke to the man to Arthan's left too.

"That's foolish!" the man on the left said to the one on Arthan's right.

"Why's that foolish?" the one on the right asked in reply.

The men were speaking across Arthan, while he, the young man, sat in the middle, waiting for either Lord-Steward Arol or Lewis to carry on with the session. All souls in the chamber above those two down there still just sat whispering of the matter, besides the pairs of honor guards at the four entryways of course, regularly standing silent during discussions, as they appeared now.

Arthan watched Grand Councilman Lewis rise from his bronze chair with wobbly legs, pointing a shaky finger at Lord-Steward Arol. *Father says Grand Councilman Lewis is regularly steady, moving like a man ten years younger than his old self, though not today, it seems.* The grand councilman was nervous, preparing to speak to the lord-steward oh so coldly.

"Idiotic, idiotic choices from an inexperienced steward. The battleground trials begin tonight, continue into tomorrow, throughout many holds of the realm. You cannot expect the competitors to battle their way through the trials, and then prepare to face each other here in Ascali with only so few days for them to make way to arrive here. The travels alone could take days upon days!" The grand councilman was finished making his argument, yet he still stood there with that shaky old, wrinkled finger of his pointed at the steward. He remained this way even though he had concluded speaking; standing there all shaky-like and breathing rapidly.

Arol gently lifted his own hand covered in shining wristbands and some black jeweled rings to place on the grand councilman's fingertip. He lowered the old man's hand down and said jokingly, "Relax yourself, young man, have a seat please, do it now."

Hunched over, old grand councilman Lewis took a few steps back over to his red-looking bronze chair, and he sat down silently.

The councilman with the warts on his face whom Arthan had met during his first time here sitting on a session, stood up from his chair. He was just a few rows below Arthan, yelling down to the steward. "Grand Councilman speaks the truth! My lord-steward, we have trials taking place upon eight or so different battlegrounds throughout Midlön, as far south as Broachenvill, and as far west to the coast at Seavill and Pirates Landing. The winning warriors should be given time to recover their strength after their trials, not having to rush the way to the arena here in the city after succeeding in the fights."

"Interesting words, Martin…" Arol yelled up to the standing man.

The councilman directly beside wart-faced Martin rose as well. "Journey from Broachenvill is a two-days' ride upon a quick steed." said this other robed man. "It's not only they the competitors who we should have concern for, it's the merchants, the out-of-city whores, jokers, and musicians. There are many out of city, and even out of realm spectators whom often attend the event. We need to give time for all to make their arrival and settle! The days leading up to the arena matches have always had the city thriving with sales; gold coming in, and out, and back in. This will not happen now, not for this tournament if we schedule for only days from now!"

"Interesting words… Hallar, is it?"

"Yes! I am Hallar!" the councilman yelled down to Arol Royce.

"Well, as interesting as both your and Martin's words might be, we have plenty of whores, jokers, and merchants in Ascali already! No need to give worry to the traveling ones. Some shall arrive in time, others shall not. You two could sit now please, and don't concern yourselves with the victors of the battleground trials and their recovery! If they're so fatigued and wounded after their entry trial matches, they can find a priest to gift them Aeon's blessings with healing hands."

Councilman Martin and Hallar sat themselves down together after they'd just been yelled at by the lord-steward.

Arol looked to Lewis. "You as well, Grand Councilman! Remember, Lewis, remember, all above! The victor of these arena battles here in the city, he or she shall become *shield* to my brother! Your king! If the victor cannot have the strength to win a trial battle and then mount a horse and ride his way here to fight oh so soon for their king, then they would not be worthy to defend him anyhow!"

None of the councilmen had anything more to say of the topic, not to argue it, at the least. Councilman George, with the hair under his ears, sitting lower and fairly close to the floor, did have some input, actually. He stood up from his seat to yell down to the lord-steward, to praise the very idea to have this tournament held so soon.

"Tournament time during this literal week? That will be wonderful, my lord-steward!" George smiled down upon Arol as if he wanted to marry the royal man. Today George took hold of a place on the benches significantly closer to the lord steward and to old Lewis than most others in the chamber, for he had seated himself placed on the first and lowest row, centered with the three of the metal chairs upon the floor below under where Arthan sat.

Arol Royce saw this queer facial expression George had let loose just now, combined with the awkward agreement of the game day being held sometime during the end of this current week. Lord Arol decided he would then make a jest. "Don't force my love upon you, George, for I only love the whores."

The chamber erupted in more laughter. Even the honor guards hadn't made attempt to hide the reaction of the humor. Arol smiled at his own jest and continued on with the horny-looking councilman, who somehow hadn't appeared the slightest bit embarrassed at any of this dialogue. "George, please tell me why you feel this decision would be so wonderful?" The Lord-Steward sat with his arms crossed, eyes closed and chin up, smiling, waiting for George to answer his question.

The councilman fingered his side hairs as his smile widened before saying, "This week, a fast decision. Competitors and spectators need to be fast to attend this royal event, just as you are fast in making decisions, and fast in combat, for we have seen you fight."

Lord-Steward Arol Royce jokingly moaned at the councilman's remarks. "Do you wish to bed me, Lord George? Or is it that you just have wish to be my most favored advisor? I don't remember you kissing King Harold's royal ass in this fashion, and it's my brother who'd be the better swordsman, please, please, I am no competition for the king's tactics. Now, discontinue kissing my royal ass please!"

Laughter from the men in the chamber spread like fast-moving flames because of the lord-steward's words and from Councilman George's now too.

George, still fondling the facial hair under his ears, said, "Oh, but the ass kissing hasn't even begun yet, Lord-Steward! I always found the most important aspect of life in the realms of the earth to be *speed*, which House Royce has always had a gift for. I feel the folk should *have* this great quality, which you and your brother possess! Make it a point to hold the tournament in such quick time from now! A new king sits the throne. Not just a new ruler, a ruler backed by a new family name, new ways of living for all, in which the realm of Midlön has never seen!" As George was praising Lord-Steward Royce, Arthan was distracted with an attempt to search for his father among the groupings of councilmen throughout the chamber. He had given in, lost focus on the discussions. The tournament meant very little to the young man. His father, Lord Edward, had told Arthan his personal care on the matters and topics would be irrelevant. As a councilman, most important of all was to obtain the power to have care *always;* to present yourself as if you had great interests for all topics of discussion, no matter how tortured with boredom you might become.

Arol Royce was clapping his hands, applauding Councilman George after he took a seat back into his chair not so far off and above the steward's. While clapping, Arol said, "Good words, George, thank you. Yes, I hope my swiftness inspires and infects all throughout Midlön. Tournament this week's end! It is decided!"

While Arol was asking Grand Councilman Lewis what the next topic of discussion would be, Arthan continued on looking upon the rows of glowing red men in robes.

"My lord-steward, we still have more tournament matters to discuss."

"What are they?"

"Grull of the Western Islands would like word."

Arol looked to the grand-councilman as if had just insulted him; Arthan hadn't expressed the most pleasant reaction to the reveal of this upcoming guest either.

What could a man of the West Islands have to ask of the council on tournament matters? Arthan silently questioned.

Arol Royce then asked Grand Councilman Lewis exactly what Arthan had been thinking, "What could a savage man of the West Islands have to ask of us? These are tournament matters you say?"

Grand Councilman Lewis wasn't looking to Arol. "Not a *man* of the Western Islands. Grull is an *orcish* of the West."

More and more bouts of laughter spread as Lewis just sadly shook his head negatively. Arol was disgusted, saying to Lewis and all, "Ehhww! An orcish has never been permitted in the Great Keep, not ever! Aside for the execution of Overlord Thraxus in the Throne Hall to end the Great-War long ago! Lewis, you've truly permitted an orcish to have word here?"

Grand Councilman Lewis explained his reasonings for permitting this foreigner, which Arol would soon have no choice but to accept in.

"Lord-Steward, Grull is *'third word'* for today, just beyond the door there, already inside the Great Keep. He waits for my call of entry, and he will certainly have it! I approved his request for word, as did King Gregory before he left for his travels. Your brother, our *king*, says that Grull will have a voice here. Remember what he said of equality amongst all-"

"Yes! Yes! Gregory and equality, his stand for the folks' rights of being equal, yes! Well, this Grull is not a folk of Midlön!"

"Might I remind you that foreigners are permitted a chance to battle in the arena, Lord-Steward! Had Grull been born a *man* of the island's instead of orcish, this would not be a problem." loudly Lewis said this in reply.

Arol stood up from his silver chair to tower over Lewis. He was attempting to make the old councilman lose comfort, and he hadn't been succeeding in it. He was sweating over the old man while he said to him, "Foreigners are permitted, but not orcish, not after the Great-War. They shouldn't even be permitted in the damn realm at all, let alone the city! Let alone the arena, and *especially* not here in the Great Keep!"

Lewis looked all the way up to Arol as the royal man stood above him. The elder challenged the young, new steward with his eyes, as he Lewis reminded his old self that he had in past observed and heard foolish words from Arol and his brother for years now on this council, in this very room. Arthan, all the way from up at the top of the chamber, watched down below as Lewis did his very best to treat the new lord-steward, just as a simple councilman as he had previously been for years.

Grand Councilman Lewis looked away from Arol Royce. "The king and I permitted Grull to have a word here, and so he shall.

Word three! Enter!" Lewis yelled to the door, straining his ninety-eight-year-aged voice.

Arol typically would have been greatly insulted, yet the sight of the orcish as it entered through past the iron door intrigued his royal self to the point of forgetting his verbal conflict just there with the grand councilman. He slowly moved away from hovering over old Lewis, walked back in front of his own silver chair, and tightened his belt up a bit. Arol crossed his arms now again, observing the orcish during his loud stomping toward the grand councilman and he.

Each step the beastly-looking soul took shook the floor, not that Arthan could feel the rumble from up there, yet he heard it. He saw the monstrous looking being from afar, could hear its heavy bone-crafted necklaces clank as it walked forward while the chains keeping his pants held up rattled loudly. *So loud!*

The honor guards at the base level where the steward and the grand-councilman were settled had seemed no less or more observant of this guest than any other in past, but they absolutely were watching closer than they'd regularly have been. Their heads never turned to watch the orcish being, yet their eyes followed its every move. Never had any guard experienced something of this sort in this chamber, with an orcish as a guest and looking so much like a potential threat.

Green-skinned Grull (looking more red here than green, in this light) halted, keeping a comfortable distance from Arol and Lewis. The orcish had the wits to not act entirely like one of these Midlön folk, even though he'd been promised equal treatment among them here and now. A step too close to one of the royals could cause a scare or be taken foully.

In what Arthan had thought to be the deepest, lowest yet at the same time loudest voice he had ever heard, the orcish said, "Steward, Grand Councilman, thanks." The orcish raised his gloved knuckles to the right side of his head, just above the pointed ear.

Arol returned the salute to Grull in the same orcish fashion, with the knuckles gently placed over the ear, and then back down.

Arol hadn't taken his seat as of yet. He was towering over the grand councilman just moments ago and now was standing across from his new guest. With arms crossed, Arol asked, "What is it you want of us, Grull? Lewis tells me your being here is of tournament matters, yet *you*? One of your kind should be the last to speak to us of the tournament, as you are not allowed entry unless as a grunt of course, although not one soul has ever asked to take part as grunt for these events."

The orcish took just one more step forward. Arol held his ground unmoving, grinning now. Arthan watched, entertained.

Arol Royce regularly appears suffering of boredom, I hear? Well, he doesn't appear to be of bored sorts now. He seems nothing but intrigued, Arthan thought.

Grull placed both his big hands along the top collar pockets on his open leather vest. They rested there while he spoke to the lord-steward. "It's why I am here. It's what I ask of you and the council. I ask for entry to the arena for play, not spectate, not as grunt." Grull hadn't needed to shout in the slightest bit; all could hear him.

The orcish raised his head now, as to speak to address the entire council, Arol, and the grand councilman at once. "Your old white king has died. I not only speak for myself, but all orcish when I ask allow us to fight with you."

"You mean to fight *us*...not to fight *with* us. You want to fight *in* the arena, you say?"

Grull shook his head negatively at Arol Royce's words.

"Fight you, fight with you, all of it. Allow orcish into your military if an orcish would desire. Allow orcish to compete in the battleground trials if an orcish would desire, to not be shamed in this realm, rejected. The new king and yourself, Steward, Grand Councilor, councilors up on the chairs! You *all* have the power to make great change."

Before Lewis or a councilman could speak on this matter, Arol said, "The Great-War cannot be forgotten. What the orcish have done, what they planned to do in those times of their failed conquest. Your kind shouldn't be treated so gently in this realm after all of that evil past."

Grull lowered himself to one knee and faced down into the bright stone floor, placing a fist up above the ear. "I ask that you not judge an orcish on his father's mistakes, on the dead and once-cruel Overlord Thraxus's mistakes. I had no part in the Great-War, for I did not fight in the Great-War. Please do not make judgment on me for what's happened in that part of time."

"Oh, rise up, please, stand." Arol saluted the orcish when he'd risen.

I would let him fight, thought Arthan to himself. *Although, would this lift of restriction result in a flood of orcish entering Ascali?* Arthan spoke to himself in his head, trying to distract from his dry mouth. Standing nine feet tall upon those giant heels of his, Grull held onto his collar pockets, awaiting to hear the lord-steward's reply or a word from the grand councilman.

A councilman among Arthan's row stood up from out of his chair to speak far down. "Even with the past forgiven, we cannot allow an orcish to compete! The size, the strength, it would not be fair. Your brother values equality! Do not make the competition unequal. I advise you to not allow this brute into the arena!"

Many of the councilmen agreed on this. An orcish being could make the strongest of man appear as child, yet as Jason would often say, *"Once you get them on their back, then you become the bigger one."*

"You up there!" Arol shouted up to the top as he stood in front of this Grull warrior. "Sit! Just sit! Orcish can be killed, that's how we won the war-" Arol now looked away from the councilman he had dismissed, and looked to Grull. "by killing lots of orcish and then their overlord, here in this very keep."

The two of them looked like they were posing for statues to be crafted down there. The lord-steward with his arms crossed, both hands tucked in under the shoulders. This Western Islander orcish holding onto his vest at the collarbone, fighting Arol with his eyes, as Arol fought back with his own two.

Arol yelled, "I'm making a point to remind all, the orcish invaded the coast! The war lasted years, now we make peace?"

Grand Councilman Lewis spoke up to defend the foreigner. "Peace has already been made back in past at the end of the war! Year 198. Gold-age, when the overlord lost his head in the Throne Hall. He died, and the war died with him on that day."

Arol took a step backwards, and then he sat down next to the grand councilman. He played with the rings about his fingers, refusing to look upon Lewis while speaking to him. Grull remained standing in his same manner, gloved hands gripping the vest. "Grand Councilman, I said I don't want him fighting, not him nor any orcish. This is always how it has been, always how it will be. I do not want it."

From not too far above the floor, standing up from a chair, Councilman George said, "My Lord-Steward, might I?" George was smiling with shining teeth, holding a hand up waving to Lord-Steward Arol. "Might I say something? My lord-stew-"

"What? What is it?"

"It isn't about what *you* want, it's what your brother wants."

Lord Arol removed his rings and placed them inside the embroidered pocket on his sleeveless top piece. He smiled and looked up to George. "I make the decisions while the king is absent. Enough with mind games! Just moments ago you had been in full agreement on the previous matter, now you go against me?"

Councilman George chuckled, lifting a fist to his mouth to hide the humor he found. "Lord-Steward, I was in agreement with you on the matter of the tournament date. This is a new matter at hand… As for what you've said of decisions… You make the decisions while the king is absent? Well, that isn't how that works here in this chamber." George laughed a bit more but quieted down when he had seen that Arol was not pleased now.

"Are you amused, George?"

"Not amused, my lord-steward. I shall remind you that you are here not to make any decisions, but to speak with us and Grand Councilman Lewis of all these importances, and to assume what the king would or would not want done with them." George then pointed to Grand Councilman Lewis's lap. "The matters upon that scroll there are not for you to take into your hands to make sole decisions. We all know our king, and we can predict our best what he wants done *together*, yes?"

Arol had scratched at his black beard violently while listening to George speak down to him just a moment ago.

Arol took a long while to ask, "And what would our king want done with this matter?"

"He would want the orcish to fight. I'm not claiming I would make that decision, not claiming I think the beast *should* fight." Grull looked back and up to George, not knowing whether to be insulted, or grateful. "But it is what your brother would want, yay?" George asked Arol from up there on that first row of chairs and men. Councilman George adjusted his view on over to his left side to see the councilman sitting there. "Yay?" he asked him.

"Yay." said the one sitting.

George yelled down to the grand councilman, "Grand Councilman Lewis, King Gregory has love for the tournament, does he not?"

"Yes..." replied Lewis.

"Then say yay! Yay for this orcish!"

Lewis shook his head in agreement. "Yay." said he.

George turned completely around and asked the man in robes behind and above him. "King Gregory has love for equality amongst all souls, yay?"

"Yay." said the councilman.

"Then yay to Grull and to all orcish!"

The chamber filled with the sounds of "yay" and a brief applause while Arol remained there, not as angry as he wanted to have been.

"Fine, disgusting but fine! Word three, dismissed. I hope you pass the battlegrounds and make it to the arena! Beast... Next matter?"

Grull saluted Arol, stomping away now with those tree-trunk legs of his. Arthan had never seen an orcish until today, not ever. He assumed he would be seeing a lot more of them, now that they'd been granted the chance to fight in the arena.

"I said next matter!"

"More tournament matters, Lord-Steward." Grand Councilman Lewis said to him.

"What next?" asked Arol to the elder.

"The prize, the winner will be selected as Shield to the King?" Arol smacked himself in the face, leaving his hand in place there.

"Lewis!" he shouted with his palm half in his mouth. "We've already discussed this during last session! My brother has stated this is what he would like the prize to be, yes."

Grand Councilman Lewis coughed and choked just a bit. This reminded Arthan of his own dry mouth. He wiped away the crust on his lips while he listened on to Lewis and Arol. "My lord-steward, I am just confirming. Typically, it's gold that is rewarded, not an oath and life service."

Arol removed his hand away from his face. "Yes, royal confirmation right here and now. My brother, the king, would have the victor of the free-for-all melee be chosen as his primary guard! We shall include a bonus of…let us give one thousand five hundred gold coins from the vault with this guarding prize! More motivation! If the king has a problem with this, it shall be undone or Greg can add to it if he feels more should be rewarded." Arol clapped his hands while the men above listened on silently; Lewis was coughing.

Arol said, "Guard service and gold! Oh, how the king would prefer Sir Jason Frauer be Shield, yet the knight's father claims this warrior son of his would have no interest in guard duties, not even for his own king!" Lord-Steward Arol shouted this while he looked above, searching through all the men in their matching robes, looking upon all the heads and small faces. "Is that true, Lord Edward? Or has Sir Jason perhaps changed his decision? Have you spoken to your son of this? Lord Edward, where are you? Could you stand?"

Arthan watched Arol await for his father to rise up from somewhere, yet Lord Edward was never seen. Lewis yelled while coughing, "Lord Edward Frauer! Where are you? Are you above, up there?"

Grand Councilman Lewis had ceased his coughing, now looking up and back behind himself, searching the rows for Lord Edward's pale face and brown Frauer hair.

Arol asked, "Did we receive word that he would be absent?"

To that, Grand Councilman Lewis said, "No forewarning he would not be arriving, no."

Shit, Arthan repeated in his mind, seeming like a hundred times. *Hadn't seen me last night, couldn't find me this morning. He's on the streets searching for me! I know he is.*

"Perhaps his kin has knowledge of his whereabouts. The boy Arthan." said Grand Councilman Lewis.

"Has he begun with us as of yet? Is he here?" Lord Arol was asking, looking up again.

No..., thought Arthan, as he already had a few eyes on him.

"Yes, he's here! Arthan Frauer, are you present? Perhaps he's absent too! He could even be with his lord-father... They're dual absences must be of relation." Lewis was prepared to send a councilman to have a search order written until Arthan at last stood up from the bench in that high, faraway row.

"I am here, Grand Councilman, Lord-Steward!" Arthan could hear the imaginable sounds of the surrounding men's eyes move to find him; of course not actually, yet the hallucinatory sound had frightened him still. It felt as if he heard an army of armored soldiers snap into their battalion formation. Arthan had just about one hundred souls here, all eyes on him, two hundred ears open to hear him...just him, only Arthan.

Arol spoke the loudest he had now all session. "Arthan, my young lord! Why is it that your father is not here this morning?!"

The grand councilman added in, "You are aware, if unable to attend a meeting, it is required that word of this must be sent forth prior to the beginning of the meeting."

Lewis wasn't yelling so harshly, yet the echo carried his voice up to Arthan loudly all the same. "My father is not here because-" *Do I tell them that I do not know why he is absent? Do I know why he is absent? I do, it is because of me.* "Because, he... My Father isn't here! For me... Because of me." Not all heard Arthan. He was nervous, oh so nervous, and would now have to repeat himself.

"A little louder!" yelled Lord-Steward Arol Royce.

"My father, Lord Edward, isn't here because of me. He is searching for me."

"And why would he be searching for you? He is aware both you and he have a session here."

"I did not return home last evening, or in the morning either! This had frightened him, I'm sure! He would more likely rather panic and rush to look for me elsewhere than think to come here! He wasn't thinking clearly, to give you word of this all, here! I'm sorry! I apologize in the name of my house."

Grand Councilman Lewis yelled to Arthan, "This will not happen again! When you do see Lord Edward, please inform him that he is to give word in futures if he is unable to attend!"

Arol bit down on one of his ringless fingers, and then crossed his arms, sitting in in his chair. He looked up at Arthan now, yelling and asking, "Why is it that you hadn't returned home last night?"

I wasn't supposed to speak at all on this first day. Why is this happening? "I had visited an establishment on Brey Street for food and drinking!" Arthan yelled down.

"Ah ah ah! A night of great feasting and drinking can always lead to drifting off to sleep in the strangest of places. Is this what happened? Did you find your way into a woman's bed last night instead of returning to the Frauer household?"

Arthan looked upon Arol down below there, then up to as many men as he could see, all gazing upon him.

"I said, did you find your way into a woman's bed?" Arol asked him again loudly and smiling.

"Sadly, my lord-steward, I do not have a well memory of last night's feast."

Some men laughed to Arthan's words. Arthan was frightened when he heard Arol scream, "Silence!" when there was a catch of the slightest sound of a humorous reaction. All councilmen discontinued with their laughter and then became silent again.

"Arthan, I'm glad you have the power to make your way through such a heavy night of drinking and still arrive here! Fresh and able! Most of us here drink ourselves to sleep nightly, yet none of us are as so bold as you are to admit and take pride in it."

What is happening? Arthan asked himself. He looked to his left where he saw the councilman staring at him so closely. Both men at his sides felt so very close now. He could feel their breath on him, but he then looked down again trying to ignore their gazing. Arthan was giving attention to the brother of the king, best he could. The only thing he could feel now was Lord-Steward Arol's eyes on him, from all the way down there at the bottom of the chamber.

"Lord-Steward, I am sorry!" yelled Arthan.

Arol shook his head negatively, now raising his hands up. "No! It's your father who should apologize. You are able to get drunk and still make it here with correct timing and the ability to attend well, which is your business and talent. It seems it's your father who isn't able to trust you with all that, resulting in him being the one not in attendance!"

Arthan was frozen. He could find no words to say except *Damn* to himself in his head, repeatedly.

"We should move to the next topic at hand. I just wish you hadn't gotten so drunk Arthan as to lose your memory of the night. I do love a good story of a fun drinking time." Lord Arol laughed a bit after he'd said that, then readied to carry on.

Arthan was preparing himself to apologize one last time and then to quickly take his seat. He would feel at ease after all moved onto the next matter, hoping the men in the red chamber would soon forget this dialogue.

"Oh, Lord-Steward…" George said, standing and waving his hand up in the air again, like a child at an Institution lesson. "For I was feasting at the Alligator Inn last night! I saw Arthan enjoying himself!" the councilman yelled. "I wasn't invited to the royal feast in the Throne Hall, and so I thought, why not go drink with the whores and the jokers! That's when I saw him and Sir Jason!" George smiled at Arol.

"And tell me, Councilman George, was it a grand night?" the lord-steward asked.

Arthan watched way down as George brought his smile away from Arol and now up to here. "*'God of Iron and the Lord of Rum'* they call him in there! Arthan was impressive last evening. Would you like to hear the story? Arthan might not have memory of the night, but I do!"

08

Violent Departure of the Village

He had his dreams of home. Mostly of the sun's yellow heat, how it touched his lands in ways it did for no other realms. Desmond dreamt of these pleasures from a time not so long ago, when his family still had love for him, when his jaw was not broken. The pleasant dreams of Eastfell, his sisters and mother, had now began to fade away as the pain in his mouth came back to him in the midst of sleep. He couldn't feel the injury if he would lie completely unmoving, breathing softly, as he was trying to do so now. He had just at this moment woken, bloodied and filthy in the corner of his small cell.

Hours upon hours ago, the first time Desmond had gained consciousness in the Willowhold dungeon, after being hit and put to sleep on the road above, were moments of the most suffering the Easterlñ had ever experienced in his lifetime. It had been the night, him taking some minutes in the darkness of the cell, trying to adjust his jawbone back in place with that wounded hand. He had sadly, painfully, failed to do this, and so he had then put himself against the wall in a back corner of the cell, defeated. He rested against the drippy stone wall instead of settling himself in the centered pile of hay, which the dungeon masters intended their captives to use as bedding. When he had first reached his wet corner, he found blood was then seeping through his teeth, leaking out off of his lips from when he had just tried to painfully repair his bottom face bones. He wanted desperately to spit the red filth outward, yet he knew such an action would bring more pain upon himself. He had sat there resting as still as he could be while the blood dripped out the sides of his mouth and down the outside of his throat and neck. *Let this dreadful night end,* he asked the gods. He fingered at the palm of his corrupted hand, the hand that the village blacksmith had put a pickaxe into yesterday. It hurt badly; nothing in comparison to the feeling of this loose jaw though. It took an hour of lying against that wall, then sleep found him and then the dreams of home had flooded into his mind.

He was awake again now; though, instead of comforting dreams, he just had his pain. The morning clouds broke away briefly just now. Sunlight poured in through the window above, bathing Desmond's face and chest in bright warmth while he sat there as still as a statue. He hadn't come to realize this room was constructed with a window until this morning! When he had gained consciousness last night, it had been entirely black in the cell. There had been no moonlight, nor light from the village to shine through this window high up. Not even one torch to be seen in the hallway of the dungeon, opposite the window, beyond the iron bars that held Desmond captive. He sat looking upon the window above, listening to the village alive with starving drunks upon the poop roads. Desmond would have thought to make an escape through that little window, yet iron bars prevented this attempt; the same sort of iron bars that prevented him from simply walking out of the cell and into the dark dungeon's hallway to find his leave. Miserable, hungry Desmond placed a gentle hand upon his left cheek. He could feel that the bottom set of teeth weren't entirely aligned with his top set. His jaw was damaged badly and would never naturally heal the same; this he knew.

The pain was unbearable, and so he stopped touching his mouth, now trying to remember the last time he ate a meal or had anything at all in his belly. During this time in the cell, the pain had been so great he hadn't even put thought to how awful his stomach had been feeling, yet now that he imagined eating, he grew angry. *I can't even open my mouth. How am I to bite into anything?* Desmond caught sight of a fat rat as he was having these horrid thoughts of eating food. The critter crawled past the iron bars that blocked Desmond in from the hallway, entering the cell as it sniffed at the moist stone floor. Even if the wounded foreign man was capable of chewing, he wouldn't have eaten the little beast. *I'm able to eat a rabbit, an uncooked rat would not be pleasant,* yet anything was more pleasant than dying of hunger. If Desmond found himself near death from lack of nourishment, he would do what needed to be done, eating anything he had to, broken jaw or unbroken, yet he wasn't quite so close to that sort of death as of yet.

When did I last eat food? he asked himself. He had consumed a small bit of ale in the Willowhold Hall yesterday, prior to that he was unable to eat the remainder of the rabbit which his dog companion, Araisha, had found in the Midlön plains, for the meat had spoiled after Desmond had let it remain uncooked for too great of time. *Araisha? Where is Araisha?* He was panicking, living in distress inside of his own head. The pain, the dreams of the East, the hunger…all these he had found thought of during his time captive, yet no thoughts of his new companion until just this moment. The last Desmond remembered of the dog was seeing her run off! Far down a poopy mud road in the village, chased by the bloodthirsty people. During that escape of hers, that little boy in leather armor tried to slice through Desmond's face with a blunt short sword, leaving the foreigner with a broken jaw. *She must have escaped as I was carried away down into this room.* Desmond had no memory of any events which had taken place after the boy had struck him, yet he knew for an absolute that Araisha was still out there living.

Days ago, Desmond had tamed this wild dog using Easterlñ magic, binding their souls together in a sort of way. He could feel her heart beating from afar and would cease to feel it if it discontinued. Desmond had experienced losing a bound creature once after he had magically tamed one. *Seeming like ages ago,* he would think at times. The emptiness for a long while had been excruciating to him after its death. When his monstrous cat had been killed in the realm of Eastfell, it had taken Desmond's mind and body a great time to heal as if he himself had been physically injured. Whatever pain Desmond was feeling at this moment in the Willowhold's dungeon cell would have been a living, flaming hell for him if Araisha had not been alive. He could feel her from afar even now, if only he could communicate from this great distance, he would have her sneakily bring some meat in through that window above. *Useless though, chewing with this mouth of mine.* A horrid and *useless* thought. Even if by a magic miracle Desmond could consume food and the beast walked her way back into the village with anything edible, she would be killed or chased out, just as she had been yesterday.

"You'll leave behind that dog of yours for us! Payment for drinking our ale and wasting our time with begging! I'll have one of the women make us a great stew!" the half-nude man referred to as the third mayor had yelled to Desmond yesterday, while he and Araisha had been making a leave of the village. The third mayor, his son with the short sword, and those two other mayor brothers had then watched from the top of the hill, standing affront the Willowhold Hall while the villagers attacked Desmond and his hound. Araisha would and should know better not to enter this place after yesterday's fight, unless her love for her master Desmond was stronger than her fear and sense of caution. Desmond was eager to be out of this cell now, to be with Araisha once more and to kill those mayors. *Just the third one. The other two would be a treat though,* he thought with a burning smile as more blood leaked from his lips. His eyes were blackening once again as his thoughts turned to horrid, bloodied raging thoughts of slaughtering those who had done him wrong. He closed both eyes, burying his dark magic deep inside; the dark magic which caused him banishment from his homelands. After some slow breaths in and outward, he came back to the light, finding mind peace once again.

Is this punishment for my sins? For studying the dark magics? Desmond was cast out of his homeland shortly after his people had discovered that he had been practicing the dark crafts in his own secrecy for many years. He had kept his studies unknown to all of Eastfell's people, for an entire decade until his blood and eyes began to run black, an effect of channeling the dark powers for long amounts of time. He had always controlled and contained the raging dark inside himself, yet on occasion (as what had happened just moments ago in this cell), he had violent thoughts, deep urges to express himself by giving in to the evil powers through wielding them, upon the third mayor now, for a great example.

With these violent thoughts, came black eyes and veins! These dark appearances were what had Desmond's magical abilities discovered, and then caused his Easterlñ neighbors to cast his sad self outward, westward down the river, to the realm of Midlön. The people of this realm unfortunately, Desmond had heard in talk throughout his years, had an even greater hatred for dark magics than the people of Eastfell had for the craft. If Desmond was to in some way survive his current struggles in this village, to truly leave and make a life in this realm, he would need to be even more cautious of his magical secrecy, more than he had been in Eastfell. If his dark powers would be discovered here, these Midlön people, they wouldn't just banish him from the realm; they would more than likely have Desmond executed.

He wiped more blood upon his looted pants, for his hand would not discontinue to leak. The fluid was black, yet luckily for him, Desmond's pants had been black too. He was not to have to worry that one could see these stains; his hand though... Desmond tore some scraps of clothing off by his ankle, using the bits of cloth to wrap his hand wound as so none would view any more of his oddly darkened blood. When he began tying the bandage, his hand didn't feel oh so pleasant. He tightened the bandage some more, while also tightening his jaw some, biting down hard before a flash of pain reminded him that his mouth could move in such ways no longer. Desmond closed his watering eyes as his new bandaging made from dark clothing was absorbing his corrupted blood. He still lay against the stone wall, unmoving now as if he had been acting as an art painting. More thoughts of Araisha came and went, yet Desmond was just becoming saddened the more that he had continued to think on his hound. He decided that he would attempt to sleep more again. Sleep was all he could do here and now, aside from thinking, and if he was thinking, it would be of only sad thoughts.

Desmond was almost off and away to dreaming; perhaps another minute or so and he wouldn't have been conscious. Sadly, his sleep was prevented by some voices. *One...two voices...no, more than two.* He could hear a pair of people not so far off. The voices were growing louder, and the hall seemed to now dimly glow. One out of the two of these men had to be carrying a torch as they had their strolling chat, perhaps both held a torch. *A familiar voice?* thought Desmond. It hadn't taken him long to come to realization that this was the third mayor's voice that he was hearing. He squinted, tightening his eye lids shut as so his whites would not fade to black. (squinting had never helped prevent, and would never help prevent this dark effect) He hadn't known this man for more than one day, yet he had hatred for him; with hatred brought the urge for the use of evil powers, and its appearances came with this urge, regardless if he took magical action or not.

The torchlight was blazing brighter now, yet Desmond still could not hear the wording of the third mayor or whomever this village leader was speaking with either. The echoes of the dungeon hall caused the voices to play tricks to the ear; he did clearly hear the rattling of the armor though. It sounded as if there had been an army marching, closer and closer with each passing second. The clanking sounds of mail and plate gave annoyance to Desmond's ears, to his mind. The language of the Midlön people was difficult enough for Desmond to communicate and translate, and so this echoing speaking of the two men under the sounds of the metal rattling was making it nearly impossible for Desmond to understand any words being said far off down the fiery hallway.

"Let me out of here, damnit!" Desmond heard a shouting man say far off.

I understood that one! thought Desmond.

Seconds later there was a loud *WHACK* sound of wood breaking on metal, followed by a scream, which then quickly turned to cries. The crying man, the two men speaking, the armor clanking, all of it was just seeming louder and oh so louder with every tiny moment that passed. Desmond closed his eyes, and then he gripped each one of his ears with dirty hands, trying his best to keep his eyes from turning black, using peaceful, calming thoughts; thoughts of *not* slaughtering the third mayor.

The man was still crying somewhere far off down the dark hallway. *Probably crying in another cell, just like mine,* thought Desmond. The sounds of the armor and weapons moving though, that ceased as did the voices of the two men. The third mayor was standing in the dim dungeon hallway, watching over Desmond through the iron bars with his king standing beside him; the king of the realm of Midlön. Desmond saw this when he opened his eyes, slowly taking his hands away from his ears.

Desmond knew with confidence that the slim man beside the third mayor was, in fact, the king: white-jeweled steel crown atop his head, the queer and luxurious apparel he wore, simply the way he stood. *Why would the ruler of the realm come to a disgusting settlement which looks as this one does? Unless all of Midlön appears as this Willowhold would?* As Desmond asked himself questions in his mind, the king and the third mayor stood silent, watching through the iron bars; behind them were standing eleven guards, wearing full sets of heavy shining armor, wielding massive spears and shields. *If I had mastered my dark crafts, I could use evil magic to make all of their hearts burst right in their very chests…* Desmond shielded his eyes, as he was in fear that his sudden thought of using dark magic to kill these men would bring his eyes and blood to more blackness. "What's wrong, Eastman? You a bit shy now?" asked the third mayor, holding a torch in one hand, a bloody wooden stick in his other.

The mayor laughed and looked on over to his king, who stood closely beside him. The king was saying nothing, only watching Desmond lie there. The mayor smacked the cell bars with his stick.

I could pull the breath out of your lungs right now without laying a finger on you, Desmond was thinking as he quit shielding his eyes and was now looking directly to the man beside this glamorous-appearing king with that bright-red cloak of his. Instead of choking the village leader with magic, he decided he would have to be satisfied with only just the thought of brutally suffocating the man. *That king has a sword at his hip, and those guards are holding spears made for slaying orcish-sized beings… They'd all kill me before I could choke the mayor to death.*

Desmond was still looking at the mayor wearing rags, cursing him with eye language.

The king spoke up now, asking, "This is the foreigner? The one that gave you a great battle, you said?"

"Yes, my king. On the roads above! Just in front of the village keep. I had told him to leave his dog for us to eat. That's when he refused, and then he attacked my folk."

The king stroked his black beard as he seductively watched Desmond bleeding from the mouth there in the cell. Desmond was watching the king watch him.

"And he gave good fight? If you could imagine there was an audience to see yesterday's battle with this one here...would they have been entertained?" asked the king to the Willowhold leader.

"I would say they would have been disgusted. The ill look of him, the way he killed my blacksmith...a horrid way. He put Rory's own pickaxe into his eye and almost out the back of his head."

"I would say that's a clever way to kill a smith. I admire this one in fact, trying to save his companion after you've sentenced it to death. Before your son had put him out, he had looked ready to continue battling with what? The dead smith's pickaxe?"

Before the third mayor answered the king's questions, he smacked the iron bars again with his beating stick. It made the same *WHACK* sound Desmond heard from the hall far off moments earlier, *this time* so very much louder; he avoided flinching from the surprise strike though.

"Yes, he killed my smith and was readying to aid the hound as my folk were trying to trap the bitch. He was approaching the villagers with Rory's pick. That's when my strong boy snuck behind him and put him to sleep to save them all."

The king shook his head to the left side and to the right side in the negative fashion. The king looked away from Desmond, now continuing his walk down the dungeon hall, saying, "Makes for a fun tale, yet if an eleven-year-old boy can put him on his bum, he'll be useless in the arena. I'll more than likely take him with me, but show me the rest, please."

The armored guards walked after the king into the darkness as the third mayor with his flaming torch had not begun following his sire as of yet.

"Eastman, think I care if he takes you out of here? We'll find that dog, we will. I got two hunters out in the plains right now, searching the grasses for the bitch."

Desmond sprang up onto his feet, approaching the iron to challenge this man attempting to provoke him. He made a great mistake though, of gripping onto the bars of the cell as he made his walk up and over to face his antagonist. The third mayor used the wooden stick to smash one of Desmond's hands gripping the iron. A knuckle broke, sending black-eyed Desmond back and down into the pile of hay behind him. He let out a small shout, yet even the smallest of sounds projected would inflict the most painful feelings in the mouth, for he had opened it a bit during this fall.

Desmond's surroundings appeared darker again as the village leader with the torch had followed the king and his guards deeper into the dungeon to inspect more captives. Desmond lay on his back against the pile of hay on the floor, one hand with a hole through it, the other with a crushed knuckle now. Captives crying, the guards armor echoing, the king and the third mayor talking of an arena, Desmond could hear it all as he lay there thirsty as ever, with a broken jaw and two damaged hands. He just wanted to sleep now! He should know better to have these thoughts of drifting off to dreaming though, for he knew that for a wounded, starving man as himself, sleeping could very well lead to death quickly.

An hour or so passed by since Desmond heard any chatting, crying, or guards in the dungeon. It was silent now, just the sounds of villagers above and outside, until the dog whimpered just beyond the window. Desmond rolled over onto his belly and then faced the opposite direction looking upward. He saw sunlight passing through the iron above again, and behind this metal was Araisha, panting. He looked into her shining eyes from the stone floor that he lay upon, raising his wrapped hand as so she would see his acknowledgment of her. He would have called her name, but his loose jawbone prevented him from doing so. *Foolish girl, how did you get back into the village unseen?*

Desmond brought himself up to his knees as he inspected what he could see of her. Some bits of hair upon her sides had been missing, torn off. On her back, she bore minor wounds from slingshots, pot strikes, and hits from pans and broomsticks too. He could see the dried blood still crusted in splotches upon the fur. She now placed herself sitting, licking the metal bars upon the window. In front of her, against one of these bars was a dead frog she had brought with her held in her teeth. She licked the bars, then the frog, then the bars again. Desmond stood up upon his feet, now walking himself over to the opening above. He leaned himself upward and stood under the window, lifting his bandaged hand up. He almost couldn't touch the opening! Desmond was a tall man with a good reach though. Araisha licked his fingertips with a rough tongue as she whimpered happily. The loving gesture felt comforting, but the wound from the pickaxe to the palm under the bandaging, felt more painful than the gesture felt comforting. Desmond pinched her nose, and then grabbed a hold of the frog quickly.

He returned himself to the center of the cell at the hay, as he then just sat upon it now crossing his legs, watching his companion through the iron above after he tucked his greasy black hair behind his ears. He sadly couldn't eat this delicious looking new raw frog of his, although he received it and brought it through the window and into the cell all the same as so Araisha would not think him rejecting the food offering, or rejecting her. He was grateful for her and happy now to see her close by him again, yet he knew if any villager up there caught sight of her, resting against the side of the dungeon window like this, she'd be chased off again, and this time, she might not be so lucky as to make a full escape again.

A brief period of time had passed while Araisha sat down, watching Desmond not eat his prize she had brought for him. Not even an hour had gone by, yet he was hearing footsteps again now. Not so many as earlier, certainly no armored men this time. Just heavy footsteps and the rising brightness of more torches in the hallway. Desmond was standing upward, bringing himself against the iron bars once again. The torchlight growing brighter, footsteps louder too. Desmond turned back to face Araisha, yet she was already up and moving out of sight. *What an intelligent girl. She knows there is danger.* Araisha was hiding out of view somewhere up in the village while Desmond was standing in the cell, smart enough to not have his hands against the metal this time.

Two men approached, one with a torch and another with dull long sword. *These drunken, starving Willowhold people and their swords that can't cut; the very reason I am still living.* The one without a sword was armed, though with a crossbow, not a blade. Desmond was not eager to learn what a bolt would feel like inside of him. He'd never been struck with an arrow before in his lifetime. Both men wore puke-stained, brown leather coats, along with matching gray wrapped rags upon their heads, *tied up to use for hats?* The one with the crossbow handed the torch off to the swordsman. The bowman removed a small set of keys from his boot, using one of them to unlock the cell door made of iron bars. Desmond took one more brief glance out the window behind him; he didn't know if he would see Araisha again, not there or not anywhere. He was hoping she would now flee the village instead of waiting to see what would come of Desmond in this horrible setting. He didn't see the beast up there, so he resumed his attention to these two new men. What they call them in this realm, Desmond hadn't known, but his assumptions lead him to believe the dirty looking beings, wearing poor scraps for hats and mismatched boots, would be referred to as dungeon masters, or prison keepers. He was correct in this!

The two dungeon masters, without speaking any words, guided Desmond out of his cell by using hand gestures, waving at him to come out towards them, and then pointing those hands down the hall. Desmond left his dead frog in the cell to walk down this hallway. The man with the torch and sword led the way; the one with the crossbow followed behind Desmond. Four times, Desmond had turned to look upon the dungeon master walking behind him, every time seeing the weapon had been aimed right at the back of his own neck.

He told himself in his head, *This is not comforting…* All he could think of was that crossbow aimed to him as he walked up that tunnel; he hadn't even been thinking of the dreadful idea that he was walking to his own execution. He'd learned through tales and talk that the folk of Midlön would regularly and formally execute the bad people of the realm by hanging them from the neck with ropes. Desmond could very well have been walking his way to the ropes just then and there, he imagined. He was rising up, higher and higher, to reach above ground, making his exit of the dungeon. Desmond wasn't thinking of ropes now though, only that crossbow again pointed to his backside.

The hallway stunk of poop, the smell coming from inside most of the cells, yet Desmond hadn't come to notice this during his walk upward. The entire village reeked from the substance because the villagers gained the habit of discarding their shit upon the roads; they've done this for years now. *Difficult to focus on these rancid odors, when you have a crossbow pointed to your backside,* thought Desmond as he finished a glance at an enormous pile of manmade dung lying within an occupied cell he'd just passed by walking; the man inside this cell was crying. Desmond climbed a short flight of stone steps made from cobble, which eventually turned to wood the further up he walked. He got closer to the above exit, trying now to see past the dungeon man walking in front, the one with the dull sword and the torch. Ahead of this walking man was sunlight to be seen creeping through the window of a heavy wooden door. When they reached this door, the leading man swung it open and stepped on through it. Out of the darkness of the tunneled hallway, Desmond had risen onto the soppy roads of Willowhold once again. It had an entirely different sort of vibrancy to it in comparison to his last experience here.

The village appeared occupied with drunken people as of the last time, *yet* these now were *happy* ale drinkers. They all spoke loud, and all appeared proud and happy to be alive. Desmond watched his surroundings as he itched at his bandaged hand, purposely causing himself pain for a reason he hadn't known. He flexed the fingers of the opposite hand with the broken knuckle while a man not so far off in bright red and orange robes, juggled four balls in front of a crowd of children. The little ones all seemed most impressed when he threw the balls all into the air all at once, and then shot bolts of fire up above from out his fingertips, making them all burst into clouds of falling red ash. The mothers and fathers cheered on their dancing offspring; these children jumping in and out of the falling glitter, covering themselves in its prettiness. Desmond was impressed, as the people were too. He'd forgotten he was supposed to be following the leading man with the torch and sword…

The dungeon master behind gave Desmond a tap with the butt of the crossbow. The keeper ahead stopped leading when he'd turned to see Desmond and the other were far behind now. Desmond was turned back, now face-to-face with this old, gray little bowman reeking of ale. *Maybe I can just bite his throat out, the old eastern way. He has no leather covering his neck there.*

"Many thanks, I'll take this one from here, masters. Bring the last two, and then we'll be off and gone out of your sight." This came from an armored man stomping through mud toward Desmond and the keeper with the bow. The man was wearing the same style of protection that the eleven guards had been fashioned with down in the cell, the guards whom stood with the king during the inspection of Desmond. The guard here carried the same shield and same sort of spear as the others did as well; that spear, Desmond couldn't keep his eyes from.

"Come to the wagon. Let's go now, yes?" The armored man politely urged Desmond to walk ahead, and so he then did that. He heard the heavy, soppy footsteps of mailed boots in the mud behind him, for Desmond had no need to look backwards to know if the guard was still following.

Clouds came in to blot out the sun once again. The day was mixed with darkness and light, the sun always in and then out again then back in, just to come out again. They quickly made their way to the king's caravan; a dozen or so wagons lined up in the center of the village, one behind the other, and the others and the other until the front of the line where it began. Bright-red banners blew hard, fast in the wind. As Desmond approached, he carefully inspected the bolts of cloth above yet couldn't make a read of the symbol upon them. He thought it might be the same black cross, the one that the *border guards* of the Midlön plains bore on their red flag; a symbol he had seen upon his first day in this realm. The winds of the gray morning were making it too difficult to properly inspect, and Desmond didn't really give much of a shit anyway, so he quit gazing high up and instead looked to his surroundings once more; to find Araisha now beside a hovel or maybe in between some of the surrounding tents. *I hope to not see her, I've decided. My wishes are that she's run off into the fields and plains; to wait for me outside of this place.*

Until just moments ago, Desmond almost had no intention of ever leaving Willowhold. Since his defeat yesterday, he'd assumed he was meant to die here. He'd hoped he could be slain in some fashion trying to go about killing that third mayor. Desmond had strong confidence that he was capable of putting an end to the mayor's life, but not without dying while doing so, or soon after he's killed him, yet now that he saw this guard's spear so closely by, if he could grasp and wield it, then he could have a surviving chance.

Desmond's most favored game in Eastfell ever since he'd been a child was his endurance challenge with the long stick. Desmond had fought off up to fourteen foes for extended periods of time with his long wooden staff, breaking noses, damaging eyes, crushing the challengers ribcages. At home, in his youth and even now in his prime, Desmond was vicious with the stick. The only difference between a long stick and a spear was that one of them had a sharpened, pointed metal instrument of death upon one end of it. So long as the weight of the weapon remained fairly the same as the stick, the tactics, the movements, and striking would all function the same for Desmond here with the spear, only deadlier.

Fourteen of my people couldn't break me. If I caused a battle now, how many would attack? The king was in the village, and along with the king came two dozen of his spear-wielding shining guards, serving riders too, and many knights. Salesmen and entertainers followed the caravan as well. All the villagers here seemed eager and ready to fight yesterday, even without arms training or magic. *Today I'd have to face them, as well as this company of the king's people.* Those men in red and orange, juggling and playing with fire, seemed as if they could use those crafts for just more than making children laugh at flaming balls and falling ash. *They could turn me into ash...* This plan of forcefully obtaining ahold of the spear now hadn't seemed so brilliant anymore to Desmond. If he had no fear of death though, it would be a legendary way to be ended, he'd said to himself, with no hopes of living beyond this day. *They'd likely sing dreadful songs, write horror tales about the massacre at Willowhold. The foreigner who came holding a spear and using dark magic, slaying a hundred villagers, three mayors, silver guards, and the king of Midlön... No, I cannot do that, for my family's honor, even if my family despises me now.*

He rubbed his eyelids with two hands, each of his fists burning with pain before he rested them down. He took another look for Araisha while he continued moving closer to the caravan. Guards were mounting up and servants too, along with more king's men with professions and roles unknown to Desmond. It seemed the company was preparing to leave Willowhold.

"Up and into the lot. King says if everyone behaves, no need to bind up anymore hands." the guard told Desmond this while he pointed his oversized spear to the cart containing a bit less than twenty or so dirty-looking men. Most sat unmoving, not speaking with free hands and nothing in their mouths. Some of them were gagged, others had hands bound with roping, even metal shackles for a few of them. Desmond nodded to the armored man, then he climbed up into the wooden cart.

"Come, sit beside me if you'd like." said a bald man without a shirt who appeared to have the darkest of brown skin, almost ink black. He had a familiar accent, yet it wasn't Easterlñ, nor had he the accent of the people of this realm either. All the men in the cart looked filthy, as did Desmond; yet this man intrigued him. He appeared cleaner than most of the others, for his skin was so dark that none could see the filth to their eyes. The people of the East had a darker flesh tone than the ones here of Midlön, and that alone gave Desmond more comfort and reason to go sit beside and maybe even trust this dark man, yet why? He knew the color of flesh on the outside had naught to do with what lay within. *Blackest or whitest, this man could be good to me, or evil, yet I need a friend now more than ever, so let's see what this one has to say.*

Desmond planted his ass in between the bald man and another being whom was sleeping with a bag over his head, hands tied to his own feet. He appeared dead, but Desmond was more focused on the man to the opposite side, the bald one with the dark skin. Desmond looked to him and then placed his bandaged hand upon his own cheekbone. Desmond rubbed at it, flinching in some pain to show his new potential *friend* the injury. "Ah, do not speak. You are hurt… No matter, you sit there. Be strong while we ride to reach our destination. When we come to our destination, that is when they will use magic to heal you, to heal any of us who need. They want us at our strongest to fight. They will not bathe us though, pity."

That accent. Where is this one from? It was almost as if the foreign man had listened to Desmond's thought. "I am of the Western Islands. A foreign man here, like you. I see from your brows and the oak skin of you, you are not of this realm. The rest here in this group is though, all Midlön men, I can see."

A one-eyed man from the opposite end of the cart decided to ask the Western Islander a question. "We're all gonna die, and you don't shut up because why? Why don't you shut it?"

All gonna die, Desmond thought he heard the man say. He heard him correctly and hadn't realized he forgot about those ropes he could have been walking his way to earlier. *The Islander said they'd heal us all, so we'd be at our strongest to fight though…* Desmond had no desire to be forced into fighting or battling any people, animals, or creatures, as well as no desire to hang by the neck. He decided he would not wait to find out which either of those two would be a worse outcome, so he said to himself in his mind then and there that he needed to take action. *The sooner the better for me.*

As the bald man began defending himself against insults from the one-eyed man, Desmond heard from afar the third mayor desperately yell, "My king, you must not leave as of yet!"

Desmond heard this from just down beside the caravan, not too far off. When he turned to look at the verbal conflict, he saw the king climbing up and into the saddle of a black horse covered in a heavy set of red plate armor.

"Don't give pressure into telling me what I can and cannot do. That is harassment. That's assault! In the old days of the Golden-age, you'd have been beheaded for this."

"My king, my bothers and I…this village! We are the mayors here! Our people do not expect a lot from us, but they do expect some. Willowhold brews the most loved ale. It's drank in every corner of the realm and beyond. Why do we see no support from the capital? We receive nothing from Ascali's treasury nor food deliveries anymore, not from anywhere."

The king sighed and wiped snot from his nostrils, flinging the filth aside into the road. Without even looking upon the mayor, the king said to him, "You, your brothers, and all the folk here consume more ale than you produce. I don't care if it's the most beloved ale in the realm! You are supplied with a *massive* weekly import of ingredients to produce your drink, yet over half of the ale that is made here just goes right down your own throats. You don't grow ingredient supply to make the ale… Any halfwit brewers could make such drink with a simple hold of your recipe."

The third mayor's brothers watched from beside a hovel as the argument took place, as did Desmond from the cart filled with captives. The third mayor tried his best to defend himself from the wounding words towards him and the honor of his village. He was doing his very best to be cautious not to speak aggressively towards his king. The man wiped sweat from his forehead as he looked upward to the crowned royal person atop that black horse in red plating, matching the red cloak flapping from the day's wind. "My king, yes, it is true. No souls enjoy the Willowhold ale more than the very folk of Willowhold, but please… We starve! My son, it's hard to admit, to say *'a man cannot feed his own son.'* Where is my boy? Son! Where ar-"

"Enough, oh please! Stop this, you sound and look as if you are a beggar." replied the king.

Desmond watched the third mayor turning around to look to his brothers for support, yet the large one (the second mayor) with his walking stick only shook his head negatively. The little long-haired and bearded mayor just sat himself down into the mud, drinking from a horn filled of ale. The king looked at the third mayor in his eyes now, saying, "When Harold Apollo grew sick, as the steward of the realm, I was the one to make the decision to urge the council to lower the stock sent to you. The council agreed on this as Harold lay in bed ill."

Out of a crowd of onlookers appeared the little eleven-year-old boy, wearing that same pink leather armor, bearing that same blunt short sword that knocked Desmond into the mud. The blunt blade was hung by the child's tiny hip. The boy watched his father begging to the king, as did the brothers.

When the king caught sight of the little one, he looked as if he almost would wretch. "I hate the sight and sound of children! Why would you summon him?"

The third mayor stood tall, upward now, as tall as he could appear as so his son would see him in a better fashion while speaking with the most powerful man in the realm. "I wanted to present my son to you, to introduce him. My son is my heir, and an heir to a fortress as Willowhold requires *strength*. My boy cannot grow strong if Willowhold never sees shipments of foo-"

The king stopped the third mayor in the midst of his speaking, giggling a bit as he made his interruption. He humorously and insultingly repeated the third mayor's term, asking, *"Fortress?"* then went on saying, "Haa! I dislike you, attitude and appearance and all. As for the realm's use of you, you and your brothers manage this village poorly even *with* proper food supply in order…and yes, it is a *village*, not a fortress! I've heard tales that you spend more time here with your balls out in the breeze than covered. Whys is that? Why roam your own village in which you have charge of with no pants on?"

Desmond watched the red-faced village leader frowning to the mud below, as if that was whom he was having his conversation with. Before he could answer the king's humiliating question, a knight wearing dull-blue iron trotted up beside his king, interrupting with, "Sire, am I to ride with you once again in your carriage?"

"You'll do well not to interrupt me while I speak to the king!" shouted the third mayor up to the blue knight.

The blue knight drew forth his hidden long sword out from under his matching cloak covered in a pattern of white stars. Desmond had never seen such a golden sword, matching such golden hair. The blade didn't match the armor, but perhaps that gave a sort of beauty to this warrior's appearance. *Armor colored of the seas, locks and sword colored like the sun.*

"Father!" shouted the boy in leather.

When the third mayor looked away from the armed knight atop the horse beside the king, he saw near and coming from his own son the short sword; it was flying his way. It flopped just in front of his feet, sinking into mud and filth. The bald man from the Western Islands leaned back into Desmond's arm as the captive with the one eye was trying to throw jabs at the dark man now. Desmond had almost forgotten they were arguing as he was readying to see the third mayor battle this armored horseman. *Battle him and die doing so...*

The mayor picked up his son's dull sword in the road, now forming a fighting stance while the knight in blue laughed atop the horse. The king spoke before the two men could clash, yet Desmond was having difficulty hearing the words, as these fellow captives beside him were wrestling so close to his ear.

"The two of you will not do this. Marcus, I need you ready and at your finest to duel *me* in the upcoming days! Mayor, put that toy you call a *'blade'* away. This is Sir Marcus Magic, Knight of many Magics." The king introduced the knightly man in blue to the village leader.

The golden-haired knight sheathed his long sword while the third mayor lowered his own weapon toward the road. The king would then explain why the mayor and the armored man were not permitted to battle each other as of now; only Desmond wished he'd heard this all, as he could not focus on any talk with the two men still wrestling beside him.

"Sir Marcus here is to duel me as a bonus event for the viewers; for the upcoming tournament at the capital, you see, an event in which King Harold never would have taken part in. You see, on my travels here to Willowhold, I visited the Guardians Guild just on this rainy morning. That is when I had seen this dangerous, magical man fight in the battlegrounds held there! It was there that I decided the realm should be dazzled to see a man of talent such as Sir Marcus here collide blades with a fine swordsman as me."

The mayor bit his lip hard as the king spoke to him from high in his saddle. The king and Desmond watched him place his son's sword into the belt loop at the hip; Desmond still struggled to watch this though. The two wrestling men had now been shouting as well as grappling in the cart while all other captives looked upon them.

Desmond did his very best to ignore the conflict beside him. He had such great hopes that this encounter between the third mayor and that knight in blue armor would lead to a battle. *The mayor wouldn't last against a foe with an actual sharpened blade, covered from neck to toe in iron protection.* Sadly, there would be no clash between the two of them, Desmond saw. He wanted the third mayor dead, and how convenient that would have been to see such a thing without having to lift a finger of his own for it.

One of those shiny-armored guards carrying the oversized spears stepped up and onto the cart to end the fighting of the men struggling with each other beside Desmond.

"End this at once! Before King Gregory sees!" The armed, armored guard stepped over some captives to make his way to Desmond's corner to the fighting men. "And yes, indeed, you'll be riding with me, Sir Marcus. Find one of my servants to ride beside your horse. We have much to discuss!" said the king loudly.

Marcus didn't hear his sire's words though, for he was distracted by the fight taking place in the cart of captives. The third mayor was turning himself around, walking through the mud to his brothers and son with a saddened look upon his face. Desmond closed his eyes, *Mother, sisters, even if you reject me in this life, I will still love you in the heavens when you pass, please find me there. For the East!* He opened his eyes.

The guard was pointing his spear to the dark-skinned captive's head as this foreign man had his hands wrapped around the one-eyed attacker's throat. He was suffocating the man while the guard shouted threats and curses above with the spear, until Desmond grasped the weapon with both of his damaged hands. Desmond stood himself high up to equal level of his new foe in silver, then he crashed his forehead against the front of this guard's helmet, sending the armored man back off of the cart. The guard fell, leaving the spear behind in

Desmond's possession. As the man in armor sank deep into the mud far down from the wheeled cart, Desmond stood tall and armed. Strangely, the last thought within his mind was the broken knuckle and that pierced hand, both gripping the spear tight as ever. He felt strong and ready to die fighting. All eyes were upon him; besides the third mayor, he was still walking to his brothers, who remained at that hovel. The king watched Desmond, hands upon the reigns of the scared horse. All the shining guards had their spears drawn now, as did the surrounding free-riding knights with their long swords. The villagers had their pots, shovels, and brooms equipped and at the ready to battle for their king. Desmond paid them all no bit of attention; he could leap down off of the cart and reach the third mayor before any would stop him.

Arrows could stop me though… He caught a glimpse of some children with slingshots above a hovel, then there was a free-riding knight with a longbow, a few of them now. *Two, three men with bows…that I can see.* Lastly there was that dungeon master crossbowman, ready to aim his weapon and fire upon Desmond. The master stood hunched by the dungeon, smiling and horny to shoot. The third mayor was turning himself around now to look upon Desmond, along with all others. *And if those armored guards are capable of throwing their spears with precision, this will end for me before it begins.*

The sad notion of all those warriors in their heavyset armor, sending their black spears through the air to kill Desmond the moment he leapt from the cart gave him a useful idea of how to handle the remainder of his current situation. Standing upon the cart while the captive men by his feet bent their necks looking upward to him, Desmond pointed his broken finger to the third mayor as he held the coal-colored spear with his other hand. Not just the men in the cart watched Desmond, not only the king and his defenders, all people in Willowhold gave their attention to this event as if it was a tournament or theatrical performance! The king smiled at the foreigner, then looked upon the third mayor. "I think he likes you, Mayor…" said the king.

Desmond, without shaking a finger, held the gesture with his arm extended out, now closing an eye. He focused upon the third mayor with the opened eye, then with the hand which held the spear, he raised forward while sending his opposite pointing hand with the broken knuckle, down past his own back side. When Desmond's bandaged spear hand reached far outward to the front of where his opposite hand had just been pointed to, he released his grip on the weapon. As he let go the spear, it felt as if a rush of fire shot through the palm of his hand and up through his arm, disappearing into his shoulder. Perhaps he had been gripping the weapon too tightly, as this moment of great pain would now ruin his throwing attack. His fingers flailed and flexed as he released his grip on the spear, the tips and the smallest bit of his fingernail collided with the grip, ceasing his perfect thrown spiral motion before it could even begin. The spear landed two or so foot's length away from the third mayor. This leader of the village removed the shitty short sword from his belt, ready for fighting.

Desmond stood atop the cart, breathing heavily as he tightened his ruined hands into fists from reaction to his own failure; looking at the spear stuck in the side of the hovel. He'd thrown it sadly and poorly. The king inspected the weapon thrust deep into the home, blunt end pointing up to the gray sky.

The king giggled. "Or maybe he dislikes you! Haa! Give the captive another spear!"

When Desmond looked on over to the king in response to what he had just commanded to his shining guards, the spear was already coming his way. Not sent his way to harm him, yet as a replacement for the one he had just lost to his ill throw. Desmond caught it with that same hand, the bandaged one with the hole in it. He did well now ignoring the pain again as before; he'd have to make sure he carried on with this power to better his next throw. Yet he thought now, *Why am I being allowed another chance at this?*

"Easterlñ, if you have a grievance with him, why don't you step on down from the cart to confront him? He seems ready for you." The king waved a hand toward the third mayor as he spoke to Desmond, showing him that the mayor was armed and stood prepared.

"My king? Why? You've given him another spear..."

"Mayor how is he to fight you unarmed?" asked the king.

Desmond stepped down into the mud. He took a few soppy steps forward on the road, passing the king and the blue knight, onward to the third mayor standing there with both hands gripped on the little weapon without an edge.

"King Gregory, take him with you or leave him in my dungeon. I have no wish to duel this idiot prisoner."

Desmond walked his way on closer to the village leader looking to his king, asking for aid.

"Have one of your men stop him! Someone fill this Eastman with arrows!" The king glanced to his company. He looked to them, mostly already saddled and ready to make leave, and then he looked among the villagers. "If anybody intervenes, you'll be skinned!" said the king loudly. He then gave his attention to the mayor once again, yelling, "Just finish him off! The Easterlñ is starving, wounded in both hands and the mouth. I have faith!" He giggled out his words.

Desmond, still walking forward, was close enough now to strike, and so he did; the moment the king said the word *faith*, the tip of Desmond's newly obtained spear had collided with the third mayor's short sword. Desmond went high, so the mayor went high, then Desmond went low, so his opponent blocked low. Both ends of the fighter's weapons had met and then sank together into the mud upon this second collision. Before either Desmond or the mayor attempted to remove the sword or spear from the wet road, Desmond landed a hard punch on the man. He hit him directly upon his mouth. Instead of landing another unarmed strike upon the foe, Desmond removed his spear from the earth and spun himself backwards to distance himself a bit from the third mayor. During this theatrical spin of Desmond's, his spearhead found its way past the back of his foe's ankle, slicing it wide open.

The king gasped, as did most people of the village when they saw the third mayor grimace in pain as he sank to one knee, using his dull short sword now as more of a walking cane than a weapon. The tip of the sword lay buried in the mud as the man used it to support his weight while his knee slowly sank deeper and deeper into the mud and some shit. Behind the third mayor, his heavyset brother was dragging away the boy in the leather armor; off toward the Willowhold Hall.

"Father!" the child repeatedly screamed as his big uncle, the second mayor, carried him off.

The first mayor was drunkenly asleep against the hovel as his youngest brother was about to be executed by Desmond only ten foot's length away or so.

Before Desmond ended his life, he gave the third mayor a minor jab with the spear to his forearm. After his arm exploded at the wrist in a cloud of red mist and splintered bone, Desmond waited for him to fall into the road. The man hadn't done that though; he caught himself with his other arm still intact, as so his face wouldn't sink into the mud. Desmond would have went for his other arm so he'd have no choice but to fall into the road and suffocate on his own people's waste, yet he was feeling artistic, and so instead, he thrust his spear into the man's cheek side by the mouth. He put a wide hole through one low side of the face, leading to another to be made out through the other side, yet this strike did not kill the village leader. The third mayor died soon after Desmond then pulled the spearhead out of the remainder of his mouth as blood and broken teeth poured out of the wounds. He raised the spear once more, and then directed the pointy end down into the man's nose after he'd just fallen and rolled himself on over. His life ended when the spear pushed the nostrils and bone of his nose inward to destroy his brain; Desmond just left the spear there in place.

Unarmed, he took four paces backwards as half of the villagers fled in horror. The king applauded Desmond though, and made a point to do so. "I still can't believe you let an eleven-year-old *disarm* you. You perform excellently." said the king of the realm, still clapping his hands together. "Do you all see this? If all of the grunts in that cart perform the way this one has here, we'll have a marvelous event to look forward to!"

"Not as bloody as this though, we hope." said Sir Marcus Magic atop his mount.

The king stroked at his black beard with his ringed fingers. "Hmm, not as bloody? Quite the opposite, I think, yes, hmmm, quite the opposite indeed… The bloodier the better, sir!"

The king drew forth his crimson long sword from a scabbard hidden within his red cloak. Desmond watched him point the blade into the air, shouting, "Like the old days of the kingdom! The arena shall be dealt in live steel this year and for the future years to come! The age of blunt weaponry and the tourney sword has ended. We now return to our true nature!" The king pointed the blade away from the clouds and over toward Desmond, standing there still in the mud with the dead mayor sinking into the road a few steps away. "Priestess Reya, give this man Aeon's gifts." commanded the king, of a woman whom Desmond had not known or had ever seen anything like.

She made her way out of a white carriage belonging to the caravan lot, almost seeming as if now she was gliding her way to Desmond. The woman in white silks stood beside him, in place of in front of him as so she wouldn't step upon or too closely to the third mayor's corpse. Desmond turned to her so their bodies faced each other. He felt as if this was some trick; she was too beautiful for this to have an outcome for Desmond to benefit from. Her hair was almost as golden as the blue knight's was there beside the king, though hers more silver than sun colored.

Desmond looked into the woman-in-white's eyes as she placed both her hands upon his, interlocking their fingers. The wind came, sending her hair and robes speeding against the air during her service. She closed her eyes and whispered some words to herself. When she opened them, her eyes were glowing of the brightest white Desmond felt he'd ever seen. A pure white, just like the dazzling white of an uncolored star of the legends. When she removed the black bandaging from his palm, the wound was gone, nothing more than a scar now. He made a fist with the opposite hand. Where he should have felt pain in his crushed knuckle, he felt power. Before he could even think on how to thank her, or perhaps this king for sending her, she placed two hands upon his hairy face, touching his cheeks beside each ends of his mouth. The woman leaned in close as if she would kiss Desmond, only she hadn't. She whispered more words unheard to the foreigner, and when she removed her hands from the hair on his face and stepped backwards, Desmond thanked her. "Thank you." said Desmond, massaging his freshly healed jaw with clean, smooth hands of his own.

The woman's whitened glowing eyes had returned to their previous color tone. She walked her way back up to the caravan as Desmond gazed upon her backside.

"Easterlñ!" yelled the king as he sheathed his crimson steel sword.

Desmond quit watching after the healer, looking upward now to this king Gregory. "Yes, King..." replied Desmond.

"What is your name?" asked the king.

"Desmond." he said back to him.

"Desmond, get back in the cart. Everyone, we're off! Back to Ascali we go!"

09

Pre Battlegrounds

Jason held both of the unfamiliar short swords, one in each hand crossing the blades together in a common defensive stance used to dual-wield such weapons. The wet dirt among the training yard grounds made the arts of footwork far more challenging for Jason than the typical dry surface would have, as was this irregular fighting style with two swords instead of wielding only one. He took light steps backwards across from Lance as this opponent of Jason's twirled his own two short swords together, that long face of Lance focused as if the battle was real. Jason could never maintain a stern expression like Lance was projecting just now, not during any kind of combat training. When dueling for practice, Jason would tend to find himself smiling or with a tongue dangling out like a joker. *This is not the day to be a fool though.* It had been a difficult morning for Jason, as it also had been for his knights training with him. *I have not felt this ill in many years…horrid,* thought Jason, *not* smiling for a change as he practice dueled here and now. The head sickness from last night's drinking, the early task of the Eagle Party seeing off the king before he'd left the city! Swinging swords under the rain in the ill weather now, Jason soon ending his training session with bruises from failing to defend himself against his own knight; all of it horrid.

Lance, in his own preference, would always use his beloved two short swords for the combat crafts; blades that have lived to see every generation of the Flux family since the Gold-age. Hours ago, after the party of knights had watched their king depart as the sun was rising, they had made for the training yard where they'd spend most of their time of the rainy day. Early in the training session while they first begin to practice duel with each other, hitting wooden dummy's as well, and shooting arrows, Jason caught sight of his knight Sir Lance swinging such two swords, as he'd seen him do a thousand times in these yard sessions and upon questing. Jason had stood there in the rain, droplets falling upon his plate mail, gazing at Lance all the while with the sounds of *clck, clk, clck* ringing in his ears from the effect of water hitting the shoulder pieces. He stood there still as a statue, thinking. He never understood how some warriors would use two swords at once, when most like himself preferred to wield only one. Jason tried to bring himself to feel adventurous, to aid himself in bearing with the ill feelings of the morning.

"Lance, let me fetch myself two shorts! I'd like to give your methods a try." Jason had loudly told Lance this from across the damp yard. He sheathed his white long sword at the side of his horse, Pax, by the small yard gate, then briefly left the rain to search the weapons chest in an armory cabin built within a side of the training yard wall.

When Jason had returned to Lance in the rain as the remainder of his men continued on practicing their striking and shooting (all except Sir Alec, for he had drank too much rum last evening, and was now seen resting beside his training companions), he arrived beside Lance with two bronze tourney swords. One of these temporary weapons that Jason carried had a nasty chip at the upper end of its dull edge, the other sword missing leather at its grip.

The friends clashed blades thrice, then Lance had come to realize that the superior craft of battle was within him, the power to easily put Jason into the dirt, whereas Jason was regularly the more skillful warrior in the duels against his knights. Lance's realization that god was favoring him made the winning warrior confident and filled with a joy he'd never felt before, yet Lance would not express this feeling, only focused more closely. Water running down his face into his black goatee, he looked upon Jason, using stern eyes while twirling those two pieces of steel.

Jason's blades were crossed still. He was waiting for another attack, yet Lance was only toying with him now. With Jason wielding the two smaller weapons, in place of one long sword; he was not at his finest, and the four others in the yard knew this as well. Brandon,

Borran, and Martin had now stopped their practicing to spectate Jason and Lance's simulated battle. Sir Alec had even risen his head and opened his eyes up to watch the two clash, him lying down head sick, wet, and trying his hardest not to vomit again.

Jason, with his eyes on his opponent's moving feet, watched for the right-side attack to come; Lance saw this observation, and so he hit Jason with a strike coming from the left. Jason's plate mail saved his elbow from being smashed to dust, but the pain of the landed hit still hurt a great amount. He ground his teeth hard together, danced backwards to regain his balance, then moved about the yard fast, yet not toward Lance. Jason briefly took leaping laps around the yard to enhance his senses, *"Find blood flow,"* as the rogues would say.

"Ah! I'm ready! Let us dance, let us dance." said Jason, then rushing in making ready to place his three overhead strikes upon the foe; one attack with each of the swords, and then a third and final strike, set with both.

Lance's own two blades defensively caught the first hit, and then the second as well; either the swords would have caught Jason's third, or Lance's shoulder would have been damaged badly. Even with the knight's heavy gray armor, lined with those strong golden rims, Jason's hit would have injured the fighting man, yet neither the blocking or landing of the strike took place. Instead, Lance dodged forward, avoiding the strike from above with a sly roll through the soppy dirt. When he'd risen from the ground after his hasty move, he stood up upon his feet behind Jason; this was when Lance made his strongest attack against him at his side, just under an arm.

Did he just break a rib of mine? Jason thought with his back facing Lance now. His plate armor was strong enough to stop Lance's sword from cutting him open, yet the opponent's attacks carried the painful force of strong impact all the same. He couldn't think about his possibly broken rib anymore though, not after Lance then hit his left kneecap, not only once, but twice, with hard slashes followed by the singing sound of sword edge scraping on armor.

Jason fell to the dirt from the immense pain. He couldn't imagine what a successful landing like that could feel like without his knee guards! He'd seen it before, done it to men himself in battle and when questing, yet never imagined the pain of it all. This hurt well enough *with* an iron covering, without one...he'd hope to never know; though he felt the more he'd think on this horrid hypothetical worse injury now, the more his current pain would lessen. There Jason was in the dirt with the clouds drizzle landing upon his white armor, mind on about how much worse that his situation could've been if he had no protective wearings.

"Do you surrender?" asked Lance with one of his swords pointed at Jason's neck.

"I surrender, you fool..." Jason slapped the short sword away from his own throat, bit his lip, and rose upward to his feet, his knights behind him quickly resuming their practicing during this. Martin was silently and accurately loosing arrows at a barrel target thirty yards off, while Brandon and Borran practiced their long sword combinations on each other. Jason was envious of the two, working their strikes over there past Martin; their long swords ringing and singing. "If I had *my* sword, you'd be on your ass right now."

"You didn't have your sword though." replied Lance, pointing over to Pax, standing at the gate on all fours with Jason's steel long sword sheathed within the saddle.

Lance gave Jason a comedic tap on the armor by the ribcage where he'd just hacked at in the end of their duel. "Ahh, you fool! That doesn't feel so well, joker, haa! Ahh... Thank you, Lance!" Jason dropped the bronze blades, then limped his way over to the side of the armory cabin where he could hide from the rainfall as Lance followed. "My knee doesn't feel the finest." said Jason to Lance as they relaxed their backs against the wall of the cabin armory; Alec sleeping in the rain, sprawled over a wooden table not only five feet off in front of the two.

"Alec, don't dwell in the rain if you would not practice war-craft. You'll catch sickness if you don't get moving about some." Lance told this to his fellow knight.

Sir Alec, with his eyes closed, replied with, "The rain suites me. I feel warm, and I'd love to become cold again. I fear last night, I went and had too much elixir before we drank the rum." Alec let out a wet burp as the very thought of rum and the elixir was now making him become ill again.

"There, there, fall off to sleep then." said Jason.

Alec placed a fist upon his lips and turned the opposite way from the two, eyes still closed as he lay there constantly swallowing mouthfuls of saliva.

Lance sheathed his swords, wiping away some of the rain off from his forehead. "I'm warmer than I should be as well. I didn't have much elixir even. My blood is still boiling though." said Lance.

Jason sighed, looking upward, getting rain in his eyes. He blinked hard, saying all the while, "I gave a bit of the elixir to my brother before we arrived at the Alligator Inn. The vial was sort of divided by seven, not six this time around so you've truthfully had less than you regularly drink. My brother takes quite big gulps. If you're warm now, it's because of this weather. It rains, yes, though, it is strangely warm for this time of the year."

At the opposite end of the training yard, Borran yelled to Jason, "That's why there wasn't as much? How in god's name did you convince Arthan to sip from the elixir of pleasure?"

Jason was removing his white iron shoulder pieces, leaning against the wooden wall as he spoke on over to Borran. "He didn't know it was the elixir. I'd told him it was a potion of different sorts, to help with head sickness for in the morning's after drink."

Alec stood up from the wooden table and leaned forward to wretch into the yard.

"The elixir makes you feel nothing but worse in the mornings!" Borran laughed before continuing countering Brandon's oncoming sword attacks.

Jason yelled toward the two sparring knights, "How did he seem this morning, Brandon?"

Sir Brandon put an end to striking Borran, standing still now in the rain removing his helm to speak to Jason, yet when he took the armor off of his head, he couldn't find his words. "Brandon?" Jason called his name.

"Umm, well, sir, when I'd woken this morning, Arthan was gone."

"Gone? To his council session, I hope! When did you last see him?" Jason asked young Sir Brandon.

"After you left the lot of us, he only spent a bit of time with the she-elf. Her servant said to your brother he was too drunk and she'd wanted him to remember the night if they did anything special! Sounded like nothing but excuses to me. The two of them seemed in love, they truly did, even though she was a mute. I don't know what dear Arthan coulda done to ruin the night, but she left him, bringing out with her that servant of hers who does the speaking for her." Brandon spat into the yard as his mouth began to become dry while he spoke.

Jason was feeling impatient, not angry though. He asked again sharply, "When was the last you saw of him?"

"After the she-elf left the inn, I told Arthan he could have at kissing one of my three women I'd be bringing up to the bedroom. Alec was off to another inn to gamble and continue on with more rum. Martin and Borran found their leave by that time in the night, not just you, sir! Your brother's elf lady lover was gone, so your brother, me, and the women all went on up to bed to enjoy each other."

"Then?" asked Jason.

Brandon said, "Then he was insisting he had to bathe first so he went to find the tub, and well, he bathed, I presume! I'd say we then had our way with kissing the women, and he woke to go off to his council, yet I cannot remember too well though. Your brother and I had drank too much of the rum with that elixir, not enough water."

Jason trusted Brandon to take care of Arthan for the remainder of last night's feasting and drinking after Jason himself was unable to do such a thing because of a lustful distraction. Sir Jason had decided he would be bringing a heavy-chested woman back to the Frauer household whom he'd just met there at the Alligator Inn that very night, so he wasn't so eager to watch over Arthan any longer past that mark in time. At the city inn, toward the end of this night of many drinks, Jason drunkenly had said, "Cheers! Arthan, you're in Brandon's hands now! I'll be sneaking this big-boob beauty back home past Mother and Father. Brandon, I expect to see you just before sunrise at Gold-Gate for farewell to King Gregory, along with the rest of you! Be there at the correct hour, my lovely knights! Please, Brandon, be sure my brother doesn't drink too much more of that disgusting rum. He must wake for his council party tomorrow morning… Farewell world! Come, my lady…" And after those wise-sounding words coming from a drunken Sir Jason, he was off with some lady clinging to his arms, both of them walking up Brey Street to make for the High District.

Borran swung his long sword horizontally, with speed and force. Jason watched his two warriors from afar. An unarmored foe would have been bloodily cut in two, yet Brandon wore his irons alike the other training knights. The collision of Borran's strike upon Brandon's armor sent the young man soaring backwards upward, and then down into the damp dirt.

"Ahhh! Coward! Wait for me to put my helm back on my head." Brandon moaned out. He lay down gripping the plating upon his left side, tearing up in both eyes as he swayed his legs from one direction to the other.

"Is that rainfall or tears? If you're crying, then *you're* the coward." Borran laughed, swinging his sword through the air, now striking at imaginary foes as he would wait for Brandon to rise and resume.

Jason heard Brandon yell up to Borran, "If you had hit my neck, I wouldn't have a head as of now!"

Jason observed his knights argue there, Brandon on his backside and Borran slaying what looked to be invisible opponents. Old Sir Martin silently shot his longbow as he would regularly do so, and Lance just stood deep in thought beside his captain here. Jason was now removing his plated gauntlets. The two against the wall of the training yard stood comfortably silent until Lance began a conversation with, "Jason there's something we must speak of."

"What is it?"

"Tonight I ride for Dain Squares. In fact, I mean to leave before sun fall."

Jason had a notion of why Lance would be journeying north to the town, yet he played along as if he hadn't assumed the man's reasons. "Why go to Dain Squares? Are you finally going to give whoring a try? You can find one here in Ascali just as easy."

"No, it would be for the battlegrounds. They're holding trials there at the squares, and I would look to partake."

And so Jason was correct. Lance had intention to make his way into the upcoming tournament, just as Jason had as well. "Why travel there? Battlegrounds are being held here tonight in the city, this you know."

Lance crunched up one side of his face with the muscles under his skin, leaning his head one way and then to the other side. "Yes, eh, well, I'm aware you'll be attending and entering in Ascali's trials. I go out of the city to compete, because I do not wish to fight you in battlegrounds, not before we could properly duel on game day for the tournament. If I attend the trials at the squares to the north, I will thankfully not have the chance to face you tonight, if you'd be attending trials taking place here."

Jason placed his gauntlets down atop his shoulder pieces which lay low beside him in the yard's dirt. A quick imaginary scene of a one-on-one duel with Lance in the sands of the arena while all watched on had flashed through Jason's mind. Jason wondered if he'd still maintain his regular comedic grin upon his face if he had to duel a knight he's commanded: to fight one of his men in the tournament or in the trials. *It would just feel as if we were training… I'm always ahead a few strikes during our dueling training; when using my long sword, of course.* He was confident he could defeat Lance, as he always was able to with his long sword, so his friend's reveal here of this attempt on the entering of the tournament hadn't made Jason come to sadness, anger, or fear. *If* Lance was capable of defeating Jason though, perhaps Jason would react differently to this statement from his knight to him, yet only very few in the realm could defeat Jason; Lance wasn't one of these souls.

"You won't have the chance to face me in the battlegrounds, true, yet if we both come out victorious in these trials of ours on this night, then you may have the chance to face me on game day of course. You are prepared to do such a thing?" asked Jason.

"Of course, of course!" replied Lance, continuing with, "I'd rather face you in a glorious arena match with two thousand eyes upon us, than in a trial duel with only a hundred."

Jason crossed his arms, watching Brandon far off rise from the ground to practice with Borran some more. As he watched, Jason said to Lance, "If it comes to that, I bet we'll put on a damn good performance. I won't be using short swords, I warn you."

"You would be a fool to… Perhaps though if we do pass our trial matches, we might not cross paths in a duel on game day, though we may find each other in the battle royale for the final event, so long as we are victorious in our own one-on-one matches. God will aid us, this I know."

Now Jason was finding some greatly positive thoughts in this all, after just hearing those very words from Lance. Jason had great love for theatrics combined with war-craft, and so he said, "If we make it to the battle royale, then what we do is we look for each other in the sands. We make our stand backside facing backside, and we hold our ground until all combatants fall before us."

"And after all foes fall?" asked Lance.

"After they fall, which they will, that is when we give the crowd a duel between you and I that they'll never forget." Jason smacked Lance's shoulder piece as this black-haired knight he called *"friend"* smiled with water dripping again from the hair upon his chin.

"Lance, you're to be the first of my knight's to face me in the arena. Every year I enter while the lot of you lie back, yet I knew this day would come eventually. I don't know if it's my many victories that have stopped you all from entering the battlegrounds or if you'd all think me to become angered at you potentially winning and stealing the prize from me, or maybe it is that you all do not wish to strike your captain, but-" Borran must have been listening on to Jason speaking with Lance from across the yard again. He halted on countering Brandon's attacks, yelling to his captain. "I strike you in training often enough! I'd have no problem dueling with you in the sands! I just dislike tournaments for-"

Borran was interrupted from the hard sword strike to the groin. Sir Brandon's sword made a loud *ding* sound against the plate in front of Borran's dick. The big knight grimaced and gripped what lay in between his legs. "Bitch!" cried out Borran. He hastily shook off the pain, stood tall, and then he tackled tiny Brandon into the dirt after flinging his own sword aside and away.

"Why is it you choose to fight this year suddenly?" Jason asked Lance.

Lance's grin from the thought of the glorious two of them standing off against all other foes in the free-for-all had now faded away as he thought of his homeland. "It's Castle Alhert. My father struggles with the dam. The stones are rotting, after the last storm not so long ago, well-" Lance began removing his armor as he spoke; training for the day was coming near end. "The stones are crumbling. We need gold to fund a new build plan." said he.

Jason told Lance, "I understand. I regret to say, though, reward for this year's games would be the honor to serve the king as his protector. It does not come with gold."

Lance held his shoulder platings under his arm now as he spoke. "Rumor is, the king and steward are to be persuaded into rewarding gold *as well* as this role of protector. The majority of the councilmen apparently are in favor of this and will speak up of it today to Lord-Steward Arol while King Gregory is about his travels. Your father and brother will tell you of this all, I'm sure, unless the steward does not find the gold reward suggestion to be a wise one."

Jason nodded, thinking of this gold. He'd already had enough gold in his life, enough gold to buy anything he could possibly desire; only he already owned everything he felt he could want. He'd won vast sums of money with every one of his past arena victories; therefore, this gold prize wouldn't feel unfamiliar for him. Jason would only compete this time for the honor to be Shield to the King, he'd thought at the least. Winning gold would be nothing but a bonus, a bonus which he nor his family had need of, and so he said to Lance, "If I am victorious, I will gift you the gold winnings as I step up as Shield to the King."

"Thank you, though I would decline in advance, for I would feel foolish, childish even, for accepting your won prize."

Jason gathered his shoulder plates and gauntlets, readying to bring the armor over to his mount to tie up beside his sword at the saddle. As Lance was beginning to walk beside him to the horses,

Jason asked him, "Don't you need to pay for men to place these new stones?"

As they walked, they talked.

Lance replied, "No, it's the *stones* we need pay for, not the men to place them. My father, as we speak, is within the Great Keep, awaiting to see the steward at today's council session. He would ask of him masons for this task, yet he does not have the courage to ask of him to supply funding for the stones themselves. If the steward agrees to send these workers to Alhert, we'll have no material for them to replace the dam with."

Jason approached his horse, Pax, to fasten bits of armor to the side of the steed. He did this as he listened to Lance speak more on his family's dam and his reasons for desire to enter this year's tournament.

"If I win this tournament, I shall politely decline the offer to be guard to King Gregory. I'll spend the gold reward to restore my family's dam."

"What an insult that would be to the new royal family. Lance, you cannot simply decline this as if it's an offer. It's a reward, *the* reward, it's a sentencing, as some would consider it. The whole very purpose the king wishes to hold this tournament is to find his permanent guard to stand beside him! Forever! You cannot enter with the intention of *not* swearing the oath as Gregory's shield upon a win!" Jason tightened the belt which held his platings in place upon the side of Pax as he awaited for Lance's reply. "What say you of that?" asked Jason after Lance silently looked to the yard grounds for a brief moment of time.

Lance looked upward to his captain now. "What of you, Jason? Each year you enter, *'The White Knight of the Arena of Ascali!'* mostly victorious, claiming your gold after ringing everyone's heads as the crowds watch on. What of this year? You intend to win again, yet this time abandon your role as leading knight to the Eagle Party, to become a guard?"

Jason slicked his hair back and out from the front of his eyes. He looked to the gray sky and inhaled deeply as he never thought of how soon this dialogue would come. He'd only heard first word last evening at the inn, word that the reward of this year's tournament event would be a lifetime role of guarding the king.

Jason loved his realm *and* his arena play and so had last night upon gaining this new information, immediately and drunkenly decided he would look to become victorious in the event still, and he'd let all folk occupying the Alligator Inn know his plan for it. He remembered now, standing atop a table in the establishment, him shouting, *"The most skilled assassins, rogues, and would-be kingslayers shall tremble before me! I will become the greatest shield whom has ever served the crown!"* taking large gulps of willow ale in between his sentences while the crowd of feasters watched on, Arthan and the eagle knights in motley included amongst them all. *"I will be victorious as I always am in those sands, yes! I'll, I shall win another year! I'll guard King Gregory from that winning day, until my last day alive in this world!"* Jason had then drawn forth his long sword, holding it high, piercing the tip up into some hanging candles above. With the other hand he brought the horn of ale to his mouth to drink from as hot wax dripped into his hair from overhead. As he gulped, the inn's folk applauded him with laughter and cheers; half the occupants thrilled with the heartwarming drunken speech, the other half mocking the renowned knight wearing this red joker's attire that reminded all of devilry.

After Jason had climbed down from the table, he recalled spending some time trying to persuade Arthan to become romantic with an elvish being. When he had eyed the little foreigner, he'd soon forgotten he had even heard word of this reward of the *"guard role to the king"* as his mind was clouded from the potion the "*Elixir of Pleasure*," as well as from all of the ale he had put down his throat that evening.

While he continuously had tried his very best to convince Arthan to show affection toward the small cat-eyed foreigner with her dumb little pointed ears, he'd so quickly forgotten that he'd brought himself up standing upon that table to pledge his sword in winning the upcoming event. It wasn't until he was halfway on his walk home with the heavy-chested woman that he gained his recollection. *If I'm to win this next tournament...I'll never have the freedom to be an adventurer ever again,* he'd thought to himself as he stumbled up Silver Street, accompanied by an even drunker person than himself, struggling to keep up with him as she attached her arms to his. Sad drunken thoughts of never questing with his knights, not ever again, it made Jason's face redden as he walked in the night. He didn't want these ideas of this future to ruin the remainder of his evening, so he had brought his gaze to the woman and her large chest as so he'd forget all about the tournament and what would come after it, after he'd win. He'd distract himself with pleasures that night, just to sadly suffer in thought through the morning.

Just two hours before sunrise, he lay upon his bed inside the Frauer household, with the woman in his arms, the entire scenario looking as if he'd known and been in love with her for years. If one would have seen him there, fingers gently in and out of her hair while she breathed heavily in her sleep, they'd think him to be in deep loving thought of her, him embracing her. Jason was only thinking of his knights and how he would tell them that his days as captain of the Eagle Party would be over. Even while brushing her hair he hadn't even remembered he had this soul in his bed; he didn't even remember her name. He was playing with her hair almost as if it was his very own, deep in thought of how to explain to his five men how he would be leaving them to stand guard for the king until the end of time. Jason assumed he would be having this talk with them *after* his victory in the arena, yet here he was in the training yard, explaining himself before he even won.

"Knights, assemble." said Jason, past Lance's head, behind him to the four others.

Alec wiped vomit from his mouth, rising to walk to Jason and Lance. Martin reached them first, followed by the dazed Alec and then Borran and Brandon, those last two now removing their helmets to listen in. The five knights placed themselves in a circular formation to speak with Jason as he stood with his horse beside him. He brushed Pax on the side, wiping some rain off of his coat before he began his dialogue.

"We've all come far since the beginning, yes?" Jason said. "Not a single one of you has ever faltered out in the wilderness, not that I've seen. Our experience and travels together, they're being written into stories and grand tales just as we speak this very moment! Death has never taken one of you from me, and none of you have seen more than one captain. Sadly, our time will soon come to an end though. As you all know, as I've said last evening…I do plan to be victorious in this upcoming tournament, and with that victory comes a price, not a reward."

Four of the knights looked down to the dirt as Jason spoke, besides Lance who looked steady on to his captain.

"Last night wasn't just drunken words from me upon that table. I did mean what I had said… I will be guarding the king until mine or his death. My days with you, the days of adventures and training, they are coming to an end."

Borran reached on over to pat Jason upon the chains of his shoulder. "You shit. I hate you yet love you at the very same time. I pray Aeon sends me a new captain just as fine as you, and many foes for you to defend Gregory from." Borran stepped back after Jason placed the same gesture upon his big shoulder in return.

Jason then turned his head to Martin. "You won't have to pray for any new captain, as Martin will take over to be leader of the Eagles when I become Shield to the King."

Martin brought his chin up high and looked upon Jason. The aging knight gave his companions each long, hard glances as well. He looked into Jason's eyes when he spoke to him. "Are you sure this is what you desire, sir? If so, I have the same wish as Sir Borran, for Aeon to send you many foes to fight in honor of and for King Gregory, else stale guard's work will cause your mind to rot. I know you'll soon be eager to be on the road again with the wind at your back alongside us, hunting those who've wronged the realm. I will say that, and thank you, sir…if this is your true wish. I am honored and grateful that you'd choose me for this."

Sir Martin placed his longbow about his backside and then gave a salute to Jason. "You deserve it Martin, and I love you. You've seen more of this world than any of us here… Three wars you've lived to take part in, killed four times as many foes as I have. When the five of us here were but babes or yet not even born, you stood here in this world, skillful and experienced."

"You're an elder killer, Praxus." said Borran, interrupting Jason.

Jason resumed speaking, "I'll be fine beside the king, no rotting of my mind shall take place. I'll enjoy knowing you are doing well in your parts out upon the roads and in the wild. If you do your jobs good enough out there, then I should see no such trouble for the king here in the city. I'll be satisfied with that. I do not need to be slaughtering foes all and every day." Jason extended his arms outward to welcome old Sir Martin Praxus in for a warming hug in the rain.

"After the tourney, I'll have to get looking for a worthy recruit for a sixth." Martin said to Jason as they took a step backwards from each other.

Lance spoke, "I wish to express my love for you all as well, for I too am entering the battlegrounds to fight and in my hopes, win to go on to the tournament, sadly to leave you all in the same manner Jason would, I suppose, if I'm victorious."

Borran smacked the plating upon his belly, laughing. "Ah, so it's *you* we might lose to royal guard service, not Jason."

Lance nodded to Borran, then gave his attention to Brandon, as the young knight asked, "What if you're put up against Jason here? You can't beat him."

To that question, Borran shoved Brandon with those big hands of his, causing the young knight to slip and fall upon the wetness of the dirt. Looking down to the fallen young man, Borran said, "It will be a glorious match, regardless of the outcome, Brandon!"

Jason was readying to end the dialogue with his knights but was interrupted by Sir Alec raising his head up, staring off, watching the gate, pointing a finger to it.

"What? What are you pointing to?" asked Jason of the wobbling man.

Alec was so sickened he could hardly speak, so Borran spoke for him. "It's your brother."

Behind Jason was Arthan wearing pink, striding toward the six of the knights. Jason turned around to view his brother hastily making way for him in the rain. "Has the council session ended?" Jason asked him.

Arthan raised his fist high and swung it as hard as he could at Jason's face. Jason caught his brother's wrist, then grabbed a hold of the flailing elbow with his other hand. He twisted Arthan's bony arm downward as so the upside of his hand would face the dirt, bringing his brother's knuckles down low. "In front of my men? Arthan! Are you finished!?" Jason held onto struggling Arthan's arm, trapping him in place as he yelled down to him. "You haven't done that since you'd been…ten years old! What is this?" Jason yelled into his brother's ear.

All knights appeared silent during this embarrassing act, all besides giggling Borran and vomiting Alec. Jason released Arthan when he ceased all his movement after he'd discontinued to resist Jason's grip.

Standing there with robes soaked in the rain, Arthan looked from his brother to each and every one of the knights. Martin finally broke the silence with talk. "Training is near end, yes? And well, sir, it seems you and your brother here have a discussion that needs to be settled."

"Yes, indeed, Sir Martin." said Jason, eyes still on his brother. He watched Arthan closely as he dismissed his men. "You, Sir Lance, must make haste if you are to reach Dain Squares by battleground time. The rest of you, return to your homes. Find rest and pleasure." Jason gave Lance a quick hug and bade him good fortune in his duel at the town to the north. "Best of luck. Win out there so we can find each other in the arena here on game day. Now be off!" Just after Lance mounted, he asked Arthan from above, "Word of the tournament reward, Arthan? Has gold been promised?"

Arthan nodded yet he looked to his brother, instead of the knight on horseback asking the question.

Lance rode off; Jason winked at Martin, his soon-to-be successor, then saluted the remaining knights as they all saddled up. Now Jason gave his full attention to his saddened, angered brother.

"What have I done to cause you to come throw a hit at me in the presence of my knights? Do you know this makes our family appear as if we're all ill-minded?"

Arthan took a step toward Jason while the knights rode off through the small gate of the yard. He thought his brother was readying to attack him once again, so Jason made ready to send him to the grounds of the yard. Arthan didn't make an aggressive move though, only breathed heavily until he put the palms of his hands into his eyes. "Arthan? What's happened?"

Arthan removed his hands from his face to look upon his brother. "You left me in the night. Alone with your crazed battalion of drunks, did you not? You told me you'd watch after me so I could make my council session in time without tardiness. Today was my first day!"

"You remember nothing of the night?" asked Jason.

"No, I do not recall entering or even the journey to the inn." Arthan sat down into the dirt, just beside a puddle of Sir Alec's still warm vomit.

"I will remind you that you desired to stay there while I returned home."

Arthan rubbed his eyelids as he sat upon the yard. He spoke to Jason while he dug into his eyeballs. "Why would I dwell at such a place? Why stay with having early business woven into my schedule for the morning?"

Jason grabbed ahold of the horn upon his saddle, mounting the horse. "Early business or not, you stayed for a woman, an elvish one she was." he told his brother from high up. "I brought a lady to my bed at home. You stayed to seduce yours at the inn. We're grown men, Arthan. I cannot alter your decisions once you've made them, nor should I try to."

Jason removed an apple from a saddlebag and rolled the fruit off into Pax's mouth at the right side. "Mount up with me. Pax will take us home." Jason told his brother, in a sort of commanding verbal fashion. "He's angry with me that I've left him hitched out front the inn last night. But the more apples I feed him, the more he forgives me. I wish I could feed you apples in exchange for your forgiveness."

Arthan stopped rubbing his eyelids and looked upward to his knightly brother, seated upon the white horse chomping on the apple in the rain with those big teeth. "I refuse to climb atop any horse with you ever again. I didn't care to ride with you last night, nor do I today." Arthan came to his feet.

Jason sighed, stepping down off of the mount. "Then we walk home. Come, Pax, Arthan?"

The saddened brother then followed Jason, whom was leading the horse through the training yard gate on foot.

They walked together with Pax, across a busy street of the city's Military District. After crossing the cobbles of the Street of War, trying to avoid rain puddles, they walked upward through an alleyway beside an armor shop. The alley eventually ended, then after walking up some painted stone steps, they passed right under a small rising arch entrance to Silver Street where they'd find the Frauer household sitting a few blocks off westward.

Jason thought hard as he walked, hard on what he'd say now to Arthan. Jason wasn't as angered though as he felt he should have been with his brother. Any leading knight should be furious at such an insulting act committed while the men whom he commanded stood as witness to it in that manner. Jason decided he'd think on this all more as a caring brother than as an insulted company leader. He was more concerned with putting an end to Arthan's deep sadness, not having an urge to discipline or reprimand him for his actions, not even a bit. *Twisting his arm down was enough,* he thought as they walked with the horse in between them trotting along. He looked under Pax's big neck to get a good watch on his brother. Jason despised seeing him this way, dragging his feet, shoulders low and face frowning. It's moments such as these grim ones, where he wished Arthan had chosen the life of swordplay, whoring, gambling, and adventuring, so he could have ridden beside Jason these past years as one of his five knights, the way those men had done so, *happily!*

He observed Arthan while they walked in the light rain. *My sad, sad brother. New robes, vomit upon them, rum, blood, and now yard dirt too. Why come and try to hit me and then sit in the mud to cry? Did he truly feel so betrayed?* "Did you miss your council meeting this morning?"

"No, I attended."

"Had you been late upon arrival?" Arthan wiped some rain off of his forehead and brow.

"No, I was early, in fact."

"Did you wretch?" Jason asked.

"No, I don't believe so." replied Arthan.

Jason wasn't becoming angered, just tempted to aggressively express to his brother that there was no true reason to come and commit such actions toward him beside his men, if no ill events or outcome had taken place this morning.

"Damnit! Then why be so negative? You enjoyed a night of drinking, great food, and gazing at beautiful women, *and* you've still brought yourself to wake to do your job the morning after it all."

Arthan wiped more rain off his face; it was dripping into his eyes now while he spoke to Jason. Arthan was saying, "I believe it was the fear of not knowing what had happened. I never wish to lose my memory to rum again. Today, it brought me to believe you had wronged me." Arthan tilted his head far downward while they walked together. Perhaps he was keeping his face out from the rainfall or he'd just been so, so saddened; maybe even both.

"Is this your way of apologizing? If so, you don't have any need to. I just don't want my men to think less of you or of our family name, thinking we fight with each other." With water running into his eyes again, Arthan raised his head to look to Jason. With Pax in between them partially blocking each other's views, he said, "I am sorry for what I had done in the yard. Today I should have had the mind to come find and thank you, whereas instead I came to raise hand to you. I'm a coward for doing such a thing, for I believe I had only the courage to attack you as I had known that you would never truly strike back."

"Why would you come find me today to thank me?" Jason asked his brother as they came closer to the Frauer house upon the north side of Silver Street.

Arthan said to him, "You'd given me a sip from your vial before we'd mounted and left for the inn. If I hadn't taken from that, I'm sure my head would have been pounding in pain this morning. It already had been, in fact. Couldn't imagine how much worse it would have been without the curing potion."

Jason grabbed hold of the last apple in the satchel strapped to the side of his dear Pax. He fed the red fruit to the animal as he listened on to his brother explain the appreciation of this good deed.

"So I apologize, and thank you. I love you."

Jason was preparing to reveal to Arthan what the true contents of the vial from last night had been. *Elixir of pleasure* it's named: a strong substance Jason and his party of knights consume frequently when in the company of women and when drinking ales and liquors. On this gray and rainy day though, Jason never told Arthan of what truly sat in last night's vial, which the poor, deceived young man thought to be filled with a medicine for morning head sickness. Jason *intended* on informing him just then and there as he brought Pax past the small black gate in front the house but hadn't done so after they'd seen their lady-mother sitting out beside the front door.

"Mother?" called out Jason as he led Pax into the miniature stable while Arthan looked upon her silently.

She was sitting on the skinny rocking chair, smoking a pipe filled with burning wizard's weed.

You could smell it. That isn't just commoner's leaf, thought Jason. He'd partake in the smoking of wizard's weed occasionally; very occasionally though, as after ingesting elixir of pleasure as often as he does, one wouldn't find much joy in the smoking of wizard's weed any longer. He wondered why his mother felt the need to begin enjoying such mind-altering delights as this, *Unless she has been puffing away on that pipe for years without my knowledge of it.*

After shutting the front gate, Jason approached and spoke to her with Arthan following behind. "Who's pipe is that? I didn't know you smoked! If you need any help finishing with that there, I can be of assistance, although I'm told I'm a horrible smoking companion. How are you on this evening?" Jason gave her a kiss on the cheek while she exhaled smoke into his eyes.

"Woah, I yield! Oh my!" Jason said, his eyes watering while his mother smoked on some more.

"It's my pipe. I'm well. How are you, my love?" asked she of her son.

"Oh, Mother, my body craves sleep. Saw King Gregory off just before sunrise, spent a full day at training. This ill weather doesn't help me feel any more awake either. Drank many cups of ale last night too…"

"Hello there." said Arthan to her from behind Jason.

"Evening…" she replied.

While Arthan picked at some crusted vomit upon his apprentice robes, Jason spoke with their mother.

"So, my beautiful mother, what is it we're feasting on? Sun is setting."

Lady Sophia took in a great amount of smoke into her lungs, yet she sat uncoughing. When she let loose the fumes through her mouth, she smiled. "Had the stew on bubbling since morning. Beef, garlic, lots of potatoes and tomatoes, so it's all juicy red, just how you like it." She smoked some more as she spoke. "Was going to roast that turkey before it spoils. Thank Aeon I've decided on the stew, though; simpler…quieter. Let the turkey rot." The chair rocked to the back and then went forward, again and again while she smoked on. She sat silent now with lazy eyes while Jason looked upon her, her moving rhythmically with the chair, smoke surrounding these three Frauers on the porch.

"Mother, are you well? Has something happened?" Jason asked her.

"Everything is well, so long as I ignore your father and your little brother with their theatrics in there, then yes… Just well, very well, indeed." She smoked, watching across the street, upwardly gazing to the red stars revealing themselves in the blackening south sky.

"Be well, my beautiful mother. I love you. Come, Arthan."

The brothers entered their house while Lady Sophia sat outside finishing the contents of her pipe. Before Arthan had even shut the door to the dimly lit entrance hall, the two of them heard the loud noise of the wood upon metal, close by the hallway past the kitchen.

"Father?" Jason called out as Arthan shut and locked the door behind them. While Jason moved forward through the hall to follow the sounds of the commotion, Arthan was remembering that he'd forgotten to tell Jason of their lord-father, how Arthan saw he was not present at the council session, and the way that the lord-steward made mention of the absence for all councilmen to hear.

In the pink-colored hallway leading to the bedchambers and washing room, Jason and Arthan found Lord Edward, jabbing upward into the ceiling, using a large broomstick to do so. Without discontinuing to repeatedly slam the hard end of the broom into the metal lock above, Edward looked down the hallway to his offspring to greet them with, "Hello, my sons."

"What?" came a squeaky voice from the above ceiling.

Lord Edward lowered his broomstick and spoke up to the attic's lock. "Not you, Dallion! Just a moment longer! You're doing well!" Jason watched his father thrust upward at the lock again, once, twice and a third time before he decided to intervene. "Stop, Father. What's happened?"

"Dallion went and locked himself in the attic." Lord Edward said to Jason and to Arthan.

"How's he gone and done that if the keyhole is on the outer part?" Arthan asked his father.

"I don't know. Got himself up there, and now it won't open." Edward said just before giving another good jab at the old black lock above.

Jason grabbed a hold of the broom, looking upon his sweating, drippy father. "Let me, please..." Jason released his hand on the broom and then grasped a hold of his long sword's grip. He unsheathed the steel from the matching white scabbard and with a hard stroke upward, broke the lock right off of the attic latch. The iron fell down, as did a set of collapsable wooden stairs. Jason sheathed his sword, and down came little Dallion, filthier than ever, yet merry all the same.

"Haa! It makes me happy that we're wealthy. I'll fetch us another lock tomorrow." said Jason.

The little brother covered in dust climbed down the staircase with two tiny hands upon each piece of wood as he held a shining steel dagger within his teeth.

"Give me that!" yelled Jason. "Where did you find this?" Jason asked while Lord Edward picked bits of spider webbings out of his youngest son's hair.

"I found it under your pillow. I've taken it without permission!" Dallion spoke loudly and with a smile.

Jason made a hard, stern frowning face downward to the boy, saying, "Why would you have done that? How did you find yourself trapped in the attic?"

Dallion eagerly went for the dagger in Jason's hands, so he slid it into his belt at his back side so it couldn't be reached.

"Tell Father how you became trapped in the attic and why you'd steal from me." Jason commanded to his little brother while the child laughed.

"The best rogue is the best thief, haha. I took the knife to fight the goblins in the attic, Father. I heard them in there, I swear to Aeon! I'll kill them. If you bought me a knife, I wouldn't have to steal Jason's nice white one." Dallion looked to the wall now. "I took Jason's, and he didn't know I was going to take it…then I got stuck." Now looking back to his father, he said, "But the goblins are real! I have to kill them. I was sneaking…"

"Ahh I've heard enough, my sons." said Lord Edward as he looked to Jason and as he brought Dallion in for a hug.

"Dallion is safe and doesn't possess a blade anymore. I'm well with that if the rest of you are, yes?" Jason squatted himself down low to brush off some dust off of Dallion's tunic. "Me, Dallion, and Arthan are well with it. Mother outside doesn't seem as if she is all too happy though." said Jason down low.

Arthan put in, "Smoking her pain away."

"She's not in pain, and she won't make smoking a habit. Just she's a bit annoyed at all of this *rogue* nonsense. With this attic scenario now, I'd say it has gotten a bit out of hand." the lord-father spoke this as he ran his hands through Dallion's shaggy brown hair to mess it up even some more. He said to his small son, "Which is why Sir-Paladin John is going to have a very long discussion with you. To put an end to this goblin-hunter business once and for all."

"Don't you wish to be a knight like Sir-Paladin John and I?" Jason asked Dallion.

His father stopped Dallion from answering his older brother's question. "Shh, not now, Dallion. Now isn't the time, Jason, rise. He'll speak with John of it tomorrow... Now we feast! Let us prepare the table, for the stew will be ready shortly."

Jason stood upward, now tucking the collapsable staircase back up and into the ceiling and then sliding the unlocked latch in place. As Jason was doing so, Edward Frauer began his walk down the hallway to the kitchen, though placed a hand upon Arthan's shoulder as he passed him. Arthan in wet robes followed him after Edward said, "And *while* we feast, you can tell me where it is you've been this morning. Not a good look to it, missing your first day at the council."

All together, the three Frauer brothers and Lord Edward walked into the dining area beside the kitchen. Arthan was preparing to defend himself in explanation of today's struggle, but Jason spoke for him before he could collect his thoughts to find a voice.

"Father, Arthan *did* attend the council session today." Jason told Lord Edward this while removing five glass bowls from a drawer beside the oven; his mail rattled as he moved about the kitchen. Jason continued on, "I brought Arthan with me to the inn last night for feasting. We shared a room, and then came morning, he went off to the council chamber whilst I went off to see the king leave for his short journey." Jason put the bowls down in front of where each chair rested at the table. He then went back to the kitchen to find the eating utensils as his father looked to him, and then looked back to Arthan repeatedly.

"You attended today's session?" Arthan's father asked him, taking a seat down.

"Yes, my very first session. I refused to miss it. Attended it just as planned. Although I admit, I hadn't intended to spend the night before *sleeping* at the inn."

Dallion leaped up onto the chair beside Lord Edward as Jason finished setting the table with spoons, knives, a plate for bread, and lastly a jug of wine with four oversized stone cups too.

Edward rubbed at his eyelids. "We hadn't discussed it, though I imagined we'd trot our way to the chamber *together*, the way we had when I brought you in for the session before you were made apprentice."

Arthan sat himself down across from his lord-father while the man still sat there rubbing at his eyes. "I imagined that too, as father and son. I wanted you to share the experience with me for the arrival and during the session at my side for my first day, and even all rest of days. I'm sorry I did not inform you I'd be arriving there on my own for this first one though. I wish you had thought to come find me there! I could not have missed the session, not for anything, not after you've made the king grant me in without the proper schooling. I prayed while the session was in progress, that you had been there as well. I did look for you amongst the rows of councilmen, I swear it."

Edward stopped rubbing at his eyes to look to Arthan now. While Jason listened on, Dallion sat battling imaginary goblins with his spoon and knife all the while. "I was out looking for you upon the streets. I thought perhaps Benjamin Drake's son had stuffed you into a fish barrel again. Thought maybe you'd gotten lost, fallen into the sewers! Or a wizard aspirer had seductively attacked you… I thought the worst of thoughts, along with the assumption that you had maybe just been off to sleep somewhere too, losing track of the hour again. So there I was upon Brey Street calling your name, *'Arthan! Arthan!'* not knowing if I'd be horrified to find you beaten, dead, or if I'd be disappointed to find you'd slept through the morning. I underestimated you, my son, as the last place I thought of you to be was the very council session itself. By the hour I had reached the chamber, the honor guards had told me the session was ended, and mostly all would be well on their way to their homes by that point in time. I came back here to the household to check if you'd be inside, only when I arrived, I found Dallion had been trapped above in the attic and your mother furiously looking for her old pipe."

There was a viciously loud banging sound coming from the front door to be heard as Arthan spoke, seated with his father. *BANG BANG BANG*—a fist slamming on wood, again and again from the outside.

"Goblins..." whispered Dallion.

"Is that your mother?" Edward Frauer asked his sons.

Arthan must have locked the door behind himself after entering the home, a common habit of his. He leaped into the entrance hall, throwing himself to the door to unlock it. As the banging sound continued, he gripped the handle, then turned and opened.

His mother said and asked, "Fool, you see me out here. Was this you?" She carried a skunk-like odor within her clothing, also releasing it from her breath as she spoke to Arthan, entering the family home now. She walked past him into the dining area before he could answer her and apologize. Walking through the dining hall, carrying her pipe and a blue glass jar; she spoke to all four of her family. "Jason, remove your armor before you eat, my love. Dallion, stop with the play fighting. Edward, I've forgotten to bake the bread, sorry. Arthan, take those disgusting robes off, then you may sit back down."

Jason and Arthan made for their rooms to change attire. Dallion sat ignoring his mother, swinging his spoon and knife above the empty bowls.

Lord Edward sat at the head of the table massaging his temples while his lady-wife cleaned her pipe in the sink. With eyes closed, facing the opposite way, away from the kitchen, he spoke to his wife while she scrubbed at the ash upon the wooden device. "Sophia, it smells foul! Do you no longer have care?"

"I'm past the point of caring, Edward..." she said back to him while beginning to dry the pipe off with a white towel, now tinted yellow after her use of it.

What a joyful woman I have for a wife, thought Edward, elbows rested upon the surface of his household table. He sat and waited for his sons to return, and for the food to make its way to him.

His sons came; the stew never did though, not from Lady Sophia. As Jason and Arthan began taking their seating wearing fresh house tunics and trousers, Edward turned his head around after hearing his wife remove a glass bowl from beside the window at the sink. "My lady, we have bowls here." said Edward.

She scooped a mighty portion of stew out from the pot, dumped it into her bowl, and left the serving spoon behind atop the oven. Carrying the steaming bowl of food with a small spoon sunken into it, she made her way from the kitchen, towards the back hall where she would walk to find her and Edward's bedchamber.

"You are not dining with us?" Edward asked his lady-wife.

"I'll be taking my meal in the bedchamber. I have a great desire to hear the sounds of silence." and with that last bit of talk, she walked away.

Jason stood up from the seat at the table to walk on over to the kitchen. As he made his way to get the pot of stew for his brothers and father, he spoke saying to them, "I hope she isn't too saddened. Nothing ill came of Dallion's goblin hunt in the attic. I do not see why she'd be in such a mood."

"Such a mood? You know your mother, my son. This is what we live with every day, her sweet misery." Edward spoke while he grasped ahold of the jug filled with wine. Edward was saying now, "Luckily for us, a little wine in the belly will make us forget all about her and her *'mood.'*"

Jason brought the pot to the center of the table. He used the serving spoon to fill the bowls for Dallion, his lord-father, and lastly Arthan.

"Thank you." said Arthan.

"Yes, thank you." repeated Edward.

Dallion sat violently eating as fast as he could allow himself without burning his face off.

While the three Frauers sat enjoying Lady Sophia's steaming stew, Edward reminded Arthan that he'd have to now inform him of what was missed during his absence today. "You'll have to tell me all that was spoken of. How did Arol perform in substitution for King Gregory?"

"I thought he did well. He seemed quite filled with boredom, one would think after a long gaze at the man." Arthan told his father everything in which he remembered hearing in the council chamber on this morning. He began with informing him on the amount of gold for the new cathedral donation, telling Lord Edward, "Arol stated that the royal family is to now pay the priests a year's worth of gold, in place of monthly donations."

Edward nodded as he packed his mouth with chunks of the slow cooked beef. "What else?"

"Kief from under the city had asked for some men to help shovel waste: military men Arol decided to send for the task."

To that, Lord Edward asked Arthan, "Kief asking for word today? Was anybody else present for requests?"

Arthan recalled the lord of the Flux family requesting word for talk of a dam, though Lord-Steward Arol never saw to the lordly man; this all Arthan told his father as Jason listened in.

"The steward never accepted Lord Flux in to speak?" Jason asked Arthan with a mouthful of hot stew.

"No, he seemed to be very impatient with these folk entering to have word with him, word with the council."

Jason dropped his spoon into the half-filled bowl and sighed to Arthan. "How is he to receive his masons if the steward would not even let him speak to ask?"

Arthan asked Jason, "How do you know of Lord Flux's request?"

To that question Jason replied, "Lance Flux is my closest knight. I've known the old lord Flux for years, been to Alhert many a time. The family is known for that great dam. Arol needs to send these masons, or the king must upon his return tomorrow."

Arthan assured his brother that all would be well with the Flux family and their dam. He told Jason, "Arol did make decision to send the masons. He just didn't care to hear Lord Flux's voice is all that I meant. The grand councilman informed Lord-Steward Arol of the dam situation, of what Lord Flux would ask of the royal family and council when he would enter. Arol agreed to the request without even hearing the Lord. Seemed Lord-Steward Arol was eager to be done with the session as fast as he could be."

Jason gulped down some wine after hearing his brother speak. Jason said, wiping his mouth, "Well I'm joyful for them, I suppose, the Flux's. A bit insulting though, isn't it? The man coming all this way southeast from Castle Alhert to have word with the new steward and has to be sent home without stepping even one foot into the council chamber." Jason drank more wine before he continued on with the remainder of his hot meal.

Edward spoke while chewing, "At least Lord Flux left the Great Keep knowing his request would be fulfilled. What other matters were discussed?"

Arthan used his spoon to shuffle bits of tomato about in his bowl. He then went on to tell his lord-father of the enormous orcish who sailed from the Western Islands to have word with the council. "Permission to enter the tournament." said Arthan to his father.

As Lord Edward chewed on spoonfuls of stew, Jason asked Arthan, "Was he angered when he was declined?"

"He was accepted to fight in the battlegrounds. He was not declined."

Again Jason dropped his spoon into his bowl, splattering some stew against the jug in the center of the table this time. "An orcish? In the arena?" Jason gulped down some more wine with widened eyes as Arthan nodded to his brother.

"I'd never seen an orcish before. Huge, he was massive. Green-skinned beings they say, yes? Yet I couldn't catch well sight of the tinted skin I've heard so much of, not with the new torches within the chamber…which reminds me, not a serious matter, yet I would tell you, Father, as so you aren't surprised upon your next entry. Arol has put an end to the silver torches high upon the walls of the council dome. They now glow the color of House Royce."

"You mean they glow the colors of Retilliath…disgusting." Edward said, spooning chunks of stew into his mouth, eyes in his bowl. Jason was grabbing for another bowl's worth from the pot with the serving spoon as Arthan was saying, "It is not their fault that the colors of their house are of the same scheme as the demonic religion's."

"The silver torches had beauty to them. Keep in mind, we are still within the years of the White-age, my sons. If this torch nonsense is the start of the new royal family's attempt to begin a *Red-age*, I think I might just die right here and now; kill myself with my own spoon." Edward raised his mug of wine after he'd just spoken and then gulped almost all of its contents down into his throat.

Jason raised his own mug, saying, "They're only torches, Father. Rested king Harold's White-age will last for decades still." Jason drank the purple sour as did Arthan too from his own mug.

Edward allowed Dallion to finish the last sip of contents from his mug, then the child resumed eating stew and fighting fake foes simultaneously; wine dribbling down his chin now.

Arthan had his left elbow leaned on the surface of the table, hand keeping his head up as his chin rested in his palm. He *was* eating his meal, just eating slowly. He told his father more of the council session. "Arol permitted gold be given as a reward, along with the honor of serving as Shield to the King for the upcoming tourney. The last matter that was spoken of was about House Orange, not paying tax for months now. A battalion of soldiers will be sent to collect the gold immediately. Before the council spoke on this last bit though with the Orange family, the king called for *you*, Father."

"Called for me?" Edward asked his son.

"Yes, your absence became known within the chamber. Arol quite literally called out for you. You were asked to speak in on a tournament matter."

To this news, Edward closed his eyes, shaking his head shamefully. "Well, that certainly is embarrassing." said the Frauer father.

Arthan seated himself upward now.

"Don't have a worry. The councilmen soon forgot you, as the attention was then brought to me. They'd asked me where you'd been and I myself felt filled with stupidity when I told them I hadn't truly known. I did say that I had presumed you were out and about searching for me. Perhaps I should have kept my mouth shut in telling that part. I was soon asked *why* you'd been searching for me, and to that I told what I could of my evening, last evening. I felt embarrassed myself, as I could only tell them little of it. I informed Arol that I had drank too much rum at the Alligator Inn and that my memory had been clouded."

Jason hadn't known if Arthan was finished with his tale or not, yet he spoke anyway, adding to it, only trying to make matters better in the eyes of Lord Edward if he could do so. "I brought Arthan to the inn, with my knights for our *'motley night.'* Sir Alec likes to drink heavily and persuaded Arthan here into having as much as he, only Arthan drank even *more* than Sir Alec!"

Arthan ignored his brother, continuing on explaining to his father, "Oh, how it gets worse. Just when I'd thought it would end there, me revealing that I had a lack of memory, Councilman George stood up to speak to Arol while all listened on, claiming he'd been at the inn, with *us (us, meaning Jason and I)*. Arol said he'd *'love a good tale on a night of drinking'* after I claimed to have no memory of last night's event. So George then decided he'd share his account of it all."

Edward chewed, swallowed, and then reached over for the spoon to grab another serving for himself, nodding his chin up and then down in reaction to Arthan's tale.

"And?" Lord Edward asked Arthan. He wasn't angry with his son, although anytime within the past when Arthan had ever had an ill night, or had have acted a fool because of drinking, Edward would express his disappointment. "And what did George say?" asked Edward.

Arthan used the table rag to wipe bits of drippy supper off from the sides of his mouth before he spoke on about George and what he had told the steward and all councilmen. "He told all of what I'd done, the embarrassing acts. Perhaps he'd thought I would take pride or find amusement in the tale? In what I'd done. He told of how the knights and the folk of the inn had been harassing an elvish woman, well a she-elf I should say. George had claimed I'd tried to save her like a hero in the stories of old; blind to her ugliness only. That cruel Councilman George said I'd been so drunk I hadn't even noticed all laughing on behind me as I fell in love with the violet creature.

"George hadn't said who's blade it had been, apparently later in the night I was struggling in swinging an iron great sword about, standing on the bar top, continuously matching that Sir Alec in drinking cups of rum and then failing to lift the iron sword any higher than above my belly. Did this all happen, Jason?" Arthan stopped telling George's story of the night to ask his brother if this had all been accurate.

"It's true, was the owner of the inn's sword you swung; had been mounted upon the wall. Heavy, yes. It wasn't even sharp though! Still a danger. As I said, Sir Alec can easily persuade one to perform foolish actions; especially upon first time drinking with the man."

Lord Edward Frauer pushed his half-filled bowl away in front of him, he was finished eating already. He said, "George, his goal was to make you sound a fool; it's in his character to do so. All of the councilmen will soon forget this, either that or you will be known as Arthan the drunk, youngest of the council."

Jason put in, "They already have a name for him at the inn... God of Iron and Lord of Rum!" Jason gulped down the remainder of the wine in his cup and then refilled it immediately.

Edward asked Arthan, "Why was I called for? Before my absence was known, you said I was to be asked...something? What was it?"

Before speaking, Arthan swallowed down the last bits of stew that had caked into the bottom of his bowl. "I believe the king's brother was to ask you once more why Jason would not want to serve as Shield."

This would be the third time during this meal that Jason has aggressively thrown his spoon down to splash into his portion of stew within the bowl. He squinted while looking to his father and then back to Arthan, then back to Lord Edward; Dallion just sat trying to blindfold himself with the table rag. "What? *'Ask once more why Jason would not want to serve?'* Who says I do not wish to serve as King's Shield? The king has asked of my service for this?" Lord Edward leaned back into his chair there at the head end of the family table, crossing his arms before he replied to his son. "Don't tell me you wish to be the king's squire and guard... Yes, King Gregory made it clear to us all you'd be a great choice. I spoke against it, as I knew you would not—well, I *assumed* you would not want it, this lifetime sentencing. I see I have assumed wrong."

Arthan spoke toward Jason after Edward was finished. "The tournament reward for Shield to the King wasn't decided as *the* official reward until days ago, after father told the council that *you* would not claim it. Perhaps you can speak with the king now?"

And to that, Jason placed his face down upon the wooden surface of the table, fingers of both hands interlaced within his hair at the back of his head.

"Jason! Are you dying?" Dallion asked his older brother across from him.

Jason raised his head, asking his father now, "So now I must battle my way to earn a reward I would have been given anyhow? Father, I love you dearly. Please don't speak for me though. There would be nothing but honor in serving as the king of Midlön's guard and squire!"

Edward was struck with a bit of confusion but soon understood. "You say you must battle your way to earn this reward? So you *are* entering the tournament this year? I must be the realm's largest fool. I thought for sure you'd lie this year out, my son, especially after hearing the reward this time is nothing but the punishment of having to guard King Gregory's stupid self forever, and ever and ever."

Jason loved his father but had great love for the realm as well. He felt he needed to defend Gregory Royce, as the *father* of the realm is the king of the realm! "Might I be excused, Father? I've heard enough ill talk of the king; the man I intend to spend my days guarding *forever*, as you say. I have a trial match to prepare for. I need to make ready."

Edward burped, trying his best to hide the gesture before he'd give his son some warnings. "The battlegrounds are this night? Do be careful, Jason. Arthan mentioned the orcish today whom spoke to the council. If it's true, and that western islander plans to make his way into the Arena, he'll more than likely partake in tonight's battlegrounds here in the city."

"I'll be fine, Father. You know I've killed orcish before." Jason then stood from his dinner seating, patted Arthan on the shoulder, and then walked off to his room after bringing his mess into the kitchen to leave in the wash bin.

From inside of his bedchamber, Jason could hear Arthan and his father continue on speaking at the table as they finished up as well. Jason lay there now, drinking from the wineskin he'd use on nights when he couldn't fall off to sleep. He needed to relax now, and the sour purple delight would always bring a relaxing pleasure, yet time was of importance. He left the comfort of his bed to drink as he buckled his white shin plating back upon both of his legs. He applied his chain mail in a rush. Next came another swig of wine, then all four of his thigh pieces; two for each leg. Then that massive leather belt, huge in size but so tight. After that would be the largest of the full set, torso plating; two-enormous pieces, for his chest and his backside. Another huge gulp of wine, then for the shoulders. After the shoulder-plating adjustment would be each of the matching white top-arm pieces, then each of the forearm pieces and of course some more wine in between each of the fastenings.

He sat there upon the chair beside the oak desk close to the bed, white helm in his lap and wineskin in his hand. He took his last gulp of the precious purple fluids, then used his tooth scrapper in the desk drawer to remove the grape colored crusting from his very own lips. As he brushed away the dried layer of wine from the rim of his mouth, his bed chamber door crept open. Little Dallion came running into the room! He leapt up upon Jason's bedding, settling into his pillow; staining the cloths with stew markings from supper.

Dallion said, "I know you'll win your battle tonight." After saying that, he asked Jason, "Then I will watch you in the big arena again, yes?"

"Yes! If I'm victorious in my duel *tonight*, then I'll be dueling in the arena!" Jason moved his ass from his chair, over to his bed beside Dallion to mess with his shaggy brown hair.

"And you'll win your duel in the big arena and be best champion!" little Dallion shouted into Jason's face when he came close.

Jason said to his little brother, "Only if I then win the battle royale. That's where all of the winners of the duels meet at the same time in the sands to fight until there's only one warrior left standing."

"I remember the last one! You were beaten."

Jason had great hatred for being reminded of his losses, the very few he'd had. Dallion was so young though and hadn't known this subject could have been sensitive for his older brother, so he'd show the little one no ill attitude at the mention of this.

He shook up Dallion's hair once more. "I've only lost two in my lifetime, Dally! This one I shall be victorious like I have many a time before." Jason slipped his pearl-white handled dagger out from the side of his belt. He handed the weapon over to his brother, saying,

"If Father finds this, you say you've stolen it from me again, yes? Now wish me luck for my duel and go run off to help Arthan clean! I need to be away to the Square now."

Dallion sprinted down the pink hall as if he was being chased by monsters. During his little brother's loud theatrics, Jason found himself slipping off down the hallway behind him, but then past the kitchen and dining area. His fresh set of clean armor clanked, chains rattling as he made his way past a little table close to the wall by the door, though Dallion's running and shouting throughout the house had been much louder for all occupants to hear, so Jason remained unnoticed. Arthan and Lord Edward had their backsides facing Jason as they stood scrubbing the bowls and returning cleaned mugs back into the cabinets. He gently opened the front door, and then out of the house he was! quietly closing the small-black gate behind him now after leading Pax out of the household stable and past the passage in the iron fencing.

Jason sat atop his mount, riding away from Silver Street wondering why the horse was swaying so far to his left and the right. "Steady, Pax." said Jason, patting his coat.

"The White Knight!" cried out a woman wearing stained commoners clothing. "Bless you, Sir Jason!" she yelled as he rode further ahead and away from her.

Am I already out of the High District? Jason had looked to his surroundings, watching the folk move about. Whores, jokers, false knights, and poor folk, *Ah, I'm halfway down Brey Street oh so soon. I hadn't realized; gone and drank a bit too much wine at supper.* Jason spoke to himself in his mind as if he was having a conversation with another soul. He rode southward upon the street within the city, passing the entrance to the Wizards District on his right side, then he trotted beside the Alligator Inn on his left, waving to some jokers in motley out at the front benches along his way.

"Hello!" Jason shouted to the folk in their rainbow silks.

"Off to the Square for the trials, are ya?" one of the men in colorful motley yelled back to Jason riding atop Pax.

"Beat them bloody, Sir Jason Frauer! You make it into that arena!"

Jason turned his neck, looking back to the man from behind as he now had passed him upon his horse. The joker was now juggling four balls in the crowded city street. Jason saluted to him, but when he turned back around to continue on riding forward, the man yelled, "Do not falter as you did four years ago and last year! Good luck, Sir Jason! Haa!" The fellow jokers surrounding the juggling one joined in for laughter. Jason heard the warning, or the jape, whichever it had been from the man, Jason heard it clear; reminded once again of his past two losses.

I drank all that wine to forget this nonsense, thought he, riding on forward almost upon the Square.

When Jason reached his destination, he'd seen that the typical stage where announcements, pyre burnings, and hangings took place, had been removed once again as it had every year for the trials. It was replaced with a temporary fenced off yarding, perfect in size for two men to battle within. The sands, same kind used for the flooring of the city's arena had been placed down for the combatants to step upon during their matches. Jason looked above as he trotted his way through the crowds. He looked to search the sky for Aeon's blue stars, yet the clouds of the night had blocked the sight of them; only the red stars of the south-sky shone brightly through the light drizzle of the night. He removed his gaze from the darkness above to search the crowd of spectators to find familiar faces. The combat yard was occupied with two fighting men while over two hundred surrounding folk watched on as best they could; another one hundred of them among the crowded Square too, selling food, and drink and pleasure potions. Jason was on the lookout for that big shining golden breastplate settled upon the chest of the giant man who trained him. It took him a minute or so, seated atop his horse watching the clusters of city folk, but he did soon find the man he was looking for.

Sir-Paladin John was easy to spot, a foot taller than every other soul watching the duel, and he'd be wearing his breastplate as he always would. Jason trotted his way through the crowd as if there had been nobody in front of his horse. All folk moved aside as the beast made way closer and closer to the large knight and his son. The match had just ended when Jason reached the side of his old friend spectating.

"Miss anything fun, have I?" Jason asked John as the man swallowed rum from a sack, then handed the bag back to his son (him too named Sir John, though not a *paladin knight*, like his father's held rank, simply a standard knight).

Jason watched the superior warrior in the battle yard raise the blunt metal sword high up into the night sky while his opponent lay under him, defeated with his hand upon his bloodied nose. "It's been fun so far. You didn't miss much though. There was an orc earlier, defeated his opponent in less than a minute." said John, looking on to see who the next pair of fighters would be.

Jason asked John, "Who are these two who just went at fighting? I've never seen these knights before."

Sir John's bearded son spoke to answer Arthan's question, "The one who'd just won here isn't a knight, he's a soldier. The one on the ground there is though. That's Sir Lewis Harper. Never heard of him either, nor has my father." The poor knight with the bloody nose rose to climb out of the dueling area to have a nearby priest tend to his bleeding.

Jason and John and younger John watched on as the victor, the military man, leapt over the fence to give his cheering wife a grand kiss upon big lips. This winner then presented himself to the tournament master to receive an ebony wristband to mark his arena acceptance for game day, just as Jason intended on doing during this upcoming hour. *After my win I don't have anyone to kiss here aside from Sir-Paladin John and his son, and that I would rather not do!*

"Boy, you'd better see Sisco before there's no more room for new combatants. Many are eager to partake in these matches tonight."

Jason accepted the advice, moving with haste away from Sir-Paladin John and his son. He trotted his way through the crowds, riding on over to the tournament master as two more armored men entered the sands to battle. "Sisco! Sisco! Over here!" Jason yelled loudly. Sisco was being swarmed with men in studded leather, plate armor and all sorts of different types of battle equipment and protective wardrobe. The warrior folk were doing their best to each gain the master's attention to ask for entry in to duel as this man Tournament Master Sisco was watching the fighting take place, as well as tending to them all for their entry requests. Luckily for Jason, he wasn't easy to go anywhere unnoticed; hard to miss! White armor, atop a white horse, shouting "Sisco! Sisco! Sisco!" louder than all others surrounding.

"Sir Jason! There you are! Thought I wouldn't see you tonight!" Sisco shouted this past a man in full iron's, helmet upon his head and all, waving a piece of parchment, listed upon it: all of his good and heroic deeds. Sisco ignored the armored man with his paper, listening to Jason on horse shouting, "Write me in! I'm ready!"

"Right away, Sir Jason! But, sir, you must wait four more matches! We have a high demand this time!" Sisco shoved a woman in leather out from his path. He approached Jason and placed his hand upon the reigns of his horse. "I'll have my servant here hitch Pax to the pillars just over there! Go, be beside the fencing for when you're called."

Jason stepped down from his mount while he watched Sisco hand the reigns over to a tall young man in yellow robes matching his master's. Before Sisco could return to the warriors begging for his attention, Jason placed a mailed hand upon his shoulder bringing him in close to speak into Sisco's queerly ring pierced ear. "Can I go at it any sooner? I'm eager…" Sisco smiled looking downward, eyes on the stone floor of the Square. "Damn you. Hop inside next. I'll shuffle the warriors. Go! This match here looks as if it would be a quick one.

Jason left Pax and the tournament master to make his way through the folk as these spectators watched one of the knights inside of the fencing fall after he'd been disarmed. Jason approached Sir-Paladin John once more as the man packed his pipe full of brown commoner's leaves. "Got in?" asked he when Jason approached him. "I'll be next."

"How'd you make that happen? You're dueling next? You've just arrived." John puffed on his pipe while he and his son watched the victorious knight reach a hand down to aid his fallen opponent in rising up.

Sir-Paladin John said, "Looks like *'next'* is now. Remember everything I've taught you, boy." John gave Jason comforting words, unlooking at him during their dialogue as he'd have a habit of doing when speaking to a soul.

Jason gave his old mentor a pat on his big armored chest.

"Love you, John!" said Jason loudly.

"Good luck, Sir Jason." said younger John.

Jason leapt through a cloud of Sir-Paladin John's smoke, over the fencing and into the sand. He had seen the past two combatants leave the battle area, so he made his entry. The Square erupted with many cheers, applauding and saluting, all for the glorious renowned White Knight of Ascali! He held his helmet within his hands as he enjoyed having the folk see that gorgeous face of his before and after his duelings. He smiled to them all, waved to some but then gave his attention to his opponent when this dark clothed ginger man with a stained cloak entered in. The cheering hadn't stopped, yet it was not anywhere's near as loud as it just had been for Sir Jason's entry only but a moment ago.

The man wore black traveling trousers with a matching black vest. His boots and gloves were colored to look as the greens of the wilderness. His cloak would have been snow white, yet years of travel resulted in it appearing more ashy than snowy here and now. Jason applied his helmet to his head.

"Sir, here!" shouted a serving man in the crowd. He threw the blunt long sword to Jason.

Sir Jason caught it, then he pointed the rounded tip toward his opponent. The man in traveler's garb moved some locks of dark red hair out from his face, revealing his tattoo surrounding the surface of his left eye and cheekbone.

A Southstread ranger, this will not be easy, but oh how it will be fun. Jason's opponent caught a flying dull sword sent his way from the crowd. He hadn't even looked to the weapon as it soared through the air yet he caught hold of it with a firm grip. "silent and steady" was their famous motto, these guardians from the cold south of Midlön.

Weapon still pointed toward the unarmored man, Jason shouted, "Ranger!" With his sword held low, the Southstread ranger began advancing toward Jason, slowly and eerily.

"Knight…" said the oncoming opponent.

Jason bent his knees and gripped his tourney sword tight in hand. He held his guard and fought his hardest while the spectators cheered on.

10

Arrival

The wagon's wheels creaked loudly, carrying the weight of Desmond and the rest of the captives. The king's company proceeded northward up the main road (this road known as Blayden's Path) passing mills, taverns, and some other structures built with their purposes unknown to Desmond. He gazed at the buildings as each one of them came and went by. Turning his head now, he rubbed at his freshly healed jaw as he looked upon the grasses of Midlön plains, thinking of the healer he'd encountered yesterday. *The woman was unlike anything I'd ever seen. Her touch was soothing…*

Desmond leaned himself over the wooden side bit, now looking to the head of the company of moving wagons and carriages. Yesterday before departure, the front head of the unmoving cart line was where the woman in white had glided off to after using her magical touch to repair Desmond's mouth in the mud road of the village called Willowhold. The magic-craft she had performed on Desmond was not practiced in the realm of Eastfell. He had the desire to thank her again for her act, and so he decided that if he and these men he shared the cart with were *not* all on their way to hanging by the neck or being forced to battle to the death, then he'd somehow find her to verbally express his appreciation once more.

"Back to Ascali we go!" shouted the king of the realm yesterday just after Desmond had briefly fought, and then killed one of the leading brothers of Willowhold.

Ascali… This famous city I've heard so much of. Desmond did not have much knowledge of Midlön, nor of its people's fashions, though all beings of Eastfell knew of its capital city here called Ascali, resting in the heart of the realm. The youth of the East, grow learning of this city's size and beauty, only Desmond was not impressed with the other smaller Midlön settlement *Willowhold, the horrific embarrassment they call a village.* If this Midlön City appears the way Willowhold had appeared, Desmond would just crave to be back in his home realm of Eastfell even more so than as of now. Further journeying north along this wide road would lead the company directly to the gates of Ascali, and they weren't so far off now Desmond would come to see soon.

At late morning Desmond thought he had caught glimpse of a massive mountain ahead straight forward up the road, only he'd then remembered quickly that there was no mountain drawn upon the maps, not in the middle of Blayden's Path here, nor anywhere near this road within the Midlön Plains. The growing mountain Desmond watched in the distance was in truth the city Ascali itself. Gray in color like a mountain, leaking the smoking fumes of industry, food-craft, and pleasures. At this distance it looked as if it had been a volcanic work of nature, the way the dark clouds drifted away from the surface of the stones of the rising constructs to disappear into the white sky. When the company appeared closer to Ascali, the structures of the mountain-like city became easier to make clear to the eye. Desmond was growing more fascinated with each passing second, now ignoring the workers upon the fields he'd just been watching before, not caring for the sight of the passing mills and field towers. He was peacefully gazing at the city as it grew larger.

His watch and thought was interrupted when the wagon's wheels slipped over a loose rock, causing the limp captive at his right-hand side to tip and fall into Desmond's shoulder. He non angrily shoved the man away, yet he pushed with great strength all the same. Desmond hadn't known if the heavy long legged being was even living, for he had his head bagged, as well as an iron chain connecting his wrists to his ankles. He sat unmoving after Desmond pushed him over and away; *had* been unmoving since even before the departure of Willowhold. Desmond was thankful to not have his own hands bound, as some of the people in the cart sadly had to suffer with. The man with the dark skin to his left side was sitting unmoving, quietly bleeding from a broken nose as he rested there sleeping with his hands tied together by roping. This Western Islander's fight in this very cart against the one-eyed man a day ago, sitting opposite Desmond and he now, had earned the two of them rope bindings for the remainder of their journey. The event of the vicious cart grapple, now had the coal colored bald man very weary, so fatigued; even *he* looked dead. Two dead, or sleeping men sitting at each of Desmond's sides while Desmond himself sat there more awake than ever. He looked upon the rising walls of Ascali in awe.

Unlike his cart fellowship of men from various dungeons, Desmond was eager and awakened as of now, for he had recently woken from a sleep that had lasted many hours. A peaceful sleep during the earlier bits of the company's short travels, finding himself now alert and strengthened. Yesterday, he had killed the leader of the village after the king had made it clear there would be no punishment for carrying out such an act. After he executed this leader, the third mayor, Desmond had then climbed his way back into the wagon after the king called for the company to make for leaving Willowhold. He experienced hours on the move northward away from the village, wondering what was to come next. He rested, sitting in the cart heading up Blayden's Path with the bleeding Westerner and rest of the men cramped together; some bound, others unbound. The time had seemed to be passing by quite quickly in his mind; a mind now greater at ease. When the sun had begun to fall, some silver guards rode up beside the cart to throw chunks of hard bread and fresh carrots in for the men to grab and eat for a sort of supper; and after that, Desmond was off to a beautifully earned sleep with a filled stomach.

He felt very at ease after killing that horrid mayor, even more at ease after the gorgeous priestess used magic to heal his face and hands too. Sleep found him easily and painlessly, so he let it consume him to silently take hold over his body so he'd regain his energy through the night and then into the morning; as to be ready for what might come next. Today is a new day, the first day he's to enter the Capital of Midlön, known by the name Ascali.

He turned his eyes to the highest point of the city, a gray tower built upon a fortress of slightly darker colored stone. *Stone fortress, giant stone walls, the tall stone tower…* Desmond was impressed, as his homeland's capital city Aildube was grand as well, yet the Easterlńs only dealt in wood; the construction through the arts of crafting with lumber only. Stacking stones was a technique which the people of the East never would master, nor attempt to in the old, present or upcoming days of time.

"King's company, passing Gold-Gate!" shouted a silver armored guard upon horse, speaking high up to the archers atop the colorless walls of the fortified city.

The wagons in single lined fashion made their way in, leaving the morning's sunlight to enter under the stone walls, passing the massive doors leading inward and outward of the city, known to all as Gold-Gate. Desmond did not understand why this gate did not have the appearance of gold. *Gold* in Easterlń language was spoken in the same word as Midlön speech, causing a great deal of confusion in poor Desmond's mind as they'd now begun passing through this gate that was plainly not made of gold. The dark metal doors to the left side and to the right sat heavily in the dirt against the stone city walls as people of the realm passed inside and out to travel upon this main road, in the same manner as of Willowhold's bodily traffic, yet tripled in capacity of moving occupants, and now with the king's company of carts mixed in as well.

People on foot unrelated to the company moved under and beside the line of wagons. Some of these people hands free and others struggling with belongings, objects, and items, etc… There were horsemen who moved about, armored ones and some with cargo too. Many carriages filled with goods, excluded from the king's company, made way inside the city, while other empty ones moved out upon the road and into the plains. It seemed all and any peoples were permitted in and out of the capital without any sort of inspection or halt for questioning. Desmond watched a family of stray cats, a rabbit and other useless animals enter and exit through this archway where this Gold-Gate dwelt, seeming more like a short-length tunnel, rather than how a gate's above archway would appear, all because of the thickness of the defensive city walls where the gate had been built within.

Sitting as comfortably as he can be within the cart of captives, he inspected the traffic some more. Desmond spotted a fat black cat and an old three legged dog, both wrestling in the center of the busy pathway down below, reminding him of his hound companion Araisha. He'd assumed that he would more than likely not see her ever again after entering Ascali, yet now that he put more thought into her possible reappearance, he'd come to realize that he had not expected these city gates to be wide open in this style. He hadn't seen Araisha since his departure of Willowhold; in truth, he hadn't seen her since his interaction with her while he was being held in the dungeon of the village on yesterday's morning. If she was alive which he felt he'd known she was, she'd follow, and so long as these city gates remained open as they had been now, she would have no struggle padding her way into Ascali to seek him out.

Desmond's tail end section of the company containing the cart of dungeon dwellers had now left the shadows of the gate's archway to enter into Ascali. This entrance portion of the city known as the Square was undeniably the most spacious and open area where one could dwell or move about here within the walls of the capital. It consisted of mostly traders traffic, all atop a stone floor, half a mile wide in every direction at its center. Upon this middle portion of the Square, working men could be seen sweeping sand and deconstructing a battle pen. All around the laborers, people walked about doing their business and or enjoying their pleasures. Many were seen entering and leaving the city, but those of whom not coming in and or exiting would be found here selling, buying and thriving; some entertaining people, others quietly resting. Aside from that main gate and the walls moving further and further away behind the company, they had all now been surrounded by many hundreds of buildings and constructs beyond the border of the Square; within the square, they were surrounded by a thousand city folk. Some of these buildings small, others taller and then taller as they went on and away in the distance beyond these crowds. They continued straight onward upon the Square. A few dozen or so yards after passing the men with brooms, Desmond saw the small buildings ahead become oh so clearly, and truly visible. Soon they'd leave the stone floor of the Square to enter the street paths in between these growing city structures.

Into the darkness they went once more. Desmond found it to be difficult to see again like Willowhold yet not from smoke and fumes such as that village contained. This visual impairment was from the high structures here blocking the light of the sun and brightness of the sky above. The company moved upward upon a very dark, yet heavily occupied street. They rode past various different tall standing shops with purposes mostly all unknown to Desmond, except for the establishment built with the gray balconies upon it's sides, occupied by half nude glistening women. The street smelled of sweat, onions and all sorts of rotted meats and stale garlic too. *Far better odors than those of Willowhold...* thought Desmond as his stomach now ached a bit more for the pleasure of food. The bread and carrots from after yesterday's victory had satisfied him for a long while, yet now he yearned for more nourishment.

Desmond rubbed at his stomach while now turning his sight away from the marvelous city to inspect the men he shared the cart with. He'd seen now that he wasn't alone in his consciousness here within the cart any longer. Desmond watched a captive man turn and lean himself over the edge to get a view at the close by passing people upon the city's street. The man seemed full of fear and curiosity; plainly a Midlön man, yet perhaps not of the city. This gazing man and that aggressive one-eyed man who'd fought with the Western Islander; he'd been awake now as well. That one sat there frowning with his hands bound by rope, bleeding from his ear where the Islander had taken a bite from during their grapple. Desmond decided to ask his question to the more peaceful appearing captive.

"Where we are going, will there be food?"

The man leaning over the edge gave no answer to Desmond, not even a responsive look. *Perhaps he did not hear me.*

Desmond asked again, "Where we're going, will there be food there?"

Yet the man seemed to not hear him for a second time again.

Desmond turned to look upon the one-eyed man across the cart; he would try his luck with this one. "Do you know, where we're going, will there be food? The place that we go to?"

The one-eyed man squinted at Desmond and then sadly did nothing more than let out a grunt before shifting away, as so they did not face each other any longer.

This onion smell from the shops reeked of heavens, as did the rotted meat; for all meats, rotted or unrotted, smelled fantastic to one such as Desmond who hasn't been properly fed for days now. He removed the thought of consuming food from his mind and decided to make an effort in beginning a dialogue with the only other conscious man once again, the one who'd been leaning over the wood to watch the city people. Just before Desmond was to attempt to ask his question, the man hopped right out of the cart to land hard on his feet upon the cobblestone street.

"Runner!" yelled some voice from the midst of the caravan.

Desmond watched a close by horseman of the company wearing silver armor trot on over. He threw his black spear downward towards the sprinting man. The weapon itself was of equal thickness to the poor running man's arm; it pierced him through the back and surprisingly to Desmond found its way into the street. The man died, held in place by the spear trapping him within the road. Desmond was far off now as the moving company continued on forward through the dark street, cart never stopping during this scenario; yet he closely still watched through the low crowds as the strong silver guard trotted up and removed his spear from the body and cobble. Not one person of the city paid these actions any bit of mind. They'd ignored the murder, all now trampling over the corpse in the shadows as if it hadn't been there.

Desmond wiped the violent visuals from his mind, now bringing his attention to the beauty of Ascali once again. He saw clearly how the architecture had been greatly changing the higher uphill that the company moved. *That poor fool shouldn't have run straight off like that.* The darkened paths began to wind, grow steeper and shift upward; with this, appearance of the constructs changed too. In place of the cart's wheels moving onward upon dirt cobble, Desmond leaned over to find the sight of smooth stone down below; smooth as the Square's floor. The buildings close by the Square's edge near to that main gate, and the one's of that dark north street they'd just left, had been constructed of mostly wood, cobble, and clay, whereas the surrounding ones now looked to be made of all and only stones; nothing more and nothing less. Desmond was now truly finding an appreciation for the Midlön crafts, trying to wipe his mind of the thought of that man who'd just died by that spear throw.

After riding up a smooth stone slope designed for wheeled carts, built beside a set of dull silver painted steps under a bright metal arch, the company had then come to a sudden and unexpected halt at this larger, more cleanly street. Desmond tried his best to look onward to see the king prepare for what he had to say to the company after leaving the luxury of his carriage to mount his armored horse, yet the other wagons ahead blocked the view; for Desmond only had visual of the tips of King Gregory Royce's diamond inlaid crown, nothing below.

As that golden haired knight Sir Marcus in blue, mounted his own steed beside his sire, the king yelled out, "This is the breaking of the company! Sir Marcus and I shall return to the Great Keep with the bulk of my honor guards, those of god to the Cathedral, all else to the Military District. Aeon be with you all! I enjoyed our short journey, for I am starving. Off we are!"

The king, Sir Marcus, and most of the spear wielding horsemen in silver armor made way further uphill, riding upon the stone road in destination to what Desmond heard King Gregory refer to as the Great Keep. One carriage containing *"those of god"* (Desmond's healer included within this covered wagon) wheeled its way down the street westward. While all those riders departed, Desmond and the remainder of the company was then escorted down a southeastern path by a handful of honor guards who would remain riding for oversight of the company. They'd ensure that any captives who might retaliate, and or attempt to run off the cart and away into the city crowds would be executed immediately.

As the line began to move to make entry into the Military District, a silver honor guard rode up beside Desmond's rolling cart;

his plate mail was half covered with dried mud, caked within the under chains as well.

"Watch yourself, Eastman." said the guard wielding the black spear; the very same spear Desmond had stolen yesterday to attempt to use for slaying the third mayor of Willowhold.

Desmond nodded in an awkward sort of agreement as he gazed at the rider's mud-crusted weapon. He rubbed the blackness away from his eyes as they began to tingle in a sort of pleasureful sensation. He turned away from the riding guard to face the chained, bagged captive. The honor guard spat, then rode on forward to the head of the squad.

The ride grew rough feeling again, as the cart was rolling atop cobble once more. Desmond used his knees to block the sleeping man from falling against him again as the cart's wheels bumped and groaned, shaking all of the passengers. More than half of the captives in the cart had awoken now, including the Western Islander; not the man with the bag over his head though.

"Easterlñ…we arrive?" After the bald man with bound hands beside Desmond had spoken his question, his nose leaked blood.

"In the city so fast, and already to Military District." he said to Desmond.

Desmond, not knowing if his speaking was in form of question or statement, asked, "You know where the place is that we're going? Will there be any food there? Are we being sent to death?"

A sleepy younger man in a prisoner's tunic, sitting beside the one-eyed captive, spoke before the Western Islander could answer Desmond. "We're going to the dungeons."

"We aren't going to the Ascali dungeons. We are going to the arena, or rather under it."

"That was my meaning, Islander. The dungeons within the arena, the arena's cells. They'll hold us there until game day." said the captive.

Desmond asked him, "What happens on game day?"

The man in the prison garb answered, "They bring us above, where we fight the competitors while they all hack at each other with blunt metal swords."

Desmond sighed and looked to the Western Islander as he was wiping blood from his nostrils with the rope about his wrist.

The Islander said, "He is not wrong. It is all true, all of his words."

Desmond asked the prisoner captive, "Will they give swords to us too?"

"Only wooden swords. The combatants get metal ones, grunts get wooden. Best of luck, Eastman…to you and to me as well. We'll just be there so the crowd gets to see more heads crack in the sands."

Desmond looked away from the prisoner to watch the clusters of city people walking through the district. He could jump off the cart and dash his way through the traffic of bodies to disappear; although that last dead man who attempted a leap off of the cart, likely had this same plan thought out in his mind.

There're fewer guards than earlier. During that man's attempt, there'd been many more. Perhaps my chances of success are greater now! Battling Ascali knights in an arena using a wooden sword while people cheered on, the notion of this sounded cruel and horrific to Desmond. He'd enjoy a nice chase through the city though; a brave attempt at an escape instead of riding as a passenger within this cart into a known doom. Though stepping down to the street from where he sat now could very well lead to a spear attack through his back, or he'd be swarmed by the armed men moving about the district here.

This portion of the city appears so different than the Square, and different from the clean district past those silver painted steps. The buildings here consisted of stone as the previous High District had, yet reflected a different sort of fashion. As they rode through the bumpy, light smoky road, Desmond observed the black painted buildings, all with that same look of iron to them, just like that Gold-Gate, which was absolutely *not* golden in color. One construct here looked to be made entirely of steel and iron, only as the cart came closer through passing, he'd seen that it was only yet again just another fine painting job done well by some working artist in the past.

Smoke filled the streets here alike the village of Willowhold, for it seemed more than half of the total of establishments along this city road consisted of smithies, armor, and weapons shops; all leaking out rising gray and black clouds. The cart passed by many forges, all occupied by strong looking men and women. This idea of escaping into the crowds no longer seemed pleasant. The city people in this part of Ascali seemed as if they'd be a grand threat themselves; more than likely they'd be eager to attack a fleeing captive coming off from the royal caravan cart. Smiths, soldiers, guards, and knights; this was where one would find Midlön's warriors, as well as where a great amount of their armor and weapons would be crafted too.

"Here we've come." said the Western Islander. The cart crept around the bright smoky bend in the street. Desmond closed his eyes and coughed. When he opened them, he saw the arena. Roofless and circular shaped, it stood surrounded by many buildings within the Military District. Bright gray, maybe sort of cream colored, it sat crumbling, awaiting Desmond and the rest of the men in the cart who would all soon be referred to as "grunts" for the upcoming game day.

The cart came to a halt when they'd all reached a welcoming yard at the brick walls within the exterior parts of the arena. "Get the scum off the cart and down underground. Store the wagon, feed the horses, then those with duties return to where you belong." This order came from one of the higher-ranking honor guards within the remainder of the company. He was overruled though when a copper-skinned man in yellow robes stepped out through a black tunneled entrance built within the side of the arena.

The robed man said to the guard on horse, "I'll take them now, sir. Here, send the horses to Quazzy in Wizards District, my thanks." The man in yellow used his thumb to flip one, two, and then a third platinum coin up and over to the honor guard.

The horseman in silver caught all three with his mailed hand, careful not to drop the money. "Well, thanks, Sisco."

"Of course. The steeds, they need proper bathing and meals, I can see. Quazzy will have it done. Any leftover money you have there you just spend on some of that good wine you'll find at that new shop across from the horse-care establishment. Erick Butterhair sells an enchanted vintage which makes women lustful. After you use the coins there on the care for the horses, you should have plenty leftover to buy yourself a few barrels for back at the household; for your riding companions here as well."

"As I've said, thanks, Sisco." The honor guard trotted up beside the wagon of captives after leaving the copper-colored man. "You heard your master, off the cart!" yelled he upon the horse, holding his black spear in one hand, new set of high valued coins in his other. Desmond was the first to jump down, followed by the Western Islander, and then the rest of the captives one by one.

The few men who had their hands bound with rope soon were cut free, as well as those with chains about themselves; they'd had their irons released and dropped by the honor guards. Desmond saw the man with the bag over his head was, in fact, alive after he'd watched a silver guard climb into the cart to release his metal bindings. The being stood himself upward to rise upon his feet after the metal was unlocked, then ripped the black bag off from his head with haste and strength, yet without aggression or a struggle. Pointed ears, hairless jaw, and a mop of sandy colored hair. Emerald-green eyes burned bright as he inspected his surroundings, stretching his muscles too, flexing and cracking his finger bones. The odd ears, the lack of hair upon the face, those naturally sharpened finger tips... All could see either this man's mother or his father was a full-blooded elvish being. Desmond lined up beside the rest of the captives, watching the pointy eared half-breed leap down from the cart to join the rest of the weary and hungered men.

The caravan's cart, guards, and horses had been away now down the street, leaving this man called Sisco practically alone with the captives as they stood there in a sort of sloppy formation. Sisco cleared his throat as he held a bit of cloth up to his moisturized lips. After he spat and then tucked the fabric away into his robes, he spoke out to the line of men. "Welcome! I am Tournament Master Sisco. I'll begin with saying that I'll be good to you all now, so please don't be violent, I ask. You're my responsibility, meaning I am expected to treat you with kindness, yet I must be sure you'll all conduct yourselves accordingly. The king's honor guards are leaving us, only don't be so easy as to slay me just yet, for we're currently in the Military District, where you can see there are plenty of able men here willing to defend my good self and this city's purity."

Desmond looked behind his own self where the street was found, occupied by hundreds of passing men, making armor, selling armor, as well as weapons…buying swords, bows, and trading spears and maces. Sisco was reminding Desmond and the others they were not in a friendly location here.

"Do we have an agreement? Don't attack me or run away, and you won't be cut up… I'll take your silence as a yay. Let's make way to your quarters! Come, come." Sisco turned his back to the line of men, leading them now into the blackness of this arena tunnel.

The one-eyed man led the way for the former cart dwellers, following directly behind Sisco. Desmond made sure he'd be last to enter into this gap in the arena wall, for he did not want a companion walking behind him as he made his way through within the line. He'd known these men, including himself had been marked as dangerous beings, for they had all been found in dungeons for committing crimes; it would be the right mind-thought to not want one of them strutting behind him, not in that tunnel nor anywhere.

Seconds before entering, Desmond looked behind to be sure his backside was clear, and this was when he'd seen the true man of danger, more dangerous than any of the cart captives could have been. He was an elder, yet he wore heavy bright iron armor, rimmed with crimson-colored edges. His cloak was blood orange; it covered a pair of bulky pauldrons. Under all the platings, rested a maroon leather coat ending down at the knees where Desmond saw his high-top red boots, matching a pair of red leather gloves that he wore. As Desmond inspected the possible threat, this old man placed an iron helmet atop a head full of graying hairs. The exposed bits of his face through the helmet were covered in black shadow. Within that dark side slit crafted for the wearer's vision through the helm, the elder's eyes grew bright, appearing as red stars would when they'd shine in the black sky.

"Follow in with them, Eastman." commanded the armored elder.

Desmond stood his ground, unmoving as the rest of the captives followed Sisco inside. Desmond turned back forward to watch the Western Islander enter in the arena tunnel. He then looked back at the armored man with the burning eyes. The man raised a gloved hand, making a tightened fist. When he released his grip and opened his fingers wide, his palm became alive with flames. The man possessed the same form of elemental power Desmond had seen before, wielded by flame entertainers in Willowhold, magical Midlön jokers; this form of the craft though was undoubtedly for deadly force. *This is no entertainer...*thought Desmond as he turned himself around once more, now walking his way into the arena wall. Whatever lay ahead inside would be more comforting than being burned to death by a fire wielding Midlön warrior.

He found himself yet again, underground walking his way to his possible doom with another unfriendly man at his back; only this time the unfriendly man had the force of fire to use against Desmond in place of a crossbow like the dungeon keepers of Willowhold had. Of course being unhurt should be his greatest desire, hope and thought here, yet he constantly visualized himself either being burned alive by this elemental man, or struck in the back with a crossbow bolt by a dungeon keeper. As Desmond took each anxious step forward, he was consistently reminded of the fiery man shuffling behind him as the light of his glowing torched hand brought most of the tunnel to view. If he didn't put thought into being roasted alive, his mind went back to the imagery of having been shot in the back with a pointed bolt. This glimmering at his back, creeping behind him; the heat from it too...very discomforting to Desmond. This elemental man was the only true source of light for the occupants of this cobble tunnel, until a boy in the same matching yellow robes as his master, approached Sisco down at the far front of the line. Desmond tried to get a view at what was happening down at the front there, but was so far back. The boy could be seen handing his master off a flaming torch as so Sisco could lead his way easier.

They proceeded one by one, lower into the earth in single fashion. The tunnel under the arena here seemed endless, and all too hot even for Desmond's liking. With his dripping backside, the Islander in front of Desmond finally came to a halt, as did the entire line of sweating men ahead. Torch bearing Sisco with the boy beside him, unlocked a door at the end of the tunnel. He brought his apprentice companion along with all of the captives into the feasting room where they'd find tables to take their meals at when the time would come. When Desmond stepped foot into the low ceilinged chamber, he took in a great deep breath of air, for the walk in the dark tunnel with the hot flame at his backside had caused this underground world to spin in circles within his head.

The fire-wielding elder behind him closed and locked the wooden tunnel door after extinguishing the flames he channeled with that red gloved hand. He walked around Desmond, leaving him with the line of men standing, all of them wondering what's to come next. The armored magical man now stood beside copper-skinned Sisco and the younger one with the same styled yellow robes. Sisco took a seat down atop a bench by one of the many long tables within the feasting room. He sat gazing at the men, as did the armored elementist, his gloved palm placed gently upon his other gloved fist, seeming ready to burn anyone who'd move inappropriately.

"Well…here we are my guests. My *grunts* as a matter to be, until your time within the arena is ended. So well…yes. You are all formally now my grunts." Sisco called the boy to his side to whisper a command into his ear.

The boy dashed away through a door, and just after his disappearance there was the man with one arm among the group of former cart captives, he'd spoken up to ask a question to Sisco.

"*When* is our time within the arena ended?" The boy returned almost instantly, holding a golden goblet filled with purple wine. He served the drink to seated Sisco, trying not to spill any of the goblet's contents, and then after that act of service, he returned to stand in between his master and the fire warrior.

Sisco answered the one-armed man's question with, "After game day, and game day, as it happens is tomorrow, beginning early in the morning." Sisco clapped a hand against his thigh as he sipped on the wine. He told the group, "You are some of the luckiest guests I've ever taken in. Grunts are commonly tortured with the boredom of dwelling here for days and or even weeks, waiting for that dreadful time to come to fight above in the sands, only they don't know until after the tournament's end, that waiting *days* here to partake as a grunt, is worse than the actual game day itself. For you lot, here you are standing now, and in two days after the event, here you will *not* be."

Sisco sipped on some more of his wine. "You'll be given a meal here tonight at midnight, after which you'll be brought back to your cells to sleep until sun comes. And then off to the armory! That is where you'll collect your weapons and apparel for the fighting. The duels of the day will conclude at midday, and the battle royale will then begin. The doors will open and out into the sands you will walk to conquer each other as well as the armored and armed competitors."

All men were silent, all looking upon Sisco sitting there drinking purple colored wine with his ass on the bench and his back against the table.

"As for what is to immediately come next, I'm going to take my meal here while Battle-Mage Bishop and my apprentice show you the way to the quarters. I'm famished... I'd like to wait until you all leave me before I begin. Are there any questions before I dismiss you?"

The half-elvish being among the line of men asked, "What happens after the tournament ends?"

"You'll all be forgiven for your crimes in which you've committed that had caused your captivity in wherever it was that the king had found you. What your crimes had been I don't know or care to know, as it doesn't seem the king does, so why should I? After the tournament, if your heads are still in one piece, you'll be set free to dwell with the city's poor folk within the Low District, or you go and return to wherever it is you've came from... You'll win no money, nor glory, only the reward of freedom. Any other questions?"

A serving woman in yellow brought forth a platter of fish, potatoes, and asparagus. Sisco would not touch the food until he was alone within the feasting room. "My thanks." said he to the servant before giving her one golden coin.

Sisco then asked the men in line once more, "Any other questions? Dismissed then. Please sleep well! Priests will be visiting within the armory on game day if any wounds need addressing before the fighting takes place. Aeon be in your dreams!"

"Come, grunts." said the battle-mage. He led the men around Sisco's table and through the feasting hall to a door made of brass.

The apprentice moved so very close by the old mage's side during the walk in between tables. This boy in yellow robes unlocked the brass door with a big brass key he had tucked in his clothing, and then down the cell hall the lot of them all walked; calmly and peacefully with the mage leading the way.

The boy in yellow locked up the metal door behind all of the men as they walked in single-line through a hallway made entirely of cobblestone; the floor, all walls, and the ceilings too. The crumbling hall was lit by candles resting upon many small wooden tables in between the entrances to each personal sized chamber. The boy put the key back into his robes and then continued to follow the men, Desmond directly at his front side; Desmond himself once again, last in the line of walking men. As he made his way down the hallway, doorless rooms rested at both his right and left sides. More and more appeared as the men continued their walk past tables with the candles atop their surfaces. He turned around briefly to inspect the fearful boy at his backside. Weaponless and scrawny looking the young one appeared. *He could have anything under those robes though. He could possess a blade, a body of great strength. I refuse to underestimate anybody in this realm after the youngling from Willowhold had put me down in the mud. This boy in yellow might even possess magic to wield as the mage leading the line carried inside himself...* Armed or unarmed, this boy gave Desmond more comfort at his backside than the battle-mage would have or a foe with a crossbow.

The man ahead of Desmond came to a halt, as did the one ahead of *him* and the half-elvish and then the next man, and so on and on. The mage was leading each of them into their own rooms; rooms consisting of wooden beds, a single table with a lit candle resting upon it, and a bucket in the corner to drop dung and drip piss into. He peeked around the head of the man at his front. He saw down the hall, the Western Islander walking into one of the rooms at the left side of the hall with the mage accompanying him, then the mage walked out from the little chamber to lead another man into one on the right side across from the Islander. This happened rapidly, each one of the grunts silently being assigned to where they'd temporarily dwell, until lastly it came Desmond's turn. The boy in yellow stood behind Desmond as the armored mage walked to stand at Desmond's front. "Let's find you a bedchamber." said he, now moving away to guide Desmond to one of these doorless rooms.

"Give me the wand, child." commanded the mage.

The boy ran around Desmond, leaving his backside to join the superior. Out of his robes came a wooden stick, no bigger than a bit of small tree branch. The boy handed the device to the magical elder in armor. While the three walked, this battle-mage named Bishop had the stick raised a bit now, not so high but raised upward to point at his own chin; chin covered by the iron helm he still wore. His elbow extended out some, the tip of the stick an inch or so from where his mouth would be if not covered by the iron. Desmond inspected what he could of the wooden stick, as it now appeared slightly different than it had when the boy brought it out from a pocket hidden within his robes. From what Desmond could see from behind this man wielding the *"wand,"* as he had called it, just moments ago, the device had begun to pulsate slightly, seeming alive with a glowing veinlike texture. It was dim though, blue one second and then red or green the next. If the mage and this boy hadn't been walking through the hallway so quickly, Desmond would have had an easier time inspecting the magical item.

The mage spoke out, his voice louder than the sound of lightning strikes, echoing throughout the cobble hall to flow into all of the rooms occupied by these men. "Grunts, sleep well. Midnight's time is in thirteen hours. The door to the feasting chamber shall be unlocked and opened then. You'll enter in to dine when this happens."

Desmond dug through that greasy black hair of his to cover his ears with his fingers while they walked as the mage talked into the tip of that stick.

"Each bedchamber has no door. Try not to fight or fondle each other while you're left here. Do not fool with my candles, or I'll kill you with them. You will speak with Master Sisco after the door is unlocked for feasting."

This elder fire warrior, Battle-Mage Bishop then handed back the wand to the young one, and inside the yellow robes the magical device went to live once more.

Desmond came to a halt after the mage and the boy stopped moving forward. They all discontinued their walking to stand now in front of an empty chamber, more looking like a cell in truth, now that Desmond peeked his head inside. *An improvement from the last cell I had rested in.* Desmond looked to the walls and ceiling where he'd seen no windows, as this captivity hall had been built much deeper into the earth, compared to Willowhold's dungeon. Any hopes of his companion Araisha seeking him out had begun to diminish now that he'd realized how far under the ground he'd been here.

As he stood there upon the sandy cobble, thinking of how his hound could get herself into this tunnel to find him, the mage spoke in his ear. "Enter." said he.

Desmond walked into the room, and then he turned himself around to face the boy and Battle-Mage Bishop in the hallway; although the mage hadn't been in the hallway, he'd entered the room following in behind Desmond.

"What magic do you practice, Eastman?" he asked Desmond.

"I do not use magic." Desmond said to him, badly lying.

"No use in telling me false truths. Any priest or mage in Ascali will sense the power in you. Your aura is strong, dark though. No matter, magical beings are permitted to partake in tomorrow's event. Best not use any of the craft though. King Gregory will have the honor guards spear you to death while the crowds watch on, amused."

The young apprentice in the hallway behind the mage said, "Master Sisco will want us back now. It's time we've returned to him, Battle-Mage."

The mage was still standing there in his shined iron helm, dripping and sweating from the weight of his armor atop his fiery colored leathers. He finally moved in silence, striding out of the chamber and down the hallway. Sisco's apprentice followed the man hastily. They both made their exit through the brass door at the far end, locking it behind them to leave Desmond and the rest of the newly made grunts to sleep in their doorless rooms or to dwell in this lonely, dim hallway Desmond had been standing in now.

He had immediately left his personal chamber, to watch Bishop and the boy in yellow shut the door. After hearing it's locking, Desmond moved a few steps down the hallway past a bright table covered in candle wax and burning wicks. He reached the first room beside the one he'd been placed in by the mage. When he'd taken a look inside, he briefly caught sight of an old man with no hair, sitting upon the wooden bed set, scratching at scabs upon his arm. The man caught sight of Desmond, now yelling, "Out! Out of here you go! Go!" yelled the elder.

So out Desmond went. Across the hall he brought himself, and that was where he saw the half-elvish resting peacefully upon the wood inside his room. One would think he'd been sleeping on a beautiful feather bed the way Desmond saw how he breathed heavily, deeply yet gently. Both of his enlarged hands rested upon the center of his chest, the pointed nails aimed to his chin. *How could he fall off to sleep so fast? How could any of these people rest on these slabs of wood when we're faced with battle tomorrow…*

He quit gazing at the useless, sleeping pointy-eared being. Into the next room he went but quickly left its entrance to make way back into the hallway after he'd seen a man half-nude, squatting in the corner of the chamber to poop into the wooden bucket. Desmond found the Western Islander sitting upon the wooden bed planks in *his* room, beside the one he'd just exited with the man on the bucket. Palms pressed against his eyes, this dark man sat obviously saddened, defeated looking and ready to weep.

"We must leave here." Desmond said to the sitting man as he stood in the entryway.

The Islander removed his hands from covering his eyes. "There is no leaving this place." said he.

To that, Desmond told him, "I will not accept a battling in an arena. I do not want that."

"None of us *want* that. We have no choice in this, you see. If we do not fight, we will be hurt by them; burned by the battle-mage or hanged by the neck in the Square. Best we fight our hardest, then enjoy our freedom after we've finished." The Islander placed his face back into his hands, elbows resting upon his knees as he just sat there, waiting for Desmond to speak, or to leave him.

Desmond asked, "Have you fought in this city before? In the arena above?"

"No, but I have viewed the fights once before. Grunts do not do well in the battle royale. The knights and the armored warriors all battle each other at the same moment, while grunts roam the sands with wooden weapons only to be easily struck and attacked for only more joy to be given to the crowds; for added amusement to the event. Sisco will put us at disadvantage on purpose. We're meant to violently fail tomorrow."

Desmond understood well, which was why he had then said to the man, "This is why we must escape. Will you help me?"

The Western Islander removed his hands from his face, then he looked to Desmond one more time. "No… Too dangerous. Leave me please."

Desmond sighed, then he left him there to return to his own room and wooden bed.

He sat alone now, unmoving and lost in thought as he lay flat on his backside against the splintered wooden bedding. He thought of home, then of Araisha, and then of how he could possibly escape here. Thoughts of food and thoughts of violence and the upcoming battle. More thoughts of food, more thoughts of how to escape. There was no food though, nor was there anyway of leaving this place as of now. Perhaps he could use his strength or the power of dark magic to attempt to kill this fire warrior, and Sisco and that little apprentice. All he would need to do would be to wait for that brass door to unlock, then he could make his surprise strike. *Avoiding tomorrow's fight, with a fight in itself tonight…* It just didn't seem to make any bit of sense now to escape through using violence, when the purpose of the escape itself would be made to avoid game day's violence. It seemed either way, Desmond would have to battle whether it be at midnight tonight during an attempt to leave, or during this upcoming tournament event.

It took Desmond all of six hours of ceiling gazing to make his decision; the decision that he would not be attempting any form of an escape from here or this city. He came to remember Sisco's mentioning of the aftermath of game day for the grunts. "*After the tournament, if your heads are still in one piece, you'll be set free to dwell with the city's poor folk within the Low District, or you go and return to wherever it is you've came from...*" From those words coming from the tournament master, he'd made it seem as if the grunts would be treated with peace after the event; a reward of sorts or pardon for those who'd previously been in captivity for crimes. It would be a pleasure to look to hope on, although Desmond was not satisfied with this, as he considered his imprisonment to be false, unfair, and an act of cruelty. He had been sent to the Willowhold dungeon after refusing to let the leaders of the village cook and eat his hound companion. Now he'd have to fight to earn his way to being a freeman. *How unsatisfying,* he thought if he had the brain to be a storywriter like his youngest sister in the East, that this tale would make for a legendary inspiration for an epic journey story or even writing for comedic material; sadly though, he was not a storywriter, and this was his reality, not a myth, legend, comedic tale or poem.

He lay there upon the wood, lost in thought and hungrier than ever. At midnight Desmond heard the sound of the brass door unlocking, far off down the cobble hall. He thought he'd been the first of the captives to hear this, until he'd seen the half-elvish in the hallway peeking his head out from the chamber. Some more grunts revealed themselves in reaction to the sound which came from the metal door. It crept open slowly as the men gathered; almost all had left their doorless chambers now.

"No plot to rush the door? Peaceful grunts, yes?" A hand waved through the opening of the door, sleeved with a yellow robe.

Sisco used the hand to open the door wide as he sipped from a golden goblet of wine with his other. The brass door was now fully opened and there he stood alone in the feasting hall. "Ah, yes, good. Some years the grunts find this the perfect opportunity to ram that door open at the sound of its unlocking. It's why a part of me always fears feast time. Please find seating! Come in, come in, peacefully, of course, please." Sisco took a step backwards, deeper into the feasting chamber. The grunts funneled in, one by one, sitting themselves randomly upon the benches at the long tables.

Desmond felt the heat before he'd even entered to leave the cobble hall. When he stepped through into the feasting chamber, he saw Battle-Mage Bishop standing just beside the opened brass door, one of his red-gloved hands on fire. Of course the mage had been making it appear as if he was needed there with his flaming hand as so the occupants of the chamber could see and dine without a struggle with impaired sight, though all knew he was there as a source of security for the master Sisco. Desmond gave the mage a glance from head to toe; the old man seemed the same as before, armored and alert. Desmond tried his best to appear uninterested and absolutely not afraid, so with dead eyes and a forced yawn, he looked away from the elemental warrior, gazing now upon the tables to find where best he should take his seating. He searched for the Western Islander, as Desmond's preference would have been to feast with him, the only other foreigner among this lot, the man here he's shared the most dialogue with. The Western Islander had already been seated, as were most of the men now. The Islander's table was entirely filled with occupants though, benches overcrowded in an uncomfortable cluster, so Desmond chose the next best option he had for himself, a table with only one occupant seated at its edge. He preferred either to sit with the friendly Islander, or among as few of the captives as he possibly could. After Desmond finally sat himself at this lonely table, across from the man with the one arm, then all in the chamber had been officially now seated; aside from the guarding battle-mage, of course, and Sisco, who was now calling out servants through a bright small hole in a stone wall.

Women wearing black-and-yellow robes, carrying heavy buckets of smashed potatoes, entered through a wooden door. Sisco had his apprentice boy enter in as well to pour more wine into the goblet he held. Sisco stood smiling and sipping as he and his apprentice then watched women bring potatoes, and now trays of thinly sliced meats into the chamber, presenting them to the grunts. Sisco was laughing now as he saw some of the men hadn't even the patience to wait for the wooden utensils to reach the table top. Most dug into the buckets of potatoes the moment the women had placed them down, devouring the food from their own palms and in between their fingers after scooping with bare hands. Desmond watched the one-armed man calmly grab slices of the thin beef to slowly chew on with a mouthful of rotting teeth. Desmond ate in the same fashion, calmly and nonhastily, as the three tables of men beside him consumed their meals as if they'd been crazed animals.

A young woman with half a mustache approached Desmond's table. She handed him a wooden spoon and a fork, smiled and then walked to the one-armed man, presenting him with the same utensils and gesture.

The women served, the grunts ate, Sisco watched with wine… until he was unexpectedly needed above for unknown reasons. A serving woman spoke to him by the doorway, too far off for Desmond to hear the wording of their talk, yet he saw Sisco nod his head and then wave for Bishop to attend to him. As Desmond ate his meat and his portion of potatoes, he saw straight in front of him, Battle-Mage Bishop tapping the tip of an unlit torch mounted upon the wall. He touched the wood with his flamed hand, and of course now the torch was blazing bright. Bishop extinguished the fire surrounding his hand and wrist to walk on across the chamber to Sisco. Sisco, the servant, and Bishop, all left into the tunnel pass through the wooden door for reasons unknown to Desmond or any of the grunts. *Not that anyone here is noticing these sorts of bits except for me… They're in love with the food they've been given.* Desmond was cautious, fearful, in fact. If there was to be a slaughter, a grand execution of some sorts, now would be the perfect moment. These eating men could have been ingesting poison, or fed to become distracted so they could all be roasted to death with fire magic or even feathered with arrows. The only thing keeping Desmond from believing those outcomes could happen, was the sight of the boy in yellow at the doorway. He remained behind, awaiting his master and the protector battle-mage. *They wouldn't flood the room with death with that boy here to suffer, or perhaps they would… I do not know these men of Midlön just yet and their forms of cruelty.*

Desmond chewed on more potatoes, then he grabbed himself another serving of meat with his wooden fork. He was inspecting the exits of the locale, the brass door leading to the cobble hall where the chambers could be found. Secondly there was the wooden door where the captives themselves entered through after the walk through the deepening dark tunnel from the above street. He quit watching the wooden door; he had been waiting to see when Sisco and the mage would return through it. He stopped gazing because he was joined at the table by the Islander.

"Could I sit and eat with you? We're already running low at the table there." said the man, dried blood still upon his nostrils.

"Yes, sit, friend." said Desmond.

The Western Islander took a seat beside Desmond, across from the man with one arm. All three of the men were happily chewing their food at the table, this was until a muscled shirtless man with oversized ears approached them. He was standing very still now, holding his wooden fork with a firm grip. Bare feet, he had no torso piece and ripped pants hardly covering any skin below his upper thighs. The brute of a man stood flexing, eyes fixed on the Western Islander.

"I'm gonna eat here." said the chiseled, veiny man.

With a mouthful of food, Desmond said, "Join us, yes." to the standing man.

The man pointed a scarred finger to the Western Islander. "I will, and you will leave the table."

The Western Islander chewed and swallowed what remained of the food that had been within his mouth. He looked to the man above him, then he slapped his hand away. "I'm not going anywhere." said the Islander.

The big man wrapped his entire pasty hand around the Western Islander's throat. While he choked the air out from him, this attacker high above used the fork he held as a weapon, stabbing the Islander now in between his legs with a hard, piercing strike as he suffocated him still. Desmond leaped up and back from the table in horror, now against the stone wall and unable able to think, unable to act, only to witness what's to come next, oh so horrified. The one-armed man fell backwards, vomit spraying from his mouth as he fumbled on the floor choking. The remainder of the grunts arose to witness the fight. That was when the young one in yellow robes threw the wooden door wide open to yell down the dark tunnel, "Help! Come!"

There was no time for help though, not for the Western Islander.

With one hand around the Islander's neck and the other hand dug twisting into his dick with the fork, the big man brought him high up and into the air. He slammed the poor foreign man against the wall and held him there in place just beside where Desmond was leaning. The bleeding Islander's legs flailed; he kicked and kicked at the huge shirtless one, even tried to grab him by the face, to attack at his eyes; he was unsuccessful in this though. The man was too strong, and the Islander had not one breath of air inside his lungs, and he had a fork sunk deep into his ball sack, pinning him to the wall.

The brute released the fork, but only to slam it back in between the smaller man's legs, and then he released the fork once more to just jab it back in and then outward and in and out and in and out of the man's groin, again twisting the fork more. The Islander would have screamed but was unable to with the muscled man's hand wrapped so hard around his throat, so the rest of the grunts screamed for him. Some yelled in horror, and others cheered on as if they'd been spectators for the upcoming arena match. The room was loud with the sound of man terror.

Should I have aided this man I've just called "friend"? If I act now, can he be saved? Desmond thought this out as he literally still witnessed the dark man being stabbed repeatedly with the fork against the wall. *These Midlön people with their healing priests... Men live after castration even in Eastfell without holy magic! He could be saved!* Desmond grasped his own fork from the table, hoping he could be as strong as this heavyset shirtless man was. He'd take the fork and pierce it right into his neck. *For even the strongest of men will die from bleeding.* Desmond wanted so much to be cautious and uninvolved, should be cautious and uninvolved in a scenario like this here, yet he felt that he had to aid this suffering Islander. *He is a foreigner like me... If I watch over him here and now, he will watch over me when my time comes for need.* As Desmond was readying to intervene, his own eyebrows were practically burnt off his face when the bolt of fire passed him by maybe a foot away from him. Battle-Mage Bishop had sent a ball of fire past a dozen of the grunts to land right at the backside of the shirtless man. The man screamed, then he let go his grip on the Islander, then the Islander finally got to scream a bit…

Battle-Mage Bishop absorbed the flames back into his palm, sending them off and away from the scorched brute man. When the fire had left the big being, he fell to his knees, dropping the Islander. A layer of skin had melted off the big man's backside. The Islander lost consciousness, which could come back; his manhood would not though. Both of them lay unmoving, unawake and silent as half the men in the chamber cheered on still, the other half trying not to wretch; Desmond was one of those in horror.

Sisco approached, finishing the contents of his goblet and wiping his mouth with that rag of his that he used so often. He held the cloth to his nose, now saying, "Ah, well. Did they at least get the chance to dine? We'll get them back into their quarters, and they'll be good as new after they're healed by the priest on game day before battle."

Sisco put the cloth into his robes and then walked his way over by the wooden door to lean against the wall and gaze at the men; his apprentice joining him at the ready while Bishop began to carry away the Islander past the brass door. Sisco sent the boy away to fetch more wine for his goblet as he made ready to speak again.

Sisco said to the grunts, "Well…either return to your chambers for rest, or continue to dine more! Go on, go on."

Desmond looked over to the brass doorway where he saw Bishop now dragging the brute-like man on his belly, as so his raw back would not scrape against the cobble past the door.

Sisco continued speaking, "Either way, grunts, eat or sleep. Game day begins at sunrise. You'll want to be full and rested for it."

Desmond sat to continue on eating, ignoring the smell of burnt man flesh.

11

Dallion's Quest

When Dallion opened his eyes, he saw the sun had already risen, brighter today than it had been these past few weeks. The ill weather had now faded away from the look of the rays piercing through the stained window above Dallion's bed here and now. The children sized set of drums in the corner of the room, perfectly visible and shining, as was the blue carpet as well as all four green walls. Dallion knew, if he could see his bedchamber clearly as he was lying there, and the contents within it, then that would mean the sun had risen, and if the sun had risen, then time it was to make ready for the day's institution lessons. He threw the blankets off of the bed set and then jumped onto the carpeted floor. Dallion broke his fall by landing upon his feet, as well as his hands; his entire body sprawled across the floor as if he'd been a spider. He made attempt to crawl his way out of the bedchamber and into the washing room, except his strength had failed him when he'd made it only halfway out of his room. He collapsed onto his belly, then took a couple of quick deep breaths inward. He pressed his palms to the floor to push himself up and onto his feet to stand as he exhaled his breath outward with a smile upon his face. While placing a shirt over his head and shoulders, he waddled his way down the house hall to make way into the washing room so he could leave poop in the privy pot and then clean his hands, hair, face and mouth; only he was distracted with his morning preparations when he'd heard noises coming from the kitchen.

Dallion walked barefooted down the hallway, very sure that he would find some goblins thieving from the cabinets to take food from his household to bring back down and into the city sewers.

My knife! I don't have my white knife! screamed the little one, in his mind of course; he was very careful not to make any sounds as so the enemy raiding the kitchen would not detect him engaging in his rogue-craft. He had always hunted for goblins in the household attic when he'd been able to find ways inside of it; the very same for at visits to other households not of his own family's. During all his goblin hunts, Dallion always had made sure he'd been armed, whether it be a knife from a kitchen or even a weapon as simple as a stick or some tool; only now that the little boy truly had *finally* heard some goblins, he had nothing to attack these foes with. His excitement almost turned to fear.

Every one of Dallion's little classmates had been frightened of the rumors of the goblins living in the Ascali sewers, their household attics, cellars, and the ones under their beds too…not Dallion, though. He'd always been eager to find them, to fight them! As opposed to hiding deeper under the bed's blankets as his classmates claimed to do so when they'd heard the creatures in the night. Alex Forkworth told Dallion and the class that he had cried, calling for his mother and father after hearing the goblins attempting to enter his bedchamber through the window of the Forkworth household on a rainy night. Ever since that day he'd told the tale, the children of the school had all always verbally tormented poor Alex, constantly claiming he'd been a coward and a tear baby. Dallion decided ever since hearing the class harass the boy, he would not only show no fear of the Ascali goblins, he would hunt them and kill them all!

Little Dallion Frauer feared embarrassment and neglect far more than he feared the evil goblins, yet now that he truly caught sound of one in his own household kitchen, perhaps he began to think that his classmates have been smart in this matter; in fearing the creatures. Before he could possibly think of fleeing though, he'd have to see the being with his own eyes at the least. Dallion would have to be brave, to poke his head around the corner of the wall here so he could tell his class that he had gotten to look upon it, alone and with his own eyes before summoning mighty Jason in to slay the beast. *Jason has killed orcish before…says goblins don't exist, but I know he's lying. He's killed them too, I know it. If Jason isn't afraid, then I'm not either…*

The last soul that Dallion had expected to encounter there in the kitchen was his brother Jason. Dallion was readying to get a glance at the goblin, and then sneakily retreat down the hallway to retrieve Jason to have him slay the creature, possibly even call for Jason with a shout if he had to…except there *he* was, his brother Jason Frauer, bandaging his wrist at the sink. Dallion was half relieved and half disappointed that these sounds he had heard earlier and currently were not of a goblin intruder, but now he was more curious than he was relieved or disappointed.

Dallion stood itching at his backside while watching his older brother cleaning a wrist. "Why are you in armor? Are you going to battle?"

Jason turned around to face his younger brother. Dallion saw his nose was cut across the middle, above the nostrils; a very thin opening of a tiny wound, yet leaking much blood.

"Came from one." Jason said to him, waving a newly won ebony-made wristband for Dallion to view. He smiled and then turned himself back around to face the sink where he was tightening the bandage across his hand.

"Your trial battle? That was last night, after supper." Dallion said to his brother, confused.

"I went to the Alligator Inn after the duel, got some food with the women, and the jokers… I've just returned."

Jason discarded an older bloodied bandage into the waste bucket under the sink, then he steadily walked past Dallion to sit down into the head chair at the dining table; he was trying not to spill the contents of a mug filled with ale all the while. Jason's white armor clanked when he collapsed his ass down at the seat. The bandages upon his wrist appeared fresh and clean until he wiped at some blood leaking from the top part of his nose with the wrapped hand. Jason had seen that the blood soaked into his fresh bandagings, so he said, "Ah, shit."

Dallion walked over to the family table where he climbed up to have a seat down next to his older brother. Dallion asked him, "Did you win your fight?"

Jason took a long and healthy chug of the ale. The foam clung to his upper lip to mix in with some blood there. Jason said, "Yes, I did." Then he slammed the mug down onto the table, spilling a small bit of drink onto the wooden surface.

"Yes! I knew you would. You can fight tomorrow?"

"Yes, I can. You know the rules: win the trial duel, you fight in the arena."

"I mean can you do it? You don't look well."

Dallion was scared, more scared than he appeared (he didn't appear frightened at all; in fact, only appeared curious). He had never seen Jason move so slowly, the way just before how he sat down into the chair; walking to it with almost a sort of limp. Dallion knew Jason was the strongest man in all six realms of the earth, which meant seeing him in this condition, gave his little mind great concern for his wellness. "Why don't you visit a priest? Or have John-"

Jason interrupted his little brother, "I have no love for holy magic, nor for priests, and certainly not for John putting his fat hands on me. I love John, but I would rather bleed." Jason groaned with a smile as he rubbed at his ankle.

"How will you fight in the arena tomorrow?" Dallion asked him.

"I will heal all myself with time, not with magic. I'll be fresh as new by tomorrow… I only bear bruises. This cut here, like the bite of an ant." Jason poked at the mark at his nose where the tip of a sword must have bit into his face, just barely. "God aided me in the duel. He'll aid my body in recovering. See this?" Jason again poked at the minor wound above his nostrils. "My opponent scraped me right here with his sword's tip. The sword was blunt, still took some skin…and even so, a blunt sword can destroy a man. If I had been half an inch closer to this ranger's sword stroke, my face would have been split wide open. I could have lost a nose, perhaps been blinded or even killed…or worse, left dead in the brain like a zombie."

"But none of that happened. You won! Just the tip cut you? Weren't you wearing a helmet?"

Jason leaned back into his father's chair; smiling at Dallion before he spoke. "Fell off my head after I made a roll through the sand. In the end, Aeon granted me victory. Now Aeon will heal me. I don't need a priest or paladin to quicken the process."

All this talk of battle, winning the fights and war-craft, these dialogues were making Dallion eager now; eager to fight too, to goblin hunt, to go on a dangerous quest! Dallion slammed his fist down onto the tabletop. "When I grow bigger, I'm gonna win as much as you when I fight!" He spoke loudly, forgetting that his mother, father, and brother Arthan had been asleep still on this bright-gray morning.

Jason tilted his head backwards now, facing up to the wooden ceiling, smiling. "Is that so?"

"I almost had a fight this morning, with a goblin. But then I saw it was just you here. I didn't have the knife you gave me. I would have died if it wasn't you, if it was a goblin. I should keep the knife with me always, even in the house because I would have died if that was a goblin, if it wasn't you." Dallion looked to Jason as he awaited for his reply from him.

Jason closed his eyes and exhaled air from his lungs. "If you wish to be a good warrior, you need proper training, as well as proper rest and proper sleep."

Dallion reached over to grab a hold of Jason's mug so he could have a look inside of it, maybe take a sip of the ale while his brother's eyes had been closed. The mug was empty though, so Dallion placed it back down. "Sleep? Yes, I love to sleep. Arthan came and woke me from sleep in the night to speak with me, only…I forgot what he told me."

Jason chuckled at that, eyes still closed and head still placed far back as he sat limp there in the chair. Jason said, "Arthan? Awake in the night to speak with you? Doesn't sound like our lazy Arthan to me."

Dallion scratched above his ears. "Yes, maybe I was dreaming of it all in my sleep. Arthan is a lazy man. Are you wanting to sleep now, Jason?"

Jason practically choked on his own spit.

Dallion's brother sat upward, leaning over the table now with his hands placed over his face as he gagged, one hand mailed, the other naked and bandaged at the wrist. “Yes, perhaps I should get this armor off and rest before game day tomorrow. You...should be making ready for lessons, little one.” Jason coughed as he gently smacked Dallion in the face, right at the cheekbone. He would do this frequently, gently and humorously. Always Dallion would respond by punching Jason as hard as he could in his thigh, even if he was wearing his platings, and so he did just that.

Dallion struck Jason with a hardened little fist upon iron, and then off Jason went down the hall and into his bedchamber to remove his armor. Dallion went down the hallway as well to find the chamber where he would poop and then clean himself.

Into the washroom he went, and then twenty or so minutes after, back into the hallway the child took himself, with clean and drying hair and a minty mouth, leaving behind last night’s dinner in the privy bucket for his lady-mother to discard when she would waken. Once more and with haste, the little Frauer boy entered his own bedchamber, retrieving his weapon which Jason had gifted him. He slid open the desk cabinet at the opposite side of the room where the drums sat. *For defense against goblins...this morning in the kitchen was just too frightening. Leaving the house without my knife would be a great risk.* Dallion reached into the desk cabinet, grabbing the dagger and the belt for it, then shut the cabinet and left for the hallway wearing unlaced little lord’s shoes.

Dallion hid the weapon within the belt under his big tunic, passing all three bedchambers of his family mates while he made his way down the pink hall to find leave of his house. During this short walk, the boy was tempted to enter Arthan’s bedchamber. He wanted to wake Arthan, to ask his older brother in there to remind him what it was that he had said to him last night, after he’d woken Dallion from the midst of sleep; a very unlikely act for Arthan to carry out in the night. When Dallion approached Arthan’s bedchamber, he creaked the door open ever so slightly. The boy was low in height, but he could still easily view Arthan atop his bed set. He was in the midst of deep sleep, Dallion could see. *Dead looking...* And so he decided to leave his big brother to peacefully rest undisturbed. *I’ll ask him about it all when I return home later today.* Dallion shut the door, leaving his snoring older brother to sleep; *sleep,* known to be Arthan's foolishly favorite activity.

Dallion opened the front door of the household gently, and then after his exit, he shut it all the same, very gently as to not disturb his sleeping family. Dallion climbed up upon the rocking chair beside the door outside the house. He sat here awaiting Sir-Paladin John, as he did every morning on lesson days. Rocking and rocking back and forth as the city folk of the High District passed by in front of him, beyond the garden and little gate to the family's property. Perhaps Dallion should have worn a tunic made of lighter fabric, like the silk blue Frauer House ones he and his brothers possessed; as he felt uncomfortably warm already. The day was not only brighter than of norm, surprisingly it had been hotter as well. *It will be nice and warm for the arena fights tomorrow,* thought Dallion as he sat in the huge chair, shifting his weight back and forth and back and forth.

Finally Sir-Paladin John approached, wearing his coat and silly golden breast armor atop it. *Even though it's hotter than the inside of a volcano today!* When the knight approached the gate to the family's house, he unlatched the top bit of the black iron entrance, opening it wide.

"Come, boy!" yelled John.

Dallion hopped down from the moving chair and jumped all the way past the wooden steps down to the front pathway hoping his belt wouldn't come loose. He walked through the little garden area pulling his pants up, ignoring the sad and lonely steed Pax inside the miniature stable to the left side. The horse neighed as Dallion passed the small structure containing the animal. When Dallion approached the knight, he said up to him, "John! It's hotter than the inside of a volcano today."

Sir-Paladin John closed the gate after Dallion went through it, and then down Silver Street the two of them walked, westward to make way to the Institution.

"Jason won his fight! I thought there was a goblin in the kitchen when I'd woken this morning, but it was just Jason returning from his fight."

The child and the knight spoke as they walked through the crowds of the rich folk upon Silver Street. "I know, I saw the entire duel, my boy; a *duel,* not a fight…call it what it is."

Dallion was struggling to keep up with Sir-Paladin John, so the child reached his hand out to grab ahold of the knight's. With a gloved hand, John led Dallion to the school as they walked and spoke to each other.

The knight asked the boy, "So your brother was just returning home before I arrived just now?"

"Not so long ago, yes. I thought it was a goblin broken in."

John spat and wiped some sweat from his forehead. Dallion thought perhaps John's big graying yellow beard was just damp from a mornings bathing, but now the little one saw it was all sweat. "So then your brother spent all night celebrating and into the morning, when he should have been spending his time resting. I hope he's recovering now, getting some good sleep, as he'll need it for tomorrow."

Dallion walked faster to keep up with John's long strides, trying his best to hold onto the man without being dragged like a dead animal after a hunt. The traffic of folk for today had been much denser than the average lately. "*Fine weather brings out the folk from their homes,*" his father, Lord Edward, would say. Dallion just remembering this now.

So many folk, so difficult to move through their big bodies and still manage to grip on to John's giant hand. The suffering soon ended, and Dallion was able to give his little legs a rest when they finally approached the front steps to the Institution (or "*school,*" as many folk would refer to the structure as).

"I'll retrieve you in six hours, boy. Enjoy today's trip."

Dallion turned around after jumping up upon the first of the steps. He only saw John's backside, him walking further and further away. "Goodbye, John! Where are you off to today?"

John was quickly gone, though; lost in the crowds of Silver Street. Dallion rubbed at his belly, realizing now how hungry he was.

The child jumped up and up like a rabbit, hopping up the steps of the Institution. As he climbed, the little one was thinking of the breakfast to come and thinking of what John had just said too right as he left him. *"Enjoy today's trip."* Dallion had to think very hard on what this meant, what it could mean. He came up to the last step, at the very top by the big entryway doors. This was when he finally remembered what this *"trip"* was that his mentor had referred to. *I'm silly... The class is to journey to the Great Keep today.* Dallion had forgotten all about his class trip to the king's house.

His father would have greatly wanted him to wear finer clothes for a journey such as this; for Lord Edward Frauer said one should always represent the family house when inside the Great Keep. Dallion's House Frauer silks were his finest attire; sadly, today he dressed himself in an old woolen winter shirt he'd acquired when he'd been seven years of age, along with his sleeping pants that he had never changed out of after awakening from his bed this morning. *Mother would be angry with me, Father disappointed. Why didn't John say anything of my outfit? He'd known where the class was going today. He'd seen me in this unfit garb!* Luckily Dallion's mother and father had no knowledge of today's upcoming class journey. As Dallion made his way into the school, he decided it would be best to not mention this trip to Lord Edward and Lady Sophia, not ever. When they catch sight of what he's wearing for the day, after telling them of his visit to the Great Keep after his return home later, that was when they'd make harsh comments and perhaps even punish Dallion for this sloppy attire choice.

He quit acting like a bunny rabbit and quit thinking of his family and his current wardrobe. Dallion waddled through the thick unlocked doors to find his classmates in the entry hall of the school: a grand hall with a dome shaped ceiling. This ceiling, and all walls, thriving with color from artwork crafted by the hands of the very children that the Institution had taught throughout the decades. Dallion looked to the far end of the hall by where the privy tunnel could be found alongside the circular wall. Just beside the door to this tunnel was where Dallion's contribution to these walls art had been made. He painted a knight slaying a goblin with a blue sword! He always felt the need to get a good look at his portion of the wall's art when he'd pass through this entrance every morning. He gazed at his goblin now, yellow skinned, bringing a war hammer down upon it's foe, a white knight as the hero stabbed it to death.

"Dallion! Come, come, fall in."

Dallion looked away from the wall to Instructor Nicky. Dallion obeyed his teacher and walked right up beside his classmate last in line, making himself now the very one to be last in the line of students… *Better this way. If ever I have to sneak away, being last in the walking line would always make such a thing much, much easier; all rogues would think this way.* "Instructor Nicky, it's hotter than the inside of a volcano today."

The teacher ignored little Dallion, but a classmate was eager to greet him.

"Hi, Dallion."

Dallion greeted his classmate Barry who he stood beside. "Hi." said Dallion to the fat boy.

Big Barry asked Dallion, "Are you excited for the class journey?"

"No, it will be boring. I don't care about the keep."

Instructor Nicky said, "Dallion! Don't speak in this way. We won't have you spoiling the mood for the rest of the class."

Stupid ginger…, thought Dallion. That was what Jason called him at home, whenever Dallion would tell stories of this teacher; a *"stupid ginger."* Dallion knew not to repeat these words to his classmates; and especially not to call Instructor Nicky this name to him.

Before Dallion could apologize for his sentence, old Instructor Maya shouted, "Instructor Nicky, finish organizing them up please!"

Nicky turned away from Dallion to reply to his superior. "That's the last of them… We leave on your word."

"Then be gone! You stay sharp and keep a watchful eye. Class, remember, most important of all, have a joyful time, and learn lots!" The barefooted old lady clapped her hands together once, and then walked away down the dark hall to the music chambers. Instructor Maya left the young, stupid ginger Instructor Nicky to escort the thirty-six children out of the school to lead them northward up Silver Street, where they would find the Great Keep for their visit.

The instructor brought the class outside, down the steps of the Institution, and out upon the crowded street in the High District.

Instructor Nicky held onto Daisy's hand tightly, the tallest student in the class. She held hands with Alex behind her, Alex held onto Demii's hand, and on and on it went. Each one of the thirty-six students locked fingers all the way down the line until it came to Dallion at the end there, with nobody behind him; only big Barry in front whom he held hands with. The instructor trusted each of the students not to let go of each other, not to break off to walk away. Effortlessly any one of them could have kept their hands to themselves, leaving the line, breaking it to drift off, yet they didn't. The children politely obeyed like peaceful little Midlön city folk, undistracted and eager for an adventure to visit to where the king lives!

The street began to steepen the more they walked northward on the winding path. The heat of the sun and this hill-like path was uncomfortable, most all students felt. Dallion's hair from his morning washes had just begun to finish drying, but now appeared all wet again.

"It's so hot..." Dallion complained to Barry walking front of him.

"Won't be long, Dallion!" replied the friendly little thick being.

They held on to each other's sweating little hands so tightly. Dallion felt like he'd been gripping a raw oyster the way Barry's palm felt. He soon forgot all about the boy's sweating sausage-like fingers and oyster-feeling hand; he was dazzled with the size of the keep's tower, growing above, seeming to become higher and higher. Of course Dallion had always seen this tower every day, like most all Ascali folk, yet now that he approached its base... He never truly appreciated its size, its beauty. He couldn't have known how big it truly was, not from his house or where he'd spent his time in the city living, and now he'd finally gotten to see.

"I've never been so far north in Ascali." Barry told Dallion as he held his hand still, still moving forward with the entire class ahead of the two of them on the street.

"It's so big, isn't it, Dallion? So pretty... I bet the tower is more than one hundred feet tall." said Barry, gasping for a breath of air, yet happy as ever.

The children of the Institution moved upward through Silver Street in single fashion, until finally they came to a small path taking them in-between two grand buildings, perhaps shops or taverns (Dallion could not come to realize the purposes of the establishments after his brief inspection of them). The class had left the crowds of Silver Street to now enter the welcoming yard of the council chamber. *Where father works his profession, now Arthan too.*

"I thought we were going to the Great Keep!" shouted bucktoothed little Kevin in the middle of the formation of children. Instructor Nicky had organized the students in a line once again, them now appearing like how Dallion had found the class when he'd entered the school this morning.

After Instructor Nicky grouped the children in this formation, he answered Kevin, "The council chamber *is* a part of the Great Keep. We will enter in through here, for the king is engaging in a private meeting being held within the Throne Hall."

Tall Daisy appeared saddened at what the teacher had just said to Kevin. "So we won't get to meet King Gregory? Or to see the Golden Throne?"

The stupid ginger sighed, looking down to his toenails as he made his reply to the student. "Sadly we will not. The king is busy, and busy *inside* the Throne Hall, so we are unable to enter. But come! There are so many more places within the Great Keep that we can explore! Let us enter, and oh, we shall breakfast here as well! Grand Councilman Lewis says we shall feast on the fine foods from the king's own kitchens. Come."

Instructor Nicky waved the class on over toward the doors to the dome-shaped council chamber as he was walking his way there himself, barefooted like an idiot.

"Hello, sirs." said the instructor to the two spear-wielding honor guards at each side of the iron door.

The guard to the left told Instructor Nicky, "We've been expecting you and your students."

Dallion watched both men in silver armor stomp the butts of their spears to the yard grounds once. The black iron doors swung open immediately, and so the instructor then led the class into the dark tunnel with red glowing lights at its far end. Some students held hands once again, others didn't. It didn't seem all so scary or strange until the doors behind them all had shut! The only light now was the red light at the end of the hallway…or tunnel, what it was called, nobody had known or asked Instructor Nicky.

Dallion heard one student ask the teacher as they walked, "Have you been here before?"

Instructor Nicky said, "No, this is my first time too. I'm just as excited as you all are."

"So how do you know the way to go?" that same child asked the teacher.

Nicky said, "There's only one way to go, silly man. It's a hallway, and we're halfway through, see. We go forward."

Another minute of walking until finally the class came to the glowing red archway, or one could call it a doorless entryway. Dallion, last of the class to walk through this arch, had been just as amazed as his classmates too at what he found past it. As the children walked down the many steps and beside rows of empty seating, most all had their heads tilted upward, admiring and appreciating the beautiful architecture of the room. Ceiling, dome shaped like their school's welcoming hall yet tippled in size here. Upon the rounded ceilings and walls lived many, many torches of pure red flame. The chamber glowed a deep crimson color, not dark or dim though, yet bright and oh so red! *Like the reds of the fire-elementists' garb,* thought Dallion as he descended behind the rest of his moving class. At the base of this chamber sat three lonely metal chairs, all three of them glowing bright red; as was every object, student, guard and piece of wall, floor, ceiling, and the seatings in the chamber too.

Sadly Dallion was soon suffering from boredom the moment he'd been finished inspecting and appreciating the chamber's ceiling and decorative fashion. He had happily gazed upon the beauty as he walked just moments ago, though now only stood bored and craving a form of fun or new sort of amusement.

Daisy said, "I don't like it… They're torches from hell."

Instructor Nicky walked beside Daisy, patting her on the shoulder to comfort her as the students swarmed to gather around the chairs upon the floor. "They are work of the fire-elementists, child, not devilry."

Daisy's best friend, Ellisaria, walked beside her and Instructor Nicky, telling them, "Retilliath torches shine black flames, not red. The king put red torches here because he loves blood so much."

"There's no such thing as black fire!" shouted bucktoothed Kevin, standing atop one of the metal chairs, jumping up and down.

Nicky told Daisy and Ellisaria, "The king chose red-flamed torches because the primary House Royce color is red." Nicky looked on over to jumping Kevin, surrounded by his classmates and friends trying to pull him off of the chair, them all making these actions apart of a sort of game now. "Down from there, little lord!" shouted Instructor Nicky.

As Dallion watched Nicky shuffle past his students to reach Kevin, Barry poked at his arm. When Dallion gave his attention to the fat little boy, Barry said, "Isn't it great? These chairs are for the king, and his brother, and the grand councilman."

Dallion ignored Barry, trying to watch Kevin kick classmates in the shoulders and their chests as they tried to pull him down from jumping upon the seat. Finally, Instructor Nicky reached the boy, grabbed him by the collar of his shirt, and brought him down off of the glowing red chair, gently but quickly. "All of you, calm yourselves!" yelled Instructor Nicky.

None of the children seemed to hear him though, only chatted louder amongst themselves; some began to sing.

"Line up! Line up!" he yelled, clapping his hands together repeatedly as he spoke out loudly to the children. They eventually fell in and went silent. "Peacefully quiet, yes? Say it with me…"

The students, as well as Instructor Nicky, all repeated his phrase, "Peacefully quiet."

"There…thank you for being extraordinary! You are all very well behaved young lords and ladies." The instructor looked to his high surroundings, briefly inspecting the pairs of silent honor guards stationed at all four entrances of the massive chamber. He returned his gaze to his students, telling them, "Well, Grand Councilman

Lewis was meant to meet us here upon our arrival, yet I do not see him." Instructor Nicky tapped at that weirdly oversized chin of his.

Plainly Dallion could see that the instructor was struggling with making some sort of decision, speaking to himself in his own head the way Lord Edward would do at times.

"Very well, yes. We have quite a schedule today, my young lords and ladies. The tour is long, and we still have much to learn back at the Institution scheduled for after we make leave here." Nicky turned himself around to watch the guards up at an arch past the stairs there, then he quickly turned back to the students once again. "Yes, yes. I will search for the grand councilman. Perhaps there's somebody I can speak with whom knows his whereabouts. I expect all of you to behave. Otherwise, these honor guards here, they'll tell me of it! Look at them, they don't look like you'd want to make them angry." Instructor Nicky pointed to the sets of paired silver guards, high up in the distance by the doors in the walls.

Jason has better armor than theirs.

"I'll only be a few minutes. Behave or you will not have breakfast served to you! Remember, *peacefully quiet.*"

Instructor Nicky ascended a flight of steps. He ran up and up, past many rows of benches for where the councilmen must seat themselves during sessions.

Dallion watched him have a brief word with the honor guard at the exit. *They look more like statues than real men…* And then he watched Nicky go through the arch. Immediately after their teacher had disappeared, the class began chatting once again, quietly though and without climbing upon the chairs at the center of the grand room. Dallion heard Alex talking to Daisy just a few heads over in the line, but he was unable to see the two. "No, Alex, the guards will hurt us."

"They won't hurt us. You just think that because you're a girl! They'll only do something if we try to leave through up there." Barry poked Dallion in the arm. "Dallion, isn't this room-"

Dallion shoved the boy's hand away, trying to listen in closer on his other classmates speaking. "I could escape if I wanted to… I'm not afraid to try. I'm not a coward, you little girl." Alex told her.

Sadly, Dallion's painful boredom caused him a craving for some satisfying conflict. Dallion stepped out of the line of students. He walked closer over by Alex and Daisy. "If you're not afraid to try to leave, then do it, Alex." Was Dallion attempting to provoke the boy? Attempting to impress Daisy by antagonizing little Alex? Not even he knew; he was just truly bored and deciding to act a fool. *I'm Dallion Frauer. I can do anything I want…just like Jason. I do what Jason would do.*

Alex said, "I'm not afraid. I just don't want my mother and father mad with me, you idiot."

To that, Dallion said, "I think you're just scared, like how you're scared of goblins. Why would you talk about it if you're not gonna do it?"

Alex's eyes began to glisten slightly, but the boy managed to wipe the upcoming tears away before they'd been able to drip out onto his cheeks. He said to Dallion, "You leave here if you aren't scared to try then. You always say you're secretly a rogue? Prove it, idiot. If you really do assassinate bandits with your brother, then you show us your rogue-craft! Idiot, idiot, liar."

Dallion looked away from Alex standing there beside Daisy. He backed himself up three paces, now inspecting the set of guards high above all the students, far up those steps. They'd been guarding the archways, standing there as still as statues, same as the set of guards behind Dallion at that entryway up there too in the back, and the ones to the left side of the chamber, and also the pair the right side at that gap in the rounded wall. Dallion looked to his closer surroundings. There was an iron door at the base of the room here, low by where all the students were standing just now. It was built directly in front of the three chairs in the center, with no guards stationed to watch it.

Dallion looked to Alex, smiled, and then looked to tall Daisy, smiling even bigger now. He waddled over past the chairs to inspect the door closer.

"It's going to be locked." one of Dallion's classmates had said from the line of standing children.

Dallion tapped the iron with his knuckles and then pressed his ear to the big metal door. A year ago, he'd seen a painting at the museum of a thief breaking into a secret chamber to find treasure; this was what the thief had looked to be doing in the painting, listening in on a vault door.

"Dallion, what are you doing?" yelled a girl from the line.

"He knows what he's doing." said Kevin, reminding the class, "He's a rogue!"

Dallion pressed his palms to the door, praying to Aeon, *Please let it be open, please let it be open…*and open it was. He used a little force to gently push against the iron. It creaked open a bit with a slight hissing sound of the iron on stone sliding.

Dallion smiled, turning around, whispering "I've unlocked it."

The class was in awe! Dallion took a moment to look upon the honor guards up top there, them not paying Dallion or the class any bit of attention, only strangely guarding their entrances. *Perhaps Alex was right? Maybe the guards will only act if I'm to attempt to leave through their exits up there?*

Dallion refused to let boredom consume him. Even if this meant getting into trouble from Instructor Nicky, so long as the man didn't inform old Instructor Maya or the Frauer family. *Nicky never tells Mother and Father anything I do. He's too scared of Jason.* Dallion took one last look upon his classmates standing there in the line, and then he was gone! Slipped right through the cracks of the iron door, and then shut it right behind his little self. He blinked once, twice, and a few more times to try and rid the redness from his brain. It took a minute or so for his eyes to adjust as he stood there with his body weight pressed against the door he'd just walked through. He was leaning against it, closing his eyes and then opening them over and over again until he no longer saw the color of redness woven into all within his sight. The torches of this hallway, *thank Aeon*, had been blazing a standard fiery color, not that disturbing crimson of the council chamber. As his eyes were still adjusting, Dallion could faintly hear the voices of his classmates speaking inside the chamber beyond the door at his back, as it was still opened slightly. "Why's he tryna escape?" Dallion smiled, enjoying hearing himself being talked of. "He's not escaping. He's hunting goblins!" said some boy from the class.

Dallion finally removed himself from the door to begin walking forward down the stone hallway. Many doors to the left and to the right had been built within the walls of this hall. The boy didn't even know where he'd been going or what his desired destination should even be. He wasn't looking for his stupid instructor; the ginger would just become mad if he found Dallion away from the class. He wasn't looking for gold or jewels or any valuables to steal… *I'm a rogue of the light. I do not use my crafts for the darkness of evil or for wicked thieving reasons,* Dallion had to remind himself this after he took a glance inside of a room with an open door. The little chamber was filled with tables topped with statues of knights all the size of children's toys! Dallion looked away and resumed his walk down the hall before he was tempted to take one of the statues to examine and maybe play with for a little bit of time. No time, though; he had to find where it is he was walking to and why. *I am hungry, though!* thought the boy.

At the end of the hallway Dallion came to a flight of stairs leading up one level, with another flight beside it leading downward. There was another turn to enter a hallway to the left side and the same to the right as well. Dallion randomly selected the stairs leading higher for reasons unknown even to him. He walked up and came to a hallway matching the one he'd just ascended from. His options were to walk straight ahead down the hall or to walk down the one to the left, or right…or descend back down the steps, and lastly to also continue climbing up and up. Dallion chose to walk up more stairs; he did this passing six floors, until he was finally too tired to continue on upward any longer.

He rested against a wall and on his butt, breathing heavily trying to regain some strength. As he sat there dripping sweat, he listened in carefully to some echoing noises coming from above. He tucked some of that curly hair behind his ears as so he could get a better listen. *Voices…footsteps…louder, and louder!* There were two men making their way down the stairs, the stairs that were only a few feet off away from Dallion. Now he would absolutely need to use his rogue-like skills if he wanted to remain undetected. Dallion hastily yet quietly ran down the hallway as far off as he could, away from the staircase. He ran and ran, quickly yet light on his feet as so he wouldn't make loud noises. He ran past a small red carpet and around the corner into an entirely new hallway. He discontinued running when he made his way past this corner; now resting flat against the wall, he stood waiting to hear where the folk would move to next after coming down the flight of steps. He was too far off now to hear anything though, so he peeked his head around the corner. At the opposite end of where he stood now, Dallion glimpsed two men in brown robes descending, probably councilmen or servants. They walked down the steps onto the level Dallion had been upon now, but then they simply continued walking down more steps, descending further to the below floors now out of view once again.

He was satisfied with himself now, confident he could move anywhere he wanted throughout the Great Keep, unseen. *I've evaded them successfully!* he happily screamed to himself in his head. His happiness soon turned to shock and a bit of fear maybe when the door beside him burst open (in truth, it didn't burst open or open irregularly in any way; Dallion only felt it had violently slammed open because he had been so very near it and obviously hadn't expected such a thing to happen just then and there).

"Who are you? You shouldn't be here!" yelled the servant man wearing beige robes, carrying a silver tray with bones atop it. Dallion did very well not to hesitate. He ran right through the man's legs, almost tangling himself in his dangling robing. The man still held the tray, head turned around like an owl as he stood there with his legs spread wide. He watched little Dallion sprint his way down the hall; he was speechless now.

Dallion's fear soon tuned to a strength rush. He found his blood flow! He wasn't fearful at all now, only craving to run and run until he could no longer do so. Shortly after he discovered this satisfying strength, though, he sadly let fear enter his mind again; a different sort of fear though, one seeming unfamiliar, yet very familiar too in a strange way. The sprinting boy wasn't afraid of who could be chasing him, or who he would find to discover him; not of who would punish him for this foolishness and not even of any goblin encounter or conflict with dangerous guards. Dallion was becoming scared of the Great Keep itself, as if he'd been trapped in a bad dream where the walls and very floor was the enemy. Here and now, no matter which hall he turned down, every one of them looked the same. The same halls, same doors, and very same long carpets in the centers of each of them. He felt he'd been lost in a maze from a horror tale. Each hall felt like a duplicated illusion of the previous one. Dallion tried to escape the frustration of it all by checking some doors, searching for another opened one like from when he had seen that room containing all of those fascinating statues. Every door that the boy tried to enter through though had been locked tight; except for a privy chamber, only that didn't lead anywhere! *Trapped...* thought little, panicking Dallion as he stood there watching water drip from the sink used to clean one's self after pooping and or pissing.

Dallion left the privies to find another route to wherever it was he was intending to go. *I don't care if I'm to be in trouble anymore... Perhaps I should try to find Instructor Nicky.* Though, Dallion came to realize he was just thinking nonsense anyhow. By this mark in time, his teacher was more than likely searching for him already. Instructor Nicky wouldn't have noticed Dallion's absence when he would return to the council chamber with the grand councilman... but Dallion's classmates, he assumed, would instantly tell the instructor what Dallion had done, how he had left through the big metal door. *Nicky probably has had the grand councilman form search groups for me. They'll find me soon.* Dallion was too eager to just sit and wait to be found and punished though. *If I search for them while they search for me, then I'll be found faster.* Dallion resumed walking down the hallways, checking doors to discover if they'd been locked or not.

Dallion ascended some more stairs, continuing to walk in search for his classmates or Nicky or anyone now who could assist him in finding a proper route to...somewhere. He found another iron metal door, though! Very similar to the one that he had left the council chamber through, only four times as small. *Maybe this leads back to the council chamber?* Dallion asked himself as he pressed his palm to the iron to see if the metal would move. Sadly, Dallion had been nowhere near the council chamber, yet he hadn't known this terrible fact. He hadn't known truly how far through the Great Keep he had been moving about all this time. All his running, climbing stairs, and turning down so many different hallways, he was far off from where he thought he had been. This familiar feeling door though, and his great hopes...all of it had led the boy to believe this door could very well have brought him back to the council chamber where he would find his class, his friends, and Instructor. *If I'm lucky...the class will not have told Instructor Nicky anything of my disappearance. If that is what has happened, then perhaps I can sneak back into the formation without him even having notice! I'll have left and returned unnoticed... just like a true rogue.*

Dallion pushed both palms against the door, finding that, unfortunately for him, it had been unlocked and opened for his entry. He stepped through the door into a black, unlit room no bigger than his washing room at home. At the opposite end of this dark room, there'd been an archway to a balcony; a balcony with much light shining upon it. Dallion quietly slid the iron door shut behind him, then he walked his way through the darkness to step through the archway into the light of the sun. There wasn't any light from the sun though, only more torchlight. Dallion walked onto the little indoor balcony, disappointed; another route led to an end just like the privies. He was too small to see over the railing of the edge, but he could see through it! They looked like stone bars, like bars from a dungeon cell, only huge and made of rock instead of metal. In between the gaps of these stones, Dallion could see what lay below. He couldn't view the entire chamber, but he saw the hall was massive. Under the balcony, Dallion could see bits of the giant golden chair. *The Golden Throne,* Dallion kept reciting in his head.

In front of the golden-colored chair were three men, two of them sword fighting, and one of them just watching the battle. *I'm in the Throne Hall! Daisy will be so excited when I describe this to her. After I tell the class I had broken into this room, I'll be known as the sneakiest man in the city.* Dallion held onto the stones with each hand as he watched the fighting men. *Is that the king fighting?*

Dallion watched a man in a full set of blue plate armor, swinging a golden sword as if the weapon weighed the same as feathers.

The bald man he swung at wore a maroon leather chest piece, as well as red leather boots, matching gloves, and hideous tiger pelt pants. His cape was the most noticeable piece of his attire, *crimson* alike the torches of the council chamber. Sadly for the man with the cape, he had stepped upon the moving fabric while trying to dodge an attack from the one in blue armor. The caped man fell backwards, landing his ass right at the steps of the Golden Throne beside where his brother stood over him.

"Ready to try without the cape?" Lord-Steward Arol Royce asked his brother as he stood over him, this brother of his, the king, flat on his back and without breath.

King Gregory rose as quickly as he could, using his sword to support his body weight as he stood himself back up to his feet. "I'll be wearing the cape as well as the crown! I want to practice with the crown."

To that, Dallion heard the king's brother say, "No crown. You should be focusing on the dueling, not keeping apparel from slipping off your head."

The king spat upon the floor of the Throne Hall as his opponent in the blue constantly twirled his sword throughout the air across from him.

Arol Royce said, "Should be focusing on *pretending* to duel, I should have said."

The king looked away from his opponent, to his brother who just had insulted him. King Gregory took his brother's advice, though, peacefully…sort of. "Fine!" shouted the king. "No crown." The king unclasped the hooks upon his shoulders. "No cape." The crimson-colored fabric fell to the granite floor. "I don't look very *kingly* now, do I?" Gregory Royce asked his brother and the blue knight.

Arol Royce answered his brother before the knight in blue could. "It wasn't my idea for you to fight in the arena tomorrow… or play fighting, pretend fighting; whatever it is you call this game of acting that you're so fond of."

"Might I remind you that I led the rescue at Pirates Landing?" the king said to Arol.

"Still never cut a man." Arol said in reply to his brother.

"I've had truthful duels before!" the king shouted back, throwing his sword to the floor.

Arol shook his head negatively. "And you've still never been cut nor been bruised."

The knight in blue removed his helm, asking the king and his brother, "Are we taking a rest?"

The king said to Arol, "I've dueled Lucifer Gray."

Arol laughed, saying to that, "Which wasn't one of your truthful duels you speak of… You had paid Lucifer to allow you to win, and he was foolish enough to accept the payment, just like this joker here."

The knight in blue sheathed his golden sword, the sword matching his golden hair. "Don't call me joker… I'm Sir Marcu-"

"I know, Marcus Magic, Knight of Many Magics. King Gregory and I, we've done this before, as you know, and all of your sire's past opponents had tailored their fighting styles for what makes the best of shows. After the time comes for my brother to disarm you three minutes after first strike, do not retrieve your weapon from the floor so quickly. Tomorrow you must roll through the sands, dodge some of my brother's attacks with strafes and some of those sidesteps you did before. The battle will truly intensify if you spend as much time as you can, unarmed."

The king asked Arol, "I'm supposed to be the one impressing the crowds… Perhaps I should be the one who's to be disarmed?"

What these three men had been talking of down there, Dallion hadn't the slightest bit of notion. Just a minute ago they'd been dueling, and now they were just standing there chatting! *So boring…* He continued watching them as the three of them spoke on, waiting for them to resume the fighting. Sadly though, Dallion had seen that the one with the gold hair in the blue armor had put his sword away into his belt. This blue knight was speaking now.

"How am I to disarm you though?" Dallion heard him ask.

The king said, "The same way I would be meant to disarm you, a strike to the knuckles, light though, of course."

The knight told the king, "I would rather not. Even with a mailed hand, my golden sword could still damage you. I would strike you with a tourney sword, though. I do not think the decision for this year's event to be dealt in live steel was so wise, not if *you* are to be partaking."

The king's brother looked annoyed now, even Dallion could see from way up there on the balcony. Arol said to Marcus, "You aren't being paid to give your input on the matter."

Marcus smiled with his hands placed upon his armored hips. "You aren't paying me gold to be your bitch either, so don't speak to me like one, Lord-Steward."

The king's brother approached the knight in blue. "The *gold* is for you to take in return for letting my brother, your king, destroy you in the sands tomorrow, not to question his decisions. I will remind you this gold is to buy your silence as well, for if you speak of this to anybody, you will suffer the most dire consequences. You seem like a proud man. I'm a bit in surprise you'd accept money for a planned loss."

The king approached Arol now to stand in between him and Sir Marcus. "Don't speak to him like this, Arol, for I've enjoyed my time with Marcus here." The king placed a gloved palm on the knight's shoulder plate.

"I seem proud? Well, I think gold sounds more fun than pride, wouldn't you brothers both agree? I love gold, and I love kings..." Marcus said, grinning.

Arol spat. "Disgusting, horny men." he said to his brother and Sir Marcus after taking a few steps away from the two of them.

Marcus smiled, looking to the king, yet speaking to Arol who was now standing back by the throne. "Don't have worry, Lord-Steward, any secret of the king's is safe with me. If that grim Lucifer Gray can keep a mouth shut about play dueling your brother here, I can too. How many men have you done this with, Lord-Steward? Sire?"

Dallion couldn't handle himself, the boredom, the suffering. Only seeing the last bit of the battle below not only a few moments ago! He felt he was teased. It was unfair and all horrible, so he decided to try to convince the king and the knight to fight once again. *They'd just been doing it, and the swords are right there. Maybe they'd do it if I tell them!*

Arol Royce said to Marcus, "Too many times… There's a reason why the realm thinks Gregory here to be one of the finest swordsman alive."

"FIGHT! FIGHT!" shouted Dallion down to the three.

His voice echoed throughout the entire Throne Hall oh so very loudly. Dallion was not expecting to hear himself at such a high projection; gave himself a bit of a fright. The faces painted upon the men below had also not felt so pleasant to the boy. Confusion and anger flashed through the eyes of both Royce brothers, and Marcus Magic just stood there not particularly happy or saddened, just trying to piece together who he'd been looking at up there. Suddenly Dallion felt he had made an error. He removed himself from in between the opening in the stones so he would no longer be seen. He stood frozen for some seconds, trying to think on his options, how many he had, if any at all.

"Marcus, get him." Dallion heard the king's brother command.

Dallion glanced through the slits in the stones once more. The king stood down beside Marcus there, until…the blue knight had vanished, leaving behind a cloud of violet smoke! Dallion was horrified when regularly he would have been dazzled at such a sight. *What is happening? It's all so fast.*

Dallion removed himself from the stone once again so he could now make his escape. He only had one route he could take, and that was back through the arch behind him, back to the iron door past the black room, into the hallway and then…to where? He hadn't known, but he knew first he had to get himself into that hallway. *Step by step. Don't try to figure it all out at once,* thought he, turning around to run. When he made to take his fourth step, the air in front of him came alive with many sparks; irregular sparks, colored blue and pink. A cloud of smoke had pulsated outward and surrounding the sparking lights now, and within its horrific beauty emerged the blue knight. He stepped out of the clouds, completely revealing himself fully now. He hastily knelt down, gripping Dallion by his little arms.

"Got you!"

A blue flash of light had blinded Dallion briefly. He could see again now yet was distracted from choking on smoke. When the boy wiped the tears from his eyes, he'd seen now that he had been standing in front of the Golden Throne. He felt as if he had to vomit, and so he did, yet only fluids spewed out from his mouth, as his stomach contained no food within prior to his retching. He breathed heavily, hoping no more vomit would come forth as the knight stood behind him with his iron hands placed over the boy's shoulders. Dallion's mother would always tend to him with a rag and a fresh mug of water if he ever had retched. These three men had not acknowledged the boy becoming ill.

"How long have you been up there?" Arol asked Dallion.

My head is in pain, and I am so dizzy.

Arol approached red-eyed Dallion, now gripping his mouth with a hand of ringed fingers. "Speak! Who are you?"

Dallion began to tear in both of his eyes. His legs gave out, and he almost fell, saying, "I feel ill."

Marcus held him in place, him doing his best to stay silent but failing in that now. "Be gentle. He's not even ten years old. How old are you?"

Dallion twisted his head away from the lord-steward's grasp on his jaw, ignoring Marcus's question too. Dallion placed his palms into his eyes to absorb his leaking tears.

The king asked, looking away, "No family emblem on any of his clothing?"

"No, probably a servant's son or visiting student from the school." Arol said this to his brother.

The king looked Dallion in the eyes now, harshly, and then he quickly looked away in disgust. "Better no emblem… Don't ask his name again nor his age. I want him gone, Arol. Make him gone… It seems even my own Throne Hall isn't suited for private times."

Arol turned to his kingly brother, asking him, "Do I look like a sorcerer, a wizard?"

"You've made people disappear from this world in the past, for me…for us. This would be for us too. Now that we're in positions of true power, well, it just makes carrying something like that out all the easier, does it not?"

"Sire, Lord-Steward, participating in a pretend duel I would be a part of, *this* I would not; if I am correct in thinking on what it is you're speaking of." Marcus let loose Dallion, and so the boy dropped to the floor to land on his butt.

Arol's flesh went from warm to hot, veins popping at the neck. He had appeared as if he'd been ready to attack the knight. Arol turned his loose hands to fists, now saying, "Moments ago you claimed any secret of my brother's would be safe with you, yes?"

Sir Marcus stepped backwards a bit away from Dallion lying on the granite. "I'm a knight of Midlön. I cannot take part in this. Do not attempt to persuade me with more gold either."

The king walked to his brother to stand closely by him. King Gregory put his hand upon his brother's chest, and then he briefly placed his head upon his shoulder too, in the same precise manner as how Dallion would place his head on his lady-mother's when he'd been sad. The king removed his head from resting upon Arol, and then he looked to him in his matching maroon Royce eyes. After this brotherly gaze, King Gregory brought his attention to Sir Marcus Magic.

King Gregory stepped right over Dallion to walk to Marcus, eyes on the knight, never on Dallion again; refusing to look upon the crying child.

"Sir Marcus, our time together was magnificent… I will hate to see it spoiled over this." A tear fell from the right side of King Gregory's cheek. He approached Sir Marcus Magic for a hug, sobbing into his golden hair.

Arol gave Dallion a brief inspection as the king gave the knight a grand hug. Arol shook his head again in the negative fashion, and then he walked around the boy to approach the hugging men. "The ride to the city in my carriage… I've never felt more comfortable with somebody in my entire life, Marcus."

While King Gregory grasped Marcus tightly, Arol walked up beside the two of them with his red dagger unsheathed. He pierced the tip of the dagger into the knight's neck. Marcus bloodily squirmed, still standing as the king held him in place while his brother Arol removed the dagger from Marcus, and then put it back into his throat again. Dallion witnessed much of the murder. The boy's cries diminished to silence as he sat there watching the knight die. Eyes widened and mouth sealed shut, Dallion sat there as the struggle was brought to the floor. The dying man's shaking legs eventually stiffened. He spat up a gulp of blood, then died as his throat leaked more of the red fluid from the many freshly made holes.

King Gregory stood tall now, wiping blood from his hands and tears from his face. Arol was rising off the floor, removing his overcoat as it became drenched in Sir Marcus's gore. When he came to his feet, Arol told his brother, "We need to be sure nobody will enter. We'll be in here for quite some time."

Arol looked to Dallion, and that was when the boy found fear of the answer to this bad question he thought on now, *Does he want to hurt me?* Dallion had never seen a man die…nor looked into the eyes of a grown man who'd wanted to hurt his little self. This had been perhaps the most fearful moment in the boy's time alive in this world. He asked himself, *What would Jason do?* Jason told him that when a man was afraid, he could be at his most dangerous. *I'm afraid now, so that makes me dangerous?* He kept asking himself in his head as the steward Arol walked closer to him, *What would Jason do? What would Jason do?* Dallion removed the white dagger from his belt, hidden under his white tunic. He found his strength again! Rising now as quick as he could onto his feet, he screamed as he rushed at Arol, the dagger pointed straight for the man's belly. He ran as fast as he could past the king, right at the armed lord-steward, ready to do what Jason would do.

12
GAME DAY

Lord Edward Frauer was seated upon the head chair, sweating at the end of the family table. He watched the entrance door to his household, tapping his finger against the wood which he sat behind. Arthan brought the jug of wine to the table, filling three mugs for himself, Lord Edward, and Lady Sophia. Arthan poured, then seated himself close to Lord Edward, the same moment Jason with a pot of potatoes in hand approached the table. After placing the pot down upon the surface, Jason took his seat across from Arthan beside the empty chair where Dallion regularly would sit. "Don't be so negative in thinking, Father. He's at that little skinny one's household, more than likely. Mother, what's his name?"

"William." answered Lady Sophia. She walked to her husband and two sons at the table, carrying a tray of bloody, undercooked mutton and onions she had just pulled from the oven in the kitchen area. She placed the tray down for the family, excluding Dallion, to dine on its contents.

Jason used the copper fork to pierce a slab of the pink flesh. He brought the bit of dead animal dinner to his plate from the tray, cutting into it the moment he set the bit upon the ceramic.

Jason spoke as he ate, telling his lord-father, "William, yes. He'll be at William's now."

Lord Edward served himself a piece of the meat, as did Arthan, and lastly, Lady Sophia grabbed herself a large forkful.

Jason was still speaking, asking his mother now, "He spent four days and nights at that one's house some weeks ago, yes? Slept there each night and never came home?"

"That's right." said Lady Sophia, crunching down on the almost raw onions.

Jason continued on, "Well, there it is. He's having another night party with his little friend."

Edward thought to himself, *Only, Dallion always tells us of his plans for his "night parties" prior to the night of the event...* Edward nodded with his son, then took a sip of wine before beginning his night's meal.

Before the sun had fully lowered on this day, Sir-Paladin John had made visit to the Frauer household as he did most days during the hour of darkening, bringing Dallion home from his lessons learned at the Institution. Today though, Paladin John made his appearance without Edward's son in his company.

Where's he gone off to? Edward had asked the holy knight when he arrived there alone at the front steps of the house.

John had told Lord Frauer, *"When I saw the boy wasn't out front the school waiting, I went in to find him inside."* The young instructor in the welcoming hall had told Sir-Paladin John that he nor elder Instructor Maya had made notice of Dallion gone at any mark in the time during the day's class's trip or during the return, nor had the students made mention of anything in relations to Dallion sneaking off or misbehaving.

"Well where is he then?" Paladin John had demanded to know from these teachers.

The instructor older in age, the one named Maya, reminded John that, *"When the students are dismissed, they're free to leave... If you aren't present out front to retrieve the child at the dismissal time, well then, that seems an error on your end, does it not? Sir-Paladin, this is why you should have yourself out front side before the dismissal bells are rung... Otherwise, the child could go off anywhere within the city.*

Before John had left the Institution after Maya's words there, the redheaded instructor, the one younger in age, said to the paladin, *"The child more than likely went home with another one of his classmates. This happens often with the students. They're eager to spend recreational time together after dwelling in these halls throughout the morning and midday."*

After John told this entire tale to Lord Edward at the Frauer household doorstep, Edward had welcomed the paladin inside to speak while they awaited Dallion's return. *"Best I take walk to find the boy. I'll double back to the Institution, get a list of the children he's close with amongst the class. I'll head to their household's to find which one he's having his play at. If we're false in our thinking, and he isn't dwelling at another one of these households, best to know early rather than late."*

Edward let John go walking after that, thinking, *What a grim way to end a dialogue... If Dallion isn't questing for goblins at a friend's household, then where would he have gone to?*

When John had left him to make way westward on Silver Street, Edward immediately returned inside to brief his wife and sons on the matter. Jason had stood in the kitchen consuming a filled jug of water, laughing while saying, *"Wherever he is, he'll return home eventually. Little adventurer that one wants to be."* Jason resumed drinking his water.

Sophia only said, *"All children return to their mothers."*

It was only Arthan that gave Edward a look of any shared concern. That was all hours ago... Edward sat now at the head of the table as the four of the Frauers consumed their late dinner. He had been watching the door for a while now, waiting for Dallion to come through happy as ever to tell tales of goblin hunting.

Jason chewed his food hastily, still speaking as he took each bite. "Come to think on it, I'd prefer he didn't spend repeated days in a row as guest within these other family households. It's the fathers that worry me... Some of these family men this day of age, they love little boys a bit too much. I'd slay a bastard if I found Dallion is sleeping nights in another man's house so often 'cause he's been getting touched, enjoying it so that—"

Lady Sophia stopped his speaking, "Enough of that! Why speak that way?" She sat asking her son.

Jason finished the contents of his glass of water, then he apologized. After his apology, he said, "I must piss. Excuse me!"

"Jason!" yelled Sophia with a stupid sort of smile upon her face.

"Sorry, Mother, all of this water is making me leak every ten minutes!" Jason excused himself from the family table to make way to the washing room found in the pink hallway.

Edward sat silent, as Arthan was too; both of them trying hard to enjoy their sort of raw meals while they thought on where Dallion could possibly be. Sophia sat eating happily with her mind on her new found idea of knitting scarves for all three of her sons, her husband and herself too; for the upcoming winter of course. Jason, all day and night, had his mind on tomorrow's upcoming game day he would be partaking in, prepared to win the title of *Shield to the King*, after successfully defeating all foes in the battle royale! Jason and Lady Sophia, though, now joined Lord Edward and Arthan in bringing their minds to missing Dallion, after they all heard the hard knocking sound coming from the entrance door.

They'd been midway through the dinner meal when all four Frauers heard the *Knock! Knock! Knock!* all thinking of Dallion. As Sophia was turning herself around to get a glance at the door, Arthan had already risen, walking to unlock it from under the handle. *Knock! Knock, knock!* Edward stood himself up from the table and chair, almost spilling the contents of his drink. He watched his son slide the latch to the side, then grip the handle above it to open the door…all actions seeming to happen ever so slowly. Lord Edward's eagerness had made the world appear to operate differently, slower.

Knock! Knock! came the sound again.

The lord of the house took a deep breath inward, then he let loose the air within his lungs after the door had fully been opened by Arthan, revealing the guest. He seated himself now, sipping more wine as he watched his tall niece there in the doorway, hugging Arthan with a big smile planted upon her face.

"Cousin!" said she loudly and happily, gripping Arthan so tight that his face and neck reddened.

"Tillsy!" Arthan yelled, struggling to breathe as he choked on the hairs of her bear fur cloak that was smothering his face.

Tillsy Frauer remained hugging Arthan at the doorway, yet began greeting the remainder of the family without letting her cousin loose first. Still hugging Arthan, she yelled at the dinner table, "Aunt Sophia! Uncle Edward! Hello, hello!"

With a mouthful of half cooked dinner, Lady Sophia said to her niece, "Tillsy, hello! I love your new hair. It's almost as short as Jason's." Lady Frauer unknowingly spat out half her dinner as she spoke toward Arthan and Tillsy at the entrance. Tillsy Frauer used her foot to kick the door behind her shut. Her grip tightened on Arthan as she asked to all, "Where *is* Jason?"

"I'm here." said he, coming round the corner with wet hands from the washing room. Tillsy let loose Arthan, shoving him to the wall so she could run to Jason.

Edward drank more wine as he watched his niece go to hug his son by the hallway. Arthan was returning to the chair at the table, trying his best to catch his breath back while Tillsy now smothered Jason, briefly though. She took her head off from Jason's shoulder, letting loose her grip on him. She took a step backwards to look upon him, saying, "Most combatants heal every cut and scratch before game day, but not you?" Tillsy tapped Jason right on the center of his nose where his scabbing slash was, a minor injury.

Jason flinched, then said to her, "You know how much I love those priests." Jason pinched her ear, then he slapped her cheek the way he does to Dallion for play. He then he returned to take his seat at the family table to pour more water for himself and to resume dining.

"Help yourself to anything. We have food and drink plenty." Edward told her, forking more meat.

Tillsy hopped like a toad over to Lord Edward to place a kiss upon his cheek, then she walked her way to her aunt to place a kiss upon her as well. Both Lord Edward and Lady Sophia wiped the red lip paint from their cheeks after the girl walked away from the family table to make her way to the kitchen area.

"Jason, what are we having?" Tillsy yelled, asking him as she searched for the cups within the cabinets beside the oven.

Jason chewed his food, swallowed, then yelled back to his cousin, "I need to fill on water for the tournament tomorrow. It's water for me!"

"When I visit, we drink ale or wine! Jason!" Tillsy returned to the table with two empty ale horns. She made an exaggerated frowning face, expressing it to the sitting family. "Jason will not drink with me?" asked Tillsy, pretending to almost cry.

Edward said, "Come, have a seat and Arthan shall pour you wine. Relax yourself… You've not even removed your cloak or footwear. Take that leather armor off, if you'd like. You can put it beside Jason's mail in his chamber."

Tillsy kindly retrieved an ale horn filled of wine from Arthan at the table, now bringing it with her into the hallway of the house to search for the door to Jason's bedchamber. Edward gulped down the last bit of wine within his mug, looking for Arthan to pour him some more. *Now if I am to have to endure my brother's daughter, I will need much wine in me.*

Edward sipped his newly poured wine while he looked at Arthan and Jason. He said to his family, "Well, this was an unexpected visit. Your uncle, he raised an interesting lady…"

Lady Sophia added in, "And still beautiful as ever. I mean it when I say it, that girl will never grow ugly even in elder days."

From the hallway, and inside Jason's bedchamber, Tillsy shouted to them, "I can hear you all in there! No more compliments!"

Within a minute or so, she returned to the dining area now without her boots, nor her half-cloak; she still wore her leather armor though as if prepared to battle. She took a seat beside Arthan, holding out her half-filled ale horn toward him.

While Arthan dropped his fork to give more refreshment to his cousin, Lord Edward said, "Take those gauntlets off. You're making me nervous. Are we to expect a battle?" Tillsy took a long gulp of wine, holding the horn wearing those leather studded wrist guards and fingerless travel gloves. She wiped her mouth with her wrist-armor. "We're to expect a battle tomorrow, isn't that right?" she said, looking to Jason, smiling.

Jason rubbed at his ankle, saying to Tillsy while smiling back to her, "Not a battle, a slaughter! I'll ring their heads in quicker than ever this year. I've been practicing new technique."

Tillsy raised her horn of wine, drinking more of its contents. Lord Edward raised his mug for the same gesture, and then he drank same moment she did.

Tillsy inspected the empty chair beside Jason, across from her. "Where's Dally? I expected him to greet me at the door all happy and wildlike." Tillsy looked underneath the family table, then brought herself back upward and yelled, "Dallion!" aloud.

Arthan said to Tillsy, "In truth, we actually don't know where Dallion is."

Tillsy laughed at her cousin, then looked to Jason, then to Sophia and then lastly Edward. She glanced at each of them for reassurance that Arthan was jesting. Lady Sophia dropped her utensils into her plate, gripping her mug tightly while telling Tillsy, "William's house or perhaps one of the others, Barry's, or Olef's household or one of the girls even. He's having a night party, more than likely."

When Tillsy finished another gulp of wine, she wiped some droplets from her red painted lips before she spoke. "Oh shit, so you truly don't know where he is?" Tillsy looked to Arthan again.

Edward said to his niece, "He'll be home shortly, or in the morning before the tournament. If we do not speak of it, then we'll soon forget it, causing his reappearance to seem to come quicker. I won't dwell on it. It's making me a bit nervous not knowing his precise whereabouts. There, I've said it. I apologize to you all if I don't appear calm."

Tillsy turned away from Arthan to smile to Lord Edward, raising her horn while doing so. "Cheers, Uncle, what would *you* like to speak of?" Tillsy sipped her drink while Edward thought of a gentle topic of discussion; the rest of the family ate quietly.

"How does my castle?" Lord Edward asked Tillsy.

"You mean *my* castle…my *father's* castle?" she asked him, correcting him and smiling.

Lord Edward winked at his niece. "Ah, it will always be mine, in truth. He still doesn't know half of the hidden passageways throughout the east end of the fortress."

Tillsy then said to him, "Knowledge of hidden passages or not, you passed Bluewood on to him when you chose to live out your days in this fine, fancy house on this fine, fancy street."

Jason looked to Lord Edward, saying in a half-joking manner, "Would have been nice to inherit Fort Bluewood one day from you, Father…" Jason laughed.

Tillsy grabbed a tiny bit of potato and threw it right at Jason's forehead. She said, "No! Mine, mine, mine, my castle." She threw another piece of potato, striking Jason in the nose. He cried out an exaggerated yell of pain as Lady Sophia burst out into laughter.

The family soon then began discussing Tillsy's father, his health, and of the women in his life. "Healthier than ever, and with a new wench every next week." she told them.

"Glad to hear our uncle is doing well and enjoying his time." Jason said to her.

Tillsy explained to the family that her lord-father would have been present for the current night, and for the tourney on the morrow, only he was unable to make visit and attend because of his duties upon the Frauer land where Fort Bluewood sits.

"It's just too much now, for him to leave the lumber yards only for the men to tend to. They're skilled cutters and gatherers, but Father says when he's not round, they act fools. I'm sure he'd love to see you duel, though, Jason. He knows you'll win anyhow. He's seen it before."

Regularly dinnertime would last thirty or forty so minutes, yet this night it seemed to go on and on, unending. Tillsy continued drinking on, which had encouraged Arthan to do so too, attempting to match her pace. On all occasions, chatting had never seemed to end when in Tillsy's presence, and so as the dialogue continued on with the family, so had the drinking. Sophia joined in on the wine consumption with Tillsy, Arthan, and her husband; Jason remained with his water. They spoke, they ate, they drank, but mostly, they drank.

None of the family seemed the least bit weary, even long into the night, that was until Lady Sophia brought Jason out to the front steps with her smoking pipe. Edward, Arthan, and Tillsy were seated upon the chairs at the family table, eating raisin-filled cookies while they spoke ill of the new king, mocking his idiotic, newly shaven head, harshly making comments of his awkward voice and his flamboyant mannerisms. Jason and Lady Frauer had stepped back through the entrance door to the house, reeking of wizard's weed.

"Without me?" Tillsy cried to Jason when she'd smelt them coming inside the household.

Lady Sophia said, "Good night, Tillsy. You can sleep wherever you'd like."

Tillsy watched Sophia dragging her feet into the hallway with reddened eyes.

Jason said, "We'll smoke tomorrow. I'm off to sleep too. It's later in the night than I realized. I'll be off to the arena before the lot of you will even be awake on the morrow. Sleep well, and wish me luck. Tillsy, glad you're here."

With veiny eyes and that rancid smoke odor upon him, Jason walked off to rest within his bedchamber. This gave Edward the notion that perhaps he should gain some sleep as well, and so that was what he now intended to do. He gulped down one last full cup of the purple wine, and then he arose from the head chair.

Tillsy looked at Lord Edward while he stood himself upward. She then snapped her head opposite him now to hastily look Arthan in his eyes. She grabbed her cousin there by his shoulder, tightly, saying to him, "Don't you leave me too. We have much more wine to intake."

Arthan nervously said, "Of course." to his cousin Tillsy.

Edward burped and inspected the plates upon the table. He decided he would clean tonight's mess later in time, perhaps in the morning. He patted Tillsy on her back, saying to her, "You can take the big chair over by where your aunt reads her books and knits. Often she naps there, or you can go sleep upon the bed in the guest chamber, although that chair is often comfier to sleep upon than that old bed in that damp back room. Either way, I'll leave it to you to decide. Good night, Tillsy. Good night, Arthan." Edward left his son and niece to continue their drunken night gossip.

Lord Edward took heavy steps, walking upon the floor of the pink hallway so ready for sleep. He took entry through the blue door, into his bedchamber, all the while with a satisfying belly full of wine. His skunk smelling wife, Sophia, was already deep asleep from her effective act of smoking from the pipe with Jason. Edward blew out the candle beside the bed before burping once again. He collapsed down beside his wife, not caring to undress or set himself under the blankets. Edward Frauer was off to sleep not a minute after his head hit the pillow. A dreamless sleep took hold of him and so off to snoring he was. When he woke to piss, he'd seen that the sun had risen.

I think I may still be drunk… Edward thought, as he lifted himself upward to inspect the spinning bedchamber for sight of Sophia. She was nowhere to be seen within the chamber, though her cooking was being served from the smells leaking through the cracks of the door. Edward wiped the weariness from his eyes with his thumbs as he stepped off from the bed. Wearing yesterday's garb, Edward walked out of his bedchamber and into the washing room. He pissed out all the wine in him, washed his hands, and then his face. In the mirror he watched himself, water dripping from his stubbly chin. Lord Frauer was not happy with his appearance. *I look of hell…* he said to himself in his mind. *Why did I go and drink all of that wine?* he questioned but soon remembered that it was to put his mind off of his missing son.

Edward left the washing room after a fresh face shave, now rushing into the kitchen in hopes he would see his entire family preparing for breakfast; *entire,* meaning Dallion too! From the sounds of it, all in the household had been awake and present in the kitchen or among the dining table. *Much could have happened throughout the night and early morning… Dallion could have appeared!* Edward turned the corner to see Sophia working the frying pan, and only Arthan and Tillsy occupying the table; they'd been playing card games. Dallion was nowhere to be seen, and Jason was away to the arena as he should have been.

"Any word of Dallion?" Edward stood by the hall, asking any and all in the kitchen and dining portions of the house.

Sophia answered, "No, nothing yet."

Edward walked into the kitchen to find some water to have a drink of.

Tillsy said, "Morning, Uncle Edward!"

As Edward passed the table by, he'd seen that his son was half asleep there holding some cards as a bit of drool dropped down to land upon his own leg. Tillsy threw a handful of cards at Arthan's face, then he sprang alive in surprise.

"Ah!" yelled he, knocking over a small mug of goat milk off of the table.

"Arthan! Clean that!" shouted Sophia.

Tillsy said, "Wake up, we're not finished with this game here."

Tillsy took in a gulp of ale from her horn as Arthan cleaned his spill. Edward approached his wife and placed a kiss upon her cheek as she stood there burning the bacon in the pan.

"Good morning, love." said Edward after he pulled his lips away from the side of Sophia's face. He asked her, "My lady, are you not worried of Dallion?"

"He will be at the tournament. He is so very excited to see Jason duel. I know he won't miss it. We shall find him within the arena. If he isn't there, well that's how we'll know there is truly something foul happening."

Edward leaned beside the stovetop where his wife was almost finished with her cooking. Edward told her, "I think that is an ill way of thinking this in. Even *if* Dallion makes an appearance at the arena, there will be thousands of folk there today. We won't find him. If he *isn't* in attendance as you say *could* happen, and there is a problem at hand, wouldn't you rather we know this now than after returning from the arena much later?"

Tillsy decided to throw more cards at cleaning Arthan before giving her input on the subject to her aunt and uncle. "What you say is true, Uncle, but imagine Dallion shows in the arena audience, and then the four of us are off searching the city for his little self while he's there expecting us!"

Sophia said after Tillsy spoke, "Yes, we aren't becoming absent of Jason's duel due to Dallion's foolish tampering with the day's schedule."

Edward appreciated the positive view on the situation from his wife and niece, though for himself, taking no action and carrying on with the day's event as if nothing was out of the norm…felt unsettling.

Edward approached Arthan at the table. He'd been wiping milk off from the deck of cards as his father placed a gentle hand upon his shoulder. "How are you?" Edward asked him.

Arthan answered with, "I'm sleepy."

Sophia brought a tray of burnt bacon and a bowl of oranges to the center of the table. Arthan continued with, "Yesterday morning, I woke feeling dreadfully tired as if I hadn't gotten a good night's rest."

Edward asked him, "Did you recover by acquiring a good night's rest last night?"

Tillsy laughed as she sliced open an orange with her bronze dagger.

Arthan said, "Didn't get to try. Tillsy and I never went off to sleep… We played drinking games out front, waiting to see if Dallion would ever show."

"Arthan wanted to go off to sleep, but I refused to let him! I even wanted to leave the house to go searching for the little demon imp, but Arthan held me back, so we mostly just waited out front there to see if he would ever show."

Edward watched Arthan in his sleepy and saddened manner, consuming his bacon and drink from his new ale horn filled of fresh milk. Tillsy was ripping through the orange skin with her teeth now, juice running down her chin and neck.

Edward assured his son and niece, "We'll find him. He'll be at the arena with one of his companion friends and their family, more than likely. I wouldn't be in surprise if we find him there with Sir-Paladin John. Could even be he's been found by him."

Edward removed his hand from his son's shoulder to make way to the window by the entrance door. He'd been viewing to see where god had placed the sun in the sky now. *A hot day from the looks of it. A bright day, and an early one still…would be a perfect one if Dallion was present in my sight.* Edward gently slapped himself at the sides of his shaven face with the palms of his hands after he finished inspecting the sky out through the glass. He was still trying to rid his body of last night's drinking effects. He turned himself around to tell the family, "Eat quickly, we must be off to the arena soon if we're to find proper seating to our liking."

Sophia gave Edward a look of disgust as she stood scrubbing the pan in the bin of water; Arthan and Sophia sat eating oranges. "Ed! You aren't dressed yet."

Lord Edward brought his attention down to his garb, the apparel he'd slept in through the night. He acknowledged his error, then said to her, "I'll only need a moment, then we must leave."

Lady Sophia said to him, "They can finish eating. They'll only *need a moment."*

"I'm well to depart when you lot are." Tillsy said, sheathing her uncleaned bronze dagger, then lacing up her boots. She said, "I'd prefer some arena food and rum in me anyhow."

Arthan brought the empty plates as well as the remainder of the breakfast food from the dining area to the kitchen wash bin. By the time Tillsy had finished drinking her ale and Arthan had finished assisting Lady Sophia in cleansing the dishes and utensils, Edward was just arriving back into the kitchen, dressed in fresh attire. He'd worn a sleeveless brown tunic, almost colorless, matching his graying hair and eye color. Upon the fabric, in the center of his chest was marked the blue tree of House Frauer. His pants were light silk (light in color, *as well* as in weight) and his sandals were ugly, but they kept the hot air from becoming trapped at his toes.

He reminded his family, "We must leave now, though you three could take a moment to go and dress for warmer weather, for it looks to be a hot day."

Tillsy gripped and shook the leather armoring upon her shoulder. "Nonsense, let us be off."

Arthan and Sophia remained silent, looking at Edward, waiting for him to open the door for them all to take leave.

Edward was the last to exit, shutting the door and locking it behind him. The three passed through the black gate by the garden. Out upon Silver Street they brought themselves, squinting under the light of the sun.

Edward recommended, "Should we search for a walker? Get us four ponies?"

Edward searched the crowds of city folk to find the yellow cloaked men with their rental ponies on the leashes, though there were none in sight. Was difficult to search through the folk to get a good view anyhow; the crowds of the day were thick. *These bright days, how I dread the crowds they spawn,* thought Edward Frauer.

"Forget ponies, Uncle Edward. Let us walk with our legs. Before we come to realize, we'll be right at the spectator gates."

Edward nodded to his niece's quick decision; Arthan and Lady Sophia hadn't seemed to care to give input.

The Frauers made way toward the southeast, down into the Military District, passing by many buildings of metallic appearances. Silver Street smelled of perfume, the Square and Brey Street smelled of foods, whereas the Military District always had not only the *smell,* but the taste of a forge in the air. Ash, iron, coal, and sweat, the four of them embraced it all.

"The Street of War, my favorite portion of Ascali," said Tillsy, smiling at a cluster of wet, hairy men of all ages, crafting shields.

"Smells like Jason's armor." Lady Sophia said.

They approached a familiar winding bend where the four of them knew the arena would be found behind a set of tall twin buildings. They painfully caught notice of the crowd ahead, thickening more and more every second because of the event taking place.

Patiently, the four of the Frauers moved slowly like the way a turtle would make its progress in travel. Many folk were gathered for entry into the arena. Making way inside, depending on time of arrival here, could cost one some great waiting lengths. Finally, they reached a young woman wearing black and yellow robes who held a heavy sack in hand by the walls where the gate was. An inch behind her stood an honor guard with one of those heavy black spears. These two were placed a foot in front of an opened gate meant for spectators to enter and leave by. When they approached her, Lord Edward handed the woman forty golden coins, ten for each of the entering spectators. Through the gates they went and up many flights of stairs with folk completely surrounding them, moving all the while with them. Through and around a sloped, long window-filled hallway bend now they all walked; at its steep and highest end, an honor guard was revealed pointing a spear in the direction of a doorless entryway. The entry led to the roofless center of this grand structure. They were now in the arena's spectator areas, and just in perfect time!

Tournament Master Sisco was making his way to the center of the sands below while folk cheered on, others chatted, some drank, others ate, and some did all four of those actions at once.

"We must find seating fit for a nice view!" Tillsy eagerly shouted.

"What of Dallion?" asked Arthan.

Lady Sophia led the way up some steps, steps leading to more seating choices. She found five empty chairs high up within the crowds, pointing to them for the three to catch sight of. She looked upon Lord Edward and Arthan, telling them with her eyes that was where she decided they'd be dwelling for the event. When they reached the chairs, she had been the first of the four to sit down.

She had told the family as they took their seats, "Five chairs is perfect. If Dallion finds us, he can sit here beside me." Lady Sophia scanned the crowds of folk in search for the walking merchants who sold refreshments, leaf, and weeds. Edward wiped some sweat from his forehead, trying to ignore the thought of Dallion now. It was Jason he was here for… *Jason made plan to be here though. Dallion, wherever he is now, I so do hope he planned to be there, wants to be there.* Lord Edward did not bring his mind to think on how he would punish Dallion for this overlong quest of his. He only wanted him back in his sight to beg him not to leave him this way again… *No punishment necessary.* He was glad Sisco down in the sands had been preparing to speak to the crowds of spectators, so his mind could be taken off the subject of Dallion, possibly in peril. Edward wiped more sweat from his hair, readying to listen in.

A girl wearing yellow and black robes, no more than thirteen or fourteen years in age was seen running to Sisco in the center of the arena down there. When she had reached his side, she halted abruptly, raising a green painted wand to his chin. Sisco spoke into the tip of the wooden device so all spectators could hear him loudly and ever so clearly. "Folk of Ascali, of Midlön, and from realms afar.

I, Tournament Master Sisco, present to you the eighty-ninth tourney. It's game day!" Sisco raised both fists up high into the sky, as did most the viewers. Their cheers had been almost as loud as his magically projected voice. Tillsy joined in, in raising her gloved and tightened hands high up, shouting with the rest of the surrounding spectators. Sisco continued on, not waiting for the cheering to discontinue before he spoke again. The power of the girl's wand below him sent his voice into the ears of all; even folk few yards outside of the arena could hear the echoes of the tournament master upon the sands.

"As many know, King Gregory was to partake in a special event *within* the event which no other king has done anything like… The king was to duel Sir Marcus Magic, for you all to witness! This will no longer be happening, sadly."

Boos, cheers, and laughter echoed throughout the arena. Even from afar, Edward Frauer could see Sisco smiling down there, standing in the sands. He gave the folk a brief moment to continue on with their reactions this time. Lots of whining and complaint-filled shouts came from the mouths of the folk. Some already had begun throwing their food, which was regular behavior for the arena events… Typically the duels had begun though by the time the food throwing had.

Edward thought, *Of course there would be an excuse for the king to not commit to a planned duel. If he did, it would be a hidden mock duel anyhow.* Edward was not surprised to hear this; though the *excuse* coming from Sisco was strange… "There has been an incident, resulting in Sir Marcus's inability to duel on this day. Because of this, your king has become saddened and sickened. His royal self remains in the Great Keep, where the lord-steward is comforting him. I am to host today's games, in place of the king and Lord-Steward Arol."

Most of the women cheered and clapped, praising the copper-skinned tournament master! Most of the men yelled phrases like, "On with it!" or "Begin the games!" or the frequent chanting of, "DUELS, DUELS, DUELS!" Sisco joined in with the clapping, applauding himself.

The women love him, thought Edward as he pulled his wet tunic away from his chest. The sweat caused the fabric to attach itself to his body. Tillsy was clapping and making whistling sounds.

Edward asked her, "Tillsy, you think he's a fair man to look upon?"

Tillsy laughed as she cheered on for the fights. "That one? I have bigger balls than he. Looks like a woman in that yellow dress, with that luscious ink black hair... ON WITH IT!" Tillsy was now screaming as she grabbed onto Arthan's arm just beside her. She squeezed it tightly as she continued cheering, now jumping.

Sisco continued on speaking through the magical device held for him. "This year's winner has the honor of acquiring the title of Shield to the King AS WELL as a beautiful prize containing a chest full of some gold."

More cheers, more whining and lots of food throwing could be witnessed among the crowds. Sisco paid it all no mind, continuing on telling the folk, "Forty competitors stand in the armory within the pit walls here... Forty warriors, all victors in their battleground duels made for the honor to fight before *you* all fine souls. Forty warriors, twenty duels, twenty winners...whom will then continue on to all face each other in the battle royale!"

All became loud now, in positivity and not of complaint. The battle royale had always been the most loved portion of game day. "The winner of the battle royale shall stand victorious as Shield to the King!"

Tillsy yelled to that, "You've said that! Let us see a duel!"

"Our first duel of the day!" Sisco began.

The crowds grew louder, yet the magic of the wand held at Sisco's throat kept his voice from being overpowered by the spectators. "Sir Arthur Mullen of Hemgrue Keep versus Sir Tallion Glade of Maul Squares."

All thought Sisco would then dismiss himself to walk on off up to the hosting booth, leaving the fighters to enter the sands. He left the crowd with a last surprise before he wished all combatants within the armory much luck, and the spectators his hopes for a pleasant show.

Sisco said, "Lastly, this year's games shall be dealt in live weaponry! Aeon give your protection to all combatants. I hope you all enjoy the show!"

Edward and his wife covered their ears from the overbearing screams of the surrounding spectators. Sisco with the magical girl, walked away and into the armory gate within the walls of the pit.

Tillsy's cheering had died down to nothing more than a wide-eyed stare down upon the sands as Tournament Master Sisco walked through the gates to disappear. Now she looked to Edward, asking him, "Is Jason prepared for live steel? Did the competitors know this?"

"If Jason knew sharpened swords would be used today, he certainly kept it hidden from me. Have you heard anything of this, my lady?" Edward asked his wife.

She answered, "No, hadn't heard a thing of it. He'll manage."

Arthan said, "Me either." biting his nails.

The Frauers and all spectators watched as the two warriors exited the gate, side by side. The armory was then shut and locked behind the two opponents, now squaring off from each other. They stood fifteen paces apart, the knight named Arthur, suited head to toe in orange plate mail, carried a two-handed steel great sword.

"That looks heavy." said Tillsy as she remained gripping Arthan's arm.

The other warrior, the knight from Maul Squares, wore the same style armor platings yet unpainted. He carried a steel short sword in one hand, and a heavy shield made of some wood on his opposite arm, but mostly made of iron alike his own armor. Both knights' weapons sharpened to cut flesh. The knights positioned into their battle stances, the horn blew, and then it was clashing time.

Sir Tallion Glade with the shield rushed inward, yet without striking. The knight in orange plate swung his great sword with a mighty sidestroke toward his oncoming opponent. Sir Tallion the knight in the dull irons, leapt backwards not daring to block the attack with that shield. Tillsy said to her surrounding family, "If that great sword is real, the other knight's shield will be useless!" Tillsy Frauer had been absolutely correct in her statement. The knight in orange armor raised his two-handed weapon overhead, bringing it down upon the direction of Sir Tallion's helm, though again, Tallion had evaded the attack with a leap; this time to the side, not backwards. Sir Arthur was hasty to send another strike towards Sir Tallion, a strike which Tallion would not maneuver out from. Sir Arthur approached now, rushing in attacking from the side, alike his first strike during this duel. Sir Tallion would have jumped backwards and away to evade the attack, yet the walls of the arena pit had been now close behind him. The knight in dull colored armor could have rolled away, perhaps even ducked low, yet he chose to foolishly block the oncoming sidestroke with his shield.

The crowd cheered when the wood split, shattering splinters to the sand. The iron of Sir Tallion's shield had bent, wrapping bits around his arm with some chunks of wood trapped within his mail at the wrist. The crowds cheered as Sir Tallion inspected his own arm. Sir Arthur approached, readying to send another attack toward his opponent, one which would cut him in two, even with iron protection. The knight lifted his great sword high but was dazed and disoriented when Sir Tallion collided what was left of his shield, with the front part of Arthur's helm.

"Oh shit!" yelled Tillsy, along with one hundred other spectator folk of the arena.

Down to the sands went the knight in orange. Sir Tallion stood over his downed opponent as the shamed knight attempted to rise. Tallion struck him in the back of his helm with his short sword. A spark burst from the back of Sir Arthur's head as he returned down into the sands.

"Surrender?" shouted Sir Tallion.

Sir Arthur made an attempt to grab ahold of his great sword within the sands, an action which Tallion had caught sight of. Sir Tallion struck Arthur eight times in his helm, each hit, white flames and bits of what looked like lightning had exploded from the armor. *Sparks,* the alchemists and elementists call the bursting effect.

Enchanted weaponry? Edward inspected what he could of the knight's sword from up in the crowds here. *This year is quite different than all previous games*, thought he. The short sword glistened, dazzling as Tallion raised its beauty while the folk cheered on his victory. Arthur lay unmoving underneath him, until four men in yellow robes came through the rising gate of the armory.

They dragged the knight away as Sisco, with a wand held to his neck by his little servant, said from inside his spectator booth high, "Tallion Glade wins! We'll be seeing you in the battle royale! Sir Arthur shall be seeing the priest for healing."

Tallion raised his sword high and low, high and low as if piercing the clouds repeatedly. He stomped away toward the armory as two more combatants entered the sands through the very same gate in which Tallion was headed for to take leave by.

Edward looked upon his family beside him. Arthan was sweating as Tillsy dug her nails into his arm. Sophia was calling a huge woman over to the family, a woman who had been walking the crowds, selling barrels of wine the size of melons, and little cups for purchase as well.

Edward spoke over on to the three. "No sight of Dallion, nor John, though there are thousands among us. They could be here. Are you all well?" Lord Edward asked them this as Sophia received three small barrels, placing two of them beside her feet, and handing one down to Tillsy. Sophia paid the woman in golden coins, and then Tillsy let go of Arthan's arm to enjoy some of the warm barrel wine.

Edward asked his son, "Are *you* well, Arthan?"

Arthan looked to his father as he rubbed at his elbow under his silks. "I feel ill." said Arthan.

"Have a seat down." Edward told him.

Arthan said, "If I sit, then I cannot see past the heads."

Sisco, from the comfort of the hosting booth, announced to all, "Sir-Paladin Reese Callum of Ascali! versus Daetherian Ain of the realm, Reitina!"

Edward said to Arthan, "Wave a merchant who's selling water." Then he tossed Arthan a coin before resuming his attention to the upcoming duel.

These two opponents looked drastically different from each other, in stature and apparel; facial and body features. Last duel consisted of two combatants who'd been *both* knights of Midlön, equipped with swords and or shields as most knights would regularly use. Both clad head to toe in iron platings, performing using standard Midlön sword-craft… This knight, though, a *paladin* alike Sir

John. He was fastened with golden rimmed platings. The main color of his holy knight's armor consisted of beige paintwork. Sir-Paladin Reese stood tall front his little foreigner opponent, Daetherian Ain of Reitina to the north. Not only was this Daetherian a *foreigner*, all could see he was of the elvish folk, the *pure* elvish. Half the height of a regular man, the creature walked its way barefooted through the sands, holding a short spear in both its claw-like hands. The elvish had his blackened hair shortened around the tops yet braided at the back bit; the hair hung low and his ears pointed high. The paladin wore no helm either, showing a headful of hair just as black as the elvish's. Alike Sir Arthur of the previous duel, Sir-Paladin Reese bore a two-handed great sword, *his though* with a golden pommel. The paladin knight held his sword in one hand, resting its edge on his pauldron, blade almost touching his ear.

Sisco said through the power of the wand projecting his voice, "Reminder! Sir Reese, none of that holy magic. Daetherian, no elvish magic. I expect a nice, clean battle, using the natural crafts of strength, speed, and arms."

The elvish squatted low, squinting those bug-like eyes of his and showing a mouthful of razored teeth. He looked to be hissing, but from the distance in which Edward and his family stood spectating, they'd not been able to hear. The holy knight bent his knees and dropped the sword's tip to the sand, him side facing his opponent and appearing to be holding his weapon lazily, though it was all in great tactic. The horn was blown and for a brief moment the competitors stood in place still, each of them waiting for their opponent to make the first move. At the same time mark, soon then they began circling each other. The elvish moved like a strafing duck, holding his spear as if it weighed the same as a feather. The holy knight took wide steps, dragging his great sword through the sands as he walked round. The crowds cheered, louder when finally the elvish made the first aggressive move. The purple-colored little being slid forward through the sands as if he weighed nothing. Bits of the arena grounds splashed upward as his body weightlessly moved forward, his spear held high. The paladin swung his sword striking low, himself as well sending sand rippling upward into the air as the tip of the blade stayed downward, ripping through the sand grains during the attack. The crowd was awed after seeing the elvish spring up from sliding, now to jumping as if shot into the air through a dwarvish cannon. The knight was pierced in the shoulder by the tip of his opponent's spear as the little thing leapt overhead. The elvish had one hand placed on the Knight's head and hair, the other gripping the spear as it's tip dug into the iron pauldron; both its bare feet pointed up to the sun. When Daetherian landed in the sands, his opponent's backside had been to his face. The knight was quicker than he had appeared though; he was soon turned back around facing the elvish as it crawled backward through the sands like a spider; somehow managing to handle it's spear steadily all the while.

Tillsy took a sip of wine from her horn, as well as did Lady Frauer. Tillsy said to Arthan, "The agility of an elf, it's not fair! The paladin has no chance."

Arthan was still patiently waiting to find a merchant who'd been carrying water; so far here he'd only caught sight of the one's dealing wine and ale. Edward was paying no mind to Tillsy, his son, or his wife; he was very engaged in the inspection of the fight. Edward was trying to get a glimpse at any more sparking coming from the collisions of the weapons.

The paladin took a glance at his shoulder piece, seeing nothing more than a scratch from the attack of Daetherian Ain. The elvish would have to use his spear to find the joints, cracks, and bits where the chain separated the plating within the foe's armor; otherwise, these attacks would be wasted strength, which could be used for the better. Daetherian pounced forward in the same manner a cat would toward its prey. It swiped the spear sideways with haste, though it's opponent gently lifted his great sword upward, blocking the attack. Once Sir Reese's sword had been risen though, after the blocking of the spear swipe, that's when the knight had begun a spree of deadly combinations. One would think he had been of the elvish himself, the way he moved with that haste, only using the great sword with one hand where as men regularly needed two, and even *then* typically still struck slowly. The elvish did well in blocking the attacks though, successfully being able to land a hit upon his opponent after each parry. The knight would strike, the elvish keeping a safe distance and jabbing at the blade during each swing. After each time he'd tapped the sword with his sparking spearhead, he would then rapidly poke at the paladin somewhere upon his armor; staying as low as he could all the-while, still appearing to walk sideways like a duck, and at times backwards like a spider.

The elvish countered impressively, but Tillsy even made mention of the fact that, "Its attacks are doing nothing. That spear will never penetrate those irons."

This truth had been why the elvish was piercing the plating so often and hastily, as so it could locate these vulnerable bits, which it had now successfully found. The knight swung the sword from high, to low. He missed, the blade now sunk deep into the sands of the pit when the elvish dodged this heavy attack. Before the knight found his strength to remove his weapon from the sands so he could make an attack once again, the elvish had sent his spearhead into the surface of the holy knight's leather belt at the front. Underneath this belt is where the front torso-plate, met the thigh-piece plate. The leather split at this gap. This breaking, the elvish combatant felt through the grip on the spear, and had seen it too with his bulging eyeballs. The paladin now used both of his hands for the first time during the duel, lifting his great sword out from the sands with much might. Sir-Paladin Rees's belt dropped down when the elvish removed the spearhead from the broken leather. Before the paladin could swing his sword downward after he had risen it, the elvish jabbed the spear into the chains where the belt had been covering just moments ago. The spear pierced the chains and pants beneath and, of course, the flesh of Sir Reese Callum. The holy knight dropped his weapon to the sands, groaning in pain and trying to get a hold of the spear. Daetherian gripped the spear hard though, and now pointed it upward through Rees's thigh, to his hip, trying to twist it into find the insides of his lower torso.

Edward took a glimpse at Arthan, who surprisingly hadn't been looking away from the event. Tillsy was smiling, entertained as ever as she happily spilled her wine while drinking it from the tiny cup. He looked to his wife, she seemed neither unhappy nor saddened.

Edward looked back to the sands where the elvish had his spear thrusted into the paladin still.

The paladin struggled to pull the weapon out from his own body, so he discontinued grasping for it and so he grabbed a hold of his opponent instead. With one mailed hand upon Daetherian's shoulder he held him tightly. With the other armored hand, he sent a hardened punch to one of the elvish's big eye's. After the creature had been hit upon its face, its grip on the spear had loosened; Daetherian went entirely limp after this strike to the eye. The elvish may have even been stricken to unconsciousness right there at that moment, but none would ever know after what actions would quickly then take place.

Daetherian would have fallen to the sands if Sir-Paladin Reese hadn't kept him afoot with his grip upon the shoulder. The paladin held Daetherian upward while removing the spear from his own gut. He flung the elvish forged weaponry away, then placed his freehand upon the being's hip. He used both of his armored hands to hold the creature high, as high as he could bring him in the air. One hand held the elvish up at its shoulder, the other hand upon it's waist! Down then the creature was thrown. Paladin Reese brought one of his knee's upward during this rough action. The elvish's backside cracked upon the beige iron of the paladin's knee armor, then the foreign being was dropped into the sands, broken and split in half from the inside.

Edward heard Tillsy throw up while laughing all in the same time. He looked away from the dueling pit and to his niece, past her where Arthan was watching her puke. He saw Arthan look back to the sands at the bent elvish's body, then back to his laughing puking cousin.

"That was amazing..." said Tillsy, wiping vomit from her chin and trying to refill her horn with more wine.

The paladin was stomping away making for the armory, dragging his sword as he gripped his wound, leaving behind trails of blood in the sand. Edward observed the four men in robes walking to the downed elvish being. He was readying to tell Arthan not to watch the men carry away the broken little creature.

The men approached the being, unmoving in the sands. When Edward took another glance at Arthan, his son was swaying as if moving to the rhythm of slow music. Arthan's legs went limp, and so he collapsed downward.

"What? Shit." said Tillsy.

"Arthan!" yelled both Lord and Lady Frauer.

A melon merchant waved over the closest honor guard his old self had caught sight of. Arthan's eyes had been shut, mouth wide opened when the knight in silver approached as the melon man walked away to make more sales within the audience. Edward was gently patting Arthan upon his cheek, attempting to make him wake!

"He's alive, yes?" Lady Sophia asked everybody.

Tillsy placed her fingers upon Arthan's wrist under his silk sleeve. "Alive, yes. Just got too hot more than likely."

"Seen too much violence?" asked the old honor guard.

"Arthan? Arthan?" Edward tried to wake his son by calling his name into his ear. The guard fastened his shield and spear to his backside with strappings.

He said, "Give him here, this happens lots. A priest will wake him."

Lord Frauer and Tillsy stepped out of the path of the elder knight in silver. "There's a man of god in the armory." the guard told them. He grabbed a firm hold of Arthan and slung him over his shoulder so he'd rest upon armor during the carry.

"Gentle there!" yelled Tillsy to the knight as two more combatants had entered the sands below.

The honor guard said to the three Frauers, "We should have the healing priests out here, the way we have the refreshment merchants. This happens too often, folk knocking out as they watch. I'll send the lad back here when he's woken."

Edward watched the old, but strong honor guard carry his son away to the stairs beside the family's seatings; view of the two now lost in the crowds.

"What do you think has happened? This isn't his first tournament he's watched?" Tillsy asked her uncle.

"No, but the first time he's seen a back be broken in that fashion, and I'm sure he's thinking of this year's change to use live blades, hoping Jason won't be cut." These were, in fact, Lord Edward's current hopes and thoughts. Jason was known to be a renowned, winning champion of the arena, but never before had he fought front the crowds against a foe equipped with a weapon which could kill him; his son had saved that sort of battling and dueling for questing and defense on a journey, never for game.

The upcoming duel below consisted of two warriors, one man wearing leather, of Ascali's military. The other combatant was again a knight in unpainted armor. After the duel of these two, it would be Jason Frauer's time to fight.

13

Duelings

Inside the armory of the arena Jason stood, shouting at the man with the lazy eyeball behind the slab of wooden countertop. "If we are using sharpened steel, then I'll be participating holding my own sword! You cannot expect me to duel with one of these foul things!" Standing in line close behind Jason was his knight and friend (and potential upcoming opponent) Sir Lance Flux. He waited in line while Jason argued, waiting alike the combatant behind him, and him and so on and on down the line of soon to be fighting souls. Lance placed his mailed hand upon one of Jason's white shoulder pauldrons. He reminded Jason, "You're to duel next." Jason looked backwards nodding to Lance after the knight removed the light grasp of the hand on armor, then Jason turned to look beyond the iron bars within the wall at the left.

Past the metal gate, two warriors stood in the sands under the sun and thousands of eyes as their names were being announced. Jason turned his head back to look at the man behind the wood again, sitting there slumped upon the stool with many weapons behind him mounted upon the wall; some dull, some sharp, each one various styles and fashions.

"I only use *my* sword." Jason repeated to him.

"You've used tourney swords before, I remember handing them off to you many times." the man argued back.

"Yes, but if *this* year we're playing with edged weaponry, I'll be using my sword and no other." Jason slid the white pommelled, white gripped diamond inlaid sword from his scabbard; scabbard also colored white. He held the weapon high for the man to look upon, not with his lifeless eye though, that stayed looking downward. He never even looked upon the sword with his good eye either though.

He would only look upon Jason still, now telling him, "Then as I've said, Sir Frauer, dip the sword in the barrel of spark oil and you're all set for your duel."

Jason bit his lip. He angrily replied with, "AND AS I'VE said, the oil is bad for the steel. It causes cracking!"

The crowds above the ceiling, past the seven feet length of stone, were roaring and applauding, all warriors below standing here now could hear this rumble. The tournament master had announced the names of the two within the pit, telling all spectators where they'd come from in origin as well. The dueling outside soon began from what Jason could hear past the iron; he was running short of time. He let out a groan, then he spat on the gravel floor in front the counter before asking the man, "And why spark oil this year?" The man replied, "Don't know, sir. King Gregory wanted a more violent, loud, smoky, sparky show. Things old King Harold never cared for."

Jason slammed his armored fist upon the slab of wood. "The king isn't present in the arena today, so I hear."

"Sir Frauer, I will continuously repeat myself if I have to. You cannot be allowed to duel unless the sword you participate with is enchanted with the oil. It's only temporary, sir. If you do not wish to have your weapon there enchanted, I can enchant and rent to you any you wish that lies behind me."

Jason bit his lip again, squinting his eyes. He tried his best to paint his face with a threatening appearance to cast fear upon the man; though Jason had been horrid at his attempts for the menacing facial expressions, so he used his words instead.

"I *cannot* be allowed? Who's to stop me? You?"

The man pointed a finger towards the silver honor guards by the door beside the benches to Jason's right, and then the same finger to the other set of honor guards at the iron gate leading to the pit at the left. Jason quickly looked upon each set of silver-mailed men, and then he began smiling at the pointing man with the dead eye. "You don't think I can handle cutting through a few honor guards? Do you know who I am?"

"Jason, don't speak this way. Settle this quickly, peacefully." Lance told his captain in front of him, placing another hand upon his armor again. Jason brushed his friend's mail away, defeated, saying, "Fine." refusing to look at Lance.

Jason gently held forth his white sword, presenting it for the man to take hold of. "After you place it down behind there, don't you touch it nor let anyone look upon it."

"Surely." replied the man.

He wrapped Jason's sword in a cloth and then gently tucked it under the counter, never leaving the comfort of his seat while doing so. He then asked Jason, "What will you be using? Something similar in size and weight? A long sword to match your scabbard's hold?"

"It will never be the same, but yes." From the man, he then received a heavy-oiled steel long sword. Its pommel gray, blade tinted beige. "I accept it, though I will not enjoy bearing this." Jason was sounding exceedingly more *"bitchy"* (as his mentor Sir-Paladin John would call this form of attitude) than he ever had appeared in his lifetime. Perhaps he'd been expressing his anxiousness and some nervousness, releasing it from within him in this sort of ugly manner, whereas most other combatants had been expressing these emotions by sweating, pissing themselves and whining.

Excluding the green-skinned orcish fighter, all forty of the competitors within the armory (the twenty grunts as well) had been startled, stricken with awe and fright after their arrival, when Tournament Master Sisco entered in before they'd begun having all of the weapons enchanted. *"This year, not only will you all be playing with spark oil, you'll be using live weaponry as well! I'm preparing to tell the audience this in just few moments. I made sure you duelists would hear it first from me. If you haven't brought one, a lethal weapon I'm speaking of, as you'd more than likely been expecting tourney sword's and staffs be given, then a bladed weapon shall be provided here for you. In place of staff's, spears will be used and for the first time in all years, axe's and hammers of any style are approved; whether it be a war hammer or smithy's tool, battle axe or axe for lumber. All weaponry must be capable of lethality and enchanted with spark oil here; oil generously purchased by our king from the dwarvish alchemists from their realm afar might I add."* The soon-to-be fighting men looked at each one and another to confirm that they've heard the master correctly.

Real swords? All shared the opinion that this just seemed so impossible for a public event as this one. Men have died even from the swing of the tin tourney-swords. Even the blow from a wooden grunts-sword in past has broken noses, ribs, wrists and fingers.

Tournament Master Sisco finished with, "No fighting in here, or you'll be charged in the name of the king." The yellow robbed master had then bid all good fortune in the fights to come, then exited the armory through the gate leading out to the pit; this is when the first conflict within the armory had begun.

Jason had watched a knight in full blackened plate mail approach the countertop where the man with only one good eye sat behind. the sitting man was handing off weapons to those who had need of them, and enchanting weapons of those who had brought their own. The knight removed his ink black helm, saying, *"I wish to use my sword, though it's at my home."*

"Nobody is to exit now that you've all entered, sir. Even if you were permitted to leave, before the time you return from your home, your moment to duel could have come and then here you won't be." The knight had argued loudly with the man. *"Others here brought their weapons. I want mine as well. My household is on the Street of War, so very close. I'll be back quickly."*

"You aren't permitted to leave." the man had to tell the knight in black once again.

The crowds above had cheered on as the tournament master then walked his way back into the armory while the first pair of combatants had made to enter the sands with freshly enchanted swords. *"What is the problem here?"* Master Sisco had asked the man behind the wood. The knight holding his helm answered, *"He won't let me leave to fetch my sword."*

"We have swords for you." Tournament Master said back to the angered knight.

"I want mine!" screamed he.

Sisco had asked him, *"When do you duel?"*

"I'm sixth." the knight answered.

Tournament Master Sisco sighed and then had walked to the doorway that led into the arena's sloping halls. During his walk to leave, he'd said, *"By the time you return here with your weapon from wherever home is, your time to battle will have passed. I won't let you willingly forfeit and ruin the schedule for your opponent. You hadn't even known you'd be allowed to use your personal weaponry before you arrived here. You awoke this morning coming with plan made to use one of our provided swords anyhow, so do as you've planned and select one from the wall as is done every year past. Have no worry, they're sharpened just as the one you own…the one sitting useless within your household right this moment. Perhaps for next year's event, you'll remember to bring your sword with you here. Don't most knights carry their swords with them everywhere they walk and ride?"* the tournament master had asked his last question there, looking to Jason. Jason had nodded his head in a '*yes*' style to that question, *"Don't most knights carry their swords with them everywhere they go?"*

Master Sisco then sighed at the furious knight in black armor, and then he went out the door to take his leave. The knight in black unclasped his torso piece from the clips by the shoulder plating. He threw the huge piece of armor out the door toward Master Sisco. It looked as if the plating had been a shield spinning through the air! Straps flailing and dancing as the metal soared with it. Master Sisco ducked low, grinning. The knight screamed in anger after Sisco successfully dodged the incoming iron. The knight's backside platings fell off him to land on the floor behind. After that, he then sloppily threw his blackened helm at Master Sisco, but Sisco danced away sideways, laughing at the knight's frustration and ill aim.

Jason remembered the two honor guards at the doorway in front of Master Sisco, springing forward to grab a hold of this angry knight. One of the guards had used his shield first, to strike the frustrated knight in the throat. Jason had watched as the black warrior had went down choking after that quick hit. The honor guards dragged him away into the hall by his blonde hair, ripping his platings off him so they'd be able to beat him easier, to punish him more effectively. At that time Sisco had still been laughing, watching the guards drag the man down the hallway as they threw his armor to bounce off of the stone walls; sending punch after punch to his throat and shoulders. Tournament Master Sisco said to himself, "Assault on the Tournament Master… I hope he enjoys his beating there, and the judgment session to come. I wonder if the knight has enough gold to get himself out of this one." He laughed more, walking away up the sloped spiral hallway to find the hosting booth within where the spectators stood and jumped repeatedly, happily watching the first duel of the day take place.

As Master Sisco left the lot of fighters, two more honor guards had come in to replace the positions of the ones who'd left to punish the naked knight somewhere off within the lower and deeper parts of the arena.

Soon after the conflict with the black knight had ended, Jason had immediately begun his own verbal battle with the man behind the wood slab. That too had been resolved now; Jason extremely unhappy with how though. With one eye closed he inspected the rental blade as he held it outward.

He said to Lance, "Balanced and the same length as my own."

Lance sat beside him upon the bench, gazing at his own two matching weapons. "Spark oil cracks the steel, you say?" Lance asked Jason. Lance collided his steel short swords together. The blades sparked as if a tiny cannon had exploded at the mark where the edges touched, leaving smoke and steam to drift upward to the low ceiling of the armory.

Jason tightened the strap of the mail at his ankle, tightening it wondering why the foot had still been in pain. *My trial duel was two days ago, and yet my foot still feels afire from the ranger's wrath.* He rubbed at the plating covering his calf, as if that would help make his heel feel uninjured. "Jason?"

"Ah…yes. Yes, the steel. The spark oil, not good for a sword. Yes, cracking can happen."

"That must be after much, much use of the substance, yes?"

"I don't know." answered Jason, rubbing at his leg with the new sword upon his lap, waiting for the duel to end past that gate front him so he can get this event of the day on with!

"How's your ankle there?" Lance asked Jason.

"Pains me, though I've had much worse to deal with in past."

To that, Lance said, "Perhaps when taking injury in questing, this though, there's no reason why you shouldn't be at your finest before a planned duel. Would you like me to ask the priest if he'd come here?"

Jason raised his head as he picked at the scab upon his nose, looking to the back of the armory where another line of men was formed. Both combatants and grunts the line consisted of, all waiting in turn for the holy priest sitting upon the chair there to use his light magic, healing them of any wounds or sicknesses they might bear. Lance knew Jason's answer before he'd even spoken his question.

Jason gagged and looked away from Lance in disgust, still rubbing his own ankle. "No priests." said Jason.

In the back of the armory, the orcish combatant thanked the priest for his service, then stomped away, chain belt rattling with each step it took. When the beast passed by to make for the barrel of oil, Lance got a view to watch this man in white cathedral-robes with his palms pressed to the one-armed grunt's backside. His hand's glowed against the skin of the shirtless grunt. This magical man clad in white wasn't and couldn't *grow* the grunt's missing arm back, though he used magic to close and clean some open, leaking wounds which this man with one arm possessed upon his back. After that magical action, a new man approached for the touch of the healer.

"I know you dislike them, but now is your last chance." said Lance.

The crowds above then cheered loudly, as one of the duelists had just become victorious. "No priests." Jason repeated, rising now with his unfamiliar sword in hand. "No chance." said Jason, standing now.

Through the gate came the combatant in leather armor, the one of the city's military. The military warrior had been softly weeping, holding the stump of where his hand once had been before his duel which he'd just lost. His wrist, and entire forearm was bright red and shining. The priest in the back of the armory quickly left his chair, leaping from the back there, on over to where the combatant with the missing hand had been walking, dazed and in tears. The priest put an arm around his shoulder, gently repeatedly patting this combatant upon his cheek side at his face, walking him to the door to find a more quiet area to treat his wound and wipe his tears. "There, there." said he to the bleeding loser.

Through the gates to the sands came the knight whom the military man had fought. The knight removed his unpainted helm, threw the bloody, oily sword to the man behind the counter for him to catch and clean, and then this victor walked to the benches to enjoy drinking from a skin of wine after removing his shortened cloak.

When the priest made leave of the armory, Lance said to Jason, "Don't get hurt. Now you truly don't have a priest among us here to heal you if you receive damage."

"And I won't. Have no fear, Lance. You and I were meant to fight side by side in the battle royale. I won't be losing this duel here."

Jason's opponent was already at the opened gate, watching Jason, waiting for him to join him so they'd be able to make their entrance into the pit at the very same moment together, beside each other. Jason and Lance gave each other a loving hug. Jason's white armor scrapping upon Lance's gray plates crafted with lines of gold in certain portions; gold rims Jason had always been envious of. Jason Frauer left his friend there to stand beside the combatant dressed in sea garb.

"Ready for this?" Jason's opponent asked him, holding a razor-sharp short sword. Jason beside him, gripping his own deadly but unfamiliar weapon tightly too.

"Indeed." replied Sir Jason with a smile.

They both took their first steps out of the armory, matching speed, striding together for the crowds to cheer them on.

The White Knight of Ascali walked within the pit holding his helm by his belly, raising his beige sword high to the sky. Beside him walked his opponent, bearing no helm nor armor of any kind. *Not even leathers?* thought Jason as he stepped through the sands, doing his very best not to be seen inspecting his foe. Jason enjoyed smiling to the cheering folk a bit too much, as he could have been using this time to observe his opponent for weaknesses, or points of advantage for himself. From his side gaze here, and brief moment of interaction within the armory earlier, Jason had seen this foe of his had worn nothing for protection. He was fashioned in the garb of a journeyman whom travels the seas. A red but also sort of purple-tinted coat he wore, it was filthy and torn, ripped up at each of the sleeves. His undervest was green as were his boots, pants were ink black like the angry knight's armor had been colored. His sea captain hat, maroon and slimy-like. Jason got a good view of this man now as they squared off, facing each other while they both took many paces back.

Jason watched his opponent backing himself away, Jason thinking, *I could cut through all of that with even a lazy stroke.* Jason Frauer was still trying to piece together how any warrior could be so brave, or so foolish as to duel willingly with no protective coverings. Jason was thinking that maybe had the combatant known of this year's change to use live weaponry in place of tourney swords, perhaps he would have arrived clad in some armor. *No, no, one would even be fool to risk receiving the strike of a blunt weapon in that garb there. Whether it be tin or wooden sword, injury and fatality is still possible when all you wear is a sea-storm coat.* As Jason was thinking on whether or not he should swing for the man's head during this soon to be duel, Sisco was preparing to announce the names of the two warriors. *Regularly I bounce my sword off of the helmet of every one of my opponents, yet this one though… I'll behead the poor bastard if I strike in such ways.*

"We have here the White Knight of Ascali! Sir Jason Frauer, head of the Eagle Party!"

The folk erupted in heavy applause after copper-skinned Sisco announced Jason's name and title. The tournament master sat within the comfort of his booth with a wand held to his throat by one of his little assistants in their little robes matching their master's. Jason waved to the folk, wondering maybe where his parents had been seated and if they'd found missing Dallion yet. Sisco sipped on wine while he readied to tell the crowds whom Sir Jason would duel here. Jason's foe in the seaman garb, twirled his sword about the air a bit.

"Sir Bran the Cruel! Called by the dwarvish Bran the Fearless. Here he stands, coming to us from Pirates Landing!"

Half the arena crowd shouted, "Boo!" And the other half continuously cheered on as they did for the famous White Knight, not as loudly of course.

Sir Bran eyed Jason all the while.

Jason shouted to him, "I've heard of you! You don't look like a knight."

Sir Bran yelled in response to that, "Dressed as a pirate I am. I'm that also…" This knight in the seaman garb bent his knees slightly to lock himself into his battle stance. His sword had been raised as well, Jason still spoke on though, standing there in the sand holding the helm in one hand, sword in the other.

Jason shouted, "Pirate as well as knight? How is it you're able to get away with that?"

The horn for battle had then been blown, and so Sir Bran slowly took a couple paces forward. He answered Jason's question as he moved to meet him for clashing. "Not a crime if you pirate only to other pirates." said Sir Bran, approaching quicker now. Jason said no more, he spoke with his sword instead.

After Sir Jason Frauer had placed the white iron over his head and face, he gripped the sword tight with two gloved and plated hands, forming his stance for defensive war-craft. His legs straight and stiffened, chest out broad and flexed. He gripped the long sword as so the blade to be positioned in between his eyes, just in front his covered nose. The pommel of the strangers sword rested against the center of his belt, it and the entire sword, as well as it's wielder was still as a stone statue. When the pirate-knight became close enough to enter Jason's needed swinging distance, the foe paused to take a moment to watch if Jason would strike first. Jason stood though unmoving in his heroic-like position, waiting for Sir Bran's first play. The pirate-knight stood himself sideways, then leaped inward to attack, laying upon Jason a series of many jabs with that pointed short sword. When the first poke had come in, Jason raised his tightened hands high upward to his ear, sending the blade downward, tip heading for the sand casting the point of the foe's sword away.

If not for Jason's tight grip on that handle, he would have let loose the weapon from a sort of explosive fear and surprise. He had foolishly forgotten that both he and his foe's blades had been dipped in the disgusting spark oil. Two inches away from Jason's stomach, the foe's sword hissed as a white flame burst from the small blade when Jason's sword had met the opponent's steel. Jason took a step backwards through the cloud of smoke to recover his sight and to shake away the ear pain from the horrid sound of the sparking; though this is when his opponent had pressed onward with his many more jabs. If Jason hadn't countered the attacks, his plate mail at the torso front would have been poked full of holes; fortunately for him, he had avoided all of the hits. It sounded as if there'd been a loud continuation of annoyingly painful drumming of an awful musical group. Every time Jason's blade collided with the oncoming jabs of his opponent, the steel made vicious noises, flashes of sparks to be seen included.

Jason had only seen this enchantment at work from afar, he'd never engaged in combat having used the substance, nor has he ever had it used against him either. He'd been undoubtedly shocked at the effects of the spark oil enchantment, though his war-craft tactic would have remained the same nonetheless. During a one-on-one-duel, Jason's favorite method for success had been to tire his opponents before unleashing all of his might upon them, so he would regularly do as he's seen doing here now, countering and blocking each oncoming attack, playing the duel with no forward aggression. Typically, he would move backward as much as he could when parrying, yet now the wall of the pit was growing ever so close behind him; this Jason hadn't known.

Jason now used the long sword to send away the twelfth stabbing attack coming from Sir Bran, wondering while the blades met, why this knight's technique consisted of jabs, piercing attacks, when most short sword wielding warriors, tended to mostly use their slashing and cutting forms of the sword-craft. Jason should have been thinking of the wall he was soon to collide with though. His backside scraped against the stone and so he gasped. Like an idiot, he turned himself around to check the wall, as if not knowing that it was there or what he had just hit his back-plate on. When Jason made to face his opponent after this clumsy inspection, all that he saw in his view ahead was the tip of Bran's incoming short sword headed straight for his helm's eye slits. Jason for the first time in the duel, dodged an attack instead of countering it with his ugly temporary sword. He ducked and coming round the foe, he now stood balanced as Sir Bran's sword pierced the stone where Jason's head just had been front of. Three fist-sized bricks exploded as sparks burst from the blade when Sir Bran jammed the tip into the wall of the pit. He removed the weapon from the stone as Jason took a defensive step backwards toward the center of the dueling area. He almost had tripped on a bloody hand lying red within the sands, though he saw it early enough to kick it away before he could step upon the flesh.

He briefly gazed at the blackened hole in the wall behind the knight, thinking, *Did he just try to kill me?* "Did you just try to kill me?" Jason yelled as Sir Bran came closer. *I don't know if my helm would have been capable of remaining strong after receiving a blow like that.* "DID YOU JUST TRY TO KILL ME?" Jason asked again, louder!

Jason hadn't meant to switch form to aggression this early within the duel, yet he found himself leaping forward here and now. Sir Bran rushed in, though Sir Jason rushed in quicker. Bran was surprised at this change of combat style, as he now slowed his pace forward to ready himself for the deadly strikes to come from the Frauer knight. One, two, three, four swift swings with the beige long sword. The pirate-knight had dodged them all! Jason sent another six his way, two of them side-slashes leading into a thrust forward for an unsuccessful stab; ending with three downward slashes which combined, sent all the breath out from Sir Jason's lungs.

Jason stood inhaling heavily as he returned to his common, heroic styled stance. He recovered as much strength as he could, readying now to once more play the defensive end of the game. The crowds screamed in joyful entertainment as Jason posed like a statue, waiting for more oncoming jabs. The pirate-knight spat out a mouthful of browned saliva and then he ran to meet his opponent for a different form of attack.

When Jason saw Sir Bran the Cruel had raised his blade, Jason immediately had brought his grip on the sword handle upward again as so he could get an early move on a counter. Up his hands went and down his beige blade had gone to block away the thrust. Unfortunately, the pirate-knight hadn't stabbed at Jason, this time he slashed. In Jason's defensive stance to block such a strike he'd only have to raise his sword out front and forward a bit, tighten his elbows slightly to ready for the impact. In place of taking such action, Jason sent his blade downward as if the foe was stabbing at his lower torso. Sir Bran's short sword scraped against Sir Jason's right-side pauldron. The armor cracked and bent, and the straps caught flame then had exploded away off him. His ear rang in horrid pain. Jason's shoulder, arm, and hand had felt to be engulfed in flame from within the inside. It hurt at the bones. Even with the suffering of the pain to the shoulder, the annoyance of all sounds now gone from his ear, and the surprise that the bit of armor had burst off of his body, Jason had remained sword in hand and at the ready. He was moving back to counter steadily as if no hit had even taken place. *Shit,* thought Jason. Seeing truly how damaging a landing fueled with spark oil could be.

He's not wearing one scrap of armor. All I need is one gentle hit, and he'll be done with the game. The pirate-knight mixed his strikes now, a thrust forward, a side slash after, then back to the thrusting. Just as Jason felt he was becoming comfortable in reading the motions of the foe to get familiar with his techniques, the duel was interrupted when a feathered sticklike thing hissed past Jason's helm to sink into the sands, landing beside the pirate-knight's boot. With his left ear still ringing, Jason turned his body round to get a view on where this arrow had come from. Behind him, high upon the walls of the pit, stood an armored figure of a man equipped with a large crossbow. Jason thought perhaps the armored soul was silhouetted in a sort of way, making him difficult to see, but Jason soon realized this harsh view was truly because of the armor of the man, not the sun or backlight. Black as pure ink the man with the bow's armor was. The weapon was pointed towards the two combatants. Folk behind the figure in black had been fleeing, some cheering the black man on, and others not even noticing him! Most folk just wondered why the two competitors had discontinued fighting, as the bolt was so small and fast moving that most viewers hadn't seen it there flying or even now lying still within the sands at Sir Bran's feet. The competitors did not continue their fighting, just stood struck with confusion as to why a crossbow bolt was sent into the pit ever so close to them from this bowman afar.

The crowd absolutely saw the second bolt though, only after it had been fired from the bow. It pierced the pirate-knight's gut deep, leaving only a bright white feather to poke outward from him. The Knight Sir Bran never made a sound, or if he did, Jason didn't hear it after the screams of the crowds rose, some screams of pleasure-ful entertainment, others in shock and fear that there was a deadly bowman somewhere among them all, the spectators. Bran dropped to his knees as blood now not only leaked out from the wound in his belly, but from his mouth as well. It dribbled onto his chin and big beard, then leaked down to his throat; before it could reach that green vest of his, he collapsed down into the sands to suffer in a violent squirming silence. Jason was tempted to aid the bleeding man he'd just been fighting moments ago, though instead he had to prepare for if that bowman was aiming to attack *him* now! So Jason stood sword in hand, waiting to leap away to his right side if he had need to, though he didn't have need to. The man in black armor was grabbed and cast down, grappling with a lone honor guard. The silver guard had thrown his spear and shield aside to grasp and tackle the black armored being holding the crossbow. Down the two of them went out of Jason's view, behind the walls tumbling down stone stairs within the spectator seatings.

The armory gate opened behind Jason, out from the darkness came two honor guards and a priest in service for today's games; all three souls had been moving with much haste. The guards picked the bloody and limp pirate-knight up from the sands and carried him away back to the armory with that bolt in him all the while. The priest looked upon his wound as the three walked.

"What happens now?" Jason asked himself out aloud after he picked up his broken shoulder plate from the sand.

None could hear him, for most were still cheering, others screaming. Jason returned to the armory after taking a glance up at the hosting booth. Tournament Master Sisco was not inside it.

"What just happened out there?" asked Jason to all souls within the armory. He'd still been wearing his helmet, gripping his sword tight and ready to continue fighting on, though who could he duel now? Before he would have that arranged, he yearned to know who fired upon him and for what reason. "Anybody? No one knows what just happened there?"

Jason's friend Sir Lance spoke first, "Not all of us saw. I watched through the window slit there while most others behind me here had looked on through the gate."

"So what happened?" Sir Jason demanded to know.

"I was to ask you that!" Sir Lance told him.

A knight with a shield strapped upon his back was dipping the head of his spear into the barrel of spark oil as he spoke, "A knight in black armor shot two bolts down at you and your opponent during the duel."

Jason removed his helm, revealing a head full of sweaty brown hair. He shouted at the knight enchanting the weapon, "I know that. Why did he do it? I ask this! Who was he?"

A black-bearded Easterlñ grunt had said aloud from the comfort of the bench he sat upon, "Looked like you had an enemy up there trying to hurt you."

Jason briefly inspected the shirtless grunt, then ignoring his words, looked to the faces of more warriors among the armory for some more answers. The foreigner orcish leaning upon the wall by the door then chimed in, asking Jason in that ugly deep voice of his, "Did he fire to hit you or the pirate?"

Jason hadn't known the answer to the green-skinned foreign being's question, so he simply said nothing in response to him. Jason turned to face the man behind the countertop, still sitting there. "I didn't see anything." said he, after receiving Jason's stare.

The orcish repeated his question to Jason, "Did he fire to hit you?"

Master Sisco then came bursting through the doorway beside the orcish. Jason was eager for answers and still prepared to win a duel before the battle royale!

"Sisco, tell me." Sir Jason demanded of the tournament master.

The man in yellow was breathing heavily, but he quickly caught his air back. He said to Jason, "There isn't much to tell. Do you know whom the knight was with the crossbow? I come here assuming not."

"I hoped you would tell me..." Jason said to Sisco.

"Sir John took him tumbling down the stairs, unmasked the mystery man, and is now taking him to be detained."

"Sir-Paladin John?" asked Jason.

Sisco rolled his eyes to the back of his head, disappointed in Jason's simplicity. Sisco said harshly, "Did you not see? His son, Sir John the Second...the honor guard Sir John! Were you not looking? 'Twas a guard in silver who had taken down the assassin."

Jason was amused, but also fearful too. He repeated, "*Assassin*?"

And then Sisco said, "Yes!"

Jason eyed the warriors, all of them invested in listening in on the matter. One of the competitors had said aloud, "You surprise us with required live steel, now arrows are to be rained upon us as we duel too?"

Sisco turned around to face the grouping of warriors. He said to whomever made the remark, "I've just referred to this antagonist as an *assassin*. I promise the work of the knight in black was not of my doing, for the tournament party had no part to play in that act of violence. Curse me for saying, but if that was of the king's doing, my servants had no part in that. Guards are called from the keep as we speak to double on watch for the game, for I refuse to let this spoil the remainder of the event. As for how that intruder had entered the arena fully suited *and* with a weapon...I do not know how. Ranged weaponry and baggage of any kind is forbidden past the spectator entrances. Our guards, they're extremely watchful of these restrictions. We'll learn the truth soon enough."

Jason thought on this all speedily. His mind felt as if it had been a scrambled satchel of glass, constantly being shaken. *Who would do this? Of course I have many enemies... Bandits of the realm, family of men I've had sent to dungeons. Envious knights and brothers and fathers of women I've been intimate with, then had cast aside.* The possibilities of who could have fired down upon Jason had seemed endless, and there was also that other possibility as well... The bolts that had been fired into the pit had naught to do with Jason having been the current duelist. The armored crossbowman could have been aimed to hit the pirate-knight, which if he *was* his target, he'd been very successful; in his second shot down, of course. Lastly, this act of violence could have had not one bit of relation to either of the duelists. Perhaps it had just been an unlucky time mark for the two, meaning the *"assassin"* would have come and fired upon any pair of fighting men, regardless whether it be Sir Jason or the pirate-knight Sir Bran the Cruel. *I still crave to know whom this foul work was done by.*

Jason asked Master Sisco, "Was it the knight who attacked you with his black plate mail and black helm? The angered one from when you had come and spoken to us."

Sisco negatively shook his head with closed eyes before saying, "Sir Erik had the similar tinted armor, yes, but he is being held and more than likely still being beaten in the deeps by the guards who dragged him away. No soul throws and aims for me, succeeding to get away with the act unhurt."

Jason conceived an idea now after his remembrance of that angry knight in black. *Ah, this Sir Erik forfeited by attacking Sisco, so I can duel the combatant he had been scheduled to clash with since mine took a bolt to the belly.* Jason's head, a mixed satchel of glass, constantly being shaken. Jason bounced from one idea to the next, surrendering to his current task of discovering who his mysterious attacker was, to now attempting to enter the sands for a proper duel without an interruption.

Jason spoke to Sisco while all within the armory still listened on to the dialogue. "Sir Erik, whom was he to duel against?"

"Robert Nortons, apprentice of the Guardians Guild" answered Tournament Master Sisco, pointing. "Right there." he said to Jason. Sisco had his finger aimed at a combatant who wore half his armor made of pink leather, the rest mostly maroon plate mail. His bottom piece made of pigskin under his belt had skirted off as if how a robe or woman's dress would appear, and also he had bright chain sleeves resting under his iron-pauldrons. The combatant was sitting upon a bench close to where the healer had been using his magic before.

Robert Nortons had risen his head to look upon Sir Jason and Master Sisco when he'd heard his name being spoken.

He asked them, "Is there something wrong?"

Jason was oh so eager to duel. He looked from Robert to Master Sisco, saying. "I'll duel him if he has none to fight since Sir Erik forfeited by way of attacking you."

Again, Sisco shook his head negatively with shut eyes. Sisco was just readying to speak, then Robert of the guild said aloud, "Nay! I'm wiser than that to battle against one of the finest swordsman in the six realms."

"You have no choice." said Jason, continuing with, "You came here to duel, and duel you shall."

Sisco told Jason, "Unfortunately during the time of your clashing with Sir Bran the Cruel, I had sent a servant of mine down here into the armory, informing Robert here that he was declared successful by disqualification of his would-be opponent, Sir Erik."

Jason attempted to rub the annoyance away from his brain by massaging the area above the spot of his still ringing ear. He closed his eyes, bit his lip and rubbed at his hair. "I'm sorry Jason but he's already been written into the log as a victor. Perhaps you shall find each other within the sands during the battle royale."

"I sure hope not!" laughed Robert Nortons.

Jason opened his eyes and asked Sisco, "How am I to partake in the battle royale without having won a duel first?" Sisco answered, "The same way Robert there is to. When I return above, I will have you entered within the log as successful in your duel against Sir Bran. I'd say a bolt in his stomach is fit enough reason for an unwilling forfeit. Bran he is unable to continue on at the moment, so disqualified I shall consider him, what a poor soul."

Jason hadn't known what to say to Sisco after hearing those words.

"Grull of the Western Islands and Sir Lance Flux, please make your way into the pit in four minutes time for the next dueling session. All of this up and down to my booth and back here is slowing me."

Sisco left Jason standing there holding his sword and helm and pauldron, all wet from his sweating. Before Sisco had exited the armory he said to Jason, "We'll speak of the incident with the black armored bowman after the battle royale. I'll have answers for you by that time. Good luck to all!" The tournament master was then out the door and gone once again, walking upward upon the slope of the spiraling hallway to make way back to his booth.

Jason found a seat upon a bench beside where his friend stood now. He saw that Lance was looking far more pale than regular. Jason's friend covered his milky face with his iron helm. Sir Lance was standing beside Jason, inspecting what he could see of the orcish being named Grull through the golden slits of the dark head armor. The beastly being had been sharpening his axe with a stone while leaning against the wall by the door where Sisco had left from. Jason's rented sword was laying across the platings covering his thighs as he sat adjusting his shoulder armor back on. As Lance fearfully gazed upon his upcoming opponent, Jason rested his head against a wooden pillar behind the bench. He closed his eyes and allowed the rage to leave his body and mind; rage which could have been used effectively for his war-craft.

"I fight the orcish. That's unlucky." said Lance, drawing his two short swords from the gray scabbards.

With eyes closed, Jason said to his friend, "We've killed his kind before. You'll do well, I know it."

"*We've* killed, as in you, I, and the rest of the party together. Here, a one-on-one, though…" Compared to Lance, the orcish had been tripled in weight. Almost two times taller than an average man. Nine feet in height the thing stood there, his stone sliding upon the two-handed weapon gently. Jason opened his eyes to watch Lance glance at the thing. Jason said, "You know the techniques for the larger foes. Once you've gotten them on their backside, then *you* become the tall one." Jason turned to glance at the orcish duelist as well. The beast wore a huge western islander's vest, torn tightened pants, and a loose chain belt.

"He's got no mail." said Jason, looking back to Lance.

"Cause their skin is thick like armor." Lance said, twirling his blades to awaken his arms.

"I'm not saying it will be easily done, but done it can be. Strike to kill, Lance. This foe of yours won't become defeated until death takes him."

Lance spat to the graveled floor, then he said to Jason before walking off to the gate, "Wish me good fortune."

"Aeon is with you, as well as my hopes. Dazzle the spectators, for many pretty women are watching." Jason said to him, smiling.

Sir Lance nodded to Jason, then turned to face the gate.

Sir Lance approached the iron bars, awaiting for them to rise upward so he could enter the sands to begin his duel. Past Jason it came and went, Grull stomping onward to the gate. The orcish stood beside Lance, looking sideways and downward upon its knightly foe.

"Good luck, Knight." growled the green-skinned creature.

Both his hands had been placed upon the butt of his axe, the steel end resting upon the gravel by his disgusting green toes on sandals. Grull still looked downward upon Sir Lance, awaiting some sort of response from him, but Jason heard his friend say nothing to the orcish. Jason observed the two duelists standing idle for another minute, Lance twirling a sword often, Grull continuously holding his axe, breathing heavier with each passing second. After this minute had finished, the gate to the pit had opened for the competitors to pass through underneath. The moment the gate had been shut back down, twelve or so warriors of the armory had approached the irons to spectate the duel alike the folk above. Jason was eager to view this fight, yet not in any rush to be surrounded by the many sweating men. He found a window slit close to the back portion of the armory where the priest had been healing the competitors and grunts much earlier.

Jason with his helm resting in his lap and sword in hand, viewed Lance within the dueling pit. He'd been doubling his speed in walking so he could keep up with Grull's long strides. The duelists squared off from each other while Sisco began his speaking. "Have no fear, folk, not one more arrow shall fall upon anyone nor anywhere within this arena again today. Please empty your minds. Forget the incident which you've just witnessed! You all are here for entertainment! Are you n—"

Grull raised his axe with that tree-trunk-sized arm of his. He roared into the sky, so loudly that he had interrupted Sisco's magically projected voice. Jason watched from the armory as the spectators cheered on, positively enraged at the orcish's battle cry, sounding the way a tiger roar would. The spectators continued cheering on even after Grull had ended his roar. "I give you Grull of the Western Islands!"

Grull raised his axe once again, silently this time. He moved the weapon as if it was the weight of a toy.

Sisco then announced Sir Lance too. "Versus Sir Lance Flux, Knight of the Eagle Party! Coming to us born of Castle Alhert!"

The cheers died down to the standard applause and shouts; still loud the folk were, yet not as powerful as when Jason, and even the orcish had been announced their titles and origins.

The horn blew; both combatants matched a menacing walking pace toward each other. The crowds had been restless now, extremely entertained and anxious in a pleasureful and violent sort of way. They'd begun throwing food and drink again, and there even was some fighting amongst themselves; all happy though! Jason gripped the handle of his own current sword as he watched the two come closer and closer to each other; feeling as if he was in the duel himself. They came to a mark of three feet away, then the first swing was made. It was by the orcish, he'd intended to lop off both of Sir Lances feet with the duel's first stroke, but the knight jumped at the sight of the oncoming low attack. Lance didn't jump so high, but he lifted himself high enough off the ground so that the axe hadn't come in contact with him nor his armor. Grull performed with his two handed axe in the same fashion as the large Sir-Paladin Reese had, with using one hand only. When Grull had sent his axe down to Sir Lance's plated boots, he'd also sent his freehand made into a fist to crash upon the chest platings of Lance. Up went Lance from his jump to avoid the axe swing, but then away he was sent to crash backside into the sands after Grull had plowed his knuckles deep into his armor at the breast.

"Shit." said Jason, gripping his sword tight as if he'd been able to use it then and there for his friend.

Lance brought himself to his knees, then back up to stand upon his feet. Jason watched him rush toward Grull. When Lance became within reach, he sent forward a down slash using his left hand, then he'd spun around backwards so he'd been able to use more power behind a second strike, this one cutting upward, using the right-side hand. *He moves like an elvish,* thought Jason, watching his friend work at his sword-craft with great speed. He never understood how Lance fought in this manner. From Jason's perspective, the knight's tactics tended to have his own backside facing his opponents. The way Lance spun, constantly shifting stances to convert his power from one arm to another in between strikes, extraordinary yet Jason felt he could never operate in such a way where he would have his head and body facing the complete opposite direction of his foe; even if it would be temporary and done hastily.

The orcish had now been retreating as he parried at Lance's strikes with his axe, bursts of sparks hissing out from the edges of both combatants' weaponry with each hit. The orcish hadn't just been blocking the swift attacks with the axe, he'd been dodging Lance's would be hits as well. Grull's *"dodges"*—more like simple, yet long steps backwards. The creature had been so large in size that all he had need to do when Lance sent a strike forward, was take a step back and then he'd have been entirely out of range for another strike coming in. Sir Lance had to hastily take long leaps forward for every time the orcish took his moves back.

At Grull's first notice of Lance's tiring, he discontinued his defensive strides backwards, stopping his blocking all entirely. Lance used both of his swords during the same moment now for one high powered, double downward stroke forward. In the midst of the strike, Grull laid a heavy sidestroke upon Lance's blades. The three pieces of steel exploded in a puff of smoke and white flame. Lance was immediately disarmed, his blades flying to land fairly close together beside a bloody hand within the sands; Lance was seven paces away from them. Grull had the strength to not let loose *his* weapon, but the flame of the sparking had burned around one of his eyes slightly. Grull groaned and wiped at the surface wound upon his face as Sir Lance leapt for his weapons.

Lance threw himself up and back down into the sands as if intended to fly and failed. Lance grabbed a hold of his first sword successfully. Before he reached for the second one, he turned back to get a look upon his recovering opponent, though it had already seemed to be fully recovered. Grull was already fast on Lance, rushing toward him with his axe, ready to send it crashing down upon him. Sir Lance decided not to reach for the second sword, instead used the one he'd already grasped. Lance sent a slash upward just as Grull approached closely. The orcish had no time to raise his axe in defense, nor step backward in time. It used it's arm to block Sir Lance's upward strike. Lance found himself on his feet, aiming for Grull's throat, trying to avoid his arm. The creature's hand went up in time! neither competitor was happy of this outcome here though. Sir Lance hoped he could avoid the arm, to cut Grull's throat, whereas Grull had hoped he could use the hardened skin of his orcish race, to shield the attack with his forearm. The result had been the loss of Grull's finger! He had blocked Sir Lance's strike with his hand, where as he meant to with his arm.

Sir Lance ceased his attacking as he stood watching green Grull inspect the wound. Grull held his hand upward, gazing upon the redness leaking from the tip of where his fat finger had been. Jason was nothing but fearful for Lance. If there was any beings within all six realms of the earth whom could endure pain better than any, it would be the orcish. This loss of finger would do nothing but enrage this Grull character.

Sir Lance took this moment to retrieve his second blade up from the sands. All had expected the orcish combatant to be the one to aggressively engage now, but they'd been wrong in their expectations! Sir Lance was the one who moved in, more hastily than ever. He sent a combination of six different forms of attack movements toward Grull: one forward slash downward, parried by Grull. That first move led into a full spin, gaining good power to land the second strike, an upward cut, also parried by Grull. The third and fourth strike from Sir Lance consisted of a left-slash, and then a right-slash. Lance spun again, sending with it a double downward slash with both blades, and then lastly, and sadly, a double upward slash which had been interrupted by Grull. In the midst of Sir Lance's spin where he would begin raising his blades to cut at Grull from the bottom to top, the orcish had slammed the steel of his axe hard into Lance's backside; he'd anticipated Lance's attack.

Jason closed his eyes briefly, wishing he hadn't just witnessed that action. "Yes!" shouted Grull of the Western Islands. Lance lay chest side down in the sand, squirming and struggling to breathe. His armor was dented at the back piece. The golden rims at the area covering Sir Lance's spine had split and cracked. Grull approached him as he was turning himself over as so his back would lie within the sands. Sir Lance raised his hands, not to reach for his swords but as a gesture of surrender. *Thank Aeon, if he's able to turn over in that manner, no bones are damaged.* Jason was fearful for Lance that possibly he'd have been permanently damaged from that strike to his back plating, as he had seen some fighting men suffer in past. *Lance isn't meant to be a cripple. He will recover from this.*

Jason and most spectators had even been awed that Sir Lance was conscious after a powerful hit from a heavy bladed weapon such as Grull's steel axe. If not for the gray-painted irons Sir Lance wore, he'd have been effortlessly sliced in two pieces by his opponent! Now though an even worse sort of fear came upon Jason. *He's going to kill him, isn't he…* Jason stood himself upward from the bench. He gripped the stone at the slit of the window where he spectated from. *What can I do?* He rushed to the iron gate where most men in the armory had been trying to get their view from. Jason saw past the men and past the iron that Grull had been standing high over Lance, each of his green feet at the sides of Lance's shoulders in the sand. Grull lowered his axe so that it gently touched the throat of Sir Lance under his helm. Grull raised the axe, then let out a mighty roar, slamming his fist upon his own chest with the freehand. He beat on his breast, shouting again, "YES!" Jason was stricken with surprise when Grull then stepped forward and away from Lance, leaving him shaking in the sand. Lance then went limp, becoming completely unconscious as the gate of the armory was lifted.

The warriors within the armory all had hastily stepped aside, and then in went Grull to join them again. Out of the armory went two honor guards, heading to bring Lance back inside so they could take him through the door to find where the priest would be. Grull was back standing by that very same door again, breathing deeply and consuming a great amount of water from a sack. Jason watched lifeless looking Lance, helm still equipped and backside armor cracked open. The knights in silver carried him out through the door; Jason was now without a friend.

Jason had hatred to see Lance unsuccessful, especially *damaged* as well as unsuccessful. Perhaps this was for the better though, as Jason did not truly enjoy the notion of having to have dueled Lance during the end of the upcoming battle royale. Jason felt confident that if he and Lance could have stood back side to back side, and have had the opportunity face off upon all foes together, that they'd have been victorious, easily victorious. Though after all opponents fell, Lance and Jason would have been forced to duel, for there could be only one winning champion. Jason felt he'd have crushed Lance in a short amount of time; but now Lance will not participate any longer. *Better to have it done before it even began I suppose.*

Jason walked on over back to the bench with the pillar behind it. He placed the rental sword and helm upon his lap, holding them in place with his mailed hands. He rested his head back upon the wood again, closing his eyes. *How many? Thirteen or so, and then on to the battle royale.* He spent his time resting now. Not caring to view the remaining duels before the ending portion of today's event. *I've only lost the tourney twice in my life...I will not fall today. I am Jason Frauer the White Knight of Ascali, Champion of the Arena.*

14

Champions of the Arena

Of course he couldn't have known which ones yet, but some of the warriors surrounding him, he knew he would have to fight when the time came for all duels outside to have concluded. He sat there upon the bench inspecting as many of the armory's occupants as he could. Before Desmond's fighting could begin, forty of the battle ready warriors within this armory room under the arena would face each other in a single-person-versus-single-person fight: a *duel*, as the people of Midlön referred to the two warrior presentation as. Desmond had heard this term spoken multiple times since the beginning of his captivity. These armored duelists had willingly been present here, where as the nineteen grunts within this room had all been set to partake in this event today by way of threat and would be force.

Desmond rested the palms of his hands upon his knees as he sat at the bench, watching the warriors dip their swords in the barrel full of magical oil. He inspected each one of them as they approached the wooden countertop, some trading in their weapons for temporary rental swords, spears and axes. Others chose to fight with the weapons they had brought with them, dipping their owned blades and spearheads into the wooden barrel, releasing a reeking fume of metal and ash when the weapons went in and out. Desmond observed their armoring, weapon types, and even the way they had walked to inspect their footing. He and the remaining eighteen grunts were to be placed at an extreme disadvantage when their fighting time came for the last portion of the day's event, known as the battle royale.

Each grunt was required to fight bare-chested, to wield nothing more than a wooden sword as a weapon. Desmond gazed upon the warriors to inspect them so he could somewhat makeup for these upcoming struggles. *I need to know how I'm to do this, or I'm in for a brutal beating.*

A brutal beating was traditionally the common outcome of a grunt's play within the battle royale, though this year, live weapons will be wielded by the willing and present warriors they called "*combatants,*" or *"competitors"*; grunts were still to wield only wood as past tradition. With the combatants using sharpened, *real* swords and spears, Desmond and the grunts would receive much more than a brutal beating from the strikes of these attackers.

Two hours ago from the current time mark, just after the tournament master had left the armory room, a grunt was addressing lot of them to speak a plan. Some grunts sat among benches listening, others stood waiting to be healed by the priest. All the while, the combatants were making ready to receive or to make enchanted weapons at the opposite end of the room. This speaking grunt was the fattest of the nineteen half nude fighters. Balding, sweating, and tearing, though he was the only man among the captives to seem to have some sort of notion of what to do once the fighting horn would be blown. "If we stay together, we'll have a greater chance of survival." he had said to them while nervously pacing the room with his belly bouncing as he took his steps. Desmond watched the grunt approach the half-elvish, half man thing in hopes he would agree.

The pointy-eared being said, "Leave me."

"But do you not agree? These knights and them over there won't be grouping up to fight together, but we can! It's the only way we won't die. They're here to win a prize, meaning they're gonna have to go at each other, fight each other for it. We just need to survive, and we can do that together!"

The grunt was then becoming louder, as was a knight in black armor at the wooden bar top where the swords were and that oil was resting in the barrel. The reasoning for their argument over at the opposite end of the room there was unclear to Desmond. Desmond was trying to listen to both of these yelling men at once, the grunt here and the black knight over there.

The heavy yelling grunt came closer to the half-elvish. "We fight together, we live together!"

"Leave me, or I'll go for you first out there." said the green eyed half-breed, now looking directly up at the fat man. The loud grunt then became a quiet grunt, seating himself to tear some more. The man with the one eye said to the fat, tearing one, "You really should just shut it." The grunt with the prison slacks sitting against the stone wall joined in on the dialogue, "Nobody wants to fight together. Let's just get this on and over with as fast we can."

Desmond listened in on the entire talkings of the man with one eye and the fat grunt while watching the knight in black be tackled to the gravel floor after he had removed some bits of his armor to throw at the tournament master. The master had returned to the room and then was assaulted by flying armor upon his leave there at the doorway.

At that time, the knight in black was then dragged away by a pair of silver guards while the one-eyed man was saying, "Yes, let's just get this done with. Together, or not together, we got no chance against these knights in full armor with swords." The heavyset grunt with the plan removed his hands from his face to reveal his glistening cheeks as he spoke. "Their swords are real this year! We will not leave those sands alive!" cried he.

Desmond had then stood himself upward to walk on over so he could witness the duel taking place outside beyond the iron bars in the pit.

He had still been listening on to the grunts talking. The grunt with the prisoner pants said, "Have no fear, they will not aim to kill us. Most of these men are knights of the realm. Maybe that orc there could be bloodthirsty, but do not fear these warriors. They will fight with honor."

The heavy grunt went back to shouting, "How can you aim to strike a shirtless man such as us, using a sharpened sword and *NOT* aim to kill. We will all be hacked to pieces!"

“Shut it.” said the one-eyed man as an entirely new and unfamiliar person had approached Desmond by those iron bars.

This elder in white had asked, “Do you require healing?”

“Already had it.” Desmond said back to him as dueling had been taking place beyond the bars of the gate. Desmond then put thought to where the Western Islander had been as of now, for he was not present here within the armory. *The Islander will absolutely need the touch of this healer after he was attacked during last night’s feast.*

Then there was another argument taking place by the weapons and oil, this one involving a young knight in white armor. The armory was becoming so very loud, and so Desmond was forced to raise his own voice to ask a guard beside the gate there, “There to be twenty of grunts. Do you know where the Western Island man is?”

The guard in silver laughed to his friend in matching armor standing closely. “The coal-colored man? He died some hours ago. Waited too long to see the priest in here.”

The other guard spoke, adding in, “They should heal you lot after dinner, not here on game day. Grunts feasts are dangerous times… I heard he was stabbed in the dick with a fork!”

The other guard said, giggling, “Probably bled out before he could make it to here.”

The priest had again seated himself in the back of the room and had now been healing both grunts and combatants while sitting in a chair. Desmond had become saddened more at that time than he had been in his entire captivity. The souls he had been closest to in this new realm, gone. Araisha missing, the Western Islander… dead. *Araisha I still have a chance of meeting once again. The Islander, though, I best forget him so my heart does not ache.* Desmond observed the fighting men beyond the iron, thinking his last sad thought in relation to the dead foreigner, *I never got to know his name…*

Desmond gripped the gate with his hands as he looked on to the ending duel, trying to hold tears back.

“Don’t touch that there.” said one of those silver guards maintaining the gate.

Desmond removed his hands from the iron as the gate had then creaked upward, opening. Out from the sands came a warrior in leather, bleeding without a hand. The winning knight in unpainted armor came through as well. Out from the gate and into the pit then went that arguing White Knight from moments ago, and his opponent, a man wearing garb of a sea traveler.

The gate had closed, Desmond remaining there behind it, standing in between those two guards so he would be able to spectate with some men behind and around him with the same intention; these men, some knights, some of them grunts. That next fight involving the knight in white and the man from the sea had ended ever so strangely. Desmond had witnessed the duel in its entirety and most importantly, the incident high above it which caused the duel's very closing. A lone black-armored bowman had stood tall atop the walls just above where the drop to a portion of the pit was. This black figure fired crossbow bolts down upon the fighters, one bolt striking nothing but sand, the other bolt hitting the fighting seaman in his lower torso. Whence he'd seen this play out, Desmond had then moved far back away from the iron gate as one of his greatest hatreds in the realms of the earth was for arrows and bolts. The watching knights and grunts by the iron had gasped and shouted during and after this violent interruption of the event, meanwhile Desmond had seated himself upon the bench again and closed his eyes to rid his mind of the imagery he had just witnessed.

The gate opened and so the seaman was then retrieved from the sands. Desmond did well not to look upon the limp man as he was carried through the armory, bolt still in his gut. The White Knight soon came through and back into the armory once again, angry and asking all for answers. The knight continuously asked all the truth of what had happened out in the pit.

So Desmond had answered him with, "Looked like you had an enemy up there trying to hurt you."

The knight had looked to Desmond, but then said nothing to his obvious statement. He looked away asking the same question, yet to different warriors within the room. Desmond was sitting upon the bench, eyes blackening as he visualized the bolt in the belly of the man out in the sands. He had held his palms to his closed eyes, sitting awaiting to fight and not caring to spectate any longer. *There will be no advantage for me, maybe no disadvantage either. If the gods meant for me to survive, then survive I shall. If my death time is coming, then Father I shall be happy to see you shortly.*

He sat there for two hours with his eyes closed in deep thought of his past fighting tactics with his wooden staff. His eyes had been closed all this while, but he had kept his ears opened though, and now that he had heard, "After next duel, the battle royale will begin." He opened them wide.

Once again he was looking upon the combatants; all of them here now would be the winners of their duels. The green giant was among them, the orcish warrior. *I had hoped that one would lose his one versus one. It would be a pleasure to not have to worry about such a foe out there for the free-for-all fighting.*

Desmond watched the grunts too, almost all of them terrified. *The half-elvish seems calm though, why is that?* Desmond thought perhaps the being planned to use magic in the fight, for all with even the smallest bit of elvish blood in their veins bear the power of magic… though magic is restricted in the games. Desmond had to be cautious not to use his own dark-crafts in combat today. The tournament master made it clear that no magic is permitted to be used, and Desmond did truly plan to commit to not breaking this rule. The half-elvish sat, eyes glowing green as he twiddled his thumbs together with a half smile upon his face. Desmond wondered what the being was putting thought to, until Desmond's gaze was interrupted when the guard at the gate yelled, "Line up! Make ready."

The iron bars were raised, out of the gate and into the armory came limping the losing knight wearing striped armor. He was cursing with each step he had taken. Behind him a victorious man in chain mail came through. "Yes! I have won!" said the warrior in chains.

The honor guard by the door yelled, "Well then, win again! Line up there, go, go. No time to rest. Time to fight again."

Desmond stood himself up to his feet and then walked to the grouping of men behind the opened gate as that winning man in chains approached from behind for the same reason.

From the power of the magic at the master's throat, Desmond heard him outside telling the crowds, "AND NOW! Folk, to you I present the battle royale!"

"Out you go. Form a circle when you get out there and wait for the horn. Don't be sloppy!" yelled one of the guards at the opening.

The man ahead of Desmond began moving forward, as did the next one ahead of him. Each shirtless man was handed a wooden tourney-sword just before entering. Desmond with the other eighteen grunts, and the eighteen competitors, all made their way out of the armory and into the sands of the fighting pit of the arena!

Desmond walked as two thousand people cheered high above him and the warriors. They screamed, threw their food, laughed, and shouted. Half the fighters were unarmored grunts with wooden swords; the other half, lethally armed and armored combatants, most of them knights of the realm.

The circle of standing bodies was slowly formed as Sisco high up in a booth at the crowds said with the wand at his throat, "The countdown drums of the final portion of the event will begin in one minute! Combatants! grunts! folk! ready yourselves!"

They stood twenty paces apart, each warrior having another man to possibly fight at both their left and right side. A hundred paces front each of the fighters stood another foe of this grand circle. Commonly when these battles would begin, the men within the Arena's pit would play beginning with one of the four actions: attack the foe to the left side, attack the foe to the right side, attack the far foe across, or hold guard defensively. It was mostly the grunts who would stand at the guard, waiting, watching and hoping no fighters would choose them to battle with. The competitors often rushed in, attempting to impress the crowds and eager to swing. Desmond remembered hearing though that this year to everyone's surprise including the combatants, that sharpened weapons would be used by all except for the grunts. Because of this, the competitors weren't as hasty after the horn was blown compared to how they'd reacted to its sound in the past years.

Desmond stood, shirtless and shoeless. He buried his toes in the sand and gripped the wooden sword loosely. He used his quick eyes to find the closest competitor who chose a spear as their weapon for the event. Far off at the complete opposite end of the pit, stood a knight holding a shining steel spear in one hand, with a wooden shield fastened upon his other. He wore a suit of plate armor and chain mail. *He couldn't be any further away, but I'll need that spear of his.*

Upon Desmond's left there stood a grunt, the grumpy one with the one eye. Piss was dripping down his thigh as he was just standing there. When the man looked down at the wetness, he became angry again; angry and frightened. To Desmond's right there was a huge man almost as tall as the orcish being. This one was a black haired knight who wore beige armor and carried a two-handed sword massive in size, yet he only wielded it using one of his hands. This knight though seemed uninterested in most of the warriors, for he had his stern eyes placed on that knight with the white colored armor. *So long as there is not another attack with crossbow bolts from above, I should likely live past this day,* thought Desmond.

The drumming was loud! The pounding almost sounded the way lighting would. The high pitched beat continued on, ten hits in total. After the tenth drumbeat was laid and finished, the battle horn was blown. As expected, to Desmond's left side he glanced on over to see the man with the one eye, unmoving. The big knight in beige was already sprinting inward on the ring of moving men at the right side, though. This giantlike knight was looking to be making for the knight in white, only then abruptly a different combatant had appeared blocking his path to clash blades with he.

Desmond progressed forward, not hastily though. The knight in beige collided blades with his current opponent; some knight in pink armor. Past them Desmond saw the knight with the shield and spear, he was jabbing the weapon's head into a combatant wearing full chain mail. Desmond maneuvered out of the way of two wrestling grunts in the sand; them already having dropped their wooden weapons. He leaped over them, then spun around the fighting beige knight and his foe so he could reach the knight with the spear. *I need that spear, but I'll have to beat him for it with this wooden sword of mine.* Desmond never squared off with the spear wielding fighter though.

The knight with the spear pierced the weapon into the belly of the man in chain armor. The tip came right out of his backside! Desmond advanced forward as this was taking place; much, much clashing surrounding him during the time now. Before he could get to the knight who had just killed the man in chain, the knight in white armor approached the one fighting with the spear. Desmond had never seen a man move so fast! The way the knight in white swung his sword, moved his feet as if it was a dance, an art. The spear wielding warrior tried his best to counter the strikes coming from his opponent's sword, but he was sadly overwhelmed from the combination of different forms of attack.

Desmond patiently observed the spearman's failure. As he watched the fighting he was careful not to allow himself to be attacked from the backside. A quick glance behind him and he saw pure and total chaos. Almost every occupant of the pit was in the midst of some kind of battle. One grunt was seen crying against the wall, two grunts still rolling through the sands biting each other. The rest consisted of fighters on foot facing off to clash with another. *They are dropping so fast! Grunts and knights alike…*

Desmond watched the one-eyed man's leg fall clean off just under the knee after a combatant had swung his long sword low at him. Desmond made sure this knight who attacked the grunt with the one eye was not making for *him* now to attack. Desmond watched him move on over to two fighting grunts in the sand where he stabbed one of them in the ribs and then had begun chasing the other one, that shirtless man fleeing now up and running; the first fleeing fighter of the battle royale. When Desmond turned himself back around to face the knight in white and the one with the spear, he saw the white one was off away! The knightly spearman though was on his backside in the sands, weeping as he held onto his broken elbow. The White Knight was already moving fast on his next victim. When the white one was far enough gone and busy with his new engagement, Desmond finally ran to the downed warrior with the spear.

The man in pain attempted to foolishly withhold the weapon from Desmond when he was approached by him. Desmond slammed his wooden sword upon the visor of the man's helm as hard as he could, yet the man continued to struggle on and fight with that arm bone out of place. Desmond gripped the helm of the man, removing the armor from his head and then crashed the wood sword into the downed man's nose. The Warrior went limp and drooling, forced to unconsciously surrender his weapon to Desmond.

Desmond threw the wooden sword to the sand and bent on downward to take hold of the spear. The moment he grasped it, his backside muscles exploded in a horrible sensation of pain. The grunt with the prisoner's pants had struck Desmond by where his spine was. Desmond almost dropped to his knees, but he found himself able to keep afoot. Desmond turned, doing his best to ignore the pain upon his skin and within his body. The fighter swung his blunt sword at Desmond's face, but Desmond was quick enough to dodge it. When he had then risen up after the man made his failed attack, Desmond sent the deadly spear into the flesh of his shoulder. The man let out a yell while falling to the sands to cry.

Now front Desmond stood the heavy knight in beige, he had broken the pink armored knight's collarbone with a single hard cut of his great sword. The beige knight left the pink one to squirm in the sand, now seen attempting to make his way to battle with the famous White Knight, but the orcish warrior had just defeated the foe *it* was battling with. The orcish was now making for the beige warrior. The knight in beige had no choice… These larger two were readying to fight each other in the center of the pit there while all remained battling around them, or downed. Desmond watched axe meet sword as the two enormous figures fought on in front of him; the largest warriors of this year's event. The clash of the two was ended much sooner than one would have expected. The orcish used the handle of his axe to break the knight's eye socket; for he wore no helmet. After the enormous warrior was dazed and bleeding, the orcish brought the foe off of his feet by sideswiping very low with the huge piece of steel weaponry. The knight's beige shin guarding kept his legs from being sliced off, yet the orcish used such great force with his strike, so the knight's bones had cracked under his skin and leg muscles there; almost shattering. When the large knight with no helmet was on his back and disarmed, the orcish brought his axe downward upon he with great speed and force. The axe bounced off of the breastplate of the knight, cracking a few of his ribs and sending him into a silent sort of surrender. Desmond thought the orcish was to behead the defeated man in the sands, though he hadn't. The orcish lowered his axe to the knight's throat, roared and then carried on with finding a new target; luckily it wasn't Desmond.

The orcish had now been engaging in a battle with the half-elvish being, *that one* moving quickly too! The half-elvish made to block the axe strike coming from this orcish named Grull, though the steel had sliced right through the wood of the sword, and so now the half-elvish was forced to dodge and roll to evade the attacks of the orcish with no weapon to use for countering. Desmond was doing much watching and not nearly enough moving. The more still one would remain in the pit during a battle royale, the more noticeable one would become. He felt the slight impact against the back of his hair; for a brief moment thinking it was the feel of an incoming arrow, less than a second away from death. He turned to look and saw that this was only a bit of bread coming from the cheering spectators. He turned to look upon the crowds, him asking in his mind, *Araisha are you among these people?* He listened closely and heard no barking nor howling of any dog, only the sounds of men and women cheering for violence.

"Eastman!" he heard the muscular grunt shout his way; the one who had stabbed the Western Islander in between his legs at dinner.

Behind Desmond now was nothing but wall and only sand at either of his sides. Behind the large man with the muscles, the remaining fighters fought on hard and loudly. The brute man rushed toward watchful Desmond, him holding two wooden swords within each of his hands. The shirtless man was covered in blood, some his own and some the blood of other grunts. Desmond walked forward two paces, then threw the spear into the big man's heart. The man dropped both swords, then fell and died groaning. He was entirely silent when Desmond walked to retrieve the spear trapped within his half scarred and scorched body.

Before Desmond could decide on what exactly his next plan of action would be, he looked to the fighters to get a good sense of who was remaining in the pit. More than a dozen bodies lay among the sands, half unconscious beings, the other half deceased. The living who lay down within the sands were either bleeding, shaking, crying, or slowly dying, or a mixture of all four of those actions. The only warriors who remained on their feet had been the orcish being, the half-elvish, and the knight in white.

Sadly for the orcish, the knight and the half-elvish were now fighting *together* to bring the monster down. Desmond watched the knight carefully and skillfully slice at the green giant's ankles and wrists, thighs and arms. He had cut him successfully almost every time. During this, the half-elvish was climbing the back of the huge warrior, biting, scratching and choking him at the neck. Desmond walked up closer as people had been throwing food at his backside, yelling words he could not understand. He only continued to watch on to see how this struggle with the three would end. The knight fought on cutting and bleeding the orcish, the half-elvish clung on as best he could, ripping off the orcish's ear now with his teeth, that was when Grull was disarmed.

It seemed Grull of the Western Islands was far more concentrated on removing the half-being from his shoulders, than he was of blocking the White Knight's cuts. Grull dropped the steel battle-axe to grip the foe above and on top of him. Grull's arms were raised as he was reaching for the opponent, that's when the White Knight sent his most effective strike against the beast. The orcish was wearing his leather vest, yet unbuckled and wide open at the center, so the knight aimed his sword right for there. Grull's skin was thick but the sword used against him was so very sharp. His abdomen muscles were cut wide open! Grull dropped to his knees. As he bled from the belly, he was continuously choked by the half-elvish. Grull roared and then went silently to sleep, or died; none had come to know of his fate until much later into the day and night.

A crushed tomato hit Desmond in the back of the head as he watched the half-elvish rising up and removing himself from Grull the defeated orcish. Desmond did not move, only watched on forward as more bread flew his way from behind him. *Seems they want me to engage, to take some action…* Desmond was readying himself for the two remaining warriors over in the center there to make for him as a new target, the same way that they had doubled together to fight the orcish. They didn't double up on Desmond though, the half-elvish had risen to pounce right on the White Knight after Grull was done and defeated.

The knight's white iron helmet was viciously removed off of his head by his new attacker. The half-elvish had big hands wrapped hard around the knight's throat, using his sharpened nails to bleed him as well as suffocate him. The knight was reaching for his steel sword, but the weapon was out of distance and he could not rise nor move any closer with the half-elvish's man-sized claws in him; this grunt had the attributes and quality of an elvish, but full in size like a grown man. Desmond made his way closer to the fighters. He approached them, deciding to stand waiting for there to be a victor of the battle. Whether it be the half-elvish or the knight, Desmond would make his move when they had finished, not interrupting. He could have simply and easily stricken the half-elvish and then taken on the knight himself with an above ground advantage; instead of that play, he simply watched and waited.

The knight was beginning to lose consciousness as the half-elvish was allowing no air to enter into his mouth, throat or lungs. The half-breed turned to look upon approaching Desmond with those burning green eyes of his. The thing spat upon Desmond's toes, then freed one of his hands from the breathless knight's throat to grab hold of a thick handful of sand. The half-elvish threw the grains to splash into Desmond's eyes. That was an error though, as Desmond was filling with a merciless sort of rage because of these actions. The half-elvish placed his hand back upon the throat of the knight in white with no helm, but he continued to spit upon Desmond some more, now growling toward him the way an animal would defend a carcass to consume from. Desmond put the spear through the half-breed's ribcage at its left side, it split through his interiors and bones to break out of his right side under the arm. The elvish screamed for no more than a second, maybe two, then died quickly closing those wicked emerald eyes of his.

Desmond struggled to remove the spear from the body. He had never sunken a weapon this deep into any being in past. He twisted with a firm grip, but before he could pull the steel head and remainder of the weapon out from the corpse he'd just made, the White Knight was standing tall, sword retrieved and moving on Desmond. *That white armor does look heavy...* Desmond thought quickly, and quickly enough indeed. He removed his hands from the spear to step inward toward his rushing opponent. The White Knight raised his blade to bring it down onto Desmond for a powerful and lethal stroke. Desmond outstretched his left leg, as he did this he ducked low, sliding within the sand upon the knee of his right. Desmond tripped the White Knight so he would fall to the sands; and that he did, fell hard with that weighted armor clanking!

The knight's backside slammed into the pit floor while Desmond attempted to again pull the spear out from the dead half-thing. When he finally pulled the weapon free, his foe was already risen from the tripping. This knight was strong, he was fast, and he was moving forward yet again. The knight swung low, then high then low again; blade sparking when the steel of the sword would come into contact with the steel spearhead. Desmond kept a safe distance from the knight with this long and newly acquired spear. Every strike the knight in white sent against Desmond, Desmond would meet the sword with the tip of the spearhead with sparking defensive jabs.

After seven failed attempts to cut Desmond down, the White Knight retreated, shifting to a defensive sort of stance. Desmond refused to let the foe regain his strength and his stamina, so he stepped on forward to thrust the spear inward. The knight spun forward and finished his maneuver with a hard downward cut upon the wood of the spear, close to Desmond's hands. The power behind the knight's counter had shaken the spear and Desmond's arms as well. Desmond ground his teeth together as his hands and arms absorbed the painful shock of the impact from weapon on weapon clash. The sword hissed as it crackled against the spear again, sparks rising into Desmond's eyes. Desmond squinted in pain, that's when the knight took advantage of his opponent's lack of sight. The knight sent a backhanded punch to Desmond's mouth, and then backed away while slicing open a bit of his skin upon an arm using his sword. Desmond held the freshly bleeding cut upon his right arm up at the shoulder. He flexed and embraced the pain, eyes beginning to blacken.

"Yield and I won't cut you again!" yelled the sweating knight wearing no helm. Desmond groaned, bleeding from the arm, yet not unmoving. He violently leapt his way toward his target. The crowds cheered on as the two fighters continued on countering and parrying each other's attacks. They both shuffled from defensive tactics, to aggressive tactics so fast in an awkward sort of turn based method that would almost appear as if the fighting had been planned and choreographed. Desmond would take turns sending five or so spear thrusts inward while the knight blocked and dodged, then the knight would send his own seven or eight mixed forms of attack towards Desmond! This happened many times, neither of the men wounding each other anymore throughout it all as of yet, though they tried so very hard to.

The share of sparking, striking, and blocking had come to an end after the White Knight used his mailed hand to grab a hold of the spearhead when Desmond sent it inward to pierce him. Desmond gripped the trapped weapon firmly as the knight was readying to slice at him. He pulled and pulled, though the white armored foe would not release his grip on the spearhead. The knight in white raised his sword, Desmond pulled harder. *Shit.* He pulled no longer; instead, he continuously held the spear tightly and then raised both of his legs high while spontaneously jumping upward! When Desmond's knees came to his own chin, he then sent them down and outward for his bare feet to crash into the knight's face. Desmond was high in the midst of the air as the heel of his left foot bounced off of the knight's bare chin while the other foot struck him upon the plating at the chest. Down the knight fell into the sands with a bloodied mouth.

Let's put an end to this, thought Desmond. With eyes as black as starless night, Desmond ran to his fallen opponent whom was already beginning to rise. Desmond put an end to his attempt to stand by sending the spear as hard as he possibly could have downward, straight into the shin plating of the knight. Desmond used a flare of his magical strength to fuel the attack, though none could notice this from afar. With this magical darkness enhancing the power of the spearhead, and the simple truth that steel of a weapon was made far harder and stronger than iron of armor was, it all would lead to a result that would be not positive for the knight. The sparking steel spear bit right into the white iron, piercing it, the chains beneath, and the cloth under those chains as well. The flesh came next, and that was when the knight became defeated.

"Ahhh!" cried the knight in white as he sat within the sands. As the knight sat, no longer fighting now, Desmond tore the spearhead out from the front of the leg instead of burying it in deeper to find the bone like he wanted to. Desmond had known already that he had been victorious here and now, so he calmly and steadily removed the blackness from his eyes by breathing as gently as he could, accepting his win with pride. With the spear no longer in his shin, the knight thought to make an attempt to rise upward. It was a quick and sad attempt, for he lost consciousness from the pain of the spear thrust after he came to both feet, now falling into the sands to sleep after briefly squealing.

Desmond gazed upon the defeated grunts and competitors, then looked to the crowds. They yelled, cheered, and began chanting. *This is as if it was the work of great fiction. They are celebrating for me? I have won.* Outcast, to beggar, to captive, to grunt, and now standing as winner.

"Eastman! Eastman! Eastman!" yelled all!

Desmond dropped the weapon, watching the people applaud him.

Sisco said for all to hear, "Our winning champion! The man from the East! The new Shield to the King!"

The armory gate opened behind Desmond. Those who had been living, conscious and able, then walked out of the pit and inside. Moving out of the armory were many city guards assisting in retrieving the immobile and fallen so that they could escort them out of the arena and to the cathedral by way of cart, where they would receive proper healing or burial preparation. Desmond joined the wounded walking ones in entering the armory as Sisco was speaking more. "That concludes this year's game day! I hope all enjoyed, for the grunts and combatants both had fought hard for your pleasure. Safely and peacefully, take your leave of the arena! I shall see you all next year with the king retuning as the proper and formal host of the event. Goodbye, all!"

Desmond was underneath the gate and moving into the dark armory while all inside looked on him. He walked proudly and happily. Now he stood by a bench, scratching at his aching muscles. He fought for a brief time compared to his past endurance training sessions, yet he found himself just as fatigued as if he had been battling for an hour's worth of time. *What will happen next?* Desmond asked himself as he stood there not knowing exactly what he was expected to be doing at this moment after his victory. It was as if the silver guard at the wooden doorway there had heard Desmond ask himself the question.

The guard said, "You should be making your way to see Sisco."

"What?" asked Desmond.

The guard repeated, "Making your way to see Sisco. He's to present you to the king."

"Where is that?" Desmond asked him.

The other guard beside the speaking one said, "Come, follow me."

Desmond left the arena armory as many men funneled in from the sands to enter behind him. Out of the armory the two went, then the wooden door was shut by the guard.

The guard was beginning to walk, escorting Desmond up the spiral hallway. Both Desmond and the guard halted though when Sisco appeared with his little minions in matching robes. "There he is! Man of the East!"

"Hello." Desmond said to him.

"What's your name? I don't have the pleasure of knowing it."

"Desmond." he answered.

Sisco asked him, "Desmond who?"

Desmond hadn't known what the copper-colored man meant by *"who."* Desmond confusingly looked to the silver guard, then back to Sisco.

Sisco said, "Family name. What's your family name?"

Desmond replied, "I have no family name. Only name I have is Desmond."

Sisco sighed, saying, "Ah, I forgot the ways of the easterlñ's and their single names. Yes, well, Desmond it shall be then. Sir Desmond!"

The honor guard behind Desmond asked Sisco, "Sir? He's no knight."

Sisco frowned and told the guard, "Then knighted he shall be! Always has the Shield to the King been a knight. Desmond here will be knighted quickly. And you, you may leave, sir. I have nothing to fear from our champion here! Return to the armory."

"Yes, Sisco." said the leaving guard.

"Off you go, my apprentices, you are dismissed! Well done today."

The children wearing the yellow robes ran away back up the hallway.

"Come, Desmond. Let's get you that gold prize that was promised! Let us present you to the king so he can view the easterlñ man whom will be guarding his royal self until the end of days."

15

THE SHIELD'S FEAST

The silver guards at the sides of the enormous doors clapped the ends of their thick spears to the ground. The black iron swung open inward front Desmond and the tournament master. "Welcome, Sisco. Welcome, visitor." one of the armored guards said loudly.

Sisco snorted, wiping his nose with the cloth from his pocket. "This man here is Desmond of Eastfell. He isn't just a visitor. This man will be living his days out here in the Great Keep to call home!" Sisco rubbed Desmond's shoulder and then gave a pat on his sandy back with the palm of his hand.

Desmond was still shirtless and filthy from the battle royale.

"Welcome, Desmond." the guard said to him.

"Soon-to-be Sir Desmond. This here is the new Shield to the King."

"We assumed so. You may enter now, Sisco." said the knight in silver.

"Thanks, sirs." Sisco said to them both, leading Desmond through the huge doors and into the welcoming hall with the extremely tall ceiling.

High above there were men in orange robes who had been fastened to ropes, removing and extinguishing torches upon the walls, torches blazing teal tinted flames. One of these flaming sticks had almost fallen to strike Sisco upon his head just there as the two made their way to another set of doors ahead. The wood landed beside his ankle to smack the marble hard, killing the flame.

"Steady up there!" shouted Sisco.

"My apologies!" the fire elementist yelled downward to the walking tournament master.

These next pair of doors had been already opened as so painters could work upon them uninterrupted when one would need to enter the Throne Hall. The working men had been standing atop ladders, scrapping blue paint off of the surface of both sides of both of the doors; ignoring Sisco and Desmond's presence, as they'd been in such deep focus while at work. Desmond and Sisco stepped past the men and through the doors to now enter into the Throne Hall, but not until walking up what seemed to feel like five hundred stone steps to come to it. After reaching the top, Desmond saw at the center of the chamber there sat a lone chair, gold and glowing. A glass wall was built far behind the royal seat; the midday sun's light pouring through it to fill the chamber with warm colors. *The Golden Throne I've heard so much of.* Desmond looked at the marvelous metallic seating; its occupant was the king of the realm of Midlön. Sisco knelt to the bald and black-bearded king. Desmond watched the tournament master so he could repeat his actions.

"King Gregory Royce! I present to you—"

The king interrupted kneeling Sisco by shouting, "Desmond!"

"My king, you know this man?" Sisco asked, rising now.

The king said, clapping his hands together, "Did you forget it was I who rode to find the grunts? I saw Desmond inside of the Willowhold dungeon just sitting there all hurt. This is the one who murdered Mayor Fredrikson before my eyes."

Sisco rubbed the smooth skin upon his beardless chin as Desmond arose from kneeling. Tournament Master Sisco looked to Desmond now. "That was you who killed the mayor? Which of the three was it?"

The king answered Sisco's question for Desmond, "The third mayor, Jeffers Fredrikson, the youngest one."

Sisco scowled. "A foul fool that man was. Why did Desmond kill him?"

The king said to Desmond, "Go on, you may speak."

Desmond looked to Sisco and told him, "They wanted to eat my dog."

The king laughed at that. "Ha! See, Desmond here was quick to defend his dog companion. I hope he will use that same quickness if I ever have a grand time of need for protection as his dog had. Where is the dog now? Do you know?"

Desmond shook his head from the left to the right. "No, I do not. In the grass outside the city, in the city perhaps, far from the city too perhaps. I do not know where she's."

"Have no fear then. You are my new shield. If you desire a pet dog, I shall have a new one brought to you. A pup, any breed of choice."

The king rose upward from his throne to stand upon his feet. He stepped downward, descending marble steps, walking wearing those queerly made red leather boots with the high heeled backings. The king's boots were red, rings upon his fingers red too; he wasn't armed except for the white dagger at his hip, though. The banners within the hall above hanging from the high balconies were colored red. The blue torches were being swapped with red one's above by more working orange robed men fastened to ropings. *Red must be the king's family color,* Desmond assumed now. Even those border guards from Desmond's first day in the realm, they carried a banner colored red.

Just few days before Desmond's exile of Eastfell, he had heard word that the longtime ill king of Midlön to the west had died in his sleep. Harold Apollo passed from an illness he had suffered with for seven years. Rested King Harold was known to the Easterlñ's as the White King. *In the East, will they call this one the Red King now?*

King Gregory Royce placed a hand full of red ringed fingers upon Desmond's shoulder. "I'm honored to have a man of Eastfell as my protector."

Desmond was careful with his wording. "I will be happy to be your protector."

The king removed his hand from Desmond while asking Sisco, "He did well in the royale?"

"He bested Sir Jason Frauer, and how ironic that is, isn't it? Your preference on shield was initially he, was it not? Here came Desmond to us to defeat him. The two fought one on one, once all within the sands had fallen."

"Oh my! You bested Sir Jason? Truly?" King Gregory smiled while sending Desmond a lustful look of surprise; inspecting his minor gash upon the sandy arm that the Sir Jason had made during the duel. "Mmmmm…" the king made the noise while he held his palms together and wiggled his shoulders. "See, I knew I made the right decision by visiting dungeons to choose grunts. Ahh, and none thought a grunt of the royale could ever win against the competitors. I would say Aeon has sent you to me Desmond, though this fortune is of my own making."

"Aeon?" asked Desmond.

"God above, in heaven." said Master Sisco beside him.

The king told Sisco, "He worships the gods of the East. He doesn't know of Aeon, though you'll soon learn of him. We shall have you knighted in Aeon's Cathedral of Light to become *Sir* Desmond, Shield to the King."

Desmond really hadn't known what he was expected to say almost any time either of these Midlön men spoke to him. He just remained as polite as he felt he could have as so there would be no more conflict in the day, no more fighting.

"This is good. This is good fortune." Desmond told them.

King Gregory laughed, and Sisco smiled at that. When the king finished making the laughing sounds, he said, "Speaking of fortune, you have a chest of gold waiting for you inside your bedchamber within the keep's apartments. When you think on how to spend this money prize, of course remember you are to remain with me in Ascali to protect me as I rule till the end of my days. Purchasing any pleasure boats or mounts to desert me would be most unwise. Instead of all that, with this gold you shall have the freedom to buy for yourself any garb you desire; finest silks and velvets ever crafted. Armor forged of the rarest irons. You'll have luxurious meals and wines when dining with my royal self, though now you'll have the money to purchase anything you'd like at any time of…ever! Money for delightful food! For drinking, gambling, women, weapons, the buying of dogs, as I know you'll be interested in. Come, allow me to show you where you'll be dwelling in the nights. Your gold is beside the beautiful bed. If you don't think the bed or furniture to be beautiful, we'll get you something more to your liking."

Sisco covered his mouth in attempt hold back a bit of laughter; Desmond hadn't known what was so humorous.

Recovering from giggling, Sisco said, "Well, I suppose I should take my leave."

To that the king said to him, "See you back in here for feasting at sundown."

"Yes, indeed. We have much to discuss of the event today. Goodbye, my king. Goodbye, Desmond."

Sisco left the Throne Hall smiling while Desmond stood there with his mind on that sweet word *feast* that the king had just spoken.

"We are feasting when sun's down?"

"Yes! In celebration of your victory and to respect the defeated and victorious champions of not only this year's game, but all past tournaments." answered King Gregory. "They've all been invited, as has Sisco's band of yellow-robed folk."

"That is nice." Desmond said to him.

The king began walking toward the wall built left side to the throne; he was making for a door. "My brother will be there too and you shall be able to meet him. Come, I would like to show you to your chamber."

Desmond followed King Gregory through the door and up some stone stairs.

They came to a long hallway with shining new red carpets where they walked at each other's sides. "I bet you're wondering why I was not present at the arena today."

I wasn't thinking of that. "Yes, I was wondering." said Desmond.

The king cleared the snot from his throat with a groaning sound, looking on ahead as the two walked onward upon the endless seeming hallway. "There was a tragedy yesterday evening. All of the city will soon know of it."

"A tragedy?" asked Desmond. "A fatality. There was a death within the Throne Hall right where we'd just come from."

The two reached the end of the overlong hallway only for Desmond to find there was another just as long now at the right turn here. "Are you listening to me, Desmond?"

"Yes." replied he.

They walked upon the carpets while they spoke. Desmond and the king passed by many closed doors as they continued deeper into the Great Keep. *This place is grand. So large and all crafted of stone,* Desmond admired the architecture as he spoke on asking, "Who was killed in the Throne Hall?"

King Gregory looked on ahead with his eyes fixed upon the set of stairs at the far end of the hallway. He answered, "Sir Marcus Magic, Knight of Many Magics. You saw those balconies high inside the hall? It was late, late in the night. He got drunk and stumbled off the edge. Split his head open, cracked his neck, shattered his bones."

"Sad. He is famous?" asked Desmond.

They passed by a servant woman who said, "My king." nodding towards them.

The king smiled upon her and then he answered Desmond's question. "Very famous. The entire city will know of his death tomorrow once my brother announces this horror publicly. First, we feast happily though. Sir Marcus was one of the most famous knights in Midlön; still *will* be in the records. The only knight to wield all five of the magics the way one needs to acquire to reach rank of wizard! He was no wizard, though. He was knighted and preferred to battle with sword, like all the greatest in the pages."

The king went on about the dead knight as the two came to a stone spiraling staircase. Up they walked as the king spoke on of Sir Marcus, up and in circles. "Some say Sir Marcus even wielded the sixth and forbidden magic, the *black* magic, but he would never admit to having ever practicing it. Sadly none will ever know now. What a great knight he was. Had the look of the heroes. I was to duel him in the arena, but his death… I couldn't even bring myself to arrive there today; and I do so love the game day event." The king didn't look much of a fighter.

Desmond was now curious of it. "You fight well? Famous Knight Sir Marcus, he fought well too?"

Gregory smiled and looked upon Desmond's eyes from few steps above; they both were still ascending the stairs. "I am one of the best ever. Yes, Marcus was skilled as well. Shame he fell to the stupidity of drink. I knew he would have rather died in battle."

The king turned back to face forward and upward as he took his many steps with Desmond behind him. They reached a doorless entryway at the top of the stairs leading into a finer appearing, yet much smaller hallway than the previous ones down the stairs. A large door of gold, a door of silver and one of black iron was built within the walls here. The hallway contained many chairs and big cushioned seatings. A countertop with various liquors and wines rested at a corner by a window of golden stained glass overlooking the city. Desmond was led past a pair of silver guards standing by a fireplace across from the cushioned chairs; they looked as if they were statues of knights, not living men. "I just feel like weeping so very much in these horrible times. Sir Marcus's bones are being sent to his family as we speak. And here is your chamber! Sorry to leave you with such grim talks."

The king was standing at the door made of black iron, waving a *"hello"* to the guards by the fireplace there. As the king waved to the knights, he said to Desmond, "Would you like me to show you the inside of the chamber? Or would you prefer to show yourself?"

After the king asked his question, he then looked into Desmond's eyes, discontinuing waving to the room's guards.

"I will show myself." answered Desmond.

"Very well. Beside the bed is a chest with your gold prize. In the closet you'll find silk clothes of many sizes and forms. Select which suits you comfortably and tomorrow we shall rid the wardrobe of the unfit apparel."

Desmond unlatched the door and gave himself a cautious glance inside. Candles were lit, as was burning incense that smelled of copper and mint. Mostly all that Desmond could see was the bed; it was massively huge. It looked to be made for the size of an orcish.

Desmond quickly turned back to look upon the king.

"Thank you." said he.

The king smiled but covered the grin with his mouth, now giggling. When he recovered from his humorous expression, he said to Desmond, "I sleep in the grand bedchamber behind the gold door there, my brother in the steward's chamber just over there. The longest amounts of time you will not be in the presence of me for guarding is when we lie behind these doors to rest in the night. As you see, your chamber is so very close to mine. Even the strongest of men such as you need rest. That is why there will always be a pair of honor guards stationed here in the royal apartment common room. They'll keep me safe when you are at rest." The king waved to the guards at the fireplace once again. They saluted in response to his waving gesture.

The king said to Desmond, "I'll leave you now, my new Desmond. We're going to be spending quite a bit of time together. Enjoy your privacy in here. You will not have much of it for your remaining days. Feast is at sundown."

The king began walking away backwards, smiling to Desmond.

"Goodbye, King."

"See you shortly, Desmond." King Gregory said to him, disappearing down the stairs.

Desmond entered through the black door and then he shut it behind him. The room had a hearth of its own, big in size alike the bed. There was a desk, more cushioned seatings too alike the ones in the hallway outside the bedchamber. The most fascinating object in the room was the wooden mannequin beside the bed. *This is where armor is to be placed?* The bulky figure stood naked, almost the same stature as Desmond, only a bit larger in build. There was a painting nailed to the wall over the desk. The artwork upon it was of a grand, golden shield. *My prize, where is my prize?* There was to be a chest of gold for him. He found it beside the bed, now slowly opening it. *If there is to be a snake in this black box, I'll bite its head off and slay whoever laid it for me.*

Inside the black trunk was no snake or any trap of any kind. Gold ingots, coins, medallions, and nuggets filled the chest. Desmond grasped a coin to inspect it. There was an Â etched upon the side. *For Ascali? The name of the city?* wondered Desmond. *Am*

I now a rich man? He was feeling happily surprised at it all; though a part of him felt this new fortune was false. He knew even if this money was real gold and truly his own, he was not free to leave this place… *"Purchasing any pleasure boats or horses to desert me would be unwise."* the king had said to Desmond. *That means don't leave, or I'll be hunted down if I do.* He asked himself though, why he should even want to leave? *Is this my new life?* He looked to his surroundings where he gazed upon the luxurious furnitures and decorations. *I should be grateful, though this is only where I'll be sleeping… I have a lifetime of standing as a guard set for my future.* Guarding the king's side in the day, dwelling in this room in the nights. It was a better outcome than living as an exiled homeless man in the realm and a better outcome than death.

Desmond approached the wardrobe door, opening it to retrieve a black sleeveless tunic and a pair of gray silk pants. Shoes and boots of many sizes were placed inside the closet. Desmond picked a pair of black dress shoes as his footwear option, though they were so very small when he tried to stick his toes inside. He swapped them for a pair of brown leather boots that he found under an enormous red bathing robe.

He pissed in the privy pot that was built in the corner of the room. After he was done shaking his dick above the iron, he walked on over to the wash-bin where he treated himself to a well-deserved scrub with a soaped cloth upon the face after cleaning the small cut on his arm. He washed the dirt from his nose, under his eyes and around his lips. He washed behind his ears too and then decided that his entire head needed cleaning. He dunked his head inside the wash bin and then removed it to scrub, then submerged again.

There were still bits of drying soap in his black hair as he lay in the bed there now. The pillow was absorbing water leaking from his long hair but he didn't care much; the pillow was too comfortable. *I craved to be back upon my bed in Eastfell. This, though, is something entirely different. I never knew there could be such a pleasure found in a bedding.* This was the first bed stuffed with feathers that he had ever laid eyes on or body upon. In Eastfell the common person would lie at night in a tree bed or upon a mattress stuffed with hay or thick grassing. This bed and matching pillow filled with feathers felt magically pleasureful to Desmond.

Sadly he did not allow himself to enjoy the moment any further, for his mind turned on to his lost dog Araisha. *Come to me. If you can hear me, I am here waiting for you.* Desmond was still bound to her through his eastern taming technique he performed when she'd been just a stray and wild hound. *She's tamed now and she's mine, though not currently with me. I am not well at being a master.* Desmond was tired of feeling saddened, bodily tired as well. He closed his eyes and removed thought from Araisha, as well as did not allow his mind to sink to the memories of home, nor his cruel living family. He did not dwell on his deceased loving father, nor the comforts of using black higher powers to kill living beings.

The only way for Desmond to have a mind at ease now was to think on imaginative outcomes of futures. *Fiction,* as his sister would call it. So Desmond visualized a glorious war where he and King Gregory battled upon the frontlines of a great army which they led together. Side by side the king and Desmond fought slaying all foes of the opposing army who'd approached; Desmond using a spear, Gregory a sword and a white dagger. On the field of battle Desmond wiped blood from his brow as so he could see more oncoming foes more clearly, and then… Happily he heard the sounds of the imaginary instruments. The horns and the strings calling he and the king back to the city in welcome after winning a great war. In this vision, Desmond had a woman at his side, clutching his arm with a smile upon her face just as grand as his. Desmond with his lover, the king of course beside him too, and with army at their backs, marching through the Square of the Ascali as people threw flowers and cheered. *Who is this lover of mine? Perhaps she healed me upon the field of battle?*

Desmond was underneath the sheets of the bed, head rested upon the damp pillow as he now dreamed of the healing woman from Willowhold. *The priestess heals me at camp during the war. This is the same priestess from Willowhold. The king introduces me to her once more at camp after I take a glorious wound on the front line of battle.* Was Desmond dreaming or resting with eyes closed writing a story in his mind? To him it felt like reality.

Many hours passed as Desmond recovered his strength lying in the grand bed. His black hair and the beautiful white pillow, all entirely dry now by the time he was woken. There was a gentle knocking sound coming from the thick door of the bedchamber. Desmond opened his eyes slowly, wondering if he would awaken inside the chamber he had fallen asleep in. He was happy to see he was here… *Good, my victory and fortune was not all a hallucination.* Just before he was awoken, he was dreaming of having offspring with the priestess healer he often spent so much time thinking on. Now though he only thought of that upcoming feast that the king had told him of. Desmond assumed that was what the knocking was all for, his summoning for the time to dine; he was entirely correct.

The man knocking on Desmond's door introduced himself as Grand Councilman Lewis.

When Desmond had opened it for answer, the grand councilman spoke his own name and then said, "Pleasure to meet you, Desmond, am I saying that correctly?"

The little man couldn't possibly have looked any more fragile. His back was bent forward and his skin was so wrinkled up, yet tight as well that in truth he looked as if he had the face of a babe who'd just been born. His wispy, embarrassing flop of hair dangling from his scalp was thin, but his beard was thick and white. "Desmond? Is that the correct way to say your name?"

"Yes." he replied to the distracting white bits of hair.

"Good. Desmond! Right this way. The king doesn't want you late to your own feast. On with it, yes, come."

Desmond and Grand Councilman Lewis walked together down the stairway. They walked the same route that the king had taken Desmond through from the Throne Hall to the grand apartments, just reversed from that now. It had taken thrice as long as it should have with the hunchback councilman front Desmond. They descended slowly, the councilman speaking all the while, asking Desmond questions. "From the East?"

"Ya." replied Desmond.

The councilman said, "I love the food of the eastmen. We have it made here in the Great Keep, even by cooks not of the East; peppers and smoked meat and all that. How old is it you are?"

"I've lived for thirty-one years."

"Children, I'm surrounded by children. And you fight well? I wasn't present at the arena. I've never attended the event, in fact."

Desmond and the grand councilman finally made it to the bottom of the stone staircase. "I fight well." Desmond told him.

They walked upon the carpets down the long hallway; they walked in silence now. Grand Councilman Lewis began speaking again though when the turn came to make for the second hallway, the one which would lead to the chamber with the throne inside. "It's funny having one as you to be the Shield to the King."

"Funny?" asked Desmond.

They reached the door to the Throne Hall where the feasting was being prepared; many of the guests already in attendance within the hall currently.

"Yes, it's funny. People of the East being such lesser men of Midlön folk. Lesser men, from a lesser realm, yet now one is to guard the king. It's funny, wouldn't you say? As long as you have the skill, though, I don't see an issue."

Desmond's eyes almost went black, though he was able to keep the dark away by turning his ears off. Desmond made no reply to the elder, only opened the door for the both of the two to walk through, unhearing the old man if he had any more to say.

Desmond speedily walked away from Grand Councilman Lewis after he had seen what the Throne Hall had become, compared to how it was styled only just few hours before now. *Sixty, seventy, maybe eighty people in here; all of them holding cups.* Front the Golden Throne during Desmond's first visit where he stood with Sisco to kneel had been entirely cleared earlier; nothing existed but the marble floor. Now though, not only a massive cluster of people stood atop this floor, but tables, benches, chairs and many barrels of various drinks had lived there. Some of the people stood in groupings to speak, others spoke in pairs. Some guests sat in silence consuming their food and cups of drink, others leaned among the walls to take their meals and or have the dialogues. People walked, people talked; hardly any danced. *An Eastern celebration or feast would consist of much louder music, dancings of many kinds too.*

Desmond walked close by the wall left of the throne as he looked upon the drinking people in their party attire. Desmond moved his gaze from the people, to the above balcony where he saw the red banner under the stone railing. *A black cross on a red backing? What a wicked symbol,* thought Desmond.

A voice behind him said, "What are you doing Easterlñ? Admiring my family emblem?"

Desmond turned himself around to look upon the man who spoke to him. He wore a dark golden half vest, half dress. Gray boots and a black cloak, shining silver medallions were stitched over the vest where his nipples would be. He had long black hair like Desmond's, and a black beard like the king's. *He has the face of the king as well, eyes maroon like his are.*

"You are the king's brother?" Desmond asked the man.

"I am. Lord-Steward Arol Royce." He reached his hand outward to grip Desmond's.

His fingers had rings resting upon them alike how his brother wore his. Desmond grasped the Lord-Steward's hand, shaking it firmly though slowly. He inspected the red gripped dagger within the red sheath at the hip of the royal man. He wondered if the blade was colored red as well.

"I am Desmond." he said to Lord-Steward Arol.

Arol continued on shaking his hand, taking a step closer to Desmond now, avoiding some guest already drunk off of ale who was approaching behind. Arol said, still gripping Desmond's palm. "It's a pleasure to meet the man who's to be in charge with keeping my brother alive."

Lord-Steward Arol Royce released his hand from Desmond's.

Desmond smiled, saying, "I will do well."

A serving woman was approaching to pass with a tray filled with tiny cups of liquor. Arol Royce grasped a cup as she walked through the crowd beside Desmond and he. The steward drank the contents of the cup with one small but quick gulp. He placed the empty ceramic upon the table close by his butt, asking Desmond now, "Where is it you trained?"

"Eastfell." answered Desmond.

"I know you're an Easterlñ. I ask where you trained. By who? How and why? I ask how you came to acquire your skillset instead of, oh, I don't know, becoming a farmer or a craftsman. Not all men are warriors in the East, am I correct? They do have craftsmen and farmers there?" Arol Royce awaited for Desmond's response while watching the folk for another serving woman to come round with cups of drinks to receive from.

Desmond said, "My family and me farmed."

Arol put his palm into his closed eyes. He moaned as if he had been ill. He then said, "You farmed, that's great. How is it you learned to fight?"

The steward waved over a woman in beige robes who held a tray of mugs. When the woman approached, the king's brother here grabbed a hold of two of the mugs, handing one off to Desmond now and keeping the other held in his hand. He blew a kiss to the woman and then said to Desmond, "Maybe this will revive that brain of yours. Get hit too hard during the games?" Desmond tried to sip the ale, but was bumped in the backside by a half drunk man who'd been showing another guest his jewelry. The ale spilled to splash against his wrist and drip onto the floor. The lord-steward was sitting upon the table now, awaiting for wet Desmond to speak. Desmond tried to take another sip once again, this time was successful. The ale felt refreshing, alike the ale from the shitty little Village Willowhold. Desmond drank and Lord-Steward Arol awaited for him to tell where it was he acquired his fighting skills.

Desmond said, "After I lived for four years, I was put to train for the *Su-Oin En-ahkah,* the *hunters competitions*. I trained in my village with one's my age. At night, I trained with my father. He fought in En-ahkah, so he trained me well from knowing how it be for my time to hunt."

Lord-Steward Arol took a long healthy gulp of the ale as Desmond spoke. Desmond continued on, and so Lord-Steward Arol continued to drink. "My first hunt, by then I had lived for ten years.

By the time I had lived for fifteen years, I had played on twenty-four hunts."

The lord-steward removed the mug from his lips so he could ask Desmond, "Twenty-four, at fifteen? How often is this hunting competition? The arena games here take place only once a year."

Desmond took a gulp of ale. When he was finished with his long sip, he said to the lord-steward, "Hunting is once every month. I gained experience at training for hunting and experience during hunts."

"MY SHIELD!" shouted King Gregory with a stupid smile painted atop his face.

The king approached Desmond and the lord-steward while holding his crown snuggled by his breast within one arm, the other hand held a black goblet filled with purple wine; he spilled half of the liquid as he walked to them wearing his high heeled red leather boots. Behind the king stood two fully armored honor guards wielding their huge spears and shields.

To them, the king said, "You two may leave me now. I have Desmond here to guard me." King Gregory gulped down some wine as he smiled at the backsides of the knights walking away from him. The guards disappeared into the cluster of drinking and feasting people.

Gregory's red cloak flapped and spun as he turned around hastily to look upon Desmond. He smiled and raised his goblet high. "To Desmond! The very reason you all stand here drinking my wine and eating my food! TO MY SHIELD DESMOND!" The surrounding people of the hall all then raised their mugs, horns, cups and plates.

"To Desmond." they'd all said at once with lifeless voices.

The king gulped down the remainder of the wine he had in his goblet. He snapped his fingers toward a sweating serving man far off. While the king waited for the man to approach with more refreshment, he asked his brother and Desmond, "What are the two of you speaking of?"

Before either had time to answer, the king grasped the rounded collar piece of Desmond's shirt, saying, "What's this? I give you a wardrobe of some of the finest clothing in the realm and you dress as if you are preparing to go for a training run of endurance. There are many party velvets in that closet I know there are."

Desmond was preparing say *sorry,* but the king's brother spoke before he could let any word out. "He's preparing to exercise after the feast. You've chosen a damn good one here, Gregory. Desmond was just telling me of his hunters competition in Eastfell. I'd like to know how it differs from our battle royale."

King Gregory received golden wine from the servant's jug as he spoke for Desmond, "I've always yearned to spectate for the *Su-Oin En-ahkah.* That is when the—"

The lord steward interrupted the king. "I would like to hear it from Desmond, not you."

The king looked to the floor, drinking his wine while Desmond was readying to speak.

"The *En-ahkah* is twenty men. Twenty men inside the dead forest for as long as must go on. Each goes in with *ahkah rëëbund,* copper competition wristband. No hunter can leave dead forest unless with all twenty *rëëbund's.* If you leave forest with any *rëëbund's* less than twenty, you must go back in to fight to get more."

Both of the brothers drank heavily as they listened on to Desmond explain Eastfell's gaming methods. "Like the royale here, all fight each other in the hunting competition."

The lord steward asked, "So you all go into the woods to fight each other to take each other's wristbands? To win you need all twenty?"

"Yes." answered Desmond.

The steward asked, "Interesting...hunting each other. What happens if you come out with none?"

To Lord-Steward Arol's question, Desmond said, "If you are beaten or your bands taken or you wishing to play no more, this is what you do, yes. You leave the dead forest with no *rëëbund.* In *Su-Oin En-ahkah*, you leave the forest with no copper bands or with all copper bands."

"What is one allowed to fight wielding?" asked the king.

"Staffs or short stick, slings." Desmond said in reply.

Lord-Steward Arol said, "Let's hope you're just as good with a spear or sword as you are at staff and stick. I won't have you guarding my brother here with a piece of wood, no matter how often you've used one in past for these hunting games."

"Oh, he's just as good with a spear, brother. He put a spear right through Frauer's leg. He killed the third mayor of Willowhold with a spear too."

Lord-Steward Arol smiled, shaking his head in the positive manner. "To Desmond then." The lord steward raised his mug and gently collided its rim with Desmond's. Lord-Steward Arol drank, and so Desmond drank. The steward then silently walked off into the crowds to feast, speak, or drink in silence; neither Desmond nor the king knew which he was intending on doing.

"Well, my glorious shield, I'm going to take a walk on to the privy. I would regularly have you join me, though you've only just arrived, and it is your own celebration, of course. Chat with some of the folk here. Most of them are warriors. You'll make a friend perhaps. The guest list consisted of mostly past champions of the arena, perhaps a family member of theirs too or a close friend. A few councilmen are walking among this lot as well."

"Thank you." Desmond said to the king.

"This realm and city is your new home. It's best you got to learn its folk."

Off the king went skipping to a door in the wall, leaving behind his black goblet of gold colored wine on a tabletop.

Desmond felt lost in a sea of strangers. His front side, back side, left, and his right, all people existing around him; all souls unknown to him celebrating *for* him. *Maybe it's time I quit acting oh so nervous and I go ahead and enjoy my time. I smell well-made food, and I haven't had anything hot in my stomach since the feast under the Arena.* Desmond approached a table, atop it piled high was various different steaming foods. There was a chef in half white, half yellow attire who was cutting and serving roasted meats. The white was the color of the fabric, and the yellow was the color of the grease stains that covered more than half of all he wore. He served meat to people holding plates while some grabbed portions of other foods for themselves.

Beside the chef stood a fire elementist, wearing blood orange and red robing. The man of magic was tasked with using his power to be sure the food of the feast would not go cold.

Desmond stood with a plate in hand as he plucked a crisped wing off the roasted bird in the corner end of the table. He grabbed a handful of grapes beside a plate of potatoes. He strafed to his right side, working his way down the table taking bits of all kinds of foods. He broke off a large chunk of some white cheese. There was a tray of a brown substance that looked as if it was shit but it smelled similar to coca; minty too. Desmond used the spoon to slap a scoop of the dessert onto his plate. He walked down the table some more as he inspected more of the food. He was chewing through his turkey wing while he gazed upon more dishes of fruits to consume after he cleared his pate. If any people, *or "folk," as they seem to be called in this realm,* were looking upon Desmond standing there, he hadn't known. He was in love and invested in his meal and his thought of upcoming meals.

He put the bone on the plate he carried as he eyed a large cake. Desmond had never had the pleasure or opportunity to consume the famous meal he'd heard called *"cake"* though he heard how delicious it tasted. "*Most delicious food you'd ever eat.*" Desmond had heard a man of his village claim after a return journey of his back to Eastfell from Midlön. Desmond was preparing to reach on over for a serving utensil but was interrupted when a man wearing a vest that held golden buttons in its middle had blocked his path. His brown pants were held up by a belt with a golden painted buckle. The laces upon his brown boots were colored gold too. *Dressed in the color of shit, but with flares of gold. Golden shit...you can't turn shit to gold.* Desmond looked upon the man thinking, *What an ugly outfit.* Now he thought, *He's in the way of my food.* Desmond was readying to walk around the man in brown and gold but he didn't after the man spoke, and spoke on to him.

The man was a knight, though he did not wear his armoring. His hair was black like Desmond's, though cut short. He too had hair upon his face, though only under his nose and under his bottom lip at the chin. No face hair on his side cheeks like Desmond had. "Hello, Desmond."

"Hello." Desmond said to him.

"My name is Sir Lance."

Desmond swallowed the last bit of food he had inside of his mouth. He said, "Hello, Sir Lance."

The knight told him, "Congratulations for the battle royale victory. I did not have the skill of making it to the sands to meet you. That orcish eating over there had shamed me in my duel. While you had been fighting, I was sent to be healed."

Desmond now recognized the familiar face of the man Lance. He remembered him now from the inside of the armory on game day. He had worn gray plate armor crafted with dull but beautiful golden edges. Why this knight chose to wear such fearsome and fine armor, yet would dress as shit for a feast, Desmond wondered now.

Desmond asked Sir Lance, "Are you well after your duel?"

Lance nodded. "Yes, 'twas painful, though. I was healed well. Upon my backside, I bore four crushed muscles and a chipped spine. The priests were gentle in restoring me. I still am in great pain though." Sir Lance placed his hand upon his back just above his ass. He rubbed at his bones and muscles under the wool while grunting. He sipped his drink with the other hand while he rubbed the ache.

Again here was Desmond, unknowing what to speak. He said, "Thank you for the congratulations."

The knight discontinued to touch his almost fully healed wound. He drank more from his cup before he readied to ask Desmond his question. "Where did you train? Were you once a man of the Eastern army?"

"My father taught me most all that I know."

The knight took another sip from his cup. His lips were becoming stained with the wine, though he disguised it well with that goatee of his. Sir Lance said, "I only ask because you managed to somehow defeat my captain, the White Knight. This knight, this man you put into the sands, he is one of the finest fighters I've ever known. I wish to know how it is you've defeated him while I was being tended to by the priest. I didn't have the pleasure of viewing the ending fights." Sir Lance drank more as Desmond looked upon his brown eyes.

"I used a spear."

Lance laughed while leaning upon the feasting table. "Don't be smart with me. I'm asking an honest question. A spear...that makes even less sense. How did you manage to defeat one of the greatest knights in the realm with no armor, using nothing but a spear?"

Desmond did not know how to answer the knight's question. He took a step backwards to rip a leg off of a roasted baby lamb that sat upon a plate of the table. He ripped the chunk of meat off of the bone with his teeth while he thought on what to say to this Sir Lance who seemed so very upset that his captain Sir Jason was defeated by Desmond.

"Was he injured before the two of you clashed? If it was an honest fight, a fair fight, he would have beaten you."

Desmond said, "It wasn't a fair fight. I had no armor. I began the royale with no spear, only wood sword."

Lance finished the contents of his wine and then slammed the goblet upon the table. "Was Sir Jason injured when you began battling him?"

Desmond answered his question with, "No."

Lance grabbed ahold of the wine jug beside the cake to pour himself a refill. Desmond continued on, saying to him, "The knight in white was on his feet. He had his weapon ready and was ready to fight, so we fought."

Sir Lance shook his head negatively as he leaned against the table while he looked on the folk feasting.

Desmond still remained there holding his plate; his own mug just under him at the table Lance sat against. Desmond asked Lance, "Has the White Knight ever been defeated in the past?"

Sir Lance squinted his eyes as he looked on over at Desmond. He let out a random half laugh and then looked away silently, but he said, "yes" with his head gesture. He said, looking away from Desmond now, "Twice."

"How?" asked Desmond.

The knight looked upon him again now as he spoke to him. "His first loss, he was swarmed. The combatants had known his power in arms, known his dangerous skillset. Because of this knowledge, they had decided to act with logic in their play. Thirteen men grouped together to attack Sir Jason from all sides and angles. He was knocked unconscious into the sands and hadn't woken for two days." Lance sipped some more wine but then scowled toward Desmond with a mouthful of the drink. After he swallowed the liquid he said to him, "I shouldn't be telling you this. The captain doesn't like when any speak of his losses."

Desmond nodded.

Even though this knight had just told Desmond that his captain had preferred for one and any to not discuss these arena losses, Desmond asked still, "And how was he defeated the second time?"

Again Sir Lance scowled toward Desmond. The knight was readying to speak, though he was interrupted by a tall older man clad in gray leather. "Jason Frauer's second loss? That would be because of me."

Desmond hadn't thought Sir Lance could express a filthier reaction than he just had right there. His scowling before had disgusted Desmond, now this face Lance made toward this new gray-armored knight had made that scowling appear much less uglier. Disgusted was in fact the exact expression that Sir Lance had made; a look of disgust to this gray man standing beside Desmond.

Sir Lance said, "Lucifer! Listening to him and I converse with your back turned to us? Creepy old thing, you are."

The tall man in gray asked, "Sir Lance, is that the way one knight speaks to another? Is your family doing well? How does that dam at Castle Alhert?"

"Excuse me." Sir Lance said to the floor, then walked away from them.

"I am Sir Lucifer Gray. You're called Desmond?"

Desmond nodded to him.

"I looked forward to meeting you." Lucifer Gray said to him.

"Why?" asked Desmond.

The knight said, "You defeated Jason Frauer. You and I are the only men to have ever done that in a one versus one." The knight raised his chalice.

"Cheers to that." Sir Lucifer said.

"Cheers to that." repeated Desmond.

They both drank together surrounded by the guests. "Lucifer Gray? Do you share blood with the king who ruled before the White King? The one in the East we called the Gray King?"

Sir Lucifer smiled, a smile of annoyance, though. *What could I have said so wrong?* Desmond asked himself as the knight shook his head with a frown now. "No, and yes. Well, in truth, yes. King Lucan Gray was the brother of…my father, yes. I had wanted nothing to do with those fools and their wives, even before their deaths and downfall of my house. They've always spat on me, my father and his kingly brother that is. I'm happy in the end the throne was ripped from them, and happy they received death. Harold Apollo turned the Gray-age into the White-age, and he'd done it well."

Desmond raised his mug again, to drink to the memory of the knight's fallen family.

"I'm sorry they've died. Do you have any family that lives?"

The knight answered, "I'm not sorry. The Gray-age was horrid. All agree rested Harold Apollo made a much better king than my uncle Lucan had in his rule."

"Yes, but still your blood they were." said Desmond, wishing his own father had been alive today.

Sir Lucifer Gray said, "Sadly, my twin sisters still live… They're here tonight." The knight pointed towards the two blonde-haired women in matching gray dresses who were standing side by side waiting for the king on the throne to finish speaking with a councilman with funny side pieces of hair on his face. The councilman was whispering into King Gregory's ear as the king giggled; the Gray sisters just stood waiting, bouncing ever so slightly so their breasts would jiggle up and down. Desmond from afar observed the two women while their brother here stood retrieving food to feast upon. They wore matching long dresses that began at their nipples, covering them, and then ending down past whatever shoes they may have had on. They wore gray sleeved gloves that ended up at the shoulders. Both of them hair colored blonde, though one cut short, the other one wore hers so long that it fell to her ankles; perhaps it was a wig.

"Don't let them spot you eyeing them in that way. They'll climb you together. It's like they hunt for men as a pair. Shield to the King, they'll try to birth your children when they see you, knowing you posses title as that."

Desmond asked Sir Lucifer, "You do not like your sisters?"

Lucifer finished the contents of his chalice, now saying, "I hate my sisters, only because they hate me, though. They'd only been ten years of age when King Harold seized the throne. Sadly, by that time in their lives, though, my wicked father and King Lucan had already seduced them into hating me as they did too. The girls, they blamed me for the fall of our house, you see."

Desmond was enjoying this historical tale of the realm's past dramatics, though this subject of the knight's family, the knight had hatred for.

"In the East, if something same as that would happen there, then the whole family would die."

"I don't understand your meaning." Lucifer told him.

So Desmond said to him, "You and your sisters would have been killed after a new family took control of the throne, not just cruel Gray King Lucan and your cruel father."

"Ah, yes, here we almost had been. This was, hmm, almost twenty years ago now. We were only spared because of the loving nature of Harold Apollo and because the girls had no claim to the throne; so very young too, no threat. Me, I was a fighting man! I would have been murdered along with my father and shit of a king uncle, though my life was spared because all knew my hatred for my evil family. I was allowed to live and remain titled as knight, so long as I swore to never act on the taking of the throne nor thinking on such an action either."

"And have you?"

"Have I what?" Sir Lucifer asked him.

Desmond said, "Have you thought on the taking of the throne?"

Sir Lucifer stepped aside so more guests could take and enjoy food of the feast. He was smiling as he looked into Desmond's eyes while the people passed between them. Sir Lucifer stood still and steady, looking to Desmond holding the plate. Gray eyes, gray hair, gray leather outfit; the name Lucifer *Gray.*

Sir Lucifer chewed shellfish meat, swallowed it, then said, "What a good shield you are. Already looking to detect possible threats toward the king and his metal chair. I'm not interested in the Golden Throne, have no worry. I only care for the arena."

"Why not play in this year then?"

"Meaning no offense to you, Desmond. Didn't want to win the prize. I don't wish to stand beside that chair there for the rest of my life, nor guard the one who sits upon it."

Desmond and the knight stood eating and drinking as they gazed at King Gregory upon the Golden Throne, crowned and laughing as the man in councilman's robes spoke into his ear still.

"The king looks comfortable." Desmond told Sir Lucifer as they watched on, chewing and sipping together.

"That's because he's horny for Councilman George there, the one whispering in his ear while my sisters wait to speak to his royal ass. Most men would prefer to speak to two fat-bottomed sluts such as my sisters there, but as you can see, our king would rather be flirtatious with George whom looks like he's half man, half rat."

Desmond plucked an olive from a platter and put it into his mouth as he stood watching the king laugh hard as this councilman named George was saying words to him.

"My sisters have slept with the White Knight, Jason, the one we've defeated. They found their way into his bed, both! In the same night too. They bring shame to my family name, those two, though my family is known to have ruined the realm for an entire age of its history, so I suppose I don't see much more harm in them being a bit whoreish."

Desmond was extremely curious now, *Where is that White Knight?* So he asked Sir Lucifer, "Where is Sir Jason? All champions were invited to here?"

Lucifer answered Desmond with, "Ah, but let us think in terms of realism. Not all desire to show themselves here of course. Think on it, all who've attended here who fought today have failed today. You are the only winner of today's game. Look around, do you see many combatants of today's event? Most folk here are those of past year events, like myself."

Desmond looked to the people within the hall. It was true, most all looked unfamiliar to Desmond. The orcish had been present, so had the black-haired holy knight who wore no helm during the fighting, the one who battled with a two-handed great sword yet only swung it with one arm. Sir Lance, the White Knight's friend and ally, was in the hall feasting somewhere too. Many though were of past games, victors and losers both.

"Sir Jason, you think, is saddened and not wishing to come?" asked Desmond of Sir Lucifer Gray.

"I watched that spear thrust you made into his leg. Jason is probably recovering at his household, drinking wine while that family of brown-haired jokers baby him back to health."

Desmond remembered the wound he'd inflicted upon the White Knight. He almost went deeper; he could have broken past his shin bones to push the spear further in so it would come out through the surface of his calve. Desmond yanked the head out through the entry wound, though, even so, this damaged Sir Jason greatly, ending the battle royale.

Desmond itched his beard while trying to understand the healing process of these Midlön people. "Wasn't all the fighters healed by priests? I was healed by one once in Willowhold Village. It was fast, her healing touch. The knight Lance, the orcish during battle royale, they've all healed and now here to eat."

Sir Lucifer whispered a chuckle to himself as he poured some more wine from the nearby flagon to enjoy. "My Desmond, you are learning quite a lot of our folk today. Welcome to Ascali, ha. Yes, Sir Jason could have been healed, of course, though he doesn't allow priests to perform work upon him, not ever. Jason prefers to heal through the works of natural ways which involve no light magic or magic of any kind. He cries, cleans, and wraps his wounds. He allows his body to repair itself with time."

Desmond gulped down the last bit of his ale in the mug, and then he reached his arm outward so that the knight would fill it with wine from the tin jug he held. Desmond asked Sir Lucifer as he poured, "Why would Jason not want to be healed by a priest? The touch of the woman who healed me, it was a soothing touch."

Sir Lucifer Gray sighed and looked to the floor as he washed down a mouthful of olives with a gulp of wine. After he chewed and swallowed, Lucifer Gray said, "Jason was touched by a priest in his youth. Touched as in the way a man touches a woman when he wants to have his children with her. Jason and his brother attended the school where the rich take their classes, the Institution. One day of each week during schooling season, the students are brought to the Cathedral of Aeon. For many months one of the elders had been touching little Jason in inappropriate ways during the visits. Today, now Jason hates all priests and everything there is about them *and* the cathedral as well."

Sir Lucifer was correct. Desmond was learning much of the people of Ascali on this day. *All of these people of the city, they all have their stories. I will learn them all in time.* Lucifer Gray had almost choked on his wine when he had caught sight of whom just entered into the Throne Hall. "Aeon has sent him to us. Speaking of Sir Jason, take a look at who just made an entry."

Desmond and Lucifer watched him as he walked with the cane in hand and white sword at his hip. He wore a dress shirt and leather pants, both combined with multiple variations of fabrics colored blue, white and brown. He looked like a proper, fine and lordly knight, though he walked like cripple. Limping and shaking, Sir Jason Frauer was making his way toward King Gregory to line up behind the Gray sisters so he could await his turn to speak on with the king at his throne.

"You should speak to him." Sir Lucifer advised Desmond.

"For what?" he asked the knight.

"So there is no bad blood between the two of you. He is the captain of the king's private party of knights. You are the king's personal guard. You and Sir Jason need to work as one for the good of the king and the folk. I spoke on with him after I knocked his dick in the sands and tore him apart years ago. I spoke with him to be sure he was not angry with me, and if I found he would have been angry, I would have forced him to not be. Go speak with Jason. Be sure he will not hold his loss as a grudge. He's a bitchy little man."

That night, those were the last words that Sir Lucifer had spoken to Desmond; after that, the gray knight was off to chat with a group of guests standing beside the little table waterfall spouting pink wine.

Desmond approached Sir Jason standing behind Sir Lucifer's sisters. He watched Jason attempt to greet the pair of women, though they only took a quick glance back at the cane Jason held, and they saw his leg all wrapped up. They laughed and then ignored him while they awaited for the king to have word with them.

Desmond said, "Hello, Sir."

Jason turned himself around. "What could you want?" asked he of Desmond. Sir Jason's lips were colored purple. Quick the way a cat was, Desmond shot his arm outward and grabbed ahold of a cup upon the plate of a passing by servant of the feast event. Desmond held out the cup for Sir Jason to take hold of. "I want to be sure you are not angry." Desmond told him.

To that, Jason asked Desmond, "Why would I be angry with you? Have you wronged me?"

"No." replied Desmond.

Jason did not accept the drink offer from him, instead, told him, "I'm not angry with you, nor am I here to drink with you. I'm here to speak with the king. Seems everyone's more concerned with feasting rather than conducting a proper investigation."

Desmond was curious what matter the knight was speaking of. "What investigation?"

"You saw from the armory. The black bowman? It seems he's fallen through Sisco's fingers. That was his responsibility to keep him detained! Where is Sisco? Has he arrived yet?"

Desmond remembered the incident well; he had no answer for Jason's question though.

"I do not know where Master Sisco is." Desmond told the White Knight.

Sir Jason asked Desmond, "Does the king know of what happened? Does he know there was an assassin present at today's event?" *The king never mentioned anything of it, nor do I remember Tournament Master Sisco speaking anything of it to him.* Desmond felt useless. "I do not know these answers. You should speak with the king."

"I would love to, only George won't stop putting his tongue in his ear. I have to wait for these two dumb whores to talk with him too. What's George telling him anyhow?" Sir Jason glanced over and around the two sisters in gray. Jason now got his first well view of Gregory on this evening. Desmond watched Sir Jason watching the king, and oh how interesting that was to Desmond.

Jason looked to be frozen in place, entirely still, besides his shaking cane. His eyes were tightened, as if the sun was piercing his brow from above. His mouth twitched as he looked upon the king, Desmond hadn't known what this look meant; these looks. Was this Sir Jason in awe? *Is he horrified? Horny? Fearful? Angry? Why can he not remove his eyes from the king's dagger?* Desmond looked to where Jason's eyes were placed, right at the king's hip, where the white dagger rested in his belt. Desmond thought to himself, *Perhaps Sir Jason wants that dagger to match that sword of his there. The two weapons would complement each other well, as they look very similar.* Now though thoughts of his role as Shield came into mind. *I'll need to be watchful of these sorts of scenarios. Men eyeing weapons... Jason could be plotting to murder the king with that white dagger there, and it would be nobody's fault but mine.*

Desmond was preparing to ask Jason why he was seeming so strange. Desmond never asked Jason this though. Just before Desmond was to speak to him, a sweating little man came running through the crowds to have a word with the White Knight. "Captain! Captain!" he was shouting. Jason turned away from viewing King Gregory Royce to eye the running man.

Jason placed a hand upon his shoulder when he quit running and stopped right front he and Desmond. The runner's hands were on his knees, his face toward the floor as he leaned downward. "Catch your breath, Alec." Sir Jason told his knight.

"They found him, Jason." the little knight said, gasping for air in his lungs.

Jason asked, "Found who? The black knight?"

Alec fought hard to catch his breath, but he was managing; slowly, so slowly. Alec said, "No, your brother. Dallion has been found."

The Gray sisters were making their way toward the king as they'd just been waved on over by him after Councilman George finally walked off.

Jason said to Sir Alec, "Good. I'll smack him on his cheeks for disappearing for so long. Leave me now. I need to speak with the king about this arena assassin."

"No, you'll need to come now."

Jason sighed at that and said, "My father and mother will punish him, or they won't, I don't care. He's been found, all that matters."

Alec rubbed his eyelids and sucked in more air. Desmond watched on, this Alec man clawing at his own face while the White Knight stood annoyed, his cane keeping him from falling on over.

Desmond watched Alec remove his hands from his watering eyes. "He was found coming out of a sewer leak within the streets in the Low District."

Now Jason was far beyond annoyed, angered and full of frustration. "Then tell my father to bathe the sewer filth from him so I don't smell shit when I return home! Be gone, Alec, damnit."

Alec, knight of the realm, strong man to be feared…was crying to his captain now. Sir Alec said to Jason, "They found him drowned, twisted, dead."

The White Knight gripped Sir Alec's throat with extreme force. Even with that hurt leg of his, he walked Alec backwards with his hand clutching his neck all the while. The two men, captain and knight, disappeared into the massive cluster of celebrating people.

So much death, Desmond thought. *The old die, the young die too.* He gazed upon his king, Gregory Royce, laughing with the two sisters whom had sun-colored hair. Death, death… *My only purpose in life now is to be sure the king right there doesn't die,* thought Desmond.

16

CATHEDRAL OF AEON

The weather of the day was gray. Many clouds filled the sky, rain came and it went away and then came back again. If the day was as clear, bright and hot as yesterday's had been, Desmond would have been drenched in sweat under these new leathers he wore. The grand councilman had told him, *"The king will decide the style of the Shield's apparel."* Desmond, Grand Councilman Lewis, and the king had all spoken briefly in the royal apartment lounge hall by the fire outside of their bedchambers after feasting last evening. Desmond understood the councilman's words, though he had said, *"Black."* He decided to have given his input anyhow, and to that input the king went on with. *"Done."*

King Gregory had said to the three, *"Have the leathers dyed black. The kingslayers and assassins will never see you! Lewis have the leathers ready for the ceremony tomorrow morning. I would like Desmond here to be armored and armed for his knighting."*

That was all late night drunken talk after the Shield's feast. Now it was morning, and Desmond was dressed and outside in the High District. The hide material itched his neck. He was unable to scratch at the throbbing muscles because the leather was so thick, covering every bit of skin from the throat down; all besides his fingertips. He wasn't heated, though; the rain had begun to fall again now as the party came closer to the Cathedral of Aeon. The cool droplets clung to his hair and beard. He wore new black water sealed boots, matching black finger gone gloves too. The rain falling upon Silver Street had made the ride so very soothing for Desmond; leather armor which could not be pierced by water, a mop of hair so massively large and long to shield his face from the wetness. Desmond had uncommonly large eyebrows as well; though it may sound humorous, they blocked his eyes from the falling water too. He was offered a half-helm, though had refused it. He was to guard King Gregory for many days, many months, many years. He had hatred for the thought of carrying or wearing the piece of leather atop his head until the end of his days. The hide helm wasn't the only object Desmond was offered.

On this very cloudy morning the king, Desmond, Lord-Steward Arol, and Councilman George had departed the Great Keep to make way to the Cathedral of Aeon. Before they made their arrival though, the king had directed the cart driver to guide the moving mounts southward to pass into the Military District. The four men had made a brief halt to enter into a weapons shop inside of a construct on the Street of War.

Inside of this shop, the king had told Desmond, *"Any weapon you'd like. I would assume spear?"*

"Yes, a spear." was Desmond's response.

The king had then smiled and stepped aside as so Desmond could have at his choice of weaponry upon the wall. *"Anything for you is free of charge, my king."* a clerk had said to the four of them.

Desmond spent five minutes of time to gaze upon the selection of spears; he'd even asked to hold two of the fourteen. Desmond had chosen his most favored one among the rack, and then on the four men had went back outside to hop in the roofless wagon driven by the keep servant named Kevin.

They rode upon Silver Street still as the clouds gathered and dispersed and then gathered again; more would stay than would leave. The rain was coming to an end now, but it would be back within the hour. Desmond sat in the cart gripping his spear held within his lap. The handle was black ebony, the spearhead blackened steel; it was made with a strap attached as so it can be carried upon one's back.

"Why is it you fight with a spear, Eastman?" asked the councilman named George.

The steward began speaking before Desmond could answer the man in brown robes.

"Why are you here?" he asked George.

The king said, "We could use another witness for Desmond's knighting."

"Well then, why not the grand councilman? Why you?"

George laughed at Arol's sharp words. "Arol, brother. I enjoy George's company. Relax yourself." George put his hand upon the king's knee.

Desmond and the steward both had looked away from those two, eyes into the crowds of folk and honor guards riding at the sides of the carriage.

Keep servant Kevin brought the horses to a halt when the carriage came front the cathedral. King Gregory leaned himself over the side of the cart. He gently knocked on the back of the horsed honor guard's helm just beyond the edge there. "You two stay here with Kevin. We'll be back after we've had Desmond made into a knight." The king hopped over the side, walked past the horsed guards, and took leaping steps up the stairs of the cathedral. The king moved eagerly; the three others calmly stepped out and off of the cart after Arol unlocked the little door at the back.

They walked at each other's sides while the king had already been waiting at the top; he was stretching his leg muscles and shaking sleepiness from his hands as he gazed at the stones of the holy building. The construct was entirely white, and it was huge! Not as big as the Great Keep, but still impressively large. Built with all stones like the Great Keep, it stood tall; white in color, true white. The bricks of the Great Keep held more of a grayed tone; as the way unpainted iron armor would appear. This cathedral though, a pure solid and true white.

"Many towers." Desmond said aloud, climbing the many steps.

George said, looking to Desmond beyond Lord-Steward Arol's shoulder, "Each high priest gets their own tower where their bedchamber rests within, their poor knees."

The king moved away from the edge of the stairs where his brother, Desmond, and George were approaching now. When the three made their way to the top, they'd seen Gregory there front the massive green skinned beastly being.

Arol said to Desmond, “A sight as this, this is why it should be *you* to walk up stairs first before him, or at least at his side.”

The orcish, in truth, was no threat, but Arol was making a great point of advice. *The brother is right. If the king's life is my responsibility, I should know what awaits him top any stairs, even in his own city.*

Gregory's backside was turned to the approaching men as so all they could see was his red cloak and the back of his shaven head where the diamond, steel crown rested. In front of the king, the tall thing was arguing with a priest at the doorway of the construct.

Desmond heard Grull ask, “But why?”

The priest replied, “Because god's law is god's law.”

Grull said to that, “Law can be changed or can be broken.”

“Not god's law.” they argued on.

The priest at the doorway had no knowledge of the king's presence behind Grull because the orcish being was so damn massive. The priest did catch sight of Desmond though past Grull's arm there. “I have another visitor looking to enter. Step aside, orc.” said the priest up to Grull.

“I wish to enter too!” said King Gregory, clapping his hands together a few times, red rings clanging and banging as he smiled. Grull moved out of the path of the king, and now the priest finally got a look on his sire there.

“Bless you, my king! I hadn't known you'd been there. This orc here was just wasting my time with an attempt to enter, blocking my view of you too.”

King Gregory looked over and upward to Grull's eyes when the creature turned to look upon him. Gregory smiled to the beast, then he smiled to the priest. “Call him what he is, an orcish. Orcish don't like being called orcs anymore. It's offensive, isn't this right, Grull?”

“Call me what you'd like. Just want to go inside is all I care for.”

“No man nor creature as yourself whom bears false religion may enter. If you do not worship Aeon, then you may not see the inside of his house. God's law is god's law.”

Grull looked to the stone floor at the entryway there as he thought on what he should say, how to talk his way inside; the king had come to his aid though with words of his own. “Let him inside.

My primary guard here Desmond is of the East. He worships the Eastern gods. I hope you don't dare on blocking *his* passage as well."

The priest frowned in discomfort. The king asked Grull, "Why do you wish to enter if you don't believe in Aeon?"

Grull answered him with, "I am here to show my sorrow for the family of the boy who died. The arena champion, the White Knight's blood. At the feast we all heard word of his baby brother's death. It was true news. When I learned this truth, I decided to come today to express my sadness."

The priest scowled, "The Frauers have no wish to be comforted by an orc!"

The argument was becoming loud, but oh so very loud when Arol now decided he would chime in, shouting, "My brother the KING has said to allow the orcish in, so you'll allow him in."

Into the Cathedral of Aeon the five souls went, King Gregory leading, Desmond behind him, then Arol. Behind Arol came George, and shaking the floor behind George stomped Grull of the Western Islands. The king turned around as he walked, taking backwards steps, now looking like a fool in this grand house of their god.

The king whispered to Desmond, "I didn't think the damn Frauers would be here." The king turned around to walk forward properly again. They passed by many rows of birchwood-crafted seatings to their left sides and right sides too. There must have been four or five hundred of them, maybe even six. The chairs were built into each other, almost as if they'd been half chairs, half benches. Most all were unoccupied, Desmond saw this as the group of five walked onward down this main center aisle. Perhaps a dozen or so folk had been seated at the far end by the altar, opposite the door where Desmond and the royal party had come from; the remaining hundreds of seatings had been empty and cold.

"The altar is occupied, damnit. The very reason why we are here is so you can be knighted upon it there, right there, damnit." The king spoke this as he walked onward, his head slightly turned away from the folk upon the stage, or *"altar,"* as King Gregory referred to it as. The altar was made with white marble, hard marble like the floor of the Throne Hall though this was pure white, like the birch seats and the stones this very building was crafted from. In the center of the altar stood a table, upon it a glass white sphere resting. A diamond ball known as *"god's eye,"* though its purpose was unknown to Desmond. Far in front this table was the slab of iron elevated high and built on wheels. Over the slab rested a black blanket with a blue tree embroidered in its center. The blanket was placed over the dead child. Surrounding the slab was the cold boy's family and some of the close friends of the family too. Including the five souls who've just entered, the chamber was currently occupied with roughly twenty-five, maybe thirty souls; Desmond was counting them all.

Grull took a seat upon the benches to pray silently. The father of the dead child approached the edge of the altar when the king and those who followed him came close too. Lord Edward said nothing yet. He stood with his fingers interlaced, hands at his belt buckle. Desmond inspected the man's face. His eyes weren't watered, nor even reddened any bit. Edward Frauer swallowed a mouthful of saliva, and then nodded to himself as if he'd just asked and answered a question in his own mind.

"It is nice of you to come, my king." he let out.

Desmond was learning to be quite observant so very fast. He always had a sharp and quick eye, though now with this lifelong task of his to defend the king, everything and anything felt as if it could have been a threat. He gazed upon this Lord Edward Frauer from head to toe as the lord spoke on with the king.

"We've shared countless hours of word and work together on the council. Of course I would be here. Respect for you and for your son Sir Jason. Remember, he's the captain of my personal knight battalion now." Lord Edward nodded with eyes closed. Desmond looked upon his tabard. The entire torso piece was colored black, except for the blue tree at the chest.

King's family wears black and red. This Frauer family wears black and blue. King's family's art is a black cross. This family's a blue tree. He was learning quickly, though he was not inspecting the man to learn of his house, he was searching for any threatening gestures or signs. The grieving father was unarmed though, and even so he didn't seem the sort of character to attack the king at random. *Anything can happen at any moment, though…* Desmond thought. He looked downward to see the lump in the cloak at the king's hip. Desmond saw Gregory Royce still bore that white dagger of his, though he kept it hidden under his red cloak. The king was surrounded by many friends, Desmond his guard with a fresh spear, and he was even armed himself with that dagger. *Nobody is harming him today.*

Lord Edward said to them, "Please, join us on the altar if—"

But he was interrupted by the king, "We shall join you shortly. Desmond and I need to speak with the ark priest. Arol, take George and sit there to wait."

The steward and Councilman George walked themselves to a front row of seatings, the ones closest to the altar; they'd sat beside a cluster of seated and grieving ladies whom have shared past intimate relations with Sir Jason Frauer.

The king turned his back to Lord Edward standing up there upon the white marble. He walked toward a door in a wall at the left, and so Desmond followed looking above at the ceiling of the chamber. Many inside balconies were built within this main chamber of the cathedral, appearing similar to the Throne Hall's style. The back wall of the Throne Hall inside the Great Keep had been made entirely of unstained glass. The glass of the windows of this chamber…marvelous, magnificent, magical appearing and colorful. Desmond was trying to rid his mind of the thought of arrows being rained down upon them all from the above balconies by admiring the beauty of the artwork of these stained windows. The many pieces of glass on the many different windows had been colored various tints of gold, some different and odd shades of beiges and hidden blues. No torches nor candles had been living within the chamber, instead the sunlight pierced through these colored windows causing the room to glow many different forms of color as the day went on.

Desmond approached a gray door with his king front him. The king knocked his fingers on the birch, then he turned around to look upon Desmond. "I hadn't even known the Frauers lost their son. In honesty, I'd never even met the poor boy." The king sighed and placed his palm into his face. He yawned while removing it now, saying after his yawn, "Perhaps we can't have you knighted upon the altar. They'll be here all day and night grieving. This is still Aeon's house, though. Anywhere's just as good as the white altar."

The door was opened, the one who answered was a man, a priest; though he looked so very young. The king and Desmond, both two feet taller than this little gold being who had no hair. Desmond stood close by the king, they'd both been staring at the new and strange face. The king looked over the priest's bald little head and into the chamber behind him.

"Ark Priest in here?" the king was looking around the room while he asked but saw nobody inside there behind the little man in white. Desmond looked into the priest's eyes; the whites had been tattooed gold, or magical golden paint was injected into each of them… However the matte, nonglowing, golden color was put into this holy man's eyes, it was a disturbing sight to any who looked upon his face.

The man nodded to the king's question of, *"Ark Priest in here?"*

The king asked, "Where? What are you doing in his office?"

He took a step outward into the main chamber of the cathedral. The man in white closed the gray door behind him. Desmond and his king stepped backwards two paces. "I am the ark priest." said he, unmoving now. He was bald, and his lips were painted the same golden color that he bore within his eyes around the black little centers.

The king looked disgusted at the words of this man claiming to be the ark priest. The king said, "No, you are not. Where is Ark Priest Daniel?"

He replied to the king with, "Gone. He rode off days, days ago. After the death of rested King Harold."

The king put his knuckles to each one of his hips. He said, "Neither the council nor I was informed of this. Where has he gone? Why?"

The ark priest nodded his head upward and down, what for, neither Desmond nor King Gregory had known.

"Would you like the truth?" this new ark priest asked his king.

"I would expect nothing but the truth, always."

The new ark priest took a deep breath in. He slowly exhaled as the king awaited his response.

The new and little ark priest said, looking high upward to King Gregory's chin, "He told us he refuses to serve in Ascali with a Royce as the realm's king. He stole a horse and rode off to nobody knows where."

Desmond saw that King Gregory was greatly insulted at this news. Desmond watched the ark priest pull the earth's smallest golden bell from a pocket stitched into his white robe. He rang the bell with three hissing *dingz.*

The king asked, "Why was this not reported to the council? I would have had a bounty order drawn up."

"I believe we asked to speak in a session, multiple times, but we had just received word down the royal chain of command to *'be patient'* and that we shall receive our gold donation eventually."

The king closed his eyes and pinched his black beard. He whispered, eyes closed still, "I apologize, those were my brother's words. You've received the gold, though, yes?"

Down a set of stairs at the side of the altar walked two enormous knights in full plate mail, helms fully fastened and made to show no flesh of the face whatsoever. "We've received the money, yes. Though we do not enjoy being thought of as impatient by the royal family and council."

Desmond watched the men in mail approach the ark priest; their armor was schemed white and gold. Behind the knights walked an old man in white robes. His beard was as white as the grand councilman's was, though this man's stature, movement, and physic was all more well together than the old Lewis's, who was commonly referred to as a *goblin* for it, Desmond heard and learned.

Am I being tested? thought Desmond. He looked at the armored men standing at each sides of the new little, and young in age, ark priest. These men were almost as of the size of that Grull creature. Equipped upon one of the knights' backs was a huge hammer made for breaking down doors and smashing boulders and bones also. The other one's weapon was a golden long sword resting at the hip. Desmond assumed they'd been watching him, gazing upon him, though he would never know because their helmets hid their faces entirely.

"Paladins, is ex-Ark Priest Daniel gone?"

"He is." both armored men said at once.

"Have I not succeeded him, acquiring the title of ark priest?"

The paladins said together, "You have."

The ark priest nodded to the king, eyes closed again. The elder priest who came down the stairs with the paladin-knights had then introduced, "New Ark Priest Alice."

The king removed his fist from his hip to cover his mouth from the giggle. "That's a woman's name, hehe."

The paladins looked to be statues. Ark Priest Alice stood emotionless, and the elder priest scowled, then sighed.

The bearded priest brought his head back upward, and with stern eyes upon the king, he asked him, "Why is it you've come?"

The king turned around where he looked past a row of benches occupied by five knights. The king pointed to the altar, then lowered his arm back downward and looked to the ark priest. "Came to show my respects to the Frauers. Jason is the captain of my party of knights. Is that the Eagle Party just sitting over there? Those five?"

The ark priest said, hard eyes nonmoving away from the king, "Sir Jason isn't present."

To that the king told the old man, "I worked with Edward on the council for years."

Desmond decided to give a word, he was feeling the need to verbally defend his king. "Is it really place of yours to question king?" *That seemed as if it would have been something his brother the steward, Arol, would have asked. The king should think of me as a brother one day. Am I right in thinking that could happen?*

The ark priest said to Desmond, "It does seem the royal family and the city's men of god do not work as one the way they had in the older ages of the timeline, but there's no need for hostility, though."

"Agreed." said King Gregory, smiling at Desmond while the elder priest with the beard viciously looked upon the two of them.

The ark priest said, "Might you dismiss me, my king? I have much work to resume in my study. My paladins here are weary and had been on a meal break before I summoned them down just now."

The king frowned at the two armored and armed holy knights. "They do not need to be here."

"Oh, but yes, they do. My paladins go wherever I go." Both holy knights gazed upon the king through those minute slits at their white and golden helms. The king ignored the knights, commanding to Ark Priest Alice, "Fetch me a key for one of the prayer rooms. I wish to knight Desmond within one of them."

"Ah, so that is why you've come today, to knight your new protector."

The king bit his lip and squinted his eyes. "I've come today for the Frauers, but yes, for that as well."

The old priest standing among them told the king. "No."

"No? Did you say no, bitch?" The king's face was changing color, reddening and reddening so quickly.

The ark priest said, "Your Shield is a foreigner. Whether you knight him here or within your Throne Hall or anywhere, it will be an invalid, illegitimate action. He will hold a false title, equivalent to no title at all."

"My friends and allies! What is the issue at hand?" Councilman George had seemed to have removed himself from his place at the bench chairs to come speak in.

The priest with the white beard said to George, "For one to be a knight, you must be a man of Midlön, baptized in the name of Aeon."

"So have Desmond baptized!" George recommended.

The priest only shook his head negatively, though, saying, "To be baptized in the name of Aeon, you must be born within the lands of the realm. Desmond was not birthed in Midlön."

The king took a step inward, closer to the ark priest; his face was red, veins pulsating at his neck.

Before more insulting or aggressive dialogue could have taken place, Councilman George spoke some more clever words to keep the peace. "Let's have this settled properly. Rules can be broken, can they not?"

"God's law is god's law." said the old priest with the beard. The ark priest, though, was less final with his choices. "Rules can be broken perhaps if there's an offer at hand." Councilman George smiled in reaction to the ark priest's words. "As you've said, the royal family hasn't exactly been joined with the Cathedral of Light, the way it truly should be. In the Golden-age, there was no power in the crown without god's support. My king, what say we permit the new ark priest here to attend council sessions?"

To this sort of bribe, red-faced King Gregory asked, "What for? Is that something you would even desire…Alice?"

"*Ark Priest Alice*, and *yes*, it is, though perhaps in a different manner. I myself do not have the time to be attending every council session, though I have other ways of using eyes and ears to attend, just not my own."

The king sighed, saying, "This is all getting complicated. I do not understand your meaning."

The ark priest said, "Allow ten of my priests to attend the council sessions as my eyes and ears. Do this and I shall allow Desmond to be knighted."

The king looked to the floor, tapping his heeled boot. His face had still been red, actually now it was appearing purple like the color of pure elvish skin. The king said, "You do not say what is allowed and what is not allo—"

Councilman George placed a hand upon the king's leopard-patterned cloth chest piece. Desmond heard him whisper, "Peace, my king. Choose peace."

The king snorted, then asked sharply, "Why is it you wish to sit the council? Or to have your men attend? Why ten?"

The ark priest answered, "The same review will be told differently when each of these souls report back to me after a session. I shall combine all of their versions into the ultimate truth. The returning voice of one godly man is nothing compared to the voices of many; ten listeners seems reasonable."

Councilman George said to King Gregory, "Imagine the convenience of it all. They won't need to request word now for cathedral-related matters. These priests would not only be ears to the ark priest and cathedral, they can speak for him and it as well, if that is the ark priest's desire."

The king was less angered than as of just moments ago, though he was still filled with annoyance. He spoke as his flesh tone reverted back, "So long as every session isn't filled with these priests constantly rambling on of godly business, then this can be arranged surely. Ten men of god seated with the hundred councilmen? Done, deal."

The ark priest nodded gently, closing his golden eyes. He opened them after he ceased his head movement. He said with a smile, "The prayer chamber directly above me is unlocked. Bless you all and enjoy your time in god's house. Congratulations in advance, Desmond of the East."

The ark priest went inside of his study while the two paladins remained at guard standing beside the gray office door. The priest with that snow white hair just groaned, scowling walking off while the king, Desmond, and George made their way over to the staircase, passing five knights sitting upon the benching; one of them, that Sir Lance knight from the feast last evening. Desmond nodded a greeting to the knight as he passed him by, though Lance gave back no facial response, only looked back onward toward that dead boy under the cloth.

The three walked up the stairs, four of them in truth now that Arol was making his way from his seating to walk on over to follow. The stairs spiraled upward. When they reached the top they came to a long pathed balcony. To their left-hand side was built a railing overlooking the altar and the rest of the chamber. To the right side along the wall was many diamond-shaped doors. They all entered in through one of the doors in lined fashion, one after the other.

The knighting ceremony went quicker than Desmond thought it would, hardly long at all. He knelt at the king's command. He rested the knee upon the center of the circle etched in the stone floor. The walls of the circular chamber were entirely black, shelves along these walls black too with many candles upon them; hundreds resting all burning golden little flames. The steward held the king's red scabbard outward. King Gregory Royce drew forth the blood colored long sword. He rested the edge upon Desmond's black leather pauldron. "In the name of Aeon, I charge you to defend the innocent,"—he moved the blade over Desmond's head, shifting it to his other shoulder. "protect the king,"—back to the first shoulder piece he brought the blade. "uphold the good, and enforce the realm's law, now and always."

"Now and always." Desmond repeated.

The king removed his sword from Desmond's shoulder, placing the red steel back into his scabbard now. "Arise, Sir Desmond, Shield to the King." said King Gregory.

Councilman George obnoxiously clapped his hands together as loud as he possibly could have. The king was wrapping his hands and arms around Desmond, viciously hugging him.

"Thank you, my king." Desmond said as Gregory sniffed at his ear.

He let Desmond loose, smiling, fastening the weapon and scabbard to his red belt covered in golden medallions just beside his white dagger. "Let us be gone." said he.

During the making of theirs to the exit of the cathedral downstairs, Edward Frauer's wife asked her lord-husband when she'd seen them departing, "Perhaps the king wishes to say a word?"

"My king!" yelled Lord Edward.

The king turned himself around, expressing the biggest grin upon his face. "Of course!" he yelled far back to Edward, standing atop the altar with his family and close ones.

The king, the steward, the councilman, and the Shield all walked their way back toward the altar; a band of royal men, moving down the center of the isle.

They climbed the altar stairs to join the miserable circle around the slab of cold iron.

The king said, "Ah, well. Yes, sadly no. Not a yes, this is not positive. This is just horrible, a life taken so young. Little Lord Frauer will be loved forever, missed forever, and cherished forever. Neither the little lord nor his family deserved this. We shall all light candles on this night for little lord Frauer. He is now in heaven with Aeon."

Lady Sophia Frauer was sobbing. There was a paladin beside her, taking sips from a sack of liquor as Gregory spoke, sharing the bag with a younger man beside him with a similar face; Desmond assumed the young one to be son to this paladin-knight. Desmond inspected all within this circular line of souls while the king made his short speech. Beside the paladin and the son stood three men in brown councilman's robes, *Friends who serve at the council with this Lord Edward.* Two priests stood within the circle, and of course, the Frauer family. The son who wasn't Sir Jason, Lady Frauer, and Lord Edward himself; all wearing the same blue-and-black fabrics.

When Desmond finished his gazing upon all on the altar, the king still wasn't finished speaking. After he had said *"He is now in heaven with Aeon,"* he went on with, "Umm, ah. Another soul taken too early was Sir Marcus Magic, the Knight of Many Magics. He was found dead in my very own Throne Hall early morning yesterday, splattered to the marble floor after stumbling off a stone rail. Too much drink! What a tragedy. Alike little lord Frauer, he passed to heaven too, too young."

All were very happy that the king was finished speaking. They all looked upon the floor as they awaited for what was to come next.

King Gregory was readying to tell Lord Edward Frauer that his party and he now must make to leave the cathedral after just having Desmond knighted. He turned to look upon the sad man but wasn't able to tell him what he had planned because of an interruption from one of the standing priests.

"Lord Edward, would you and your family wish to look upon Dallion one last time before he is put away and prepared for burning day? You will not see him on that day. He will be covered at his pyre."

Lady Sophia Frauer answered for her husband, "We'd like to see him."

Edward nodded in agreement to her and to the priest. None removed themselves from the circular formation. The king felt he was forced to remain, and so he had, and what he would see next would come as a visual shock to him.

Desmond watched the king's eyes go wide, his lips pucker, and his cheek muscles rise and twist on upward. These expressions and reaction occurred when the blanket was lifted from the face of the dead boy. The cloth was brought down to his chest where it was gently rested by the priest. The boy looked unrecognizable to almost all, even those who'd known him well. The king recognized the boy very well, though, making the scene more of a horror for his sweating self. Desmond saw the king look to his brother, the steward. Arol Royce sent Gregory a blank expression after he himself took his eyes away from the pale water-soaked corpse. The currents of the sewers ripped much of the boy's face off, even his entire jaw was gone; but King Gregory still recognized the body and where he'd seen it last.

The king remembered how clean the child had looked before he had the body sent to be rid of in the sewage tunnels two days ago. He had thought the youngling even looked as if he was sleeping after he'd been killed, and the king absolutely did not know the child was Dallion Frauer, not until now that he's seen the corpse with the family here. The king gripped Desmond's arm, removing them from the circle, and now fleeing down the stairs of the altar. Lord Edward looked away from dead Dallion, calling, "King Gregory?"

Councilman George and Arol smiled to Lord Edward and the occupants of the altar. "Sorry." the both of them had said in turns before making to leave and to run after King Gregory and Desmond.

The entire ride back up to the Great Keep, the party traveled in silence.

"Back to the keep, Kevin!" coming from the steward was the first and last that was said after the four made their exit of the Cathedral of Aeon and back into the uncovered wagon settled outside with its driver.

The day was still early, but it had been dark and cloudy. The wagon arrived at the front of the keep at midday.

The Royal party exited the carriage. Kevin commanded the horses to trot onward toward the yard's stables, and then up the many steps of the keep the party went, excluding George. "I must be going home now. Congratulations, mighty Sir Desmond. Goodbye, my king, Lord-Steward." George left the three of them to enter the Great Keep so they could make for the royal apartment.

When Desmond, the king, and steward entered the common hall after the long walk through the red glowing Throne Hall and long standard hallways of the keep, they'd all silently poured drinks to take into their separate chambers. Lord-Steward Arol was the only one to engage in the pouring truly. He prepared three glasses of rum.

"There you are, brother." he said to the king to break the silence.

"For you too." he said to Desmond, handing him off the liquor.

Gregory said, "Oh, thank you, Arol." The king sipped and then he looked toward Desmond; Gregory Royce looked as pale as the boy's corpse had been. Gregory was far whiter than of regular.

"Do you do well?" Desmond asked his king.

King Gregory said, "I apologize. Seems a sudden illness has come over me. I shall be well soon, very soon." King Gregory took another sip of rum with that shaking hand full of rings. "I need to rest. Excuse me, please. Arol, come in to speak with me in ten or so minutes. I need to use the privy first." The king walked off to his golden door, trembling as he took his steps and drank from the little glass cup.

Arol Royce finished the contents of his little glass, then he poured more liquor in to fill it. The king had entered the bedchamber, leaving the steward here and Desmond alone with the new pair of guards stationed at the fireplace. Desmond gulped his entire glass down in a single sip. The steward offered to pour Desmond more. He accepted gratefully.

"I'll have a servant come notify you when the feast is ready."

To Arol's words, Desmond nodded his head in the affirmative, but then he quickly decided he wasn't in the mood for another feast with more people unknown to him. He craved for a quiet night, though still desired to fill his belly with some food and more of this delicious rum now that he's gotten his first taste of it. "Truly, though, I do not want to be feasting this night. I am wanting to rest in my chamber room."

Arol gulped down more rum. After he swallowed the burning liquid, he said, "Surely. I'll have a meal brought to your door at sundown. Is there anything else you'll be wanting? Remember, you are free to walk about the keep to go anywhere you wish; anywhere within the city even."

Desmond looked at that half-filled bottle of liquor he and Arol had been drinking the contents of. Desmond told the Lord-Steward, "I'd want some more of that." He was pointing to the bottle of the clear fluid.

Lord-Steward Arol handed the corked bottle off to Desmond. "It's yours. We're always having the table here restocked and replenished. Enjoy, and enjoy the food this evening. I think tonight it's duck. They eat duck in the East, yes?"

The steward was just readying to walk on over to his door of silver, but before he went in, he paused. He turned himself around to face Desmond before he himself was about to enter his own chamber across the hall, bottle in hand. Lord-Steward Arol said, "The death of Marcus, the sight of that poor boy. My brother isn't feeling the best, as you see. If he has need of you, you'll be summoned. No need to bother him if you do not hear any more words from him for the remainder of the day and night." Arol raised his glass, sipped the rum and then entered past the silver door. He shut his door, and then Desmond entered through his own, shutting that too.

Desmond lay on the bed, lost in thought for many hours, eyes fixed on the hearth inside the room. The embers were dying down he saw, and so he'd risen to put another log atop them. When he stood upward to walk off from the bedside he'd realized just how drunk he truly was. The bottle never left his hand from the moment he entered the room to even this current mark in time. He inspected the glass, within it there was maybe one, maybe two gulps left to take. Desmond walked on over to the hearth as he finished the contents of the bottle. He placed the empty glass beside the fireplace, then put a log atop the embers inside the hearth. His face warmed as the fire began to catch on the logs.

Desmond kneeled there for quite some time. He gazed at the flames as he wondered where Araisha was. It seemed though the harder now he thought on her, the closer he felt she was coming to him; literally and physically. Perhaps it was reversed though, maybe somewhere out there the closer Araisha came to him, the more his mind would turn to focus on the thought of her. All of these answers would be within certain training scrolls in the East, though Desmond never learned through the reading methods, only through legitimate approach and practice.

Desmond removed himself from the fireplace when he heard the barking coming from beyond the walls of the Great Keep. Desmond walked to the window beside the fireplace. He unlocked the latch and then opened up the panel of unstained glass. The barking was growing louder, not closer but the barking itself stronger; projected louder than just seconds ago. The barking turned to howling! Not of pleasure, nor of pain, but a sort of calling. *She wants me, she needs me, as I need her too.* Desmond put his hand upon his breast to feel his heartbeat in his palm; he felt hers too. Desmond slammed the window shut, moving on over to the door where he went to lace up his boots. His vision was slightly impaired from the massive amount of rum he had ingested, though he managed to successfully tie the laces up nonetheless. Desmond heard some sounds of movement coming from the common hall beyond his iron door, though he drunkenly paid them no bit of attention. If he had focused on them, he would have heard the king there at the doorway.

Desmond was determined to find Araisha after this new spark of confidence. He'd just heard a dog barking off in the city somewhere and he felt in his heart (literally) it was Araisha; he needed to go looking for her. When he opened the iron door to the bedchamber though, the king was standing at the doorway with a dumb grin on his face. He was holding a golden tray, atop it sat two bowls of soup; two spoons as well. "Suppertime! Might I come in? I heard you do not wish to feast in the Throne Hall this evening. Neither do I."

"Yes." Desmond told the king.

While he held the wobbling tray with an unsteady hand, King Gregory used his other to close the black door before Desmond could get a look out into the common hall.

"You smell just like rum." King Gregory told Desmond.

"I've been drinking rum." said he in response to the king's remark. Desmond was tempted to offer to take hold of the tray so his king would not have to carry it, though his weariness from the liquor just brought Desmond back to his bedside. He thought, *I was just readying to leave for Araisha, now I must stay to dine. If I do not leave quickly, I'm afraid I'll fall off to sleep from the effects of this liquor. I must make my body move.*

The king said, "Desmond, are you having a talk with yourself? No matter. It's fine, it's fine, it's fine, Desmond, it's fine, it's fine." The king placed the tray of duck soup upon the desk in the chamber, splashing some atop the wood. He walked over to sit upon Desmond's bedside with him. King Gregory said, "I've been drinking too…" Gregory put his hand upon Desmond's backside at the leather. King Gregory rubbed at Desmond's armor while he sniffed his black locks by his ear. "Why do you still have your armor on from today? Would you like me to remove it?"

"No." said Desmond, sharply.

The king's eyes began to water. The king said, "Oh." then placed his head into Desmond's shoulder.

Tears ran down the leather armor as King Gregory began to weep with his cheek planted upon him. "What is wrong? King?" Desmond patted the king on his bald head; he wore no crown this evening.

Gregory looked upward with those watery maroon eyes of his. He looked into Desmond's eyes, expressing a look of pain and fear. "I made a mistake, Desmond." After he said Desmond's name, the expression turned from fear to lust. The king raised his head upward to plant his lips upon Desmond's mouth, but lightning fast, Desmond used the palm of his hand to thrust away the king's face at the jaw.

"Ah!" Gregory yelled, falling off the bed. The king quickly rose off of the carpeted floor while Desmond watched him from the bedside. Gregory Royce immediately left the chamber, not even with the will to look upon Desmond after he'd had his own face sent away, kiss rejected. The king had simply stood upward, eyes on the floor, and then made his way as fast as he could have out of the room, holding his mouth and beard the entire time with his hands.

When the iron door was slammed shut by the king, Desmond collapsed backwards into the pillow. He thought asking himself, *Why would he do that to me?* Desmond closed his eyes, drooling as the sounds of howling poured in through the closed window. When morning came, Desmond woke to the sight of two cold bowls of duck soup upon his desk, a dead fire, and no memory at all of rejecting the king's kiss or even the offering of it.

17

The Garden in the High District

Arthan awoke from dreamless sleep; he felt exhausted. *"Aeon, god of light hear me now and today. Lighten my soul and brighten my house today. Guide me in this world, lead me to greatness today. Cast out and keep away the terrible of today. Ascend me to your heaven when my time ends, not this day. In Aeon I trust all days."* He arose from bed to piss and clean his body inside of the washing room across from his bed-chamber. After Arthan finished drying his hands, he then left the little room to find his family. He now walked out of the pink hallway and into the kitchen area while yawning. By the window, the enormous blue chair where Arthan's cousin Tillsy was meant to rest during her visit was occupied by Lady Frauer, puffing on her pipe as she gazed out through the drippy window. Tillsy Frauer was gone now though; she rode out of the city in much haste after she got a view of Dallion's corpse half hanging out of the sewer gap in the street with the rest of the onlookers two days ago. Tillsy, in truth, hadn't departed immediately after this horrible sight; she had a lengthy argument with Lord Edward first at the household here while she packed her belongings.

"Murder! He was murdered and cast in the sewer tunnels to be gone forever. The assassins hadn't planned for him to wash up on the street as he had." Lord Edward was horrified at Tillsy's theory. He'd tried calming her, called her a silly to think such things.

Lady Sophia had been more open to the suggestion and theory, especially after Tillsy made a point of, *"You saw the way his body was destroyed? So if he's found we wouldn't be able to know the true cause of his death!"*

Edward had then assured her, *"The rough currents of the sewers, him scraping against the walls. Tillsy, damnit, my dear, I'm sorry, but he was not murdered. He was hunting for goblins and had...tripped or fallen in the waters. Somehow he managed to find ways into our locked attic. He found some way into the sewers, is all. Mistakes happen. Accidents do happen, Tillsy."*

Arthan had listened on to the entire argument, so had Lady Frauer. This dialogue had taken place late in the evening during the same day of the tournament and Dallion's finding. By the time Jason had returned to the household from the Shield's feast taken place in the Throne Hall, Tillsy Frauer had already rented a horse and left Ascali, riding back northwest towards Fort Bluewood. Her last words to the family that night had been, *"I'm sorry you do not see the truth, Uncle. Dallion was murdered, and I'm telling my father news of it. I'll be back, with Frauer swords."*

Tillsy left them all there at the porch of the Frauer household. She hopped the gate and ran down the street, her big bear cloak flapping in the misty night behind her, running and running to spend all the remainder of her gold coins on a horse to rent for her ride to the family's home castle.

Jason had come back to the house twenty or so minutes after Tillsy's departure. Lord Edward explained to Jason why Tillsy had made to leave Ascali, what her reasoning was. Jason didn't make much of a comment on any of that though, as he had a conspiracy theory of his own he thought hard on in his mind; he hadn't shared this theory to his family yet though. Jason realized Lord Edward had made Tillsy appear mad in his talking of her leaving, crazed. His father would think Jason's thoughts to be the thoughts of a madman, as not only did Jason stand there believing like his cousin did, that Dallion was murdered, Jason thought that Dallion was murdered by the king himself!

That night, though, Jason kept these thoughts to himself. The knightly son's only objective was comforting his father and mother, as he assumed losing a child in this world was an ultimate pain like none other; worse pain than losing a younger brother. Constantly Lord Edward would say to the boys in the past, "*No man nor woman should ever see their offspring dead. Children bury their parents, not parents their children.*" So Jason had spent the remainder of the night being as best of a loving son he possibly could have been, sharing no thoughts of this mischievous murder assumption to his parents. Arthan knew something terrible was wrong though. He could see it in his brother's face. Jason was keeping something hidden.

What has happened? What has truly happened? What is happening? thought Arthan. Arthan heard the news of Jason's assassin as well… During the duelings of game day, Arthan had lost consciousness while spectating. One moment he remembered he had been awake watching combatants fighting under the sun, then next he remembered in the blink of an eye he was back inside of his dark bedchamber, aching and head spinning. He hadn't known how he had arrived there in the chamber or in his home; a home he had been alone within at this time of confusing awakening. His family had returned some moments later, giving Arthan the news of his fainting in the arena seats. "*A priest or paladin must have brought you back here, carted or slumped over a mount.*" Edward had assumed and told Arthan.

They then had given Arthan news that Jason had not only lost in the battle royale to a bloody spear thrust in the leg, but that an attempt on his life was also made during his dueling time. A knight wearing all black had apparently approached and shot arrows down into the sands! That's one assassin, then Tillsy claimed Dallion's death to be a murder…and strangely at Dallion's cathedral ceremony yesterday morning, the king mentioned the death of the famous Sir Marcus Magic. *Now that…sounded like a murder to my ears,* Arthan had thought when the king had made awkward random mention of the death of the knight Marcus. *A knight doesn't just stumble off of a balcony, he was thrown!* that was Arthan's thought and assumption on that matter.

That horrid night when Arthan was observing Jason there comforting his parents, Arthan believed his brother was thinking hard on Dallion's manner of death. *If I were Jason, I would be trying to connect that black bowman's attack to any relation of what Tillsy spoke on about Dallion.* Arthan yearned to know exactly what Jason was thinking there as they had all sat upon the family table to share sad cups of wine, though he held back asking. The next morning had been hell for the family. 'Twas the first day waking knowing that Dallion was no longer living. They skipped over breakfast, dressed, and made right to the cathedral; walking in the quiet rain. Jason remained in bed during all of this, not attending the ceremony, claiming his leg wound was aching greatly; though it was his poor heart and mind at ache in truth.

The family had returned home from the cathedral, miserable and silent. That night they ate a supper of olives, cheese, oats, and baked bread, hardly speaking any words to each other. When they did share dialogue, it was never in relation to the subject of rested Dallion. In fact, after the family had returned home from the cathedral yesterday, the only time Dallion had been mentioned in talk was when Arthan had asked which day the burning would be on.

After the supper had concluded, Jason and Arthan then separated into their own bedchambers without speaking to each other. Edward and Sophia silently left the dishes upon the table to enter their bedchambers for sleep as well, not sharing any words or conversation before their night of rest.

It was morning now, and all family members in the household had been awake, though so silent. Arthan watched his mother there on the oversized chair, gazing out the window as she sucked on her smoking pipe. "Mother, how do you feel?"

Lady Sophia turned her head around with those baggy raccoon looking eyes of hers.

She hasn't slept one bit.

Sophia stood upward from the chair and left her smoky corner to make for the main door of the household. "How do you presume I feel?" said she, gently shutting the door to take her blazing pipe outside on the porch in private.

Arthan opened the cold iron cabinet in the kitchen, removing a small unfinished block of cheese. He sat at the family table as the morning sun failed to enter in from the windows. The sun was high in the sky now, but the day looked to be many hours earlier than it truly had been. The chambers and halls of the house were in fact so dark, Arthan was readying to light candles for a better view. He stood upward out of the chair at the table, but then Jason appeared limping out from the pink hallway with his cane in hand.

"Don't get up." Jason said as he came closer to the table, sliding a chair away from the edge of the wood now. "Mother went outside to smoke?" asked Jason, legs shaking as he made to seat himself.

"Yes." said Arthan.

"Father is still sleeping?"

"I don't know." he answered Jason.

Arthan's brother softened his voice, bringing it to an almost whisper. "What I'm about to say to you, you must keep quiet on, for now."

"Any secret is safe with me that you have to share, brother, though I can't promise I won't react sadly if this is harsh news you are to tell."

Jason smiled a painful grin at Arthan as they both sat there in the morning's darkness of the household. He told Arthan, "You've managed to hold back tears so far these past days. These words I'm to say will not bring you to tears, but to anger. Our cousin was more than likely correct. Dallion was murdered." Jason looked backwards into the hallway to be sure their lord-father would not be approaching or eavesdropping. The hallway was clear.

When Jason turned himself around, Arthan was thinking on what words to say next, pretending almost to appear surprised at Jason's. *I had assumed these were Jason's thoughts, though why does he share this same feeling with Tillsy? Tillsy had her reasonings to believe this truth of Dallion. What were Jason's reasons for thinking this too?*

Jason indeed saw something that Tillsy hadn't. The sight of this *"thing,"* combined with hearing news of Tillsy's theory after him returning from the Shield's feast, made Jason come to the conclusion that Dallion had been murdered by the king. "My dagger, my white dagger. At the Shield's feast, just before Alec ran in and told me of Dallion's finding, I saw it Arthan. I saw the dagger."

"Where?" asked Arthan. He was horrified when he'd heard the answer.

"The king's hip, I swear it. I hadn't even heard word of Dallion's finding in the streets yet. I was there in the hall waiting in line to speak with Gregory, that scum. I saw it, dazzling and glowing, Arthan. It was mine, the white one."

Arthan shook his head negatively, though why had he? He believed his brother in his sighting of the white little weapon, so why was he shaking his head in the *no* manner?

"You do not believe me?" Jason asked him.

"I believe you. Could it not have been another dagger, similar in style?"

"There is no same dagger. I spent thousands of golden coins to have that made just for me, as well as my matching sword. The white diamonds, no other knight nor king would dare spend what I paid for a piece of weaponry as that. I saw the diamonds in the handle. It was indeed my dagger, the dagger I would often give to Dallion to play with. He last had it before he went missing. He was found naked, clung coming through some sewer bars in the Low District. The king is currently equipped with the dagger I'd last given our baby brother. We don't need an investigation for this. It's clear as ever, Dallion was killed the day he went missing. Think on it, how else could Gregory come to have the blade."

Arthan itched an ache at the back of his neck. He shoved aside the hunk of cheese as he thought on what Jason was inferring. Arthan said, "Dallion was last seen heading to the Great Keep. The students and instructors say they'd seen him at the Institution, guided him, and had even spotted him at the keep for the visit, then nothing. The students when asked say they remember nothing; hadn't seen him sneak off, nor anything of that sort."

Jason now rubbed at his leg, the deep flesh wound within his shin. Jason said, excited but not happily excited, "Precisely that. Yes, he went missing during his school visit to the keep; The *king's* own house. Tillsy was right, damnit, she was right… The king killed him and tried to have his body rid of in the sewers. Oh, I understand now, Arthan, I see it all."

"What do you see?"

"The king takes the dagger. He even wears the dagger because he does not know it is mine. He doesn't know he's retrieved it from *Dallion Frauer.* He doesn't or hadn't known whom Dallion was when he killed him."

Moments ago Arthan was believing everything Jason had to say, he still was, though now the tale was becoming oddly specific. "Now you are assuming too much." he told him. Then he asked Jason, "How could Gregory not know who Dallion was?"

Jason put his hand away from his leg and rubbed at his eyelids. "I saw Dallion that morning. I was bandaging my hand from my trial match when I saw the little one coming out from the hall right here to greet me before his school lesson. Thought I was a goblin he did..."

Arthan watched Jason there as he then silently just stared at the wooden surface of the table top. "Go on." he told Jason.

Jason blinked harshly, then he said to Arthan, "I saw his attire. He wore no Frauer emblem nor blues of our house. Dallion went into the keep, went off hunting for goblins dressed just like any other city child. The king found him and killed him, didn't even know whom he was killing."

Jason put both of his hands into each of his closed eyes now. He was holding back tears, doing well. "Why would the king do that, though?" asked Arthan.

Jason, with fingers rubbing hard in his eyes, said, "That house is wicked. Known to eat men in old ages, liars, cowards. Morbid jokesters and cruel killers. This is in the character of the family; killing a child for no true reason."

"There must be a reason, though..." Arthan told him.

"Must there? Our baby brother's dead. Gregory Royce did it, and that's that."

"You can't know that for certain."

"I can!" Jason said, shouting the words. Neither Lord Edward nor Lady Sophia came at the sound of the loud voice though.

Arthan thought on about how the king had appeared at the reveal of Dallion's corpse at the cathedral. "If only you saw him,

Jason, the way he looked upon Dallion when they showed his body at the cathedral."

Jason was confused at Arthan's words, so he asked him, "Who? Father?"

"No, the king."

Jason was interested in this information. "The king showed to the cathedral?" asked Jason of Arthan.

"Yes, claimed he was there for Dallion's ceremony, though what a plain lie that was. He was having his Shield knighted. The king didn't even know Dallion's name, kept addressing him as *'little lord Frauer.'*"

To all of that, Jason told his brother, "Go on though about how he looked upon his body. In what way had he gazed?"

Arthan took a moment to collect his memory, then he said to Jason, "He appeared to be the most horrified one on the altar, even more horrified than Mother. Didn't last long, though. He grabbed that new Eastern guard of his by the arm and ran off out of the cathedral, literally ran. The steward and that councilman named George followed them out after. Father looked so confused."

Jason silently and painfully stood himself upward from the chair. Arthan was still talking on, "I'm surprised Father hasn't said anything of it. Well, we all haven't been talking to each other much since the first night we learned of what happened."

Jason tightened his sword belt to the side of his hip. He limped to the door, saying, "We still don't know what happened."

Arthan then asked him, "Where are you going?"

"To find out what happened."

Arthan saw his brother there was attempting to play the heroic investigative knight character; dangerous though to play against the most powerful man of the realm.

"Jason, don't be a fool. Where are you truly going? Your leg."

Before Jason opened the door, he said, "I'm going to tell Mother I'm heading to pray in the garden here in the High District."

Arthan begged to know, "But where are you truly going?"

Jason smiled another painful smile to his brother. "I'm going to confront the king of this in the Throne Hall, front the steward, honor guards, and whichever of the councilmen he has there in attendance at the time. As I've said, the dagger is enough proof. He'll have it there hanging from his hip, and if not, well then, enough souls have seen him with it by now for him to deny its existence. By sundown, I'm going to have King Gregory arrested. If I can't have that done, I'll kill him myself." Jason slid a portion of steel out from the white scabbard for Arthan to view, then slammed it back into the leather. "Say nothing to Mother nor Father. The first word they'll receive of any of this scenario is when they hear that King Gregory is in chains." Jason opened the door and closed it shut just an inch from Arthan's nose; he was gone.

Arthan watched out the window Jason briefly speaking to their smoking lady-mother out upon that rocking chair. Arthan was watching through the glass as his brother limped his way over to the little stable to retrieve Pax. How Jason had the strength to resist the pain of those gallops and even the smallest of trots, Arthan could never know. *How he even managed to climb atop the horse with that wound in his leg...that amazes me.* He was proud to have such a strong brother, but a sense of dread filled his own head there as he watched his backside and the horse's ass and tail. Jason was riding off into the stormy morning, unarmored and wounded at the leg; riding away to begin a conflict with the king.

Arthan threw the curtain aside from the window, rushing to make way to his bedchamber. He donned a hooded gray cloak and then laced up some boots that he had prepared for wet and muddy days. When he left through the front entrance door of the house, Lady Frauer asked him, "Where is it *you're* off to now too?" Arthan walked past her, now stepping on downward off the porch and into the rain. He turned to face her before he departed.

He said to her, "I too am going to the garden."

"Too slow, you've just missed Jason riding away on Pax."

Arthan raised his thumb upward to show his mother his hand. A form of saying *yes.* "I'll walk." he told his mother. Arthan turned his back to her and left the property of the Frauers, past the black gate and onto Silver Street.

The miserable rain had caused these streets within the High District to appear deserted. Arthan hardly viewed any folk, for it seemed as if magically none had now lived in the city. A *ghost city,* some storytellers would call it. Even this grand garden here where folk would come to pray was practically empty. Arthan approached seeing that he would be the only soul within. Seemed all folk minded the cold of the rain besides he. Arthan in truth hated rain, but he felt the need to come to a place such as this so he could pray for the safety of Jason.

Regularly any folk whom wished to pray would typically go about doing so by visit to the cathedral. Arthan did not do this because he did not have the desire to speak to any priests as of now, and he especially felt he couldn't pray at home. Dwelling at the household this moment would mean having to face his family knowing Jason was out and about finding the king to provoke his royal self. He couldn't bear to look his mother or father in their faces while a secret of Jason's like that was hidden within him. Arthan felt his two options were either the library in the Wizards District or the garden here like where Jason told his mother he would be right now. Arthan's study at the library wouldn't help Jason in what was to come for him, praying here though might!

Arthan entered this locale where many flowers rested, colored blue and gold, surrounded by luscious, beautiful shrubbery all cut and shaped in various different styles. Regularly butterflies and torch bugs would zip through the air buzzing about here, coming and going, occasionally harmlessly landing upon folk for a greeting. The rain prevented these critters from flying through the air on this day; as it prevented the folk from dwelling here too. Arthan sat his ass down on the incredibly wet bench just beside a bush filled with red roses. He put his palms into his closed eyes to pray. Elbows met the tops of his kneecaps. He sat there hooded and cloaked looking like a mushroom or something odd of that sort.

"Aeon, god of light, hea—" Arthan's silent prayer was interrupted by a man's voice calling his name.

"Lord Arthan Frauer." Arthan *thought* this was a man at the least, though when he opened his eyes and looked onward, he saw the being was of half-elvish, half-man with pointy ears, hooded in green. Beside him stood roughly five feet in height, a full-blooded elvish. She wore maroon leather armor, protecting her wrists, breasts, shoulders, and waist area. The rest of her limbs and torso was bare exposed. As Arthan was gazing upon the smooth purple skin of hers, she grabbed ahold of both sides of her own green cloak upon her back and then covered herself so Arthan could view her little body no longer. The manly one's eyes were a bright yellow, and the full blood elvish's two eyes burned a bright blue, matching the same blue of the tree emblem stitched upon Arthan's chest portion of his gray cloak. Both of these two strangers, hideously high ears, overlarge eyeballs and lips. *Such tiny but pointed noses…usual for one with elvish blood within, though.*

Arthan was inspecting these both sort of familiar faces as he rose up to stand away from the bench. He'd remembered seeing an elvish fighter in the pit on game day, prior to his own fainting; though that elvish combatant was not a she-elvish as this one is. The one fully hooded only revealed a pale face of his, ears and bits of blonde hair too, he looked extremely familiar to Arthan. He searched his mind for memory of where the two might have been from until he realized that he had not made reply yet after the half-elvish called for his name. "Yes, Hello." he answered, looking to the both of them in turn.

The half-man said to him, "I am called Lyro, servant of family tree Ain, if you remember me, my lord. You remember Aetheria?"

Arthan used the signing hand motion to greet the low-elvish being with a *"Hello,"* though he did not have any recollection of her. He bit his lip and shook his head in the negative. "I'm afraid I can't place the two of you. I don't remember where it is I've seen you from."

The little elvish nodded, as if she'd assumed Arthan would not know whom she was.

The half one named Lyro looked down to his little elvish master with a frown. He recovered his facial expression back into a smile, looking upon Arthan now again; misty light rain falling upon the three of them there in the garden. "Ah, no matter. A second introduction then. This is Aetheria Ain. I serve her tree in the North."

Arthan smiled to the cloaked elvish with her glowing blue eyes that would have matched the color of her skin if they had been just a little bit more violet tinted. Full-blooded elvish beings weren't capable of projecting words to speak language of other race and realm. Aetheria's family servant spoke for her when she had need to use words, as she had now.

Looking upon this elvish named Aetheria, Arthan said to her half-breed beside her, "Tell her I only know the hand sign for *hello*. I do apologize, I'd never fully learned the elvish hand communications."

The half-elvish said, "No need for me to tell her. She can understand you. It's only that Aetheria cannot speak your words."

"Ah yes. Well, Aetheria, I'm sorry I do not know the signing. Otherwise, I'd watch on to…your hands." Arthan gazed upon the talon-like nails that shone past the sleeve of her cloak. Aetheria the she-elvish watched Arthan's eye movement. She covered her nails so he could not look upon them any longer. "You've already told us you don't know the signing when we spoke inside of the inn. We met you there for the first time, the Alligator Inn it's called. I'm sorry you've forgotten."

Arthan was remembering nothing of these two still, though he remembered quite well George, the one memorable councilman with that spikelike fur upon his cheeks, and the story he had told of Arthan to the council; Arthan had again heard some of this tale from the mouth of his brother later in that night upon feasting at the family table. Aetheria Ain played a big role in this tale of Arthan's night at the inn.

"Aetheria wanted to thank you again. She says it's a special thing to be the only good soul in a room filled with a hundred. You were not required to stand strong for a lew-elvish in need, nor were you expected to."

Arthan's cheeks were reddening, hers were turning from violet to pink; the interpreter almost held an emotionless look since the beginning of this encounter, though now he was smiling when he'd looked upon Aetheria's giddy reaction to what Arthan would say next. "I don't remember much of the night, but I remember seeing not an elvish in need, just I saw you. I did what I did because you are you, a soul whom needed help."

Aetheria smiled to the ground.

Arthan smiled into the clouds, face entirely wet now.

The interpreter said to Arthan, "So you do remember how you aided Aetheria atop the bar where the folk drank and feasted?"

Arthan looked on to the hooded half-man in green. Itching the back of his own head, Arthan said, almost sort of asking, "I distracted the knights and drinkers harassing her, by me swinging a giant iron great sword? *Trying* to swing it, I should have said."

"You made them laugh at you so harshly that they'd forgotten all about Aetheria. After they had finished chanting, *'God of iron, Lord of rum,'* not one of them paid Aetheria any more bit of attention. Their jokes toward her ceased. You made yourself look a fool to save her."

Arthan smiled and told the two of them, "I was happy to give help."

Lyro smiled to Aetheria once again. He smiled upon her, then looked to Arthan to speak just as he had done a moment ago too.

Lyro said to Arthan, "Aetheria wishes to know if you remember the time the three of us spent drinking the rum together after you climbed down from the bar and dropped the sword."

Again Arthan bit his lip whilst shaking his head *no.*

Lyro said, "We happily shared rum together while the knights sang and danced behind us."

"I apologize, that very well could have been my brother's knights and friends."

Lyro smiled to Arthan now for the first time while Aetheria gazed on to him across in the morning rain. Lyro told Arthan, "As I said, we happily spent this time together. You were so very saddened when you saw we made to leave. In truth, Arthan Frauer, you were saddened here to see Aetheria leave. I was mostly interpreting through the night."

Arthan hadn't known what to say to any of the half-elvish, half-man's tale, so he just smiled to Aetheria.

"Aetheria wanted to apologize. She wanted to remind you that she made the decision to leave only after we had seen how intoxicated you'd become. Aetheria here enjoyed you that night, and she wished for anything and everything the two of you spoke on about to be remembered by you in the morning and days to come."

Aetheria looked high upward into Arthan's eyes. She expressed an ugly little elvish grin, trying to hide her fangs as she smiled but failed to do so.

Lyro was saying now, "She says she hopes you'd be willing to spend more time with her again one day in the future."

Arthan smiled nervously right back down to the little thing. Arthan said, "I'd like that. I'm glad you found me, though you did not have to travel all the way out here in the rain to apologize. There is nothing to apologize for. I do not remember much, nor becoming saddened at your leave of the inn, no harm. We can begin building anew as of right now."

Aetheria Ain sighed now as she looked to Arthan. She soon removed her bulging eyes from gazing upon him to now look to her servant Lyro. Lyro sighed too, then he looked to the floor of the garden. He said to Arthan, but eyes not on him, "We followed you here so Aetheria and I could wish you our prayers and best thoughts. Aetheria says she's so very sorry that your brother has faded, as am I."

Arthan grew a fat lump in his throat, like a bulging apple trying to pierce outward from the insides of his neck. Arthan swallowed this imaginary lump and coughed a bit to clear out his throat. When Arthan recovered from coughing, he said, "Much thanks."

He nodded to the two of them as they stood there, cloaks all wet; the she-elvish about five feet in height, the half-breed a bit higher than six. "There is a bit more we have for you." said Lyro.

"More what?" Arthan asked him.

"Information, news."

"Tell me." asked Arthan, curiously looking from the elvish to its servant and then back to her.

Aetheria frowned while looking at Arthan. Her eyes were beginning to water; she held back droplets from releasing though. Lyro said to Arthan, "We were a part of the crowds when the folk gathered when your bother was found. Myself, Mastress Aetheria here and her brother Daetherian had been at the eating shelter in the Low District. We'd been preparing to make donations to the poorer lives of the city. Aetheria's brother heard a commotion out on a street. It's where there was a great gathering."

Arthan cut in, "I know where Dallion was found and identified. I've heard the entire tale."

Lyro looked to his superior again. She nodded a confirmation to him, then they both looked upon Arthan again. "Aetheria's brother says the boy didn't die from the sewers."

More folk sharing this same dreadful thought and theory…

Arthan was sadly and horribly interested in it all. Was he cruel to feel this rush of heat within him; the voice telling him to chase the unsolved story. "Why does he think that?"

"Her brother Daetherian, her too Aetheria…the elvish, they can see, they can feel certain aspects and truths without touch. Aetheria's brother saw into Dallion's body that day there."

Arthan squinted his eyes as rain was running down his brow to enter them both. He shook his head in the negative, even though he truly did understand the words of the half-elvish. "I do not understand? Her brother inspected him? How?"

Lyro was struggling to explain to Arthan, "This sight is no different from you looking upon the sun to say, *'Oh, that is a bright sun.'* It takes no effort to see what Daetherian saw, especially when your brother was found nude. His wounds—"

Aetheria sprang her left hand outward. She covered his mouth with her talons as she opened her mouth wide in his direction, showing those razor sharp teeth.

Arthan only wanted to know as much as he could of the truth. "No, what of his wounds? What did Daetherian see?"

Aetheria was gazing into Arthan's eyes while Lyro was lowering her hand and arm away from his mouth.

Lyro slowly said, "His wounds… Like all other onlookers that day, Daetherian saw the scrapes, the missing pieces of the face, the swelled flesh. Skin was torn all over, some fingers and toes had even been gone."

"What did he see that none others saw?"

"The stab wound, Arthan Frauer… There was a deep stab wound."

Arthan wasn't completely surprised at these words. "Was it the wound of a dagger?"

"Eleven inches in length, triangular tipped. Twice the blade went into the boy's stomach. There were two pierces of entry."

Arthan wasn't doubting the half-elvish, just yearning to understand this all in full.

"How could none others see this? Over two dozen souls looked on to his corpse there in the street, so I heard. Guards escorted his body to the cathedral for cleansing. If there was a mark as you speak of, they would have made mention of it."

Lyro told Arthan that, "The wielder of this small blade, the one who's slain your brother, perhaps is close with whichever priest inspected the body. As for your other question, none others saw this because Daetherian was gazing with the magical sight of the elvish eye. I know you are aware that the elvish have these capabilities. Now not all require the elvish gifts to see such things, any living soul can gaze upon a mark of a dagger on and within flesh, though your brother's fatal wound was not easily viewed because of his many other appearing wounds disguising this dagger mark of piercing. Remember, Arthan, the sewers destroyed more than half of his bod—"

Again, Aetheria placed her claws over her interpreter's mouth, silencing him once more.

The lew-elvish and half-breed then had a brief conversation with each other through using language of their eyes. None could understand this process, just accepted it; the elvish and the half-elvish beings could communicate through just looking upon each other's eyes. Some folk explained this form of elvish communication as if these beings simply just felt each other's thoughts and words, giving the ability to perform a silent sort of dialogue using only mind and magic, no vocals. When they'd finished, they looked upon Arthan. All three beings by now had been practically drenched in rain. Their cloaks withheld the piercing water, but their faces had been soaked.

Yellow eyes on Arthan, Lyro said to him, "Would you accept meeting Daetherian here at a later hour? Would be better for me to explain this all through him at my side, with him speaking to me the way Aetheria has been to me all this while. Daetherian is the one whom saw this horrible sight in truth, not so much Aetheria."

Arthan looked to her. He asked her, "You hadn't seen these wounds he speaks of? You bear the same power and gift as your brother, do you not?"

Aetheria bit her lip the way Arthan does sometimes, only she bit her flesh with a fang. She glanced quickly to Lyro, then she looked right back into Arthan's eyes.

Lyro said, "She says she didn't look upon your bother, not in that way as Daetherian had. She was too saddened."

Arthan did not have much of a schedule for the remainder of the day and night. He only wished to remain away from the household while his parents occupied it for now. Dialogue with them would be difficult while Jason was out intending to tell the king he has assumption that Dallion was murdered...by the king! He said, "I'll meet your brother here, Aetheria. When shall this happen?"

"Midnight." Lyro answered.

"I'll see the three of you at midnight then."

Aetheria Ain bowed in the elvish fashion. Lyro bowed as well. Arthan bowed low too, then he watched them glide off out of the garden.

Arthan sat into the wet puddle of the bench with his hands back into his eyes. He was beginning to resume his prayer that the elvish had interrupted; the elvish now sharing the same theory as Jason and cousin Tillsy. *Even the elvish band of visitors believe Dallion was killed. They didn't say by the king, though this brother of Aetheria Ain claims he saw through the sight of magic, the dagger wound...Jason's dagger.*

He couldn't focus on praying. Arthan sprang up off the bench and made for the street in the High District just north of the cathedral. This was the street where Sir-Paladin John's household was to be found. That was where Arthan was going, right for Sir-Paladin John. Arthan knocked on the big yellow door, harder and harder after a while of no answer. He peeked inside the gold stained window right at the porch there beside the locked entry to the house. The staining made the interior of the household non viewable. As Arthan was struggling to look inside to see if the house was occupied, John opened the door, John the Second that was, Paladin John's son.

"Sir Honor Guard John." John stared at Arthan with wide eyes. The young man's lips shook as he gazed at Arthan.

John the Second wiped the expression from his face, physically with his hand. He shook his head and hair with closed eyes as one would do after emerging from water after bathing or swim. "Arthan, hello."

"Hello." Arthan said to his *"hello."*

They stood there, Arthan at the doorway, John inside. They silently and awkwardly looked upon each other.

Arthan broke the silence with, "I'm here to speak with your father, may I?"

John the Second closed his eyes and sort of scrunched up his face. He shook his head again rapidly the way he'd just done moments ago. John said, "Yes, again I'm sorry for your loss."

Sir-Paladin John's son led Arthan inside the household. Directly upon entry, Arthan was brought up a grand wooden staircase where they would find the paladin's study. "He's in his reading room, this way." John the Second said to Arthan as he led him up the stairs.

Arthan remembered on now how Sir-Paladin John's son here was the one he heard had taken down Jason's assassin; the man in black who fired upon the combatants during the event of the arena. Arthan asked him when they reached the top, "You were the honor guard to bring down the bowman that shot at my brother?"

John the Second brought Arthan to the bronze door, now knocking upon it gently. "Father, Arthan's here!" said he to the metal.

Now he looked to Arthan to answer his question.

"Yes." he said.

John immediately took his eyes off of him whence they made contact with Arthan's.

What is wrong with him tonight? Arthan was thinking. John looked back to the metal door, waiting for his father to answer.

Arthan asked, "What happened to the killer? Who was he?"

John Second answered, "Didn't get a chance to unmask him, handed him off to another guard for imprisonment. I heard he escaped."

"Truly?" asked Arthan.

John the Second uncomfortably inhaled inward, then he turned himself around and made for the stairs.

Arthan turned as well to watch the young knight leave. That was when the metal door opened.

"Oh...boy, how might I help you? How are you feeling?" Arthan took a look through the doorway behind Sir-Paladin John's shoulder.

The office was a mess; many papers and books appeared scattered. Hardly any candles lit the room.

"Are *you* well, John?" Arthan asked the paladin-knight.

John, for once seen here surprisingly without his breastplate, had exited his office and closed the metal door.

"It's your lady-wife. She's left you as you've said she would, hasn't she?"

"Yes, she has, back to her family's castle, hating me more than ever. My wife is the least of my pain, though. Dallion is what hurts me. The thought of what's happened to him, how I couldn't find him quick enough."

Arthan was aching to tell John the information he'd received from the elvish in the garden. He assured Sir-Paladin John, "What happened to Dallion happened right after he'd been left at the school by you, during his visit to the Great Keep with the classmates even."

Sir John eyed Arthan not with suspicion but with curious questioning; as in Sir John was practically asking Arthan to *"say more"* or to *"go on"* with whatever he was inferring. Arthan was sounding very sure that he knew of what had happened to Dallion, sure of where and when. Where, when and how... Sir-Paladin John was wondering if Arthan here was sure of *how* Dallion died; Arthan told him the assumptions.

It took him all of twenty or so minutes there to get the wordings out in full. They both stood through the entire dialogue leaning among the staircase railing of the upstairs portion of the household. Time was moving so slowly, Arthan felt it had been. He spoke slowly when he told the holy knight the tale, how Tillsy cried *"Murder,"* explaining how the sewers could have been used as a tactic to hide the truth of Dallion's death, destroying his body and covering the wounds of the dagger. Jason's dagger came next after talk of Tillsy and her fleeing for Fort Bluewood.

"The king had Jason's dagger at the Shield's feast, Jason said. Jason gave Dallion that dagger… Dallion goes missing in the king's own house. Next Gregory is seen with the dagger at his hip." He told Sir-Paladin John about the elvish party in the last portion of the explanation and tale.

Sir-Paladin John had said to that bit, "Daetherian Ain? I don't know Arthan, he lost to Sir-Paladin Reese in his dueling. That's the elf who had his back bones split in two by Reese, remember? 'Twas that which caused you to faint, I've heard."

"What of it? I'm not speaking of my fainting. I'm telling you this Daetherian claims when he and the elvish group he journeyed here with, his sister too, along with all the other city onlookers spotted Dallion, Daetherian says he felt he saw these dagger wounds… With Dallion having had been given Jason's dagger, dagger that the king now holds, it just all makes much too much sense!

Sir-Paladin John sat upon the playboard table beside the railing at the stairs. Some small playing pieces of solders fell to the wooden floor, John hadn't even heard it as he roughly sat on the top, elbow on his knee and knuckles resting within his graying, yellowish beard.

After a minute of silence, the paladin said to Arthan, "We go to the cathedral." John fastened his golden breastplate atop his chest. He equipped his long sword at his hip and strapped his war hammer to his backside. Before Arthan and Sir-Paladin John left the household, the paladin told his son, "Whether you stay here or you leave the household, be cautious."

The cathedral wasn't so far from Paladin John's household. When Arthan and he arrived, they were greeted with the utmost respect and care.

"Welcome, men of god!" Ark Priest Alice greeted them from afar when they'd first entered. The day was so grim that at the far end of the cathedral chamber upon the white altar, god's eye had been lit, spherical and glowing bright to fill the room with white light. Ark Priest Alice appeared silhouetted to Arthan and John from the orb, until he came closer as he walked down that center isle off from the altar.

When they'd met in the middle, he asked the two, "How do you fare?" The golden-eyed little bald man smiled, awaiting their response.

Sir-Paladin John said, "We're here to see Dallion Frauer's body."

"Of course, you, sir, as paladin and you, Arthan, as a dear family member of the dead both have that right. Might I ask why you wish to see the body, though?"

Sir-Paladin John was sighing, but now also tightening his face, a frightening mix of expressed emotion. John answered the ark priest's question with a question. "Who performed the inspection on Dallion Frauer?"

"The king requested for his favored and now personal priestess Reya to perform the inspection."

Sir-Paladin John told the ark priest, "Bring me to Reya."

The ark priest hissed inward, his spit gurgled when he made this noise. "I'm afraid King Gregory stole her from me. She now dwells within the Great Keep."

Arthan, all this while during the dialogue, shifted his view from John to the creepy little leading priest with those black and golden eyes of his, eyes like a snake's. Constantly he looked from he, to John as the two spoke.

Arthan watched on as Sir-Paladin John was growing angry. "You mean to tell me the only soul who's gotten an inspection at Dallion Frauer's corpse isn't present here within the cathedral?"

The ark priest answered, "I'm afraid not."

John pointed onward to the door by the stairs beside the altar where the hall was found leading to the body storage chamber. "This way."

Ark Priest Alice left the two of them down the hall there at this new doorway to the chamber which contained the corpses.

"Take as much time as you need." Alice said.

After he'd left the two of them, John said to Arthan, "Come, let's learn the truth."

"No. I cannot look. I do not want to look."

John placed a big brown gloved hand upon Arthan's cold shoulder. "Come, be strong."

Arthan smacked Sir-Paladin John's hand away, then he took a few steps away from the door. "No." Arthan said as his eyes watered and reddened. He looked away from John and the door, waiting for the paladin knight to enter and perform his magical gaze upon the rotting body of his baby brother.

It took John sixteen minutes to perform his inspection; to Arthan it felt like an hour. The big knightly and holy man opened the door gently when he came back to Arthan, but he slammed it shut hard once back in the hallway. He looked to Arthan with those old and cold blue eyes of his. "There were two marks. They'd been made by a dagger."

Arthan put his palms to his eyes and sucked in a deep breath of air; he almost cried but he didn't. John went on saying, "His lungs, they'd never been filled with any water. He never drowned. The boy was gutted and thrown in the sewers."

Arthan removed his hands from his face to ask John if he was sure of this, though John was making for the doorway to leave into the main chamber of the cathedral already.

In the main chamber they stood, Arthan behind Sir-Paladin John as the big man held a finger pointed to Alice. "You send a priest as a messenger to the Great Keep. Inform Grand Councilman Lewis that Priestess Reya is to report for word here tonight, and at the council session upon the morrow. Be sure this message goes directly to the grand councilman, not an honor guard, not the steward, and not the king. To the grand councilman, yes?"

Alice looked like he'd been struck with lightning. He only said, "Yes, paladin." with his golden eyes widened and mouth made into a frown.

Arthan and Sir-Paladin John stepped down the many stairs outside the cathedral beside the Institution.

"What happens now?" Arthan asked Sir-Paladin John.

"Now you go home and you be sure your mother, father, and brother don't leave the house. Tomorrow all will be revealed within the council session when Reya is presented. I will attempt to gain word in and present myself within the council as well. Arthan, if I am not able to enter to gain access, it must be you or your father whom speaks up on this matter."

Arthan was a champion at holding back his tears. He wanted to cry so very badly right this moment, but he found the strength as always to be sure his face did not run wet. "What could we possibly say?"

Sir-Paladin John began walking with Arthan, he held his shoulder to comfort him as they moved about the street. "If I can't make it in there tomorrow for whatever the reason may be, you have your father ask Priestess Reya why she hadn't spoken up on Dallion's true cause of death. After that you make mention of the dagger. King Gregory needs to be called for his crimes while all one hundred councilmen watch on, and no other time."

Aeon forgive me for my stupidity, why haven't I made mention of this earlier. Arthan realized only now, he should have notified Sir-Paladin John of Jason's departure from the household to confront the king on all of this. Jason left at morning. It was now long after morning. "Jason left early today to have King Gregory arrested. To have him answer for these very crimes you and I have been speaking of all this while since I've came to your household with this news."

John gripped Arthan by the fabrics of his cloak. He threw Arthan hard against the iron fence beside the Institution, shouting, "No! What? No, he hasn't, boy!"

Arthan squirmed there, almost sliding out of the gray cloak as Sir-Paladin John held him on up to his own height. "Yes, I'm sorry, I'm sorry he left for the Great Keep. He's confronting the king!"

Arthan slipped right through the cloak and fell down to his ass. He sat with his butt upon Silver Street and his damp back to the fence. Sir-Paladin John stormed off eastward through the street, hammer and sword clanging and dangling, though to where he was making for Arthan hadn't known.

Arthan sat upon the fence still as the gray day went on and on; cloak in his lap and eyes in the sky. He gazed at the miserable clouds above for such a long while, he hadn't even know how long he'd been there; he looked to be of the houseless folk, or a city man of the Low District west of the Square. Arthan looked down the eastern direction of Silver Street. Clusters of children were making their way up the steps of the Institution to greet instructors. There was a chubby redhead boy who carried two school books, this boy was the closest of the students to Arthan; he was moving onward hastily and ready to learn lots at his lessons after return from his meal break just now.

"Hey there." said Arthan, greeting the child.

The boy looked to Arthan, waddling up to approach him as Arthan sat wet on the ground.

"Hullo. You're all wet."

Arthan nodded to the fat boy's statement. "Did you know who Dallion Frauer was?"

"Yes." answered the boy.

Arthan smiled at that response.

He asked the child, "Do you know when the last time you saw Dallion was? Were you in his class?"

The boy answered, "Yes" again, this time in a nervous sort of manner. The boy looked behind him to be sure his moving classmates hadn't been listening. "I know he died. You're his brother, aren't you?"

Arthan nodded to that with a sad smile. The boy glanced over his shoulder again. The child squatted now turning back to Arthan low there. "We're not supposed to say. Daisy says the goblins will come after us too if we say what happened."

Arthan removed himself from the fencing. He sat himself upward in a more firm position, though he remained seated on the stones of Silver Street.

Arthan was determined to get the full tale from the child, the truth. He asked the boy, "Goblins? Goblins got Dallion?"

"I shouldn't say."

Arthan sighed. He gained an idea though, a useful one. "My other brother Jason, you know Sir Jason, right? The White Knight? He has so many daggers and neat shiny weapons. Maybe I could meet you here one day and give you one of these as a present...only though if you tell me this secret. You could use the dagger to defend yourself from goblins, since they're killing folk like Dallion."

The boy rubbed at the flaps of his many chins, smiled, then frowned then smiled again. He decided to accept Arthan's offer.

The boy shook his head upwards and back down. "Goblins, yes. Dallion went hunting for them during our visit to the king's house. They pulled him into the sewers under the keep; that's where all the goblins live in Ascali. They use magic to teleport from their hideout in the sewers to under our beds in the night too. Dallion shouldn't have gone off after them. I told Timmy though how would the goblins know if we talked about them to anybody? Daisy would know how the goblins know."

Arthan rose to his two feet. He wrapped the drippy cloak about his shoulders, then patted the boy on his moist hair at the top of his head. "Get dry and get inside the school. Next week on this day I'll be here with a present for you."

The boy smiled up at Arthan while he made to depart from front the school. Off went Arthan, heading to an alley way which would bring him back to that garden to where he'd met with the lew and heigh elvish (*lew*, meaning "low" elvish in the Northern language, referring to the full-blooded elvish beings, and *heigh*, as in "*high"* elvish: taller, half man, half elvish).

"Aeon, god of light hear me now and today. Lighten my soul and brighten my house today. Guide me in this world, lead me to greatness today. Cast out and keep away the terrible of today. Ascend me to your heaven when my time ends, not this day. In Aeon I trust all days." The rain had ceased and the sun was lowering. Arthan sat reciting the same prayer in his mind as many hours passed by. He spent the hours praying, eyes opened looking upon the many bushes and rows of flowers.

After the fourth hour when his legs had gone numb just before the sun set, he'd risen to pace about the garden, still the same prayer playing on and on in that head of his. *"Aeon, god of light, hear me now and today. Lighten my soul and brighten my house today. Guide me in this world, lead me to greatness today. Cast out and keep away the terrible of today. Ascend me to your heaven when my time ends, not this day. In Aeon I trust all days."* He sat upon the bench as half of his face was bathed in the white street candle light, the other half completely hidden in darkness. He prayed on and on, thinking of Jason and now of Sir-Paladin John; wondering where it was that the old holy knight ran off to. *Maybe he thought to make for the Great Keep to save Jason, maybe even for home to be with his son John the Second.* Arthan prayed for Jason, then he prayed for Sir-Paladin John; now he sat half in dark praying for Dallion's poor rested soul for a long while until midnight finally approached.

From beyond a bush carved to look heart shaped, there was a sharp purring sound, followed by a tiny gargling noise. Big blue eyes blinked he saw, growing larger and larger. Leaping around the bush the way a frog would, Aetheria showed herself. She was wearing her leather armor pieces as when they'd met earlier this day, though no green cloak now. She stood herself upward from her squatting position. Even in the darkness Arthan got a proper look at her armor now in which he couldn't view in full before. It was beautifully crafted, almost matching the tone of her skin. He'd seen those little pauldrons before, her minute chest-piece and bottom bit too. Now though Arthan was able to view her elbow guards, knee pieces, and the curved short sword she carried laced up at her hip. She was undeniably fascinating to look upon, causing Arthan to wonder why the hate filled knights would act so harshly toward the poor soul.

"Aetheria." he called her name. She slowly approached Arthan, standing only a foot or so away from him. She was so low to the ground, though Arthan had grown comfortable with his constant having to look downward on her. *I looked downward on to Dallion...* She raised two of her talons and pointed them toward Arthan's direction; she kept her hands close to herself though. With her other set of claws, she put them into a fist and then brought them under the wrist of the opposite hand. She was saying *"Hello on this stormy night."* to Arthan, through elvish hand signings. Arthan understood the gesture, though he didn't know how to reply to such a greeting with his own hands. He used words, asking her, "I am doing as well as I can be. Is Lyro with you?"

Out of breath and huffing, the half-breed came running into the dark garden. Green cloak he wore, though he didn't have his hood over his head this time. Arthan got a well look at his long blonde hair as he stood there resting his hands upon his knees catching his breath back to him.

"Lyro? What's wrong?"

Lyro was breathing heavily, finally talking to Arthan. He spoke while Aetheria looked on in Arthan's eyes. "Daetherian is riding to meet you here."

"Good." said Arthan.

Aetheria and Lyro exchanged quick looks at each other. Back toward Arthan both of their heads went facing. Lyro said, "It's not good. Daetherian is angry we've told you of his sight on Dallion."

"Why is he coming here?" asked Arthan.

Beyond the heart-shaped bush, a pony neighed rushing inward. The beast bore scaled armoring alike its rider. This elvish had equipped a blue scaled leather chest piece, matching tiny scaled pants that ended above the knees. He leapt off the mount, holding a tiny spear in his hand; he had no problem showing his fangs to Arthan. This elvish brother of Aetheria's squatted low, in the same style as when he was battling that paladin in the arena.

The priests healed his spine very well, thought Arthan.

Daetherian Ain spoke using Lyro as a living way of communication. Lyro was looking into Arthan's eyes, telling him, "The Ain tree wants no part in the conflict or business of men murdering each other, nor children. He doesn't know all Aetheria has told you, only knows that the elvish are finished in Ascali. Aetheria, he wants you on the mount."

Aetheria put her hands to the cheeks of her face. What she was expressing to Arthan, he hadn't known. She hadn't looked pleased, only saddened and frightened; she looked sorry.

Daetherian with one hand only, climbed up upon the backside of the pony. He took his sister's claw-like hand and lifted her up to sit behind he. Lyro was looking upward at the two while being spoken to through the magic of the elvish.

"What's he saying?" Arthan asked Lyro as he and Daetherian looked into each other's eyes to communicate.

"He's telling me to stop speaking with you. He's telling me I'm walking back to the inn alone." Lyro looked to Arthan now as the lew-elvish brother and sister rode away out of the garden.

Aetheria had her gaze on Arthan the whole while until he was lost out of her view.

Lyro said, "Good night, Lord Arthan. I'm terribly sorry." Lyro left him there in the dark garden.

Arthan was filled with mixed, miserable emotions. He stumbled on over to that very same bench he'd been coming and going from all day and into the night. He placed his elbows upon his knees, palms into closed eyes. Until sunrise, Arthan sat awake in the garden in the High District, praying. *Aeon, god of light, hear me now and today. Lighten my soul and brighten my house today. Guide me in this world, lead me to greatness today. Cast out and keep away the terrible of today. Ascend me to your heaven when my time ends, not this day. In Aeon I trust all days.*

18

CONFRONTATIONS

He hadn't remembered falling off to sleep. Arthan spent the entire night in the garden at pray; he even had watched the sky turn from black to that early morning's blue tint. He'd seen the sun rise thinking if he'd stayed awake for this long, then he wouldn't be going off to sleep until the new night's sunset. Now though he found himself awakening, drooling into his own shoulder with his neck bent against the end of the bench. He shook away the numbness from the hand he'd spent the morning sitting on. Arthan rubbed at his eyelids and inhaled. *One more time,* thought he, then he began in his head with, *Aeon, god of light, hear me now and today. Lighten my soul and brighten my house today. Guide me in this world, lead me to greatness today. Cast out and keep away the terrible of today. Ascend me to your heaven when my time ends, not this day. In Aeon I trust all days.* He exhaled and looked upward into the sky.

Arthan couldn't judge from where the sun was placed up there: what the exact hour and minute of the morning it had been. *Still early... but how early?* It was a far brighter day than it had been of yesterday's morning; almost as hot and sunny now as it had been during the day of the arena event. With his almost dried cloak in hand, he left the garden to walk his way down to Silver Street where he would find his household; though when Arthan entered the home of his, it was unoccupied.

"Hello! Mother? Father? Jason, are you here?" There was no answer when he called for his family. Arthan lit a candle beside the table at the entrance door there. He made for the pink hallway with the blazing wax in hand to enter his own room. He placed the burning candle down upon his desk within his bedchamber. Quickly he swapped clothing for his apprentice councilman's garb. Arthan went back to the entrance door in his fresh attire, blew out the candle, left his household.

He walked eastward up winding Silver Street, it bending the more and more northward he progressed up the big sloping path. His destination was the council chamber. For some odd reason, he hadn't the slightest care in the earth if he was to be late for today's session. The death of Dallion seemed to numb Arthan's senses and reactions and expectations some. He walked within the High District here approaching the Great Keep and the dome beside it. He took his steps with emotionless expressions upon his face, making ready to have to enter the welcoming yard, having to ask the honor guards for access inside after being tardy. He entered the yard to find it loud with the sounds of talk from the cluster of councilmen waiting to be let inside for the session.

I've woken at the perfect time it's seeming. Arthan shuffled through the bodies of men in brown to make for the wooden pillars by the stable in the yard. He leaned against the oak as he watched the men front him converse, discuss, and greet each other a fine morning.

"I'm so sorry, my lord." a random and unfamiliar councilman had said to Arthan.

Arthan nodded and smiled upon the old soul. The councilman walked off into the crowd of men after he'd given Arthan his sympathy. Another man made the same remark to Arthan shortly after this, though this one was more specific on what exactly he was sorry for.

The councilman approached him. This one as well, another here unknown and unfamiliar to Arthan. "My Lord Frauer, I'm so sorry about your brothers."

Arthan squinted, looking upon the man in brown. Arthan thought, *Did he say "brothers"?* Arthan tilted his head to the left side, the way a dog would. His ear almost touched his shoulder actually. "Has something happened to Jason?" he asked the man.

The councilman's jaw dropped low, releasing foul breath from his mouth. Just before he was to tell Arthan what had happened to his brother Jason, Lord Edward came bursting through the crowd of men. He was whispering, though whispering loudly, "Arthan, Arthan." Edward grabbed a fistful of his son's pink robing and dragged him upon his feet on over behind the pillar of the stable and away from the councilman he'd been just conversing with.

"Where have you been?"

"I told Mother I was in the garden praying."

Edward ground his teeth together, now looking on toward the opening doors of the council chamber entrance there. He said as he looked upon the grand councilman coming through the iron, "Jason told your mother he was going to the garden too. Instead, he went to the Throne Hall." Edward removed his grip on Arthan's collar bit under the chin.

Arthan took a step back from his angered father. "I was truly at the garden."

Edward looked on to Arthan with mean eyes. "All night?" asked he, searching for a lie to come from his son.

Arthan asked Edward, "What's happened to Jason? Why wasn't Mother at home?" Lord Edward closed his eyes, scraping his back bottom set of teeth against his back top set. His jaw sounded like it was to break; Arthan could quite literally hear these sounds. "Jason was arrested for false claims against the king. Your mother left the household when she received news of this to request word in today's session. She's preparing to tell the king of Jason's innocence. She'll only make matters far worse."

Arthan had to now be ready for either his father's wrath on him or to see him express sadness. "It's true, though, Father. I've even spoken to Sir John. We've visited the cathedral."

"What?" Edward wasn't angered, not yet, only confused. "What are you saying, my son?" Grand Councilman Lewis was waving the councilmen inside the tunnel as the two Frauers here spoke on behind the wooden pillar in the yard.

Arthan told his father, "What Jason was on about, claiming what the king did, it's true. John and I went to the cathedral for him to look on Dallion's wounds. Have you not spoken with John?"

Edward was watching the yard begin to empty. "Nobody knows where John is." Edward told him.

The last of the councilmen were entering in to make to the chamber. Old Lewis watched on to Arthan and Edward speaking under the stable there. Arthan assured Lord Edward with confidence, "All questions will be answered when the priestess is called on. The priestess whom initially inspected Dallion, we may have to call on her ourselves if John truly isn't here. He did sound as if he predicted he *possibly* wouldn't make it here, for whatever reason that could be. This all feels horrible." Arthan peeked over to watch Lewis eyeing the two of them. Arthan removed himself from the cover of the pillar and grasped his lord-father's sleeve. He said as he pulled, "Let's go in now."

"Arthan? Call on her for what?"

The father and son walked and spoke on oh so quietly as they made their way to Lewis and the pair of silver guards beside him. "Priestess Reya is the one who inspected Dallion's corpse. We need to ask her why she hadn't made mention of the dagger wounds in his belly, and, Father, no water from the sewer ever entered his lungs..."

"Are you mad? What is all of this you speak of?"

They approached the opened gate, coming so close to Lewis now that the two were forced to cease their conversation.

They'd come to a halt when they'd reached the grand councilman as he was projecting the most oddest of facial expressions toward the lord and lordly son. "I hope the two of you aren't thinking of saying anything stupid today."

Edward curiously asked the old man, "What is it you mean by that?"

Lewis with his cane in hand and bent over spoke on as he turned away to walk into the tunnel. Edward and Arthan followed as he answered, "Lady Frauer has word today. The king is in a foul mood. I don't want either of you causing drama whilst Jason is in chains within the dungeon, and Lady Sophia's pleading in tears down by the chairs."

Edward scowled at the old man as the three of them slowly walked deeper within this darkened tunnel, that red glow in sight leaking from the far end; their miserable destination.

"We won't." said Arthan.

"Good, and if either one of you feel you *absolutely must* get dramatic, feel free to join her at the base to aid in her plea. If that is your wish, I am preapproving it now. Just say the word and you'll be dismissed as a councilman for the day and sent down to plea with her as lord only."

"Thank you." both Edward and Arthan said at the same time. Lewis still went on, "Otherwise, stay quiet. Either of you are not permitted to give input on any matters involving Sir Jason and or Lady Sophia, not as councilmen at the least."

They followed the hunchback into the red glowing domed chamber. Almost all one hundred of the councilmen had been seated at this point in time. Arthan and Edward climbed high, seating themselves in a far back portion of the chamber; meanwhile, Grand Councilman Lewis descended a row of steps to join the steward and the king at the three crimson glowing chairs, the Shield to the King standing behind these three pieces of metal furniture. The king took his seat, followed by the steward. Before Lewis sat, he pulled a scroll from his old brown robes.

"The matters of today's session include, in the following order:

"Word from Grull of the Western Islands, word from Lady Sophia of House Frauer, word from Priestess Reya. After our discussions with our guests, we shall speak on the financial matters of the construction taking place upon West Street, where the finer shops are being raised. Discussion of Sir Jason Frauer's crimes against the king need to be settled, as well as investigation of the arena incident with the knight in black. Decision on if such investigation would be continued, postponed, or ceased entirely. House Orange continues to not pay thei—"

"Sit, Lewis." said the king, looking intensely upon the gatherings of councilmen above and surrounding.

"I have not finished speaking today's council matters to our councilmen."

King Gregory said aloud, "Your order is wrong. We'll discuss Sir Jason Frauer's crimes whilst we hear Lady Sophia's word. I believe she's to plead her son's innocence. If we send him on to his final sentencing in the presence of the mother, then we won't have to repeat ourselves when we speak of it all over again all after West Street talk, agreed?"

Not anybody spoke.

"Agreed?" shouted the king.

"He's in a wicked mood." whispered Lord Edward.

Arthan, seated beside him, said, "He should be. He's about to be caught for his crimes while all here watch on."

Edward watched eagerly as he saw King Gregory gazing upon the many heads of all councilmen, searching for him and Arthan, more than likely. Lord-Steward Arol Royce was silent as ever, two red swords resting hooked at his hip. He bore his own and his king's the way a squire would carry a sword for a knight. Lewis finally seated himself after all councilmen said *"Agreed"* to the king's asking.

Gregory sat in the golden chair, tapping his heeled boot against the shining red marble with that Desmond man behind him. Red floors, walls, occupants red… The crimson torches made the entire chamber and all within it appear as if they'd been coated with a bright painting of red. King Gregory quit trying to locate the Frauers within the crimson crowd of faces so he spat and eyed at the floor.

He said aloud, "Let's get this on with. We'll begin with Grull, as you've said, yes?"

Lewis yelled, "First word! Enter!"

The iron door swung wide and out stomped Grull. The councilman beside Arthan snorted a laugh as the creature entered in down there, but when Arthan turned to look upon this laughing man he'd seen that he nor the man beside this one were councilmen. The priest looked to Arthan.

"Apprentice-Councilman." said the young man in white.

Arthan nodded a *"hello"* to the young priest. The other priest beside the one closest to Arthan leaned on over to wave to Arthan for a greeting as well. *Why are there priests here?* Arthan thought on asking himself. He thought to look to his father and ask him this, though Edward was engaged in observing the orcish approach the king, the steward, and Lewis.

Grull saluted the three, ceasing his walking. King Gregory said harshly, "What is it you could possibly want of Ascali now? I've allowed your entry into this room and Throne Hall, granted you permission to play in the arena, given you access into the cathedral! God save my soul. What do you want of us now, Grull, my love?"

The orcish looked directly on to the king, as his protector Desmond in black leather had stepped closer now that the orcish appeared nearer. Grull answered the king with, "I wish to be given opportunity to purchase property here in the city. The residency managers would not allow I inside to speak with a p—"

The king raised his finger to cover his own lips. He made a *"Shhhhh…"* sound, looking to Grull.

Grull quit speaking, allowing King Gregory to finish his sound so he himself could then talk. "Grull, I believe now you're asking much of the royal family. You've been treated ever so gently since your arrival. You've been treated in ways that no such orcish being ever has in Ascali. Now you wish to live here? I think not."

Grull frowned, or scowled, Arthan nor Edward could see from way up at the top there. They heard the dialogue clear enough though. "Perhaps one day your kind shall be allowed to dwell in a household here. I think not on this day, though. Accept your game loss and be gone back to the Western Islands."

Grull took a step forward, beginning to speak some more, "King, you—"

King Gregory stopped him before he could really make clear any sentence. "Grull, I said be gone back into the West."

Grull didn't stop his trying though. He began saying, "My king, ple—"

"Be gone, orc!" yelled Gregory.

Grull went silent and eyed the king with surprise. The beastly being turned and ascended the set of many stairs where the marble floor met the path to the seatings for the councilmen. Grull left through the top west entrance of the council chamber, opposite the far entrance where Arthan and his father came in from. The pair of guards closed the doors after his exit. Grull had gone through them, gone for now.

"Word two! Enter!" yelled old Lewis.

Edward leaned a bit upward, trying to get the best view he possibly could to see his lady-wife enter the chamber. Sophia walked fast, her fingers were interlaced together. She looked dead on to the king as she took her strides. She tried hard to ignore the hundred-plus men with their eyes upon her; she was well aware her husband and son had been viewing this.

"She looks well." said Edward.

Lady Sophia wore a blue dress and a shining silver necklace with matching earrings and bracelets. Of course his lord-father was right; she looked marvelous even from afar up here, but sadly even without viewing her face, Arthan could sense her fear and nervousness.

"Lady Sophia Frauer, here because you wish to speak of your son, Sir Jason Frauer."

Sophia replied to the king hastily. "Yes, I wish to speak of Jason."

"Well, speak on. What of him?" asked King Gregory.

Sophia lowered her head to the marble as she spoke. She talked to her king, but her mouth was facing her feet. "King Gregory, I ask that you forgive my son for what he's done."

The king smiled, entirely amused, now looking to his brother, Arol. Lord-Steward Arol was sitting with his fist a quarter way inside of his mouth, elbow upon his silver metal chair and so tired appearing. The king giggled at Lady Sophia's words, though spent more time observing the spectating councilmen than he had been watching the Lady Frauer.

King Gregory asked her, "What is it Jason's done? Enlighten me, my lady."

Arthan looked away from the talk down upon the floor of the chamber to watch his lord-father. Edward was holding the wood bits of the seating so tightly that his nails dug into the oak. His teeth were sliding against each other again, grinding and grinding. Arthan would have asked him if he felt well, though he knew the answer to a question as that, so he withheld asking.

Sophia said to Gregory, "He was badly hurt in the leg. He wasn't thinking clearly. He's accused you of murdering Dallion, I know, but we all know, the full of the realm knows you would do no such thing. He wasn't thinking correctly, looking for a villain after losing his brother…"

The king rose up from the chair to stand upon his two feet. Arthan gazed upon his belt. The dagger upon the hip, red sheath, black pommeled. Jason's was white and bright! The one equipped to the king's belt now dark. In truth, Arthan had assumed King Gregory would have this white dagger held upon and by himself no longer, for even Gregory was smart enough to have the weapon of harmful evidence no longer fastened to his side at this mark in the timeline.

The red weapon dangled against his leg as King Gregory left the chair and his guard man to come closer to Sophia. Arol and Lewis watched on from their close seatings, as did the councilmen and these new and few priests of the chamber above. The king placed a finger upon her chin to tilt her head upward.

Gregory spoke softly to her, but all heard his words still, "You sound like a dumb bitch."

No councilman made a sound. Arthan hadn't, not even Lord Edward, not until the king grasped Lady Frauer's arm with his hand full of cold, ringed fingers. What King Gregory intended to do to or with her, none would know, for Lord Edward had intervened then and there.

"Enough!" shouted he down toward the base of the chamber. Edward was standing tall. He continued on yelling, "Lewis! I am dismissed."

Lord Edward Frauer looked upon Arthan before leaving him in the seatings. "Father, the priestess…wait for her time to speak." Arthan whispered these words to his father, looking to the surrounding and close men to watch for any listeners; they'd all been listening.

Edward made no reply, just sadly smiled upon Arthan. Edward descended the stairs, passing dozens of councilmen to both his sides. He reached the base at the marble floor and walked on over to give Lady Sophia a comforting hug while the king stood not only two paces away from them both embracing each other.

"Let's just have this all settled here and now. Lewis, is Sir Jason being held in the Great Keep's dungeons here or in the Military District?"

"Here, my king." replied the grand councilman.

"Send for him." commanded the king. Lewis waved a hand off to a councilman high above whom he'd made a stern look at. The councilman went up and out of the chamber within a minute to fulfill this order.

Arthan watched on as this all happened. He looked to his parents still wrapped within each other's arms. "Councilman, your son, do you know what he claims I've done?" Edward shook his head in the negative to the king's question while Sophia buried her face within his aged brown robe.

Lewis corrected King Gregory. "Refer to him as Lord Edward. He is now here as a lord only, not councilman."

"Thank you…wise old man Grand Councilman. *Lord* Edward, your son came to me yesterday morning for a visit within the Throne Hall. He came to me telling me how I've slain your youngest, Dallion."

Many of the men within the chamber had made a noticeable reaction to these words of the king. Some laughed, some gasped, others just moved uncomfortably in their seats. Men chatted, others silently looked on for what was to be said next, which was what Arthan was engaged in. "Why Jason would think such things, I do not know."

"Nor do I, Lord Edward." said the king, shaking his head negatively in disappointment.

That rat-looking councilman George had some words to say next. "My king, you know exactly why Jason thought such things. I was there when he came to you yesterday with his claims!"

All were looking on to George now.

"Sir Jason said he'd seen you with his own white dagger, white dagger he'd given to Dallion, his brother whom went missing the day of his school's class trip to…here. Jason stated this all yesterday, do you not recall?" George was risen, standing front his seat and smiling. This councilman was placed upon a low row in the chamber, as close as he could be to the marble floor where the three chairs were sitting.

King Gregory smiled back to Councilman George. With the smile held locked in place, he asked, "What are you doing, George?"

"Helping you gather your memory, my king."

The king clapped his hands together a couple of times, still smiling to the whiskered councilman.

"Thanks for the reminder, George. As you all see, though, I carry my own dagger, not Jason's white blade."

Out of the iron door where the speaking guests had entered through at the base of the chamber came running an honor guard, jogging past Lord and Lady Frauer. When he ceased running, all could see this silver knight taking hard breaths in and outward, his whole body shaking. He had squatted beside the silver chair of the steward. The knight made to whisper into Arol's ear, though Arol leaned backward and pushed his armor away in disgust. The silver knight hopped up to stand tall once again, but almost wobbled to tip over.

Arol Royce yelled, "Ah! What? What is it? Don't enter my ear, eh."

The knight gave a glance to his king, then back his eyes went to the steward. Arthan saw none of this eye play, but he heard all their dialogue, so had the entire council chamber.

"Thought this would be best said in private, Lord-Steward, so I'm not interrupting. Got some unexpected visitors in the Throne Hall. Thought you'd be best suited to handle them to be gone. There's many, many of them."

Lewis looked angered, the king had his face in his palm, and Arol was disgustingly repulsed at the words of the knight. "Why had guests been permitted into the Throne Hall?" asked Arol.

The knight in silver armor said, "The doors, they're wide open! Meaning no offense, my king, you've had the doors to the Throne Hall left open for days as so the workers can continue applying the red paint to them." The knight was looking to the king now, as was king to the knight.

King Gregory Royce yelled, "Have the captain of honor guards tend to it."

The knight removed his silver helm, revealing a sloppily shaven head and a face half covered in scars. Arthan saw these claw markings upon his forehead and a cheek side. "I am the captain of honor guards! I don't have enough knights to—"

King Gregory lifted a hand to silence the silver knight captain. Gregory looked on to Arol sitting there in the chair beside the grand councilman's. "Have this dealt with, brother."

Arol rolled his eyes back, rising to make leave of the chamber; he handed off the king's red sheathed sword to him before stepping away. The steward and captain of the honor guards each walked their way past Lord Edward and Lady Sophia. Arol Royce gazed upon the husband and wife with his dead maroon eyes as he went on. The knight in silver hadn't been seeming to pay the Frauers much of any attention; he was moving hastily to be back to tend to the conflict taking place in the chamber where the Golden Throne rested undefended.

The moment Arol and that knight had been gone and the door shut, the session resumed almost as if it never had been interrupted. "Where was I?" asked the king, smiling above to all with sweat dripping from the sides of his crown and under his ears as he struggled to fasten his sword to his belt. He discontinued smiling to gaze upon Edward and Sophia. "Your son is charged with the act of lying to royal blood, to the crown, and to god. He's also charged with resisting arrest within the royal Throne Hall, did you both know that? It's all treason! Worst of this all is he was to be my best and private knight…shame."

The iron door opened once again. All thought it would be the lord-steward to appear or perhaps the same silver knight from moments ago. Instead it was a different honor guard or *guards*, in fact. 'Twas a pair of honor guards escorting Jason through the door to present him front the king.

"Put him beside his mother and father there."

Arthan raised his hand to cover his mouth of the horrid sight. *Jason must be terrified,* thought Arthan.

Sir Jason Frauer was half walking, half being dragged by the silver knights. His leg was still damaged badly from the new Shield to the King's spear thrust on game day; all could see the browning bandage was in need of a change. He limped as he tried to keep pace with the knights whom had hold of his arm. His hands were bound with irons behind his back; when Sophia had seen the chains, she began to cry. Jason was thrown to the marble floor; he made no sounds of pain expression, though. His hair was so dirty that it appeared wet and greasy; Sophia kissed it all the same as the honor guards stood at their sides. The guards were armed with their typical black spears, though one of them here had been carrying Jason's white sword as well.

Edward looked upon smiling king Gregory as Sophia knelt kissing the top of her son's head, him lying upon the floor still. "What now, King Gregory? Is this the look of your rule? A mother and son in despair on the floor of the council chamber?"

Gregory sighed, while smiling; if any man could project such an expression as that, it would be Gregory Royce. "Now, Lord Edward, as I've said, this is treason we're speaking of, treason coming directly from your son."

King Gregory was standing beside his chair, he glanced to Desmond, his primary guard, then took a quick look upon the grand councilman, who was struggling to not have his heart burst from too much fast action taking place within the scene. "What is the penalty for treason against the royal blood, crown, and god?" King Gregory asked this, looking for an answer from Grand Councilman Lewis, but received none. He got no word from any councilman either, nor the few and new priests occupying the chamber on this day. "Death!" shouted the king.

Arthan could wait no longer; he prepared to speak.

If this Reya priestess won't be summoned until after this matter here is settled, it will be all too late. Arthan arose from his seating, shouting, "We must hear what next word has to say!"

The grand councilman yelled far up to Arthan in his pink, "You are not to speak until after your family down here is dismissed!"

Arthan bit his lip. He closed his eyes for a brief moment. *Aeon, let this be the right decision.* "Dismiss me as apprentice-councilman for the day's session. Dismiss me..." Arthan watched the priest to the left give him a sort of comforting smile, but Arthan only looked upon him briefly. Arthan Frauer arose from the bench, now shuffling past the sitting men in brown to his right-hand side. He maneuvered to the isle of stairs, now making to descend and then stand with his mother, father, and brother. "Dismissed, apprentice. Now approaches, Lord Arthan of House Frauer."

Lewis hadn't lived to see such an exciting session as this in quite a long while; he was unhappy in experiencing it. The elder councilman watched on as Arthan approached to grip one of Jason's arms so he could bring his brother to his feet. Both brothers stood tall beside each other, Arthan tried to give Jason a warming smile, but Jason only nodded to Arthan and then looked on to the king as if Jason had been on the field of battle, gazing into the eyes of clusters of enemies. The four Frauers stood cross from King Gregory, Lewis, the empty chair of the steward, and Sir Desmond, the Shield to the King. At each side of the family stood a knight in silver, watching them ever so closely, especially watching the renowned Sir Jason Frauer. He wasn't much of a threat with that leg of his, though the knights and this Desmond knew well enough the skill that the White Knight possessed was grand and deadly. All were cautious around Sir Jason all the same, even with that wound of his made by the newly knighted Easterlñ.

"What is it you have to say, Arthan Frauer?" asked the grand councilman.

The king cut in, "I think these Frauers have spoken on enough. It's time *I speak*, Grand Councilman."

Lewis, not caring to look upon the king, just simply raised a hand to make him go quiet. Lewis, with his right hand up to shut the king's mouth, spoke on to Arthan. "You may go on, Arthan."

Arthan looked to his mother and father, assuring them with his eyes that all would be well. He went back to looking on to King Gregory now. He said so all could hear, "Word three's topic of discussion is very important for my mother and father here in terms of their argument, my brother's accusations, all of it…just… It would be all much simpler, all of you, all would see if we just let Priestess Reya speak now. Her words will help settle this."

"Reya was not approved to speak." the king told him.

Poor Arthan felt defeated. What he could say to that? Arthan lowered his head to think; his lips were shaking.

Lewis looked oh so horrified and confused as well. He said aloud, angrily, "I have approved Reya to speak!"

The king let out a nervous laugh. "Well, I spoke to her after and told her she had no need to come any longer. She had settled her matters with me in private!"

A councilman had risen to speak on down to the king. Arthan had never seen this one before, seen him speak at the least. He was saying to Gregory, "This is extremely irregular, the way you handle this sort of business. I cannot be the only man in this room who shares this opinion. Councilmen! Does this not all make you uncomfortable?"

Arthan was happy to hear this random stranger councilman speak these words. The king was not.

"Who asked your opinion, Councilman? Sit down unless you want to have your throat cut."

Many gasps of horror came from the mouths of the one hundred surrounding councilmen and ten priests.

"I joke, I joke with him." said the king, adjusting his shining crown as it was leaning to the left side.

Jason smiled to Gregory as he was fixing the sweaty piece of diamond-filled steel atop that bald head of his. The king squinted a look of concern directed at Jason. Jason, with dried blood upon his upper lip and nostrils, had been giggling, Arthan saw now. He turned his giggle into a laugh.

As Jason laughed, he said, "Ah, Greg. You'd cut his throat? Or have a servant do it for you. I bet you've never cut anyone, haha."

King Gregory spat upon Jason's silk chest piece. He continued on laughing with the saliva upon his shirt. He laughed saying, "You'd have a guard here cut his throat for you, haha! You say the punishment for treason is death! You won't be the one to carry it out, am I right? Yes, I bet you couldn't kill me. You couldn't even cut me."

To these foul words of his son's, Edward said, "Enough!"

King Gregory stepped close to Jason. Desmond equipped his spear in both hands now behind the chairs; he knew just how deadly Sir Jason Frauer could be from literal experience in fighting him. The king punched Jason in his nose, rings pushing into flesh and bone.

Jason fell backwards to the floor, though he was laughing still. The blood upon his nose and lip was still dry, some now though fresh and wet!

"Greg, you don't have the balls to kill me, and we all know how much you love balls! One would think you'd have a good big pair in between your legs."

Gregory unsheathed the crimson colored sword from the matching scabbard. The scabbard flew to the floor as he reveled the blade colored to his family's house. "Sir, give the white bitch knight here his sword. Come, Jason, let's see how well you play with that leg of yours."

The honor guard holding Sir Jason's sword had waited for his companion in matching silver to unlock Jason's iron's. After the chains had dropped, the knight would hand Jason his blade. While this was happening, Desmond was speaking with the king, asking him, "Is this safe?"

To that the king told him, "What you've done to his leg, even a child could take him down. The man can hardly walk…" King Gregory turned away from Desmond to look upon Jason readying for the duel while the councilmen above watched, half horrified and half entertained. The irons dropped, but just before the knight could hand Jason off the white weapon, Edward gently, yet loudly said, "No."

Arthan watched and heard it all, Edward approaching Jason to speak into his ear. "That leg of yours, my son…he'll kill you, even one as unskilled as he."

"I'M NOT UNSKILLED! I can hear you! EDWARD!" The king's face went from pale to almost as purple as a full-blooded elvish being's.

"Father?" Jason hadn't known what Edward was implying, not until Edward grasped the white sword from the silver knight's possession. "Father?" he said again.

Edward held Jason's sword in hand. The lord told the king, "You are unskilled, Gregory."

"I AM NOT!" King Gregory growled as if he was a kitten attempting to roar.

"Prove it then, Gregory. I'm confident a lord such as myself can slay you! Show all otherwise."

Gregory was still fueled with rage, though he found a way to let loose a laugh during this crazed mindset he'd been engaged in. "Haaa! Would be a shame to kill such a man as untrained as you."

Edward was attempting to provoke the king, and now he was succeeding; this would lead to Edward's doom. "You're nervous. You found an excuse not to play in the arena, and now you search for excuses to not duel here. Cannot simply cut an untrained lord such as myself… You must be so afraid! Weak, weak, weak, weak, You know m—"

Gregory ran in to hack at Edward. Arthan watched his father counter the strike! Gregory rushed in so fast though that he had to continue on moving forward after Edward blocked the strike, taking many steps far past Edward after this first attack he'd made; he had gathered too much speed. Gregory turned around to face his opponent once again. Edward prepared to block another strike as Gregory was rushing inward quickly.

The three onlooking Frauers felt so helpless watching Lord Edward take on this unsteady king, especially Jason. Jason was extremely confident that he could take on Gregory, even with the wound he bore at the leg here; his father he had been less confident in. Jason was preparing to rush in and help his father, until a mailed hand was placed upon his shoulder. The honor guard said into Jason's ear, "Sir! Don't! Look there." The guard pointed to Sir Desmond.

Jason had forgotten about the Desmond character, the one who'd brought him to his own defeat within the battle royale. Perhaps Jason *was* able to defeat the king here, unarmed while his father using the white blade fought him too… It would be a two on one, though with this Desmond here added to the mix of things, a victory would be impossible, especially with that wound in Jason's shin. Jason had no choice but to join his brother and mother in looking on to the brutality of what was to come next.

Unfortunately, Edward Frauer had made to block a strike that the king hadn't even made yet. Edward raised the weapon and half closed his eyes, Gregory hadn't even swung yet, though! The king saw this foolish act of war-craft, and so he sliced at the sword which Edward wielded, right at the handle. Edward dropped Jason's blade when the king's crimson weapon collided with the white handle. The red steel bit right though three of Lord Edward's fingers to slice into the white leather grip. When the three fingers dropped to the marble and Edward fell with a cursing shout, that was when Lewis decided he'd had enough of these violent theatrics.

The grand councilman rose from the chair, approaching the king, raising a finger. "This is no combat arena! Gregory, have you gone mad?"

The grand councilman placed a saggy hand upon the king's shoulder. To this touch from the old man, the king darted his free arm outward; the arm not holding the sword. He shoved the elder into the silver steward's chair. Lewis's head hit the metal hard. He lay on the floor holding the spot behind his ear, cursing and shouting. Gregory watched him on the floor for one, maybe two seconds worth of time, then he returned his attention to kneeling Edward. Edward was trying to pick his fingers up from the marble but had stopped searching for them when he saw Gregory approaching with the blade in his hand.

Arthan hadn't been focusing on them above, but the men of the council were in distress. Some had been horrified at the fast and loud sort of dueling. Most men were just worried for the safety and health of the grand councilman. Two men in brown jumped down from the seating area to tend to the old man bleeding from the ear at the chair behind the king. Three priests joined these councilmen as so the elder would receive the best and fastest healing that he could have at the moment.

Gregory looked upon these men filling the base of the chamber, though they'd only received his gaze for few short seconds. The king's eyes were everywhere; he was looking to the confused and stressed council above. He'd been looking to Edward as he was tearing and missing three fingers, bleeding ever so much. The king had to keep an eye on the three Frauers, especially Jason there. Gregory felt nervous, though safe…very safe. He had the two honor guards here beside the Frauers, and of course he had his skilled Shield at his back!

Gregory looked upon the four entrances of the chamber above; there were five total including the iron door down here. Pairs of guards lived at each of the entrances above. Gregory was in the Great Keep, and this was *his* house! So why was Arthan watching him look oh so nervous and in distress.

Gregory was sweating as he loomed over Lord Edward. Arthan kept on thinking the same exact thought, *He's never cut a man. He won't kill my father. He's never cut anybody. He will not kill him.* Though Arthan should have put just a bit more thought into his mind's speaking. Gregory Royce had cut a man; he'd just cut Lord Edward! Cut his fingers clean off.

Lady Sophia sank to her knees, pleading, "Mercy, mercy, sire!" Her hands were locked together, and she held them at her breasts. Lady Sophia was behind King Gregory, not only did the king not see her, he hadn't really heard her voice either. Gregory was so angered, so provoked, and so trapped in his own act of injustice and lies that he felt he was ready to make his first kill.

Edward hadn't looked upon Gregory, nor the red blade; he'd just looked past his killer standing there. Arthan and Jason stood side by side, their mother at their knees. Edward wanted his last sight on earth to be of his family, though his executioner king took a sidestep to block his view before he brought the blade down. King Gregory struck Lord Frauer with an overhead blow to the forehead. The king's sword landed just above Edward's nose. Edward's reaction to this would turn even the strongest of stomachs. The king was weak, his sword only bit into the thin layer of flesh upon Edward's head. Sophia shrieked in horror! Arthan looked downward to his shoes, and Jason calmly and eerily sidestepped, dragging his hurt leg so he could get a view on his father's death. The honor guards and Desmond made sure Jason would not intervene, and he had no intention of doing so. He was in a state of extreme mind shock as he stood watching Lord Edward die.

King Gregory ripped the sword from Edward's skin to raise the blade and bring it back downward upon the same mark. He'd made a new cut, this time striking a bit harder. The blade cut Edward's head at the top by his hair, sinking in deeper to crack his skull some.

Edward would have looked to Jason in these final moments though his son saw that he could not. Edward's eyes were twitching on up and up, rolling to the back of his head. Edward's mouth had been wide open as if he was projecting a scream, though no sounds were made by him. King Gregory used all the strength he could find within himself to remove the blade and then send it back down one more time. Edward's head caved inward, releasing a red misty explosion. Looked like smashed watermelon and eggshells.

Jason sank to his knees to join his mother. Arthan raised his eyes, looking away from his own shoes to watch his father's unmoving body that had fallen off to the side to lie upon the floor. He looked upon his father lying there on his own arm as his drippy, smashed-in head leaked the black appearing blood. The crimson torches caused tricks to the eye when red appearing things such as blood would come visible under the matching light of the magical flames above. The blood leaking from Arthan's dead father was black… Arthan could not keep his eyes from gazing upon this blood; the blood of his family. Somehow he could not find the will to cry. Not even a single tear it seemed he had been capable of shedding for his rested brother Dallion and now here he found he could not cry for the death of his father either.

19

The Realm's Last Council Session

Desmond was trying hard to understand if a scenario as this one presented front him was considered regular for the people of Midlön; for the councilmen particularly. He removed his eyes from the black appearing puddle of blood leaking from the dead lord's caved in face. Desmond watched the men in brown above. Two he saw now throwing their breakfasts up upon the seating and onto the councilmen at the row below them. Some councilmen had their hands placed over their wide opened mouths in awe at the gruesome execution. Most chatted dialogues to each other which Desmond could not hear from down here. *The way the chamber's people are reacting, this certainly doesn't seem regular.* Desmond had always thought the Easterlñ traditions could consist of cruel methods, this King Gregory though was making his realm and city to look be a dreadful place; luxurious appearing but dreadful in truth.

Behind Desmond, three priests and two councilmen knelt, aiding the fallen Grand Councilman Lewis. King Gregory was wiping blood from his blade as Jason Frauer watched on with hate down on his knees. Desmond looked beside the unarmored White Knight to view if Arthan the brother was projecting the same look toward the king. Arthan was only inhaling deeply as he looked upon his father's corpse. It had seemed as if Arthan Frauer had just ran a foot race and was recovering his breath. His mother beside him, the Lady Sophia was kneeling, eyes closed and fingers interlaced under her chin. She was fast at pray and tearing, lips moving but no sounds of the words coming through.

The iron door far behind kneeling Sophia and her sons had creaked open. Lord-Steward Arol Royce walked through, his long black hair drenched in sweat. He held his hands against the metal now, facing it, shutting it tightly.

"Our visitors aren't happy." all heard Lord-Steward Arol say to the iron door. He'd spoken calmly yet loudly. The steward turned himself around to view the carnage front him. "What did you do…" Arol looked on to Gregory in horror and disappointment. "You damned fool, Gregory, what have you done? Ew…" The king's face was tensing. He looked upon Arol's drippy beard and nose.

"Who was it came to the Throne Hall? Where is the captain of honor guard?"

Arol turned his head to the left and then right, in the negative.

"They beat him bloody, cut him. The intruders bear steel; they come for you, and are very unhappy."

"Who are they?" cried the king. There was a harsh pounding coming from the iron door. The two silver knights whom were guarding the Frauers now shifted their attention around in the opposite direction to the door at the base of the chamber here. They turned their spears towards the iron door; Desmond gripped his own ebony spear ever so tightly, standing about a foot length away behind the king.

The door burst open, revealing a spotted roaring horse fastened in brown leather armoring; the beast was readying to charge. Behind and at the sides of the tense armored animal stood in total forty angry footmen fastened in leather and chain mail. Armed with various weapons, they rushed inside, filling almost the entire floor of the council chamber. Their tabards were all dyed black, at their centers was stitched the blue tree of House Frauer.

Of all these intruding visitors there'd been only one atop horse, and that was Tillsy Frauer, holding her battle-axe. She whistled, riding the spotted animal with matching leather inward while more men gathered round. The beast's armor, Tillsy's, and the soldiers had all been the same matching Frauer leathers that the family was traditionally known to dress in for travel and battle. There were forty of them (including Tillsy, forty-one)! Ten of the Frauer soldiers held their weapons to one of these honor guards upon the chamber floor here. The knight was almost pissing himself, shaking his spear and shield. Another separate ten of the intruding soldiers made for the other guard to disarm him. The rest marched to secure the stairs and area above, readying to disarm the pairs of guards up above at the entrances there; though these honor guards above had been occupied with a problem at the eastern entrance.

The silver armored guards above weren't facing the commotion below upon the marble where their king was in need. *So much is happening,* thought Desmond, hoping the guards high up there with the councilmen would bring themselves down to help make a stand to defend the king of Midlön. The two below who'd been previously guarding the Frauers, now had thrown their spears down in surrender. Arol said, "You damned fool." to his brother, the king.

Desmond made to look above to signal the guards to come down, though these pairs of guards at each of the entrances above had now sadly just turned into a sloppy cluster of knights in silver, standing defending only the east entrance of the chamber in place of aiding the ruler of the realm. Out of the darkness of the arch leading into this tunnel where they'd held their spear tips pointing to came an unarmed and bloody honor guard with no helm and missing a glove. He screamed, "They're coming! Hold the tunnel!"

"Who's coming!?" shouted a councilman seated close by the cluster of guards. "The paladins! The men of god have gone mad!"

The warriors with the blue tree mark coming from one entrance down here, mad cathedral men of god from another above… This is not looking well for my king or for myself either. Am I prepared to die for this man wearing the crown?

Desmond asked himself questions in his mind when instead he should have been preparing for Tillsy's wrath. "King Gregory! You're to answer for your crimes! Murder against my cousin Dalli—" Tillsy looked as if she'd been struck in the face with a hard blow. She stopped her speaking, inspecting the corpse upon the floor of the chamber; she'd known even without having to see the garb, this had been her uncle's remains.

"Tillsy!" shouted Arthan after she jumped off the side of the horse, landing fast upon her boots. With her axe in hand, she ran toward King Gregory, letting loose a loud battle-cry! Quicker than anybody could have expected, Gregory Royce leaped forward one pace, grabbing himself a handful of Sophia's brown locks. He flexed his muscles hard as he brought her head and neck up against his own face. His nose was buried in her ear, the edge of his red sword placed hard upon her throat. With the king's blade at the neck of her aunt and Desmond's spear pointed toward her way, Tillsy made the right decision to cease her attacking run and allow Jason to hold her back and away. She was tearing, though expressed much anger through her bodily language, not sadness. Jason was standing shaking with his cousin held within his arms as Arthan sat upon his knees still gazing at what was left of Lord Edward's face. The king looked around and behind himself as he held Lady Frauer. He brought his gaze above toward the east entrance where the remainder of his security was gathered. Aside from Desmond behind him, these few guards were all the king had whom could stand between himself and the hostile soldiers here fighting for House Frauer.

"Men of the guard! Come to me!" shouted King Gregory, quickly returning his eyes back upon Arthan and Jason holding the cousin whilst men with weapons surrounded on all sides. Desmond glanced up at the east entrance to get a look on to find if these honor guards were making any movement in reaction to the king's orders.

When Desmond looked above and upon them, white light spat out through the tunnel. Four out of the cluster of guards had been instantly and maybe permanently blinded by this magical sort of attack.

"What's that?" the unarmed honor guard asked himself aloud, standing beside Sir Jason in fear for his life. Many eyes were now on the east entrance, and the guards rolling amongst the floor, armor clanking as their eyes burned in pain within their very skulls. "Help them!" cried a nearby councilman up there within the rows of the many men in matching brown. He was pointing to a priest, to direct the holy man in white to aid this blinded guard in silver. The priest wasn't giving any bit of attention to the suffering guard, though.

Desmond paid more mind to the commotion above now than he had been to the dangers below and close by. He watched the priest up there, along with two others by him now all making their way toward the east entrance. These had been three of the ten priests newly allowed into the chamber for today's session; now there'd been six grouped together. Three approached the arch closely to the wall from the right side, the other new set of three had been incoming from the left. Up the center of the isle of stairs came another priest who'd just been previously seated; he was holding a dagger. *What is this?* Desmond asked himself in his mind while he watched the holy men equip themselves with weapons.

There had been ten priests in total inside the dome for today's session. Some of these priests currently were using magic to heal the grand councilman upon the floor by the royal chairs, the remaining now were armed with daggers and white glowing wands, moving up fast. They'd been now standing behind the honor guards whom weren't suffering from the blinding magical light. Desmond knew indeed these priests were standing behind those guards up there, not to aid them but to stab them in the back; figuratively and possibly literally from the looks of those sharpened cathedral knives.

One of these priests behind the silver guards shouted, "Sirs, lower the spears!"

Four of the knights still lay helplessly in pain, clawing at their half-melted eyes, the remaining had snapped around to attention, shields and spears aiming to the priests in white. Three seconds after the knight's turned to look upon these armed priests with their little knives and pieces of magical wood was when the paladins came in through this dark and doorless entryway of the chamber.

Sir Paladin Reese with no helm and flapping black locks of hair just as long as Desmond's had leaped in first. Desmond tried his best to sense any form of attack coming from the surrounding threats down here, though he was extremely interested in the events taking place above; it was difficult to avert his eyes from this above madness. The paladin with using one hand only, swung his great sword as hard as he could to grind against the breastplate of one of the silver knights. The knight was too slow in raising his shield in defense, so he accepted the hit from the paladin with no choice. The guard tumbled down the stairs of the chamber with a dented chest piece while men in brown around watched on to the battle taking place.

Behind this holy knight came another, Sir-Paladin John. John came out from the darkness with many allies at his back whom were wearing various different styles of golden, silver, beige, and white-plated armoring. An honor guard made to block John's path, so John sent his war hammer down upon the silver foe's shield from above. The honor guard tripped after receiving the hit, falling backwards now into a grouping of seated councilmen, breaking his ankle during the tumble. John held his long sword in his opposite hand, pointing it toward the visor of the armed honor guard beside the one who'd just fallen. This silver knight dropped his spear and raised his hands for mercy, as did the other beside him. Watching this all, Desmond suddenly went from fearful to joyful after he'd heard the barking sounds through the yelling and noises of the struggle taking place.

He looked to the source of these animal sounds. Araisha was growling and barking at one of the men in silver as a paladin was clashing with he; both of the men were in a sort of private duel while this chaos surrounding was taking place. It would have been a private *uninterrupted* fight, but Araisha had descended the stairs to join the fighting men.

Desmond watched her rip a chunk of leather from the guard's boot as he fought on to his paladin opponent. The guard made to strike Araisha with a spear thrust! Her distracting bite though gave the paladin a good opportunity to ring his sword upon the helm of the knight, so he did exactly that. Araisha bit at the foot with her teeth, the paladin struck at the helm with his weapon, and then down the foe went.

Desmond eyed the Frauer soldiers again; them now much closer than they'd been moments ago. "Stay close to me, Sir Desmond." whispered Gregory as he held Lady Sophia's jaw by his own chin and mouth, pressing his sword to her throat still.

Araisha was barking ever so loudly. Now she'd been down upon the marble floor, watching at how Desmond was surrounded.

With a paladin defender at each of his sides, Ark Priest Alice descended the east set of stairs just past barking Araisha. The priest was wearing beige armor atop his white robes, matching beige helm. He gripped a white battle-staff but used it more as a cane; the device much too large for his stature. He spoke loudly, so very loudly as he walked down this isle. "GREGORY ROYCE! IN THE NAME OF AEON, YOU ARE HEREBY REMOVED FROM TITLE AS KING OF THE REALM, STRIPPED OF THE GOLDEN THRONE, AND THE CROWN OF THE KINGS!"

The king looked to his brother, Arol. The steward was silent; none paid him any bit of attention as if all had forgotten his existence.

Araisha's still making noise. She was bloodthirsty, and Desmond could sense it. She barked louder and louder, or did it just seem to grow higher in volume because of Desmond's magical binding on her? He rubbed his eyes hard while he held his spear with the other hand as her rage increased onward. His fingers were wet; he'd been sweating now wearing his new black leather armor… *Black armor, black, the black, blackness.* Desmond itched above and around his nose. The Frauer father, his blood was spilled in the chamber, and he could sense it and literally smell it, as could Araisha. She barked louder, the ark priest came closer to him and the king. The smell of blood in the air grew thicker, and Desmond's eyes blacker and blacker.

Arol was still looking upon the floor, unmoving. All other occupants of the marble base there aside from those tending to Lewis had now approached another pace inward toward King Gregory, Sophia, and Desmond; the men had formed a ring. *They'll take another step, the king will cut the lady's throat, then they'll all kill him and me.* King Gregory had many tears running down upon the sides of his cheeks. In fact, now he'd actually been hysterically crying as he held the lady there in his arms with his sword against her skin. Her knees gave out, and she dropped slightly, though still in King Gregory's grasp. She moaned and wailed. King Gregory did as well, though with words. "Don't come down here, Ark Priest! Allllll of you! Stay BACK! I'll kill her too."

The councilmen above watched on as if it had all been a theatrical performance. This was supposed to be a council session, though no councilmen gave any council to their king!

Arthan had now risen to his feet, not to speak, but to prepare to watch his mother be executed.

Araisha was barking louder, and Desmond's eyes were entirely black now. With these black eyes he gazed upon the soldiers opposing King Gregory Royce. They'd been readying to take another step inward to attempt to cease him before he could open Lady Sophia's throat. *They'll take a step, the king will cut the lady's throat, then they'll all kill him and me too.* Before they'd made to move, though, the king took a look back to Desmond to be sure he was still there defending his backside while he held Sophia's head in place there front his breast. The king looked upon Desmond, tearing. He said, "Desmond, your eyes?"

They'll take a step, the king will cut the lady's throat, then they'll all kill him and me. Desmond thought of a new scenario. He acted out his new and violent play instead of overthinking on it. He hadn't had much time left before the soldiers would take that next step of theirs.

Sophia's face was held at Gregory's chest now, not by his chin and mouth, so she'd been far enough away that Desmond's side slash from the spear wouldn't cut her head off too, only the king's. The crown was so heavy that it had dropped to the marble first, landing hard yet fully intact, unbroken and unscratched. Gregory's head somehow had been projectiled upward from this strike. Desmond's side slash from his spear sent the head up and away! When it came back and down, it bounced twice when it hit the marble and the rolled on toward the direction of Ark Priest Alice and his paladins.

"There lies King Gregory Royce." said the Ark Priest. He rested the oversized staff upon his shoulder, clapping his hands together repeatedly and looking on toward Desmond while doing so.

The next to clap his hands together too was Councilman George, smiling, flexing his gray pointy whiskers. A few more of these men in brown above clapped their hands together as well. Soon then though the clapping spread to the below soldiers whom had just been approaching Desmond and the king to save the lady. Almost all within the chamber were clapping their hands together, applauding Desmond for… *For what? Killing the man I swore to defend?* The only souls of the chamber whom weren't applauding Desmond had been Arol Royce; he'd still been silent, head bowed as if in a dream. The two Frauer brothers hadn't been paying Desmond any bit of attention either, they'd been tending to their mother covered in tears, sweat, and Gregory's blood. Few of the honor guards had been silent too, in awe of what had happened.

The applause had ended when one of these unarmed silver guards cried, "Wait! Wait! This man here, the Shield to the King has killed the king!"

Tillsy Frauer was leaning over the body of her uncle, sobbing gently to herself as she prayed for his soul. When she'd heard those words from the guard, she discontinued her prayer and made way to him. She said, "It was a justly kill…was it not?" Tillsy stopped her rushing to the defenseless guard. She looked on upward to ask the many councilmen, "Was it not? Was it not justly?"

"Aye." said a man, rising.

Another man in brown had fully risen up too, he said, "It was justly."

A councilman beside that one stood as well. "It was." said he.

All councilmen stood now, looking upon Desmond as Araisha padded on over to his side. She licked the leather thigh armor that her master wore, wagging her tail and happily doing so. Desmond felt happy too, so why had his eyes still been black. The smell of blood perhaps? The rush of the kill he'd just made? *There is nothing left to fear. These men above stand in agreement. What I've done was not the wrong thing to do…*

The harder Desmond tried to rid his mind of the blackness, of the rage and thought of death and torment, the more it all stayed within. Perhaps he was learning to accept the dark arts without letting it consume him; blackness without a spree of violence. He wasn't eager to kill anymore; he felt strangely satisfied. The worst outcome Desmond could have thought on would be if he were to lose his memory to the blackness; this had happened in past. The magical darkness would not only often cause his eyes to appear black, but they'd literally cause him to remember seeing nothing but blackness during this time of effect. This is what happened during this next and continued applause here in the council chamber.

It began from the rear of his sight, appearing how the way ink would come in when black droplets would touch a cup filled with water. He felt Araisha's loving touch at his leg, councilmen all around and in view clapping; an overwhelming amount of clapping. He saw those Frauer brothers watching him now with extreme focus. Shortly after Desmond returned that gaze upon those two who just had lost their father's life, there was nothing…only blackness.

Desmond hadn't gone unconscious; he only just couldn't remember anything that had happened to him or what had taken place after that second applause continued on. When he *woke* from this black daze, he'd seen he was sitting upon the desk inside of his bedchamber, the fireplace was unlit.

Desmond rose upward from the desk and it's matching stained oak chair where Araisha lay beside. Out of the window he watched, it was entirely dark out. Night rainclouds prevented any stars from shining once again. He felt cold as he watched the city through the window of his chamber there. He left the glass to prepare to light the fireplace so he could warm himself and Araisha. He'd still been wearing his thick leather armoring, though his body remained so very chilled. The knock came to the door just as he placed the first log in. The dog had woken from the sounds of the visitor out in the hallway. Desmond moved away from the dark hearth to answer the iron door. *Unless it had just been a dream, I do believe I've killed the king of Midlön today.* Desmond needed to be prepared for any possible threat, even though he'd just been applauded for his violent actions earlier on. He thought as he walked to the door, *It could have been a ruse…a false applause so I wouldn't see punishment coming later… coming now.*

Desmond opened the door slowly with his spear hidden in hand behind the wall. Araisha on all fours below him in-between his legs had silently watched on to the grand councilman at the doorway. His head was bandaged; aside from the wrapping's he seemed quite the same as his last visit to this chamber of Desmond's. "Sir

Desmond." Lewis nodded to him after saying his name. "Hello Grand Councilman." replied Desmond. Lewis held a wrinkly hand out to the front of the dog's snout at the crack of the door there. "Good boy." the old man said.

"She's a she." Desmond corrected him. He cracked the door open some more, leaving the spear now against the wall to reveal two empty hands to the elder. He saw now that the grand councilman was visiting alone. Desmond patted Araisha on her neck as he looked into the royal apartment common hall. There'd been no honor guards stationed at the fireplace where the cushioned seats were across from. *Good,* thought Desmond. He had seen those men in silver had been the most loyal to the king of the Midlön folk out of them all. *My corrupted self should have been the literal most loyal, and yet I was the one to end his life.*

The grand councilman said, "It's time for the session."

"What session?" asked Desmond. "What? Have you forgotten? The first-ever private council session. You are the first subject, come we've spoke of this." Lewis, with his cane and bent back, led Desmond and Araisha far down many stairs and two sets of hallways so he could show them to the Throne Hall. It took longer than it should have once again, as the councilman wasn't just an elder, he was one of the oldest souls who dwelt within Ascali; he moved so slowly. "Here we are, I present to you, the Private Council." The door opened to the sight of an entirely different appearing Throne Hall.

"Marvelous, isn't it? The torches, golden-tinted flames now, the fashion of the chamber in the Gold-age of the realm." The grand councilman pointed above to the new fire, lighting the royal room.

"Gold-age?" Desmond asked old Lewis. The elder replied as he walked with Desmond and Araisha, "Yes, the five ages… Age of Origin, Spawn-age, Golden-age, Gray-age, and the White."

Desmond nodded as he looked upon the almost fully occupied table at the center of the chamber, resting front the throne. Lewis still went on about the torches. "Most agreed that the crimson colored fire of House Royce reminded folk of Retilliath." Desmond hadn't known what the councilman was referring to when he said the word *Retilliath*. He, Araisha, and Grand Councilman Lewis almost reached their destination now. Lewis said while taking small steps, "Retilliath is the home of the devil. It's the underworld, the opposite of the great heaven. It is what we folk call *hell* in our religion. You have much to learn Sir Desmond of the East."

Grand Councilman Lewis approached the table hunched over, Desmond at his side standing tall; the hound low in between them. Six men occupied the table and they'd all looked right to Desmond and his hound upon their approach, not old Lewis, even though *he* was the one to speak first. "Sir Desmond, I present to you the Private Council. There will no longer be massive sessions held within the dome. Meeting's now will consist of discussions here, with fewer souls." Desmond looked to Grand Councilman Lewis. He said to him, "Yes." *What does he want me to say?*

"Desmond, we have here Ark Priest Alice, and Ark Wizard Spairro whom I believe you haven't had the pleasure of meeting." The leading priest with gold eyes in white smiled to Desmond, as did the unfamiliar elder beside him; this new old man wore blue robes and a pointy purple hat. Desmond waved to the two men of magic. "I also introduce to you General Julius, leader of the realm's military." The fully armored warlord saluted Desmond and even Araisha too. "I believe you are acquainted with Sisco and Battle-Mage Bishop."

Desmond said "Hello" to the copper-skinned tourney master and his defender wearing iron and red leather.

"Good to see you, Sir Desmond." said Sisco with a clever sort of smile painted upon his face.

Desmond wasn't looking upon smiling Sisco though, he was looking right to Arol Royce who was seated among the five others at the table. Lewis said, "Of course, we have Lord Arol here as well." Desmond stood watching Arol, Arol sat watching Desmond. The silence was broken when Arol said, "Hello Sir Desmond." Desmond looked away from the lordly man who's brother he'd just slain only hours ago. Lewis said, "Have a seat Sir Desmond." Desmond and the grand councilman rested themselves upon the empty chairs of the council's table; Araisha lay down upon the marble when their asses met the seating above her.

"You've been summoned here, Sir Desmond, so you can decide your own fate." Lewis told Desmond this.

Desmond nodded to the statement. Lewis continued on as all men of the table looked upon Desmond's face. "You may remain as Shield to the King as you've earned the title fairly, or you may go in peace to wherever it is you would bring yourself. You will not be punished for breaking your vow, murdering Gregory Royce while he held title of king."

Desmond asked the grand councilman, "Who is new king?"

"I will be." Arol said across at the complete opposite end of where Desmond and Lewis were seated.

Arol looked into Desmond's eyes. Desmond had not a clue what this expression could mean... Was Arol angry? Vengeful or forgiving? He just stared him on, so Desmond looked on to him as well.

Grand Councilman Lewis said, "Arol was steward and blood of the king. Gregory's wickedness had naught to do with Arol, and so a new steward shall be found. Arol Royce shall claim the title as King of Midlön and Lord of the Golden Throne. You may service him as his primary guard, or you may leave... The choice is your own."

Arol assured Desmond, "My brother was cruel and deserved death. I will not hold a grudge against you, Sir Desmond, for carrying out what needed to be done."

To that, Desmond said, "I will reject your offer."

Sisco decided it was now his turn to speak. "Lovely folks, might you tell Desmond why Battle-Mage Bishop and I are present?"

The grand councilman said, "Ah, yes. Should you reject the offer to remain Shield, Battle-Mage Bishop here will leave Sisco's service and claim the title. Since you've made your rejection, well congratulations, Battle-Mage, you shall be promoted to Shield to the King when Arol is crowned."

The elder mage nodded to Sisco, and the general gave him a stern salute. Sisco coughed a bit, holding his rag to his lips. When he removed the cloth he said, "And..." looking to Lewis.

Lewis told Desmond, "And Sisco would like to offer you the role as his personal protector, after Bishop officially leaves him."

"What say you?" asked Sisco, smiling to Desmond. "I think I will reject you as well."

"Simple and settled. Word, dismissed." said Lewis.

Grand Councilman Lewis rose to stand hunched and upon his feet. "Come, Sir Desmond, I will show you out of the—"

"I know my way out." Desmond said as he stood himself upward. He told them all lastly, "I'd like to be demoted please. I'm no knight, not truly." Desmond gave one last look upon the men of the table, as well as that beautiful golden chair over there. *I do not wish to spend my life standing beside a chair.* Desmond closed his eyes and turned his body around to face the exit of the hall, Araisha following and making for the many stairs to descend as well. After their descent, they walked past the set of massive doors as men went at work upon them, scraping off red paint, distracted by the big dog.

Desmond and Araisha walked within this next room with the high ceiling, this one as well containing warm and comforting newly made golden torches; not the ugly red ones colored of hell from Gregory's rule. They almost got to the big iron doors where they would leave to enter the night of the city, but Sisco came jogging up from behind. "Desmond, Desmond!"

"Hello, Sisco."

The copper man brushed his long hair out from the corner of his eye so he could properly look upon Desmond while he spoke to him. "Are you sure to be so quick in declining my offer? Knight or not a knight, I'd still have you."

Desmond sighed. He told Sisco, "I do not wish to be standing guard for my life."

Sisco placed a friendly hand upon Desmond's shoulder. "Guarding me…would not be like guarding Gregory, nor his brother, Arol."

Desmond hadn't known what Sisco was meaning by this, so he explained it to him. "Yes, you'll have to stand at the ready to be sure when I'm in the booth during games that nobody assassinates me. You must watch over the grunts during their feasting time to be sure they don't fight each other prior to game day. These tasks though, that's only one minor portion of the year as you've seen!"

“What happens during time when tournament isn’t happening?” Sisco removed his hand from Desmond’s shoulder to clap his two together. He clapped twice with a smile. “Travel! I travel the realm, the realms...in seek for grunts, combatants, spectators, and all. We prepare for the tournament all year long. Lots of this preparation takes place outside Ascali. I can assure you, boredom will not find you while you’re at my side. I even visit Eastfell from time to time... How would you like it, Desmond? To be able to return home for a visit.”

“I am shunned from Eastfell.”

Sisco closed his eyes, shaking his head in the negative. “You are banished as a citizen, as a freeman of the realm of Eastfell. Now you’re not only a man of Midlön, you’d be a warrior of Midlön, and you’d be my warrior, if you’d accept. What say you, Desmond? Warrior Desmond.”

Desmond stood there in his black leather about a foot away from Sisco in those yellow robes of his. The Great Keep of Ascali was cold; Desmond shivered as he thought hard on Sisco’s offer.

20

Another Sunrise

Jason received four metal pints from the tender behind the wooden slab at the Alligator Inn. Inside of these metal cups, the foaming and famous Willowhold ale. He carried two in each hand, bringing them to the largest table in the establishment, occupied by family and friends. Jason handed off the three drinks to those whom had nothing to toast with. He gave one pint to his eldest knight, Sir Martin Praxus. Tillsy took one from Jason as well as did Arthan sitting beside her. Lady Sophia and Sir Lance decided on water, the rest at the table drank the ale.

"To Dallion, to Edward." they all said at once.

Jason took his seat beside Sir-Paladin John while gulping. All souls at the table drank to the positive memory of the deceased Lord and son.

They all sat in silence, not looking among one another. Jason's knights had their eyes to the table. Tillsy was gazing upon the dancing folk moving in circles beside the girl playing the flute in the corner of the inn. Arthan was looking at the mount upon the wall, at the great sword he'd swung during his last visit here, having no memory of doing so. Arthan finished the contents of his pint and then rose upward to make for the bar top where he would receive another from the tender. He was the first to finish his drink and make to have a second.

When Arthan approached the wood, he waved his empty pint to the man pouring rum. The tender finished servicing a lady ordering and then took Arthan's empty mug. The tender opened the rum tap again, as he'd done many times this night and would do many times more. The rum filled the tin, and then the tender exchanged the pint for a golden coin from Arthan.

"Lord Arthan Frauer." said Lyro the half-elvish, half-man.

Arthan turned around to watch the hooded being in green bow low. Arthan returned the same bowing gesture. "Where is Aetheria?" he blurted out without verbally making any sort of greeting first.

Before Lyro could make an answer, Arthan asked, "How do you fare?"

Lyro answered, "I am fatigued. Our party made a great rush to collect our belongings to make ready to depart. I must be quick with you."

"At this hour? All of the visiting elvish are making to leave Ascali? You've all meant to stay longer though so I've heard."

Lyro sighed with closed eyes. He projected the negative gesture to Arthan, shaking his head; his pointy ears sticking through the hood jiggled when he did so. "After our involvement in the king's death, we wish to return to our realm at once." Arthan looked over the shoulder of the half-breed, past to the dancing folk. He saw his family, Sir-Paladin John, and brother's knights all sharing drink in silence at the table. He didn't wish to be speaking of these things with Lyro. Talking of the king Arthan had seen murdered by the Easterlñ guard; the very subject of murder he wished to stay far from, though he was curious now thinking on how Lyro said, *"After our involvement in the king's death."*

Arthan asked him, "What do you mean by involvement? Aetheria's brother happened to by chance been walking within the streets when he'd come across the crowd surrounding my baby brother's corpse. He'd seen the wounds, told Aetheria, then she told me. None need know she's relayed the information of the dagger wounds to me..." Lyro again shook his head *no* with closed eyes. Arthan sipped rum while the half-breed clad in green told him, "Aetheria hadn't just told you. That very night after her brother had retrieved us from the garden, she had made a sneaky visit to the cathedral. She had told everything she'd said to you to the ark priest."

"Of the stab wounds?" asked Arthan. He asked another question, "You were there with her?"

Before Lyro even answered his first, Lyro said, "She's familiar with the hand signing as well as is Ark Priest Alice. And yes, Arthan I went to the cathedral and saw and heard all. Aetheria told the ark priest and many listening priests of the unmentioned wounds on the belly of your brother. Even that one there, the paladin-knight of yours." Lyro turned and pointed to Sir-Paladin John sipping his ale beside Jason at the table. "He was there, making the same claims as Aetheria about the dagger theory and accusation. There was a trial taking place you see. Aetheria happened to make visit to the cathedral at just the right time it seemed."

Arthan wondered where Aetheria was as of now; his first question to Lyro had been *'Where's Aetheria?'* Lyro still never answered him.

"Aetheria is the reason for why the paladins came?" asked Arthan. Lyro smiled with a slightly tilted head. "Yes, and also no. There'd been a priestess on trial at the cathedral. This priestess admitted that King Gregory asked her to keep the true cause of the boy's death an absolute secret. She would have been punished for this, though the godly woman claimed that the king threatened her life if she'd spilled this precious secret of the wounds."

"I understand." said Arthan. "The words of that paladin John, the words of the priestess, then Aetheria comes to the cathedral with her words of it as well. The ark priest had been convinced to make visit during the morning's council session to strip the king of his title. There'd been enough evidence for it. If only they'd done it the night before, instead of waiting for the morning's session…"

Arthan was becoming dizzy. Why? He hadn't known. He sipped on some more rum and then put the pint down upon the wood. He asked again, "Where's Aetheria?"

Lyro gave a sad smile. "Aetheria's at the gate with her brother, and the rest of the twelve of our company. She sent me here to give you this. Aetheria can write in your language."

Lyro handed off Arthan a sealed envelope made of leaves. He unwrapped it, finding paper with text written upon it. "Thank you so much." Arthan put the note in one of the pockets of his pants. "Lyro, though Gregory Royce is dead. There's nothing to fear, not from anybody. Your company doesn't need to depart in haste and worry."

Lyro bowed to Arthan, unsmiling. He said before he'd left the inn, "So long as that Arol Royce sits the throne of your realm, there will always be something to fear." He left Arthan there alone so he could drink from his pint in silence.

Instead of returning to the table where the rest of the Frauers and friends had been drinking, Arthan remained leaning upon the bar. He sipped on until his pint was empty again. Arthan made to wave the tender on over, but his arm was grabbed by Jason's hand. "We don't have time for another. Just wanted to stop for a quick one on our way down to the Square. Come, we're making to leave." Arthan followed Jason out the door of the inn where the knights, Tillsy, Sophia, and Sir-Paladin John all walked in a silent group southward downhill upon Brey Street.

It was after sundown. They'd arrived at proper time for the ceremony. Many souls were invited to occupy the Square. This pyre was smaller than rested King Harold's though, and the crowd far smaller too. The Square did still consist of hundreds of souls though, just not as many as there had been for Harold's honoring; for he was genuinely loved. Gregory Royce's reign did not last long, nor did he do much good for the realm during his time of rule. The events leading up to the death of him had horrified most folk as well, causing much hate and foul talk. Many folk of the city made a point to not attend his burning here and now. Beside the king's pyre was built another, half in size. Beside that, another matching one too. There'd been three pyres for the three bodies. Dallion, Edward, and Gregory Royce. Arthan eyed his tearing mother as she stood within the crowds of folk surrounded by family. She'd wanted a private burning for Dallion and her dead husband; Sophia had hatred for the very idea that her son's burning ceremony was to take place alongside the corpse of the man who he'd been killed by and who'd slain her Lord Edward too. *"Why should Gregory be honored or remembered in any way?"* Jason had to tell his mother that Gregory's burning was done for tradition, for god, and out of respect for his family…Arol Royce the soon to be new King of Midlön.

There Arol stood, upon the empty stage wearing a red cloak. He kissed his dead brother upon the forehead while the grand councilman was ascending the stage. For Harold's burning there had been rows of chairs in place by the body, chairs for the many lords and ladies of the great houses of the realm and city of Ascali. There had been so few of the noble families in attendance for this ceremony that no chairs had even been planned to be set. Regularly the grand councilman would make a speech, speaking good words of the fallen. Gregory had shoved Lewis to the marble floor though, bleeding him before his own death. Grand Councilman Lewis wasn't prepared to say any words for Gregory Royce. He took the diamond-inlaid crown off from the top of his clam-like bald and cold stitched on head. Lewis placed the crown of the kings inside the box as Arol gazed on. Arol Royce followed Lewis off of the stage with a look of boredom painted upon his face. Down the stairs the two went, and up the stairs came the fire elementists to light the dead.

Lady Sophia let loose many tears, as did Jason and Sir Lance. Even Sir-Paladin John cried a bit for the souls; souls that would soon be at rest once the sun would be fully risen and the embers cold. Arthan took the leaf wrapped parchment out from his pocket. For the first time in many years he finally found the will to let fall a tear drop. Was he crying for Dallion? or his father? or both? Why had he only begun to let tears come now that he's to read Aetheria's letter, given to him by her heigh-elvish servant Lyro. The flames upon the stage danced on through the night as Arthan read beside his mother and his brother there.

To Arthan,

For the first moment in my life you had made me feel like a living being. I do not do well even with my own people and so was thankful to receive kindness from another soul for the first time. Those who speak to me with sweetness are only my family and servants. You are special to me, Arthan Frauer. If you ever find yourself in the North, you know where you can see me if you would like to spend moments together again.

Your friend,
Aetheria of Tree Ain

Arthan read the letter more than one hundred times as all within the Square stood silent, some praying, some watching on and others doing both. He'd must have stood reading for many, many hours. His family, along with all of the occupants of the Square at this mark in the timeline now, had looked incredibly fatigued. When Arthan looked up into the sky, he hadn't seen any stars, not blue ones or any red either. The sun was rising.

THE CITY OF ASCALI

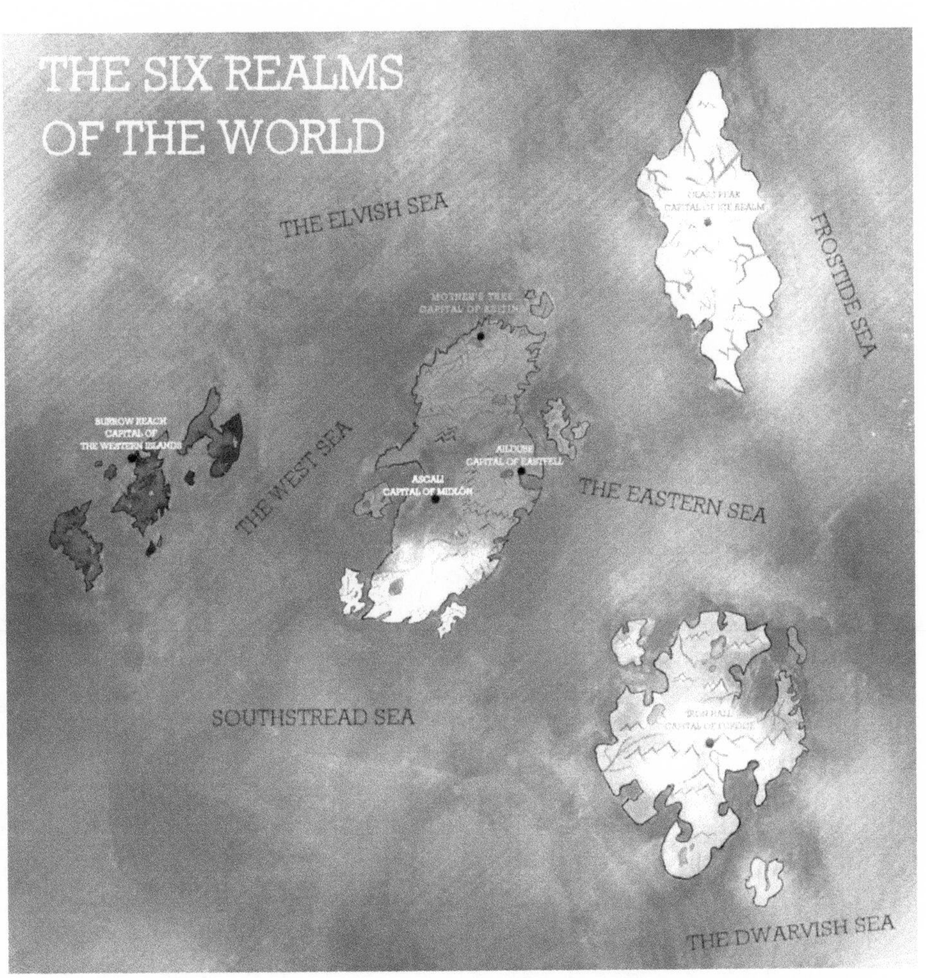
THE SIX REALMS
OF THE WORLD
THE ELVISH SEA
FROSTIDE SEA
BURROW REACH
CAPITAL OF
THE WESTERN ISLANDS
THE WEST SEA
CAPITAL OF EASTFELL
ASCALI
CAPITAL OF MIDLÔN
THE EASTERN SEA
SOUTHSTREAD SEA
THE DWARVISH SEA

CPSIA information can be obtained
at www.ICGtesting.com
Printed in the USA
BVHW070408010223
657533BV00001B/13

9 781638 819257